SOME HELLISH

A special gift from the
University of Toronto

# CHANCELLORS'
### CIRCLE OF BENEFACTORS

# SOME HELLISH

*a novel*

## NICHOLAS HERRING

GOOSE LANE

Edited by Bethany Gibson.
Cover and page design by Julie Scriver.
Cover illustration by Julie Scriver.
Printed in Canada by Marquis.
10 9 8 7 6 5 4 3


Library and Archives Canada Cataloguing in Publication

Title: Some hellish / Nicholas Herring.
Names: Herring, Nicholas, author.
Identifiers: Canadiana (print) 2022019548X | Canadiana (ebook) 20220195498 |
ISBN 9781773102559 (softcover) | ISBN 9781773102566 (EPUB)
Classification: LCC PS8615.E7684 S66 2022 | DDC C813/.6—dc23


Goose Lane Editions acknowledges the generous support of the Government of Canada, the Canada Council for the Arts, and the Government of New Brunswick.

Goose Lane Editions is located on the unceded territory of the Wəlastəkwiyik whose ancestors along with the Mi'kmaq and Peskotomuhkati Nations signed Peace and Friendship Treaties with the British Crown in the 1700s.

Goose Lane Editions
500 Beaverbrook Court, Suite 330
Fredericton, New Brunswick
CANADA E3B 5X4
gooselane.com

MIX
Paper from
responsible sources
FSC
www.fsc.org   FSC® C103567

This book is dedicated to the memory of
Catherine Herring and Stephen Leigh MacLean.

*At home anywhere, wander alone like a rhinoceros.*
   —the oldest Buddhist text in the British Library


*Only the one who knows what he wants is wrong.*
   —Georges Braque


*Is fánach an áit a gheobfá gliomach.*
   —the fishermen of Connemara

# ONE

For as long as Herring could remember, the abandoned landing craft sat along the bank of the river that flowed through Irish Montague. No one seemed to want to deal with the thing, this large rectangle of steel, tucked into the sands and grasses near French Creek, bleeding oils and diesel and rust, a ghostly series of clots, into the waters along the shoreline, while skiffs and lobster boats, sailboats and jet skis passed by. It had become a part of the scenery. A landmark that announced the proximity of the harbour, just around that last bend in the river.

Early one morning in the middle of January, he'd been driving through the village, before the plows were out, and felt the pull of it, this kind of enchantment of alloys, all oriented and slanted and seamed together. He went to it, as if drawn by a lover.

He sat in his rig for a time with the lights pointed at the vessel, a cup of coffee on the dash and the heater going at full tilt. A desperate, red face, lathered with sweat. His skin chapped and dry, hands as white and as stiff as bowling pins. The easterly winds raiding and drifting, embellishing the snows in a kind of talebearing, a seething virtuosity. He felt as if he were being cross-examined by the dominion before him.

Herring scrutinized the landing craft. Tried to make sense of the little game they were in. Its flatness spectral, and him, an awkward barrel of a man. There was the wheelhouse, its windows smashed, and on the opposite end was a little doghouse composed of ribbed steel that had an anguish to it. A set of ropes stretched loosely from the boat to the trees onshore, these swoops of fibres like the tusks of some mammoth.

Herring had a pair of Crappy Tire chest waders in the back seat. He slipped these on and tucked a mickey of dark rum into the pouch and walked out over the ice to the boat. He stepped around what had been a meagre burn pit and opened the door to the doghouse. It came off its hinges, and he tried to catch it, but it fell and twisted his arm a tad. A pain shot up through him and he cursed. Inside the shack was a crumpled sleeping bag and a few articles of clothing heaped and frozen in the corner. He kicked at these and unearthed a rimed Bible. Between the wooden studs, on the back of the steel, someone had written something in a manic scrawl with a permanent marker. Herring knelt down and tried to make it out. He thought it said, *A fragment, like a miniature work of art, has to be entirely isolated from the surrounding world and be complete in itself like a hedgehog.* He pictured a kind of mutated being, a begrimed hedgehog of human proportion, in denims and a plaid jacket, out here on this little steel island, smoking and drinking shine and eating what it could gather from the waters. A shunned creature, misunderstood by society, confused as to the true nature of its own civility, a kind of friar whose madness was a direct result of its sequestration. Its designs apocalyptic, no matter the hour. There was only the end. And the end was coming. The furnace of its eyes red, like pilot lights in a relentless twilight.

Herring sat on a junk of steel and drank his rum. He thought this could be a place just for him, where he could sit and conjecture about the world. Drink himself into an oblivion. And then he thought he'd probably never come back to this place. He watched the sun rise and push the shadows up the river. Vehicles rolled over the bridge in town, rubber and snow on frozen asphalt, their moans low and pompous, as if endlessly circling the bell of a tuba. He listened to the shifting ice, the crack of its language, long whimpers and lashes of excitement, and there was a syncopated quality to these sounds, the tires on the bridge and the ice below, that suggested a relationship, some finer arrangement.

He'd been thinking about time lately, in the middle of the night, while the winds shook the house, wrapped up, alone, in the bed that Euna and he had shared. Murphy, too. His toes and fingers so cold that they were glib vexations, smarmy, while the centre of him, his guts, were like a furnace. His mind so tired and begging for sleep. Pleading. Give me sleep. And in this kind of delirium he had begun to understand, to realize and to know, that his time was limited. That, in fact, his time was running out. That he had spent all the years of living he had managed to cobble together. That his line of credit had reached its end. There was a future version of him who was very much dead and gone, even thoroughly forgotten. He felt his mind do a strange thing, as if he were an engine, and the timing belt he required to synchronize and convert his motions was slipping. There was a tick in him that he could no longer avoid. Euna was away. Gone back to being a McInnis. She had forsaken the Herring mantle. He felt all of these things. He felt them deeply. And he didn't know what to do, how to proceed.

—

Murphy, this little Heinz 57 of a mutt they'd had for years, died a few days before Christmas, and Herring just didn't have the heart to tell Euna and the girls. He couldn't face being the bearer of so much sadness and darkness. One summer day, years ago, Euna had gone into town for groceries and come back with a new puppy and a bag of feed. At first, he hadn't wanted the dog, this sad-looking little thing, but then he took her down to the shore, and while he swam about, the thing followed him out into the water, not entirely sure how to swim, but somehow making all this panic and thrashing keep her afloat, and she nearly scratched the skin off of his back. He carried her in and Euna had been amazed at the damage done to his skin. "Forty lashes minus one," she said, her fingers on his back as if he were a tablet of braille. The blood dripping down into his swimming trunks while the wet pup shivered between his legs. They named her Murphy, and now she was dead. He'd put her in a clear garbage bag and set her in one of the bait freezers in the basement. She'd been such a noble beast, and he couldn't bear the thought of her frozen body alone, neglected, and without committal.

And so, on Christmas night, as the winds howled from out of the darkness, and after a great lack of sleep and a gutload of shine, he ran power from the barn to the century oak and fetched his chipping gun and a shovel, and he dug her a grave well below the frost line. It was slow going, and he felt like a deranged thing. With every inch he burrowed down, his mind would squabble at him to quit this foolishness. He was a miserable wretch and deserved to die. But he persisted, despite himself, because it was the right thing to do. He had to do right by Murphy, and that was the end of it. The deeper the grave became, the more sheltered he was from the cold and the winds. He'd stop his chipping and hacking and feel the sweat on his back and behind his knees, the stamina being hauled out of the centre of him like great lines of arms on ropes heaving a boat from its cribbing to the slip. How much more did he have in him? His hands braced against the sides, the soil unyielding but almost warm, like the window panes in a kitchen. He felt that this grave was a kind of wound. A wound in the earth and a wound in him. These wounds had to be. They were deeds of a sort, and they were here in order to serve a greater quality. Murphy. These marks were tributes.

He fetched Murphy from the freezer and carried her out to the grave. He removed her from the plastic and set her tenderly in the bottom of the hole. He knelt down and stroked her head. There had never been any meanness or anger in Murphy. She would look at you and seem to know all things. She listened, and her breath had always stunk. He kissed her and knew that he'd never see her again, and his heart broke in him. He cut a bit of her hair and wrapped these locks with Scotch tape. He put this in his pocket. He scraped a bit of soil and set it on her paws, and his heart, again, broke in him. He set another bit of dirt on her back legs, and his heart broke. He kissed her again, and he hated life. He swore against it. He packed the earth about her with his hands, and he wept while he kissed her. He packed and packed, and then her face was gone. His face of dirt and cables of snot dripping from his scarlet nose. Pressed her, pressed dear Murphy like a flower in the book of the world. And so, he buried her by filling up this wound with solemn deliberation, on the day of a saviour's birth, while the world was black, and the cold winds roared over the ice and the land.

—

Euna had this bar of soap that she must have used to shave her legs with, because it was so precisely hollowed out on either side that it appeared to Herring, as he sat on the toilet and it sat upon the ledge of the tub, like a dog's bone you'd see in a cartoon. He'd heard from some guys who'd done DMT that you were supposed to take a totem with you on your trip, just something to hold in your hand to remind you that the thing in your hand was real and that everything else was part of the experience. Most fellows just held onto their lighter. Herring thought that Euna's bar of soap was perfect and beautiful as it was, shaped by the shins of her legs. And, of course, it smelled like her, so as he put the bar to his nose, his heart just about crumbled in on him. He stared at it a while. This clean thing in his big, meaty hands. And then he tucked it into the pocket of his jacket.

—

He called the Fishermen's Association to see about his tags. The woman on the other end of the line was having a difficult go of it. He listened to her rustling papers and smacking at the keyboard of her computer. He felt the emptiness of the house about him. The stillness a shawl. He drew a dollar sign on the table with his index finger, and then he wondered where the desire to do so had come from. Herring stared at the hole in the floor. This gullet of the homestead belching warmth from below. He walked to the edge, stretching the phone cord to its limit, and he looked into the chasm. The stove next to the base of the chimney. The pile of chopped oak and maple on the dirt floor, harbouring a great many spiders, scuttling to and fro, trying for flies. The stack of egg cartons and coffee trays creaking and parched from the heat. These were the creatures who lived in the gut of this place. And, of course, he was here, too. What an abyss he'd created.

He heard the woman say, "Just one sec." She asked him his name again. He told her and she said, "Like the bird?"

"No, no. Herring, like the fish," he said.

—

Gerry, a sodden cigarette huddled upon the dried skin of his lower lip, said, "I tell ya, Herring, if I didn't have kids, I'd be dead or in jail." They were stood abreast of one another, a few steps past the end of the bait sheds, solemn men before the waters and the ice, still contained within the bullpen. The breeze was up and the sun was high and brilliant on this first Thursday in April. Gerry's lower back was hot with suffering from lifting all of the traps onto their berth. He had been on his arse for much of the winter, drinking himself stupid on Pink Whitneys, trying to keep out of the way of Susan and the boys, which was, admittedly, just about impossible. Boy, she was always pretty keen to lay into him some thick. She could be a tempest of a thing. "She'd walk through hellfire for money, especially my money," he said. There was a case of Schooner at their feet, near the end of the trailer, and they were well on their way to finishing it. Gerry was still kind of hungover from the night before. His gums were burned into a kind of mash of throbbing enamel and mucus and bone from the vodka and lemonade. As a matter of fact, he'd been forty minutes on the toilet that morning in some predicament, expelling all of the grains from his bowels in fiery spurts. Torrents that made him sweat and curse God and curse himself for his foolishness. If a man could buy a plug for his arsehole, Gerry would be the first in line. It was about half-three and he'd yet to even piss today. "I'm some dry today," he said. "I spose that when I get home I'll just shit like a camel. My guts'll come outta me in less than five minutes and then I'll just crack right open like I'm driftwood, I'm so dry."

Herring said, "Sounds to me like a case of the ol' barley flu, eh."

"My bowels boiled and rested not," said Gerry.

"Huh?" said Herring.

Gerry said, "Oh, I don't know."

The door to the bait shed was hindered by an uneven range of snow and ice, and they set about breaking it apart with a pickaxe and an old, yellow pry bar. They made quick work of it, all back and no knees, blinking nippily to save their eyes in the spray of ice shavings. While they laboured, Herring said, "Hateful stuff. Just hateful."

Gerry said, "Sheila was asking me to talk dirty to her there." With some considerable effort, as if only a grand heaving of his breath could scrape and liberate his interior debris, he blew some mucus out of his right nostril and let the wind take it elsewhere. "So I says, Ya take it ya mad little slut, ya. And she says, No, no, not that kind of dirty." He shifted his weight. Herring wasn't really paying attention, anyway. "Well, that was all she wrote." He admired the cigarette in his hand as if he were a doctor trying to make sense of some nearly impossible fracture. "She still needs the light off, huh."

Herring said, "Who's Sheila again?"

"My landlady," said Gerry. He picked some sleep from the corners of his eyes and studied its form, wedged between the underside of his nail and the flesh of his finger.

Herring stepped into the bait shed and puttered about. He checked some of the traps by placing his hands on the posts, running his fingers across the lace, and he poked his head up into the loft, the wet soles of his sneakers bleating on the wooden rungs of the two-by-four ladder.

"You do anything for Easter?" said Gerry.

Herring grumbled, his hands busy darting this way and that.

"What did Jesus say on the cross?"

Herring said, "Well, what?"

"I'll be back in two days. Don't touch my fucking Easter eggs," said Gerry.

They went back outside and stared at the channel. Gerry thought maybe they were looking for seals hauled out of the waters, that maybe Herring knew this animal to be some kind of augur for the coming season. Gerry imagined the man next to him in a kind of trance, seeking that elusive wellspring, that celestial voice that would make sense of all his dreams and fears, point him in a certain direction and say this is the way.

In truth, Gerry had no idea what they were doing, but he stood beside Herring nevertheless and tried to appear just as stoic, the easterly seeming to grow thicker and denser by the moment, blocked into the frame of their chests, as resistant as the anvil. They did this every year, or at least for as far back as he could recall, and he didn't want to ask the man what on earth they were supposed to be doing, lest he sort of break the spell of things. Maybe pointing out the obvious would kill the feeling, you see. It wasn't too much to stand by the fellow and be quiet and look like you were contemplating the whole of recorded history. Their bellies were full, besides, and there were assorted beers at hand, some Alpine and some Budweiser.

Gerry said, "Al's my pal, but I'd sooner a Schooner." He flicked the butt away and had a pull on his bottle. Somehow or another he had got a bit of ash into his nostril and it burned something terrible, but he didn't want to betray the moment for Herring, so he dealt with the pain as well as he could. Which is to say, he stood there and attempted to stealthily remove it with his index, crying as quietly as he could, proud that at the end of their peace he had not made a right scene, that he had not looked like a man trying not to look like he was picking his nose. He imagined that the ash, its little bit of attendant flame, might work its way into him and cauterize all of his aches, all of his melancholies, and with this image, so simple and childish as it was, a fragile conflagration in the centre of each and every man, like the beam of a miner's lamp, his spirit forgot the cold all about them. His spirit put for a kind of summer to come, a silkworm released from the palms of hibernation. Bestowed a moment of paradise. Gerry guessed that with two weeks of good weather and a fair bit of sun, the ice would be all gone. But it was only a guess. On the Island, it was not uncommon at all to have four seasons in one day.

Herring scrutinized the place, the piles and the crumbling concrete, the rebar shedding its rust over the grey blocks, the buildings and the cranes, the improvised geography of it all and the odours of neglected engines scorched with burden commingled with shit and brine. The wharf at My Bonnie was all hustle and bustle today. Of the sixty fishermen who berthed there, calling this remote harbour home, there must have been nearly forty of them out and about, either unloading traps or waiting to unload, and if they weren't doing this, they were gabbing, talking about the weather and hockey and sledding and ice fishing, about which hired man was in jail for doing what. As soon as one of them started putting his traps out, the others, as if a great dam had broken, would follow suit, apprehensive that this man, this recurrent progenitor, who was always a different fisherman from year to year, knew something nobody else knew, which was never the case anyway, seeing as they were all legally bound to start fishing on the same day. One fellow confessed that he had been calling his cork for nearly a week and all he ever got was the answering machine. He must be on the drunk, was his reasoning. Miles Mackenzie heard that another hired man, a local boy, was caught stalking an old girlfriend, driving real close, playing touch-butt with her bumper, and at curious hours of the day. Just being a real nuisance. A fright to her, which was no way to win a woman back. When the Mounties questioned him, he said that he didn't know it was her he'd been following. That it was a true coincidence. He was just out for some darts and a thing of milk. Miles then said that he didn't understand all of these shenanigans. "I don't get it," he said. "She's not even that good looking. At best she's a six, and a mainland six at that." Anyway, from what he'd heard, it sounded as if the judge was going to let him out of jail to fish for the season. So he wasn't going to learn any hard lessons, was the fact of it. "That Judge Mary Bell is a handsome woman." "And she's good at her job, eh." Some fellows got so desperately bored and lonesome for some beauty over the winter months that they'd go and steal a chocolate bar or a newspaper from Keeping's just to have a few minutes before the judge. And, of course, if you didn't care about yourself at all, you'd just get hammered and go for a drive by the cop shop. This way, you were certain to stand before her at least two or three times, depending upon how much you were able to blow over. And, for at least one of these occasions, you'd be all washed up, looking your best, real spick and span.

Herring avoided Miles as best he could. Herring would always say, "There's only two types of liars. Those who never did and those who used to. And somehow, Miles manages to be both."

Jimmy Beck and his boys were there. Dunbar Gillis was there, who only last season had accidentally killed Dick Hume and now was try-ing with pronounced futility to work unnoticed. Dick Hume had been known as Slippy Dick, for he'd been quite a chaser of women, and as with most splendid philanderers, he was patently allergic to children, had left a trail of them, a great seam that stretched through Kings County. Regarding Slippy Dick, the saying had been, "He'd trade you a piece of gravel for a piece of tail." The Jordans and the LeLacheurs and the Jacksons, the MacLeods and the MacNeils, the Daleys and the Dawes were all represented. Some of these families all had interminably high-pitched voices, as if a swift kick in the balls were a kind of birthright, or as if puberty were a nettled mistress. Some of them fished in shorts all the year, right into November when they attached A-frames and winches to their boats for scallop dragging, while the Native deckhands shivered in their oils, bewildered at the sight of this invulnerable flesh, as if the weather was of no human concern. A spiting of the elements that was downright eerie when you put some thought into it. Each clan, with its own little ways, its own minute but graceful distinctions of methodology, every man of them trying so hard to enact their own little sacraments and superstitions as a way to mislay the truth that all of these men were, in some shape or form, relatives, that in their blood flowed all of the same intuitions, all of the same appetites and furores that could not be purged.

There were other crews, the Hickens and Williams and MacLeans and Gormleys and Coffins and Pollards, from places near at hand. Gladstone and Abney, Guernsey Cove and High Bank, Cambridge and Pembroke, Wood Islands, Alliston and Albion, the Whim Road and Irish Montague. Even some fellows from Red Point and Priest Pond,

North Lake and Souris, which was quite a hike for two months out of the year. Herring didn't know the true character of these men a whit. They looked to him like trouble, were prone to displays of bluster and territory. There was one fellow from Tignish who had married a woman from Lennox Island. His name was Terry. Terry the Tiggie. And the licence was in her name. He used to be at oysters and had the financial backing of his parents. They'd sent him out of the hive to see what was what. On his boat he had a black-and-yellow flag with red words that no one was ever able to quite properly make out, though it did look like *Danger* something, and he didn't seem to understand that there were knots well below sixteen, that you didn't need to pound every tide full bore to get what you were after.

Herring could see that this was going to be the way of things. That men from up west, with capital and investors and larger, faster boats, were going to start pouring east, taking the lobsters from here and processing them back home. They wouldn't contribute one thing to this place. Hell, Terry didn't even shop for groceries down here or eat at Brehaut's. He went home Wednesdays and Sundays to fetch his meals. This kind of people, all they knew of was to take. To take and take and take.

Out in the bullpen on the shelf of ice there was an eagle, enrobed in scarlet suds, that had hauled something out of the waters. Around it thronged seven or eight other eagles, fervent and eager, waiting to see who among them would gang up to muscle the one off of his meal.

Joe McInnis, Herring's brother-in-law, was down at the wharf, too, making his rounds, shaking as many hands as he could, putting in the time, for his position as harbourmaster was something of a political one. Herring still owed him his wharf fees for the last few years.

Joe saw Gerry and Herring and waved to them. Gerry waved back, his mouth wide and slobbery, as toothless as the conclusion of a dogfight. With the barest effort, Herring nodded Joe's way. He didn't allow the man the look of his eyes. Joe had never really liked Herring, and Herring had always harboured ambivalent feelings about the McInnis clan, despite the fact that he'd married one of them, though he'd never admitted this, as such. Years back, before the new century and around the time the coho fishery out west was being shut down, when Joe found out that it had been Herring who had found his father, Joe Sr., he began to hate the man even more. And Herring had known, in his own little way, as he sailed out to Joe Sr. on that bright and lovely morning, that it was going to be like this from here on out, and there was nothing he could do about it. And, anyway, when he did think about all of the misery involved in this series of events, it seemed to make some measure of sense to him. When you bring a dead man home, you're going to get some hate.

Herring and Gerry snapped a few more beers and felt the cold touch their bones. The clouds trembled outward, flattening as much as they narrowed, like a sublime corridor demolished simply for amusement, for a laugh, just over their heads. Gerry said, "What's the shock clock say?" Herring, the curly red lappets of his hair flailing upon the mass of his skull, wriggled the face of his watch free from the band of his canvas coat and showed it to Gerry.

They locked the door of the bait shed and hopped into the rig. As they drove by the congregation huddled about McInnis, with his big, bald head and his thick and freckled fingers, Gerry said, "Baglickers, the lot of 'em," but he didn't really mean it.

—

Herring, his boots strapped into his snowshoes, cut a narrow path over the side of the long, easterly slope of the potato field. Wet from the whipping flurries, his chest grappling for breath and his back slick with sweat, he shuffled down to the bit of shore, through hushed banks of snow afforded refuge by meagre stands of pines and spruces. Something was bothering him, and had been since he'd awoken that morning, only a few hours ago. He could not put his finger on it. Sure, he was a tad hungover. There was nothing new in that. There was a rage in him, a red, molten affair, and sometimes when it rippled, when it snapped as if it were a tacked sail, he didn't know what to do with himself. Then a blackness would come, a kind of slag, and it would overwhelm him. He would see that he was tired of himself and of having to be himself, and he would desire only the destruction of everything before and around him. Walking and drinking didn't seem to unburden him of this condition. Neither did fucking. He knew that people didn't like him for who he was, for who he'd become and who he'd been, but the thing was, all those fellas down at the wharf didn't really know him as he was, didn't really know the breadth of his heart and the range of his mind. He had ideas about the world, about the constitution of progress. What was the point of it all if they could not be expressed and considered? Could a man truly escape himself? Was the point of life to come out the other side of it having been well liked? To have behaved? Likeable people were harmless. Part of him didn't care what people thought of him. But, no, this wasn't entirely true, for there was a part of him that deeply cared about his reputation. To be sure, there was something of a gulf between being a doormat and being a bully, an aggressor, and he'd lived in both places for a time. He had a sense that he needed to find the middle of things, to live as a morsel in the stomach of human notions. Not to be a beginning or an end but an in-between thing. If everyone was perfectly reasonable, would anything interesting ever happen? What would people talk about?

When he was younger he assumed that life would reduce in complexity and all of his questions would resolve themselves. But the opposite had turned out to be true. He had grown to see that his notions would and could never change the world, for most, if not all, of them were not worth leaving the space of his understanding. That to have needs and wants beyond oneself was to put yourself in immediate competition with your neighbours. That to live in pursuit of things was to disqualify others from the opportunity to do so. The simplicity of this idea sometimes took his breath away. The world was a labyrinth of hallucinations. The brotherhood of man, in truth, a conjuring. All of it.

He remembered a time, some years ago, around when he was working toward his bona fides, and he'd finally gotten in to see this dermatologist from Halifax about his psoriasis. He'd been on the waiting list for two or three years. On the ferry over, he got to thinking the fellow must be some good. He was kinda hoping for a miracle. He'd taken to praying to God to relieve him of this particular ailment, but that wasn't working much in his favour. He gave this up after a few nights. It seemed silly, doltish. They got to talking about skin and that, and Herring said that the pores in your skin will eventually grow smaller as you grow older, right, and the specialist had said no, the opposite was true. He was so thrown off by this, by the fact that his instincts had been so utterly incorrect, that after he received the script for a whole lot of ointments, which, incidentally, didn't do jack and cost an arm and a leg, he went to The Split Crow and sat there, alone, by the front window, drinking quietly with a strange, defeated look on his face till the place closed, nearly annihilated by this bland fact. How could you trust yourself if your hunches were so mistaken? He was a fisherman, after all, and sometimes your hunches were the only things that preserved your whole damn enterprise from ruination.

In the night, he had walked down Lower Water, drunk, just all over the pond, thinking how cruel it was that his pores were only gonna get bigger, while students with fine skin giggled and hollered at one another. He had felt like a marked man. Just a poxy junk of a man.

He thought of Miles Mackenzie and of how last season he'd seen the fellow getting out of his burgundy rig a few times as they sailed in from open seas, up the channel between the green and red buoys, the cans and nuns, with their trays and tanks full. The man was rooting around for his roll of money, taking only a few bills here and there, too cunning and wily to rob him blind. He'd considered going to Joe with a request to install security cameras, but in the end, he hadn't done anything. You didn't need closed-circuit television to know that Miles Mackenzie was a wretched thing. Years ago, when they were doing mussels together, and the tension had been just brewing for weeks, Herring had finally attacked the fellow with a Greco submarine. Smacked him right in the face, sending meat and mayonnaise into the air, this great sickle of condiments.

He reached the end of the field, where the rocks of the shore gave way to the ice floes, shackled to one another and creaking with agitation, and he stopped and listened to the sound of the snow meeting the buckle and swell of the stunted waves. The grey belt of the water encircling the world. This, the labour of this grating, the abiding grind of the world, as of bones meeting in a joint, was the only commandment. And though the air was mostly beholden to the precipitation, he was able to feel a smidge of joy arise as his mind registered the brine. And then he felt tired, like the fight in him was leaving the show.

From some distance behind, a white snowshoe hare emerged from a thicket and stopped briefly to watch him. Still and erect and balanced on its hinds, its thin ears like dried apricots, its youthful eyes darkly clear pans, rendered all the more so by the patter of the chalked descent, its heartbeat shuddering through its skin. The hare had somehow confused day for night, and now it was exposed, vulnerable, and it did not look over its shoulder for foxes, but rather, observed him, Herring, as if he were a totally innocent thing.

When he got home he fried up some smelts and ate them with lots of ketchup, bones and all.

—

Gerry took his father's van and drove to Scotchfort to visit his mother, Dolores. The sky was a shield of pewter, thick and immobile and nearly endless in a way that could remind a person of their insignificance, that they were nothing but a liquid in the tankard of existence, less than a plaything. A bit of snow flaked daintily here and there. He filled the ashtray and kept his eye out for any Mounties. The rear passenger-side hubcap snapped off, and he didn't stop to go back for it, content to watch the disc whirl, enact its unhinged revolutions, as if its only desire was to keep up with the van so that it could return home, and then it broke with his direction and went for the ditch.

She was in the living room having a nap in her big chair. The radio in the kitchen was on. There was a little aquarium on a stand by the window. The water in it cheerless and stodgy. She may as well have been housing a cow patty, such was the smell and look of it. He thought of putting his finger in it, just for something to do. He helped himself to a jug of pop, sitting himself in the rickety chair by the refrigerator to admire the yellowed lines of the ceiling tiles. The fizzy prickle of the cola was painful on his rotten teeth, made his eyes bulge. With each swallow he bent his knees up and away from the floor. The pleasure of this absurd little rite seemed to judder him awake, and he hadn't felt awake like this in forever. He'd always wondered how well he handled pain. He didn't like to complain about injuries. Some fellas loved to make a scene over the tiniest of scratches. Sometimes he wasn't in the mood for things that called attention to themselves.

He boiled some water and fluffed some scallops out, then got a skillet hot with butter and fried them in this, adding a bit of salt and pepper. She came in and opened the window, lit a candle, turned the radio off. She put a load of clothes in the machine, and they listened to the water going full tilt and the gurgle of sudsy clothes being spun about. Neither of them shared a word. She toasted some bread and they sat, she at the end of the table, he to her left, and ate in silence, their jaws clicking, the pump of their throats.

Through the steam of her mug of tea, she said, "Are you still fishing with Herring?" She winced a little, creasing the lines about the edge of her right eye, as if she were registering arsenic somewhere in her system. "He's a queer man, you know."

Gerry wasn't in the mood for a debate, and he wasn't up for defending the fellow, yet again. He said, "Mother, I'm just a donkey. You know it. I know it. I can't pass judgment on the man."

Dolores huffed in a bit of air. She said, "That's it. I've said my piece." She passed him a cigarette and together they sat in solitude, as forlorn as defeated vessels. He put the kettle back on and belched mutely.

They returned to the living room and watched the news. A middle-aged woman in Irish Montague had driven her vehicle through the front door of a house near the pizzeria. The man who lived in the house had been sleeping on the couch. He was an amputee and her car had mangled his electric scooter. He didn't know how he was going to get around. His mother sighed and looked away. "I can't bear the news these days."

"You don't even know why it is that you don't like the man," he said as he was leaving, his boots undone upon the shamrock linoleum of the hall.

"You'd be wise to stay away from him," she said, her voice strained and volatile. "He'd skin maggots if he thought there was money in it." Gerry threw his hands up into the air as he walked down the drive. "And you shouldn't be drivin', ya fool. You've no licence."

When the engine came alive, he waved to his mother, and she waved back, pulling a grand smile across her face, for the love she had for her son had no conditions.

—

Gerry bought cartons of smokes for himself and for Susan and Sheila. There was a patch of freezing rain on the highway, and the wipers were too rotten to do their proper work. He pulled over for a spell and sat, while the windows glazed and the lights from the highway smeared, grew indistinct, as if the world were being painted into oblivion. A fox came out of the ditch and onto the shoulder a few yards in front of the van, and then, having thought better of things, it turned and trotted back into the bush. Boy, a skunk would just shuffle out, stop, and let itself get smushed, he thought.

Gerry smoked a joint that had some crumbs of shatter in it and felt the fear rise. He thought about jail and he thought about death. And then he put the van in drive and released his boot from the brake pedal. He was bored with thinking the same old thoughts. The same old dark thoughts.

—

They themselves were little more than children when she got pregnant the first time, and while it was true that neither of them had been trying in earnest, they were both excited by the opportunity. Susan had a temper, to be sure, and in general she seemed to dislike just about everybody and everything. These were the things Gerry liked most about her. As the world before her seemed a source of perpetual disappointment, Gerry sensed that her unreasonableness could be a force of great change, and he had wanted to be near to someone with her qualities, her energy. He kept waiting for her to begin offering suggestions about how to improve the inefficiencies of the world, but they never came. Eventually Gerry realized that she was just a whinger, an A-1 moaner, and he was just too simple to give her whatever it was she wanted. Anyway, she didn't seem to know what she wanted, and it was a significant problem for her that Gerry didn't know, either. He didn't possess the confidence of knowing how an abstract problem, an *issue*, should be corrected. Of course, all of these facts would remain unknown to him for much of his life.

Susan liked to fuck. She was good at it, and she knew it. She thought he was good at it, too. The pair of them just a couple of naturals. And he knew that she had a truly healthy and mostly wholesome relationship to this aspect of her existence. Nothing traumatic had occurred to her when she was growing up. As far as he could tell there were no dark and secret places in her mind. No repressions or wounds. No damage that couldn't be overcome. His relationship to sex, to his own desire, was a tad more abrasive, though he didn't really know why. Until his first time, young Gerry had always been rather scared of the act, but then, once things got going, there had never been any notion of retreat. In fact, their undoing was precisely because the two of them had grown so good at it, at fucking. There was no longer any underlying tension, if it had ever been there at all, to inform what they did between the sheets. And Susan was the type of person who needed a pinch of hostility to keep her motor going, to prevent her interest from waning. After the birth of Robbie, they both seemed to understand that the end was near, but this hadn't stopped them from getting pregnant again, this time with Mickey. The long and the short of it was that they had just been too damn young to do right by one another. The timing was off, but only just. When, but four months after Mickey came into the world, she told Gerry about her new fella, well, he took it pretty hard, and though his dejection had not surprised her one bit, his suffering took him by surprise.

As a rule, and from a particularly young age, Gerry had a distinct and ineradicable sense that to pass judgment on a person or a thing was to miss out on a whole bunch of experience, and still, to this day, this feeling guided his every movement. He still loved Susan very much. They both knew this. She didn't ever say she loved him, or that she had stopped loving him long ago, and this love had somehow crept back into her soul, which would have been a real shocker. No, in a way he just didn't care to bother about wondering, for to do so would be to unnecessarily stir up a complicated set of affairs. Maybe it was as simple as he was too slow for her, and she was too fast for him. He moved through life as if he were an iceberg. She moved around him, about and from him, with all the liberty and consequence of a seal.

He knocked on the door and let himself in. She called to him from down the hall and he wandered down to her bedroom. She had just finished a hot shower and was standing in her room, wrapped in a towel the colour of a goldfish, applying concealer underneath her eyes. Susan looked down at his feet and rolled her eyes. She said, "Jesus, honey, take yer boots off. You've tracked dirt everywheres."

Gerry said, "Oh shit." He took off his boots and cleaned up the mess. Susan handed him her vodka soda and he had a small sip of it. She was going out on a date with an old drinking buddy of Gerry's, a bar clammer by the name of Norman. He told her where he had left her carton. It was getting late for him, and anyway he was plucked. Starting to get the spins.

Robbie and Mickey were watching television in their room. Gerry poked his head in to ask after them and they grunted back at him nearly in unison, the room a giant carbuncle of blue. He'd had them out with him for a day last season, trying for oysters up in Cascumpec Bay, but the boys weren't interested in the venture whatsoever. Their indifference had plainly hurt his feelings. His mother told him that he was being too sensitive. Susan told him that he wasn't much of an entrepreneur anyway, and that much less of a fisherman to boot. He already knew all of this. And yet he hadn't been able to shake the feeling of having been wounded, of some greater, some ancient debt having been settled at his expense. His own father had seemed to be totally uninterested in him from the moment he was born, had never taken him aside and shown him how to tie a certain knot or how to hold a handsaw, how to speak to a girl and make her feel good, and there was a symmetry to his current position that bloody terrified him. And too, he worried that there was something wrong in his brain, some switch of victimization that would not relent, and so he just tried his damnedest to stop thinking about how much of a sook he was, the bones and flesh of a casualty, and got on with the business of things.

He said, "Mickey, you still good to shear the ol' hair tomorrow?"

Mickey looked up and said, "I'll do you one better, pop. I can do it right now."

They made a little space in the kitchen, and Mickey got a towel from the cupboard and draped it over his father's shoulders. Robbie brought the electric shears and plugged the device in. Three beers were put on the table, cold and wet with condensation. Pink Floyd was turned up. Robbie tapped his fingers on the table, bopping ever so gently. And Gerry was so happy and so tired it was all he could do to not burst into tears as the blades made barren rows of his scalp, as he felt the lightness of what had been brush his arms as it plummeted to the floor.

—

"McClellan."

Gerry was quietly trying to get past the basement door down to his apartment when he heard her voice from above. He turned the knob and tried to move his feet lightly.

"Gerry fecking McClellan."

His eyes adjusted in a way that made him feel that he was in a dream. He could barely make out the face of Sheila in the dark and through the screen of her kitchen window.

His head was gloriously fresh and unbound, as if there was no division between the air and his skin, and this feeling reminded him, in the way that only meek and artless things do, that people, that all things, were suspended in the air, so to speak, in much the same manner all of the fish in all of the seas were suspended. Life was a pendulous affair.

—

She skunked him at cribbage, and he was a little sore at having lost so handily. She told him that his problem was that he didn't take himself seriously. "How is anyone else sposed to take ya seriously?" she said. He shrugged. She huffed, unsurprised. Gerry said, "Hey, what's the difference between a puppy and a lobster fisherman?" Sheila said, "What?" "A puppy'll stop whining after eight weeks." They shared a clementine and a cigarette, and then they were quiet for a while. "Don't fall asleep on yer stomach," she said. "You'll get wrinkles."

When he got up to leave he stared at the carton of smokes he had placed on her little shelf by the door. It was a sign, he was certain, but as to what, he did not know. No amount of scrutinizing the damn thing would provide him with an answer.

He walked outside and down the concrete stairs, damp and cracked things, and slept in his own bed the few hours until daylight.

—

Herring and Gerry were out in the barn painting buoys and smoking hash. The month of April was halfway through. They had a gallon of bikini-blue paint and a quart each of black and white, and they diluted the blue a bit with some turpentine. The buoys were stacked on the ground, and they had all of their trays and brushes and cans of paint set on a small green tarp in the middle of the floor. Gerry sat uncomfortably in a little computer chair on castors. Each man would grab a buoy and slather it from top to bottom with the bikini blue. After this, the buoy was hung from a spiral nail that had been driven into the joists above them. They did a coat of blue on each buoy, and then after they dried for a day or two, they would apply another. After this coat dried, they applied two thin rings of white on each buoy and then used black paint to draw the number of the dump. And finally, with large permanent markers they wrote their Canadian Fishing Vessel number, their CFV, 105098.

The door and windows were closed, and the fumes from the paint were giving both men serious headaches. Gerry exhaled a great plume of smoke and admired the joint between his fingers as if he were a kind of bird preening itself.

He said, "You remember that Thai stick we used to smoke fer seven bucks a gram. You got so high you tried putting the steering wheel on the passenger side."

Herring looked up from the buoy in his hand, his face splattered with paint, and laughed.

"Another time," said Gerry, "I was at my mother-in-law's on Colombian stick and I leaned over to take off my boots. I woke up in the morning and my laces were still in my goddamn hands."

"It's no wonder the two of you got divorced," said Herring. "I was thinking of setting traps from the front this year."

Gerry looked puzzled, and he asked why.

"Well, 'cos we got all tangled up in the prop a few times, 'member. And we lost a few traps, and we had to get Banger Chapman down in his scuba gear to swim under and cut the rope off the prop."

Gerry said, "Well, how the heck would we do that?"

Herring said, "Leverett told me he knew of some of the ol' timers filling a bucket with sand and setting it at the stern to keep all the ropes clean and free."

"Boy, I dunno. A rope'd catch on a piece of snot," said Gerry. "A rope'll catch a fart, I swear to Christ."

They went outside and stood before the hull of the boat, the *Marcelina & Marceline*. High prow and a low stern. It could even be said that there was some sensuality preserved in its form. Out of all of his possessions, Herring did his best to keep the vessel in good shape. That it was the furthest thing in the yard from ruin could be stated as fact. It truly was a fine boat.

They taped the waterline of the *M&M* with green painter's tape, then diluted the bucket of tar with some gasoline. Using a paint roller, Gerry started coppering the hull, rolling the concoction in vertical stripes from the keel to the taped border, spray from the nap mottling itself in fine formations all over his arms and face and neck like the blight of some disease. He could feel it burn something terrible, but he was used to it. He'd done this plenty of times before. It was hard not to have the stuff splash down your throat, huddled and cramped as he was beneath the hull, shuffling about like a louse. You just had to make sure that your mouth was closed, or as closed as it could be. It would take a few days for this stuff to properly clean off. He had another joint on the go, his lips dry and tingling. The sores were coming.

He coppered impatiently, sweating in the cold, his head stinging from the vapours. There was no artistry here, though the fact of this made him wish that he did have the composure to undertake a project, any task, that, with slowness and deliberate sensitivity, would evolve into something that could be considered near to elegant. If only he'd had more patience in him, Gerry knew that he could have done something truly great and noteworthy, could have tapped into all of the talent in him, those abilities he was truly afraid of. Transform his rivals, these weaknesses of his, into his strengths, you see.

Herring changed the wheel on his grinder and clamped her into his vise. He had a small cardboard box of rusted and dulled bread knives that he'd purchased years ago at the dollar store. He used these for cutting redfish and mackerel, and for cutting rope, if need be. You could never have too many blades on a boat. Herring pushed the trigger on the grinder and began sharpening them as best he could, the sound of the blade meeting the wheel thin and ghostly, a discarnate screed.

Gerry and Herring drove into Irish Montague and got some fried chicken at the grocery store. As they walked into the building, they saw themselves cast back by the tall windows. They looked like the distortions of ancient fables. The one with the blue face like a god of the sea, and the other, with his face as black as an arsehole, like some god of the underworld. Together they were conspirators of a sort who trafficked in the flesh and soul of the common man. The one would cause storms and shipwrecks and send men to their watery graves, and the other would rule over them eternally.

They ate their greasy meal out in the rig and watched the women coming and going. Gerry said, "God bless the fella who invented them black pants."

"I wanna put some dinner plates in a few of the traps. See how they fish," said Herring. And they grabbed some coffees for the road.

—

There was just something about the basement flight of stairs. When Herring thought of them he ground his teeth and curled his toes, cracked his molars and popped his joints. He could not let them go. Could not get the image of them from his mind. There was just something about having to take the stairs that had begun to bother him. To think of his weight on the treads, groaning the wood beneath, provided him with a glimpse of something bigger, some immense dread capable of consuming not only all of him, but all of everything. They seemed to him to be evil, wicked things.

He couldn't recall if it was in a fit of rage, or perhaps a fit of idleness, but in early December, in the midst of an exhaustive sweep of wet snow and razor winds, he had taken his chainsaw and cut a hole in the living room floor. Then he went out to the barn, retrieved his chain-block hoist, and fastened it to the ceiling joist above the opening. He rigged a little platform out of plywood and old carpet and lowered himself onto the dirt floor of the basement so that he could load more wood into the fireplace. When Euna and the girls got home from church and saw the hole in the floor, Euna had blown a gasket. The girls thought it was cool. He had never seen her lose it as she had over the hole in the floor. From the way her face had grown red and the somewhat vacant look to her eyes, how she was almost calm, and the way her body held itself upright, he had a vague sense that this was a major blunder on his part. And even that was putting it lightly.

Euna, for much of her life, and for much of their married life, had been an orderly person. Things would happen, problems would arise, and initially she had addressed each of these events in her life with the same deliberation. Hers was a cogitated methodology. Something would come from nothing. She would approach and begin the process of remediation. She returned something back to nothing, whether it be dirt on the floors or laundry in the hampers or a lack of food in the refrigerator or the tail light in the van. In the winters, when they were about to be storm-stayed, it was she who filled the tub with water and checked the batteries in the flashlights. To leave a car overnight in the drive without gas was utter foolishness, because one might need to get to a hospital before the garages opened.

To find the words to say to him had taken her quite a few days, and in the interim he had slept on the chesterfield, only a few feet above that fiery maw, sweating liquor and enduring terrible dreams that he could not remember seconds after waking. They avoided each other, stretching the silence between them as if it were a cat's cradle. Now, it's your turn. Now, it's your turn.

On a Monday evening a few weeks before Murphy died, she walked up to him, rather surprisingly, in the busy Montague grocery parking lot. He was immediately anxious that she might cause a bit of a scene. But somehow they ended up leaning against the body of his rig, both of them with their arms crossed over their chests, admiring the piles of dirty snow along the perimeter of the asphalt. The sun was dangled above the horizon. If one had been watching them from inside the store one would have struggled to discern the exact nature of their relationship. They were as stiffly comfortable as siblings reunited. Their mannerisms, equal parts synchronicity and something near to omniscience, and yet somehow still individual, the tilt of their necks and the stoop of their mouths, indicated that a great spell of time had been held between them, and this holding was of an intimate nature. In short, they were bedfellows. A federation of people who had lived, shaped, and changed one another in the most sacred and nameless of ways. They were, in truth, a coincidence. One of those things that happens at every moment of human experience, a laugh or a hug, a blade of grass underfoot, hands about a mug of tea, legs wrapped up in a blanket on the couch, but which is nonetheless utterly miraculous.

"My great-grandfather built that floor," she said. He knew this, and more, she knew that he knew this. He could feel himself growing rigid, his mind readying the defences. This place was familiar territory, like a caught fish released. This place was their sea. After another long silence, she said, "Why did you do it?"

He searched his mind for an appropriate justification and he came up short. He felt like a sook. And he knew this as God's fact. Her brief interrogation, its blend of serenity and warmth, confronted him with the full picture of her grace, and this allowed him a fleeting sense of all that he essentially lacked. He did not possess a system like hers by which to devise a larger, overarching series of intertwining systems. When they had married, her worldview was order, was such that one event created another event, endless swirls of creation. He had no such determinism. He saw no patterns. There had only been the stairs, and whatever it had been about them that had driven him nearly mad. He pictured the hole, the floor, weakened and sagging like a representation of gravity.

He felt his mind turning, trying to find the best, or simplest, way to say what he felt that he needed to say, and, as if in the throes of a dream, as he neared something that felt like a response, it slipped from him, backed away, returned to the current from whence it came.

He knew she understood that he needed a bit of time to say the things he needed to, and for this he was grateful. He looked from the snow piles, the jagged line of these miniature ranges, to her face, and he saw the impatience in the very muscles of her face. And then, what had only seconds before struck him as the markers of her nearly infinite grace, the shocking breadth of her tolerance, now seemed to be the fruits of exhaustion, a pure and colossal exhaustion, like the polar ice packs. Just a big creak.

There was too much between them. She knew this, as did he. If they were both honest, neither knew entirely where to rightfully commence. And they both understood that this was a delicate kind of surgery before them, that any carelessness would topple all of it. They also both understood that to talk like this, to excavate, was perhaps to topple a thing that had already toppled long ago. And, if neither of these were exactly correct, perhaps they were in the midst of a long and protracted topple. He felt the breath as it was taken from him. "Well, you were a drunken danger most of the time," said Euna. He watched her huff a grand bit of air at him, and then she laughed sternly as if all of this was so goddamn predictable.

He felt the eyes of everyone upon him. People around these parts liked to know the colour of everybody's shit. Behind him, the traffic rolled. The sun was about to call it quits. He reached for a cigarette that wasn't there, his hands shaking somewhat. He needed a bath. But man, those eyes bore holes in him. His drive home was a daze. His nerves shot. His own eyes, wild in the rearview and a clenched arsehole. As if life could leak out of a man.

—

The night of that same Monday, Herring endured a terrible series of dreams that were so vibrant and so upsetting that he woke up about quarter to two and cried for a while. He tried to recall what they had been about as he sat on the cushions, those stuffings musty with the scent of him, but all that he could recall were the smooth sides of mountains, and some prominent light source that seemed only like a kind of distant cousin to the sun, casting shadows onto the world in ways that were disturbing but within the dream could not be escaped. As to how these things had terrorized him so, he felt like an idiot, shivering and pulling on his pathetic little bottle of whiskey, trying to come to some sort of conclusion that would only ever elude him. Eventually, he began to shiver with the cold. He went to the window and stared out into the dark. A man was out by the road, stood still, observing the house. His heart nearly burst in him and he began to tremble. Though he had the rifle. Wait, where was the damn thing? Did he have ammo? And when he blinked, the man was gone, like a knot disappeared from the end of a rope by a skilful and steadied hand.

He pulled some socks on, shuffled over to the platform, and lowered himself into the abyss. He loaded some logs into the stove, the bit of web between his thumb and forefinger taking a few bothersome splinters, and he sat, swinging, like a dead man who has absolutely rejected God's mercy. He splashed a bit of diesel in. He'd used just about everything a person could think of to start a fire, and it was something of a mystery that he had any eyebrows or arm hair left on him. The logs took flame, and he let the heat isolate and outline him, demonstrate his negative, the measure of his truancy. His brow beaded with sweat, and he let himself cry once again, and this time, rather unexpectedly, he felt a little less pitiful.

Behind him, upon the stacked stones of the foundation, the flames looked like boughs of a cherry tree, distressed and nearly laid to rest by the wind.

# TWO

Gerry was outside in the dark and the cold, just shivering like a beaten pup, stood at the shoulder of Georgetown Road as if he were a monument to sorrow and misery. His lips had burst open with cold sores during the night, and the cream he'd put on them hadn't done anything more than render them as cracked and rigid as larvae paled by the frost. He thought that he probably resembled a lunatic. The wind, when it arose, seemed to come from any direction it pleased, and it took the fresher deposits of snow, banked along the sides of the road to Montague, and spun them with centripetal force, as if the whole of the universe could be forced into the hole of another dimension.

He heard the thrum of a breakneck quivering a few moments before the lights of Herring's rig, a burgundy one-ton with at least two tires in the grave, crested the road about a kilometre away. Gerry's heart quickened.

Looking at the man's clothes, Herring asked Gerry if he had long johns on. Gerry said no.

Herring said, "You need to get a dog there, Gerry, to get you up early in the morning so that you'll know what the weather is like."

The warmth of the cab felt like a vacation and Gerry rubbed the chill out of his arms. "There's nothing quite like being cold and hopping into a warm rig." He looked around. "Where's Murphy?" Herring stared straight ahead, refusing to turn his head. He put his hand into his pocket and touched the soap and the tape of hair. Gerry kept quiet for a time.

They stopped at Robin's for a cup of joe and a donut each to go. Herring, his eyes on the road and his hand trembling ever so slightly, took a sip and, twisting his face a bit, said, "Fuck me, ya could walk on that," which is what he said every time he had a Robin's coffee. Sometimes Gerry wondered if the man had memory problems. A rig passed them with one headlight out. Gerry punched the roof and said, "Kadiddle!"

Between Irish Montague and My Bonnie River, they passed a large sign, erected on a cleared-out timber lot, that declared in thick black capitals, CHRIST DIED FOR OUR SINS.

"Sheila's threatened to turn off the internet again. So I'm back to having to sleep with her." Gerry wrinkled his face a little and tapped the ridge of his brow with four fingers.

Herring chuckled, the air out of his mouth low and muted. He said, "Well, she's a tiny little thing. And built for speed, too. I'd say yer not suffering all that much."

The windows were fogging up. Gerry rolled down his window and felt the cold air wash over his face. He opened his mouth and drank of it, as if it was the remedy to hot coffee. He said, "The best bit about making kids is the tryin'. That's the fun part, eh. From here on out, she's all downhill, depending upon yer point of view, I spose."

As they drove just ever so southeast, past My Bonnie Harbour, the clouds pulled away, like grand sheaths of cotton put to a blunt knife, and thereafter the sun was a juvenile and brilliant thing. Herring said, "What the heck is that thing there up in the sky? I haven't seen that for a while." Gerry could tell that he was excited.

They got to Herring's situation along the shore road without any fuss, though the winds coming off the straits, which were strong and irreverent, lashed and drifted snows in every which way. Herring said he still had a spot of shine, and so they walked over to the furthest barn, forlorn and somewhat diminished, all by itself, and dipped two cups into a sparkling bucket.

Herring said, "This batch is called 'block and tackle.'"

"How d'ya figure?" said Gerry.

"Because when you drink it, you think you can block and tackle anything."

Herring walked him over to the century oak and showed him the little piece of concrete he had chiselled her name upon. Gerry said, "She was such a good girl." They drank some more, and between coughs and the wiping of his eyes upon his sleeves, Gerry asked when it was that Meaney was due out. Herring looked at his watch, said that high tide would be at around dinner. Meaney had said he'd be out shortly to get the boat off the hard. Herring needed to replace the toilet and fix the work lights, mumbled something about the wiring. He had a wheeled twelve-volt charger on the battery and a number of cords running to an outlet in the barn. He also needed to replace the oil filter and attach some new hoses for the hydraulics and check the housing on his transmission. A few scuppers needed attention. He was pleased that they'd been able to wax the hull and copper it beneath the waterline and attach a new anode. These little things made the *M&M* feel brand new.

Herring climbed up the wooden ladder set against the transom and over the washboard and stood himself on the deck of his boat for the first time in quite nearly a year. He looked at everything before him, the shape of the fibreglass, each angle and each seam, and how so many quiet conversations could weave and braid themselves into a sum that was this thing, this boat of his that enabled him to feed others and to feed himself, never struck him as any less than miraculous. He'd bought the boat new in 1981 from the builders in Kensington and had decided against naming it, which had mystified everybody down at the wharf shortly before it began to piss them off, claiming that its lack of designation was a safety hazard. Then Marcelina had come along, so he gave the boat her name. And then Marceline had come along eleven months later, and he gave the boat her name, too. At the time of its purchase, he was still a proper greenhorn, putting two years under his belt so that he could get his bona fides okayed by the government, and although the prospect of not being able to transform himself into a competent fisherman, of having effectively indebted himself to his own doom, truly terrified him, knotted his guts up with worry and anxiety, he knew that the boat had allowed him to stay sane out on the water, bobbing about under the watchful eyes of the cosmos. To understand his competencies, all that he had learned about himself and the tides, the lobsters and the herring, the crabs and seals, had taken him the better part of a decade. He didn't even know what it was that he knew, if he could properly articulate everything that was in his head, things that time and experience and a bit of intuition had provided him. He wasn't particularly good at communicating things, and he noticed this inability when he tried to tell guys like Gerry, and all the other deckhands he'd had on board, how to do things in the ways he preferred.

Anyway, this was a sacred moment, his little ritual, between the boat and him, the both of them perched on the world. He trusted it, he trusted the *M&M* completely. He knew everything about her, every angle and seam. When he stood on her he could feel the precise length and width and weight of her. He understood her limitations and never sought to take her past her thresholds. Years back he'd run over a tree trunk floating in the channel and had never forgotten the sting of it. And most fellows pulled up to the docks going a hundred miles a minute, because they'd got to show off as much as possible, smacking their hulls against the fenders. Herring was always careful and deliberate. He didn't mind pissing off the guys waiting in the bullpen to sell and get bait. He was going to go at his own speed for the sake of the boat. And if the *M&M* didn't trust him at this point, well, he couldn't imagine living in that world. What they had was something like faith, but not really that, either. What was between them was beyond faith, somehow deeper and more inalterable, irreducible, even.

They'd get the engine going and let her warm for a bit.

She had a 350 Cummins diesel in her, and compared with the monstrosities that were being sold as lobster boats these days, she was tiny. She was tiny and mostly white and plain. "Less is more," he said. And Gerry said, "Especially when yer doing dishes." Looking back, he'd have preferred a wooden boat, better on rough days, for they weren't as corky as the fibreglass, more stable in the winds, but he figured the money and time and effort that he saved kind of balanced everything out in the end. In a glassed boat you didn't have to worry about the thing coming apart, battling edge nails or clenched nails when repairs were needed. Wood, maple, and cedar planks were too alive for his pocketbook, because they reacted to the water, there was too much maintenance, and rot always finds a way in. Ultimately, fibreglass meant that you didn't have to nurse the boat.

Herring stepped down into the cabin. He breathed deeply and let a heavy sigh out. The floor and the cabinets were dark and sticky, begrimed. A number of squirrels had invaded and spent the winter in his cabin. There were so many holes in his blankets and his King Cole tea bags that it looked to him as if a shotgun had gone off. The things had also left enough tufts of hair in curious places that you could hook a rug with them. Numerous battles for territory had been waged. There was a tub of butter from back when he used to fish herring, and he hadn't fished herring in eight or nine years. He inspected the mess of oil gear and tools on the bunks. He couldn't remember who owned most of the jackets and pants. Eventually he'd get around to cleaning up the mess, though it seemed to him that he said that every season. He lifted up the toilet lid and found a confused-looking dead squirrel staring back at him. Its colour and demeanour put him in mind of pickled mussels, but the poor thing was as hard as a manifold of the universe. Gerry poked his head down and saw what was in the toilet. He said, "Jeez, that keto diet sure takes a man to strange places."

Herring put the key into the ignition and hit the button, and the engine turned over and she started up without too much of a fight, emitting a great mantle of blackness, as if bleak thoughts were a boil that could be lanced. Gerry came up from the cabin and together they loosened the engine hatch with a rusty T-wrench so that they could watch the thing shake and spin. Two saturnine rodeo clowns trying to muster up something, any drip of enthusiasm, regarding the mad beast before them. They smoked a bit more shatter while the engine warmed up, and then Gerry gave Herring a bit of a hug. It seemed like the thing to do. Herring didn't say anything, but Gerry could tell that he'd made the man uncomfortable. He thought that if he did say anything he'd just chalk it up to the hash and the shine, for he was feeling pretty cut, anyways, and just as he was thinking about how to explain why he had done what he had done, Meaney's canary long-haul International and its four-axle trailer rumbled into the driveway.

Johnnie Meaney was a Newfoundlander by birth, a real meat-and-potatoes kind of fellow. He was as hard on his heart as he was on his equipment, and he'd only ever told one joke in his entire life, and even he couldn't remember what on earth it had been about. Somehow or another, through the webbing of destiny, he'd found himself on the Island. Either it had been a job that had brought him here, or a woman, or perhaps a bit of both. When the old ladies at the credit union watched him march into the building to do his business and get his little book stamped, they would think to themselves, What's he still doing here? He was always going to be a CFA, a *come from away*, and he carried this knowledge like a kind of cross.

As he stepped down from the cab, Meaney offered a kind of elegant handshake. His teeth as yellow as his truck on account of his terrible addiction to pineapple pop. Herring moved back and said, "I've it on good authority that you've fleas, Johnnie." Meaney looked like he was going to burst into tears. Herring stepped forward and shook his hand, asked him how the drive had been. Meaney's voice was low and devotional to its duty in a way that called to mind the application of really thick peanut butter. He said that it was still snowing up north, but it wasn't amounting to much. The roads were good. Gerry ambled over and shook the man's hand, though he was sheepish about displaying the state of his lips.

Herring looked first at the trailer and then to his boat. He slapped his hands together and said, "Well, shall we get this show on the road?" Meaney stumbled on the first bit of his reply and seemed keen to give up entirely on any pronouncements going forward. The muscles in his face contracted involuntarily and Herring understood that the man required some form of negotiation before things could occur. "I've a few drops of shine left in the barn there, Johnnie, if you'd like," he said. Meaney held up his pineapple soda and shrugged. He preferred screech. To him, shine tasted like licking the gravel under a leaky truck. Gerry took a few paces back, and Herring took Meaney by the elbow and walked him around to the front of his rig. Standing before the grill, in the heat and throb of the engine, Herring looked at the man's eyes and sensed that Meaney was trying to dig in, however prematurely. Herring leaned over his pelvis, almost as if he was held by wires, and tried to look deeper into those damn black saucers.

"It's three hundred this year," Meaney said.

Herring said, "Why? It was two hundred the year before. And before that, it was two. And before *that*, it was two."

"I'm sorry, Herring. I can't do it for any less," Meaney said.

"You drove all this way just to tell me this? You could've called and saved yerself the diesel."

"I'm out of my jurisdiction. I mean, I have to raise the price."

"Well, Christ, I may as well get the Mersey boys to do it for me. I went with you because yer the last fellow who hasn't been bought out by 'em. Look, I understand that you've…yer telling me that you won't do it for less than three."

Meaney nodded, put his hands in his pockets.

Herring said, "A wise man once said he who puts hands in pocket feels cocky." Then he said, "I might starve if I don't get this thing in the water."

Meaney nodded again. He was clearly in a bit of pain. "And, as far as I can tell, this'll be the last year for me coming out east. I'm getting the squeeze here, eh."

Herring pulled the zipper down on his jacket and retrieved an envelope from his breast pocket. He passed it to Meaney, adding in a mutter that he ought to knock his head off. Meaney stood where he was, as still and as stiff as a moose hung for skinning, and he said, "Herring, I'll need the other hundred before I put my trailer under yer boat." Herring stepped away from the man and his truck and blinked a fleet of patters with the lids of his eyes. "Boy, yer really puttin' the fucks to me here, Johnnie. Give me one goddamn second," he said, and then he marched into the house. Gerry was over by the boat, pretending to check the state of its stands, and when Herring had disappeared he looked over at Meaney, who, after heaving himself a pull of his yellow bubbles, looked briefly back to Gerry as if to communicate the notion that this was, in truth, entirely out of his hands.

Gerry said, "Hey, Johnnie, where are all the trees in Newfoundland?"

Johnnie looked at the fellow's lips, the rile of them, as if a poached salmon got into a fight with a poached cod. He said, "I dunno."

"Between the twos and fours."

Meaney was given the balance by Herring, who had practically run out of the house as if the place were on fire, and when he gave it to Meaney, he declared that this ought to get all the insulin in the world into his bitch of a wife. Meaney's face flushed crimson, and it seemed to Gerry that the two men might come to blows, so he began to run over, but somehow or another he managed to blow a tire and he wiped plain out, falling right onto his elbows into the grasses pushing up for sun through the slighter deposits of snow. This broke the tension, and Gerry was so pleased with this turning he could barely contain himself. Herring professed that he was sorry to have included Faustina into the mix, that he was sorry for what he said. "I didn't mean it, ya know. You just had me worked up a bit, is all." Meaney was somewhat placated by the immediacy of Herring's disavowal and now, contented that the terms of their agreement had been ratified, hopped back into his truck.

The three of them set about removing the *Marcelina & Marceline* from the hard, turning and readying the trailer to back down the drive, next to the barns, through the cradle arrangement of stands and creosote timber blocks and forty-five-gallon drums, so that it lay beneath the boat's hull, its wheels grabbing through the snows for purchase. This itself was a delicate operation, enacted slowly and with about as much precision as all three of them could manage. They used an old creosote railway sleeper, maybe it was larch or maritime pine,

Herring didn't know, about four feet high or so, to prop up the bow portion of the keel so that the water could run out of the scuppers below the transom. You wanted a bit of a tilt on her, too, so that water didn't get into the keel and split your hull. In the fall it was of utmost importance that a man didn't forget to remove his plugs. Meaney, his head and left elbow protruding from the driver window, tried not to yell and fluster the other two, and Gerry ran back and forth, from port to starboard, his rubbers slipping in the snow and the wet grass, checking that the boat and the trailer were straight with one another, that the one might not topple the other, his eyes panicked and ashen droplets, arms stiff and held low as if suppressing the rising earth, a voice hard and strained, proclaiming affirmatives. Yup, yup. A correction of the wheel. Left, left, left. Yup, yup. Keep 'er comin'. Popcorn. Popcorn. A legion of clouds rolled past the sun and the whole of the world cast in red by the eyes of the tail lights.

Herring and Gerry were at their respective breaking points of stress, their adrenaline high, their system somewhat improvised because they cared not to establish a clear and direct line of approach beforehand, at best slapdash. Gerry got the cables out and as the trailer slid beneath the hull, Meaney hollered at him that the pin was in the box beneath the levers for the winch. Gerry said, "Yup, yup." He jumped up onto the trailer and slid the pin through the hole in the hull and got the cables on either side and then winched her a bit, so that Meaney could keep sliding under to receive the full weight of the vessel. Meaney would reverse and holler at Gerry to winch her a bit more, and Herring would yell from the stern that they were pretty well lined up, to just keep her going, and in this way, these increments, man and machine conspired together to see that a boat could be floated from this place to its berth. They sweated through the entire ordeal, their mouths exhausting a near-constant stream of cigarette smoke, muttering superfluous curses like generals who had been knowingly pressured into sending their men to the slaughter. It was their little dance, truck and trailer and boat, Herring and Gerry and Meaney, and though it was difficult for all of them to see things as they rightfully were, that they had mastered this romp was something of a fact.

"Strong like bull, smart like tractor," said Gerry, pretending to flex his biceps. Herring laughed. They put rubber pads on the corners of the hull, chained the boat to the trailer and secured these with binders, and then, where needed, they ran thick, polyester straps over. Meaney believed that this was overkill, but he kept his thoughts to himself. They didn't have that far to travel, really, and he wasn't reckless with the gas pedal. But he let the man have his rituals. Meaney knew the importance of liturgies. Often, they kept people sane. He'd seen this firsthand.

The two men checked the security of the boat by yanking on its fetters until satisfied that the load would survive transport. Gerry, the skin of his face wet with labour and his eyes as flushed as a domed beetle, looked at the boat set up on its trailer and said, "She looks pretty good considering she's been rode hard and put away wet for way too many seasons." He looked to the house for some sign of Euna but didn't see anything. He always enjoyed giving her a wave. She was a pretty lady and she had a way about her. She was graceful. Elegant. Big smile. Eyes like blueberries. Well, the truth of it was that Gerry had always had a bit of a crush on Euna, though he'd never dared to tell a soul. Anyway, something was going on with Herring. Murphy and Euna and the girls. Herring was the type of guy who would drown rather than holler out for a life ring because he was just too proud to ask for help. The man had this hollowed out look to him, like a fellow who has returned to his home to take stock of the damage a storm of tornadoes has wreaked.

Herring ambled into the house and Gerry found a bush to piss into. He stacked all of the stands and all of the jacks in a corner of the barn, and then, after Meaney joined them in a ceremonial snap of rum, which was always the last, said Herring, "'Cos rum's the drink of the Americas," they drove along the shore road, Meaney and the trailer first, Herring and Gerry behind in their rig, slow with the ceremony of it, even regal, the fibreglass of the boat capitulating to the golden threads of the sun and then releasing these things aslant, as if it were all a kind of colossal terminal, the disk of some beautiful sunflower. The engine just about on fire with the strain of it all. A few neighbours waved at them. A few, seeing that it was them, turned away, back to their tinkering.

The plows had taken out most of the mailboxes over the winter and at some sites a group of people were gathered, drinking coffee around these carcasses, scratching their heads about how exactly they might upgrade their particular model. One fellow near Cape Bear had his mailbox welded to a giant truck spring, which was then welded to a tractor rim. It was a pretty good idea, but the damned thing also seemed to rarely survive a winter. During a fresh snow, it could look a bit like a jilted hair dryer.

When they pulled onto Wharf Lane and passed the buildings of the fish plant, tilted like blocks of butter unbound of their wax, a bald eagle swooped down from the heavens in a western direction. "Look, Gerry, there's yer spirit animal," said Herring.

Joe McInnis's burgundy rig was on the wharf, some of his traps out on his berth. He came out of the rickety door of his bait shed, the one with the Budweiser logo inexplicably painted on it, with a clip-board in his hands, looking like a production manager or something. He walked but a few paces and then stopped, as if held there by some grave remembrance, watching, grading their performance, this dance of the idiots, as Gerry hopped out of the cab of the rig to spot Meaney as he enacted a circle in the parking lot, and then began backing towards the slip, its concrete retaining walls pasted with engine oil and barnacles, bottles of rum and braided bits of nylon rope. Herring waved to Meaney and the man halted the procedure so that Herring and Gerry could remove the chains. Herring remained on the deck of the boat, gaff in hand, to combat the mess of electrical lines that ran to the fish plant and threatened the tree of antennas on his cabin, his GPS receiver, his radio antenna, his thirty-nine-inch VHF. Some of the boys had big eight-foot VHFs. Everyone called these ones the big sticks. Herring motioned for Gerry to join him, and the latter stepped

off from the retaining wall to the washboard, as happy and enthusias-
tic as always. Herring gave Meaney the thumbs and they backed the
trailer down the slip, into the receiving waters. When the hull met
the waters a sound emerged, restrained and humble, as fine as the
line of a razor put to skin, the utterance of something being filled,
or something being taken away. This was the sound of limits being
introduced. A boat, the outer lines of a human creation meeting the
outer lines of an ocean. Two natures, shaped by one another to vary-
ing degrees, meeting, as they always did, to see what they could take
from the other. This thinness, this sibilance, was the very sound of
what mankind had said would be a quota.

They fired up the boat's engine again, and Meaney got out and did
his best not to tumble on the slip in his rubbers. He eliminated the
few straps and pulled the pin out of the hull, and then they reversed
the boat a bit, the blades of the prop churning the waters, as Meaney
drove forward to retrieve his trailer, steaming and dripping from the
cold and wet, like a great iron sword being slid from the entrails of
its foe. Herring steered them out of the bullpen and into the channel where he opened the engine up until every bolt on the deck was
having a fit, screaming with force and tension. Returning to harbour,
they slowed down and headed for Herring's berth, the hull coming
into contact with the floes and fish carcasses released by the thaw,
irritating the eagles and the gulls. Herring took the boat and enacted a few circuits in the bullpen, his throttle low and his movements
somewhat deliberate, creating enough of a wake to risk irritating
some of the fellows who were easy to irritate, the fellows who already
had their pressure washers hooked up and were hosing down their
decks, cleaning their windows and tanks and trays. Herring said,
"Jesus, this isn't a fucking yacht club." He shook his head a bit. They
berthed in front of the diesel tanks and Gerry hopped up and got the
pump going. Herring unscrewed the tank covers and they guessed at
how much she'd take. Herring said 640 litres. Gerry said 459. Each
tank ended up taking 350 litres of fuel. Herring took off his toque and

scratched his head when he saw the numbers rolling as they were on the pump display. He looked over the sides of the boat to see if he was leaking anywhere. You didn't want to get caught spilling fuel down at the wharf. Jesus, it was a hefty fine. And once you had diesel on your boots, you may as well have put on a pair of skates.

Balloons down, they reversed into the ladder, and, with two ropes, they secured the boat to the curb of the wharf. Another two ropes held the stern.

His berth was right beside Jack MacLeod. Soon enough, tape measure laid out and a marker in hand, Jack would be complaining about the lack of space there, up on the wharf. Gerry ran an extension cord from the power shroud to the battery charger.

Meaney was in the parking lot, collecting his chains and his ratchet straps, his bottle of pineapple pop on the gooseneck.

Herring climbed up the ladder and realized that he and Gerry had left the rig over by the plant, both its doors open and its heater cranked. Fools, the lot of them. Joe McInnis was still on the wharf, organizing his traps, and waited for the two of them to pass. "Hey, Herring, you dropped yer pocket there," he said, pointing at the ground in front of him. Herring halted and looked to the spot where his brother-in-law's thick fingers were steered, and, seeing nothing, he allowed his eyes to remain there, as if it were a kind of holy simulacra, as if this singular spot contained the whole of reality as it was without representation, as it was precisely.

"Hey Joe," he called.

Joe turned back to him and said, "What?"

"Nothing. Just checkin' fer assholes."

He and Gerry walked back to the rig. They watched as Meaney pissed by one of the axles, and then groaned himself into his yellowed International, and, no goodbyes offered, drove away, the fallen beads of saltwater marking his retreat. Gerry wondered if they'd ever see the man again. Didn't seem likely.

Herring and Gerry drove down the road to Keeping's Clover Farm and sat by the window of the store, drinking hot coffees over beef-and-mustard sandwiches, watching the boys come and go, the odd tractor bounce by or a lumber trailer creep up the hill, grinding through its gears. Gerry didn't enjoy eating in public too much on account of his lack of teeth, but with the right amount of lubricant he was able to compel portions of the triangle sandwich halves down his throat with relative ease. Anyway, Otis was a good chef. His biscuits were to die for.

Pretty soon this place would be overrun with the knuckle pickers from China and Mexico. Some of them boarded in the rooms above Keeping's. A refurbished school bus would pick them up in the mornings and drive them to work. Before they fell out, Herring used to drink at Clem Fraser's place on Fish Alley. He had a little barn out the back with some old sleds, and there they'd get fucked up on shatter and listen to country music, while the neighbour's chickens cleaned through Clem's woodpile for slugs and spiders. Clem would inevitably start talking about politics. He'd say, "I'm a dyed-in-the-wool liberal. I'm red, man. Chrétien was my guy. I don't get the Progressive Conservatives. Either yer comin' or yer going. Which is it, eh." The house next door had a bunch of Mexican women living in it, and sometimes a Mexican fellow would walk down from Keeping's and sit with one of the ladies at the picnic table in the yard, and they'd do cocaine and listen to Toncho Pilatos records and start petting one another real heavily. The ladies were always cooking and the dryer never stopped running. For seven months of the year the smell around their back door was a combination of hot spices and those rectangular sheets of air freshener.

Herring chugged a bit of coffee and Gerry thumbed through the *Eastern Graphic*. The "Letters to the Editor" page always got him worked up. There was a guy from My Bonnie River, a born-again Christian, who frequently wrote in and managed to connect something entirely unrelated back to the Bible. Gerry always got real bent out of shape about these. He'd say, "Stretch Armstrong would be impressed by that one."

Joe whipped by in his rig with a load of ropes and trays, his left hand grabbing the Jesus Christ bar above the door.

About the time that the co-operative had found its legs, Joe McInnis Jr.'s career in the NHL had all but petered out. He was an enforcer on the ice, just a real fortress out there, always throwing knuckles in defence of the better, finer players who just couldn't take a check or a slash, the finesse boys who made the game entertaining, even beautiful, who sold the watching of the whole mad circus, truth be told, and as such, he'd heaped up too many concussions over the years and both of his knees were blown to smithereens.

Seven or eight years ago, while Joe was limping along in the third or fourth string on the Carolina Hurricanes' bench, his father, Joe Sr., had worked to organize the co-op with a fellow from Truro, an investor, so to speak, and just as the thing was getting its legs, the fellow from Truro did a runner with just south of half a million. The fishermen were incensed, and they called for the head of Joe Sr., thinking that he must have had some inkling of what was truly afoot, that maybe he was in on the scheme. A boat out at the wharf had been set on fire. When the volunteer firefighters showed up, they started fighting one another because they were all fishermen, too. They had their allegiances. There were other things not worth mentioning that came to the surface during the whole calamity. The cops finally arrived and broke up the fisticuffs, and eventually, after things had calmed, an investigation was conducted. Lawyers of every ilk had been involved. Men called round at ungodly hours and yelled at each other on the telephone. Letters were mailed. Forensic accountants were brought out. Politicians like Lawrence MacAulay even came out to take stock of the chaos. It was pretty awful.

Joe Sr. was beside himself, couldn't find the dignity to leave his property. It wasn't so much that the wind had been beaten out of him. It was that his sails had been overtensioned and, as a result, torn. He lost a lot of weight. Started to kind of shrivel up. His wife, Agnes, stopped going to church and playing bridge at the community centre. Some people said that she became interested in the occult. So Joe Jr. came home from Raleigh, and his very presence helped smooth out the situation. Joe was good with the men. They had all watched him grow up. Joe didn't care too much about material things. He cared about spirit and about principles. He was good to his father, who really was a true melding of these qualities. Got him out of the house, got him eating more routinely. That he was back was a blessing. Nary a soul would deny this.

And then one day Joe Sr. was out in the boat alone, about a mile outside of the bullpen, just running the engine on a fine Sunday in May, keeping her warm, the boat just sitting there, an idle thing in winds less than a knot, the water gentle, rhythmic little hauls, the sunrays spackled and consistent on the face of things. A summer day uprooted, transplanted to the here and now. A great swathe of pollen out in the channel, twenty-five metres wide and a kilometre long, so thick upon the waters it looked like the wood shavings from some mill of centuries ago.

Herring had come down to the wharf for something or other. He could see Sr.'s boat out there and a real bad feeling came over him. "Real bad" was how he said it later. He hit the radio. No response. He took his boat out and found Joe Sr., crumpled up by the bulkhead in his bibs and his Hartford Whalers cap, his son's team, before it had uprooted, rebranded, and landed in North Carolina, his mouth agape and his face contorted into a look of horror, which Herring remedied with his hands, the butts of his palms and the pads of his fingers pulling the terror out of the muscles, the look of a man who had realized that the whole damn thing was rigged, and there was just no bringing him back from where he'd gone. People said the stress of it all, the swindling and what have you, because a lot of other details, quite strange and nasty affairs, had circulated in the wake of the thieving, had got to him, and just about everyone felt terrible about how things had played out.

After this, sanctified by a fatal heart attack, Joe Sr.'s innocence was accepted as gospel. Joe Jr. brought everyone back to their senses, which was contrary for a man who had made a career of fighting, but in this inconsistency was something truly touching, and sooner than later people just kind of resolved to forget about the fellow from Truro, got back to focusing on what they could, fishing and putting food on the table and dealing with health problems in the family and the like. A man did what he must to keep the lights on and his wife happy. Joe did well to keep the peace, and of this fact, you had to give him his due. He kind of steered everybody back to the level of civility and harmony that had, mostly, always been there. The natural way of things, if people don't have a bunch of reasons, good or bad, to want to kill one another. Though some people began talking about Agnes and supernatural curses.

Joe kept the licence and the gear, but sold his father's boat to a fellow from up west. Said he just couldn't imagine spending his days standing in the scene of a crime. It was this ancestral thing, because Joe Sr.'s father, himself another Joe Jr., had also died of a poor heart while out fishing, about twenty years before. Anyway, Joe bought himself a new boat and christened it the *NHL Joe*, which was mostly a terrible name.

Across the road from Keeping's was this great, white house with a red oak in its yard and a vast array of lobster buoys hung from its limbs, coated with these rather obnoxious whites and pinks and yellows, colours that were practical on the water, but when on the land they were indecorous, and when a rig or a loader rolled by, these buoys would be pushed by the swash of winds, swinging, and in certain light, when the clouds obscured the sun, they struck Herring as ominous and depressing, gave a kind of cursed feeling to the property.

Gerry went to the cooler and came back with two slices of blueberry pie. "When I was working at the blueberries up in Morell ya had to be clean shaven 'cos yer working with food, right. Not even a bit of stubble on the ol' cheeks would do. Had to be smooth. My foreman came up to me one day 'cos I had a bit of fuzz and he gave me hell. And I said, Jesus, I mean, c'mon Larry, there's some old ladies walking around here with whiskers on their faces."

Herring said, "Jeez, I hope you didn't say that with any of them around."

"No, no, I'd never be that rude," said Gerry. He chewed and swallowed some pie. "Boy, you could work as many hours as you liked. I had a few weeks where I was putting in eighty-seven hours."

Herring's first cousin, Big Arbot Herring rode up on his mountain bicycle, the face beneath his ridiculous helmet red and raw and contorted, like the bared foot of a poacher caught in his own trap. "He looks like the Great Gazoo in that thing," said Gerry. Arbot lived just outside of My Bonnie Harbour, on the road west to My Bonnie River, in a bungalow surrounded by great stacks of tires and more than a few stoves and microwaves rusting out in the grasses. Next to a stand of trees was a great formation of concrete steps all heaped and cluttered as if it were an M.C. Escher print. After a string of drunk-driving charges, Arbot had had his licence permanently revoked by Judge Mary Bell and spent a month in Sleepy Hollow. He'd escaped from the jail for a few days, and this bestowed on him a rather fleeting celebrity. Like clockwork, he cycled into the Harbour twice a day to fetch food and drink from the store, resplendent in a high-visibility jacket slathered with engine greases. As the road into the Harbour was something of a lengthy slope, Arbot just kind of coasted into the place as if he owned it, swerving from side to side with careless disregard for any other traffic. For a time he'd even taken to declaring himself the unofficial mayor of My Bonnie Harbour. And when there was actually a proper mayoral election, Arbot got his name on the ballot and lost mightily. But, somehow or another, the man had put enough pressure on the government to replace the bridge in the Harbour. So you had to give him his due for this. Some of the old folks who had a more contrarian bent would mutter, "Say what you want, but they should name that bridge after him." Just after Y2K, Euna had purchased a green Toyota Echo, and whenever Arbot saw the thing parked at

Keeping's, he would wait for her to come out and then he'd say, "You let me know when ya wanna part ways with that thing. My cousin had one and he just couldn't kill it."

If he wasn't on his bicycle, rolling here and there, or on the internet trying to trick some Filipino lady into falling in love with him, Arbot was most assuredly down at Fish Alley, drinking and watching the boats come in and out and the tide rise and fall upon the steel pans.

Herring had no time for the man, hoped that he would resist the urge to shuffle over and start gabbing on about something utterly inane. Years ago, there had been a mix-up at the post office. Euna had ordered a book about Greece, and because Big Arbot's wife at the time was also named Euna, the post office driver, an older fellow by the name of Willie Machon, had delivered it to Arbot's place. An honest enough mistake. Anyway, Euna had been wondering what on earth had happened to the book, so at last Herring went down to the post office to get to the bottom of it. Next, he drove over to see Arbot about the book, and Arbot refused to admit that he had received the package at all. Herring went back to Willie Machon, who reaffirmed his testimony. "Yup, Arbot signed for it all right," said Willie. "His John Hancock is right here." Herring went back out to see Arbot, and Arbot, his breath reeking of root beer and spiced rum, found his head crunched between the door and its frame. "I wouldn't piss on ya if ya were on fire," said Herring. And that had been that.

Herring thought that when Gerry ate he looked and sounded like a cat cleaning itself, all hunched over, guarded and contemptuous. Gerry took a heave of coffee and asked Herring what his father had been like. Gerry didn't know why he asked him this. It was just something to talk about. Kill a bit of the silence. Herring said that all he could really remember was riding around in the man's rig, watching him put away bottles of vanilla. "He drank so much vanilla he sweat brown. The sheets would be stained like a goddamn wood floor, and there'd they be, out on the line, drying, for all the world to see." Gerry looked at the line of Herring's nose just above the rim of his cup of coffee. The steam had wet the skin of his face, the wings of his nostrils sheened, as if wrapped, flattened by plastic. "And cheaper than hell. He used to make me go around and straighten nails just for something to do," said Herring. "The nail of the big toe on his left foot was gone. One time he had a horse step on it and then he dropped a block of wood onto it and these things together must've killed the root. The toe was just a round piece of flesh. Growing up, I was totally hypnotized by this toe whenever he had his socks off. How can you have a toe without a toenail? This little unprotected thing. I'd be nervous my whole life about hitting it."

"When we were kids there was a fella in Morell who had a chip wagon for a time, right by the bridge there," said Gerry, "and the thumb of one of his hands was actually one of his big toes sewn on. You'd order yer fries and this hand would come outta the darkness with your little box of fries, and you'd just stare at this hand that was also a foot. You'd wonder what his poor foot looked like. But it was a hell of a thing, for sure. I've never forgotten that hand. He terrified a lot of kids. A guy like him, with a hand like that, shouldn't have been serving people food. Maybe he lost his thumb, got his toe stitched on, and then thought, 'Boy, I need a career change that'll show this Frankenstein hand off as much as possible. I know, I'll get into the food industry.' His fries were some good, though, let me tell ya."

Herring said, "Our neighbour, gosh, I think he was a MacKay, well, years ago, he was trimming the lawn around his rose bushes with his push mower and he slipped a bit and his foot went under and got caught up in the blades. But you couldn't tell from his walk that he'd lost all of his toes on the one foot."

Gerry said, "Maybe he donated a toe to the chip wagon fella in Morell?"

"By Christ, maybe there are pails just full of 'em in the hospitals."

"Jeez, women are always telling me my toes are some handsome. I might be in danger of being harvested," said Gerry. "It's true what they say. One man's thumb is another man's toe."

"Yeah, like if he ever became a movie critic, would he give two toes up?" said Herring.

The wind had picked up considerably, and they listened to the bones of the place rasp with effort, the flag on the pole outside electric and vicious, as if it were a whip in the thralls of flesh.

—

Herring patted his gut and recalled that he hadn't had a good movement in a couple of days. The thought worried him. They were back out at the wharf, and the wind was coming from the north, the sky without a single aerosol. A storm was coming. Snow was but a few hours away.

He and Gerry set about finishing the work that they had started that morning. They were moving traps from the shed to the berth, inspecting them, the hemlock and the concrete ballasts, the snoods and the bridles, the tags. Any trap considered worthy of attention, that was beaten and injured from previous years, was carried out of the shed and set on the tattered asphalt path between the shed and the fenders of the wharf. Over the years, Herring had found that a trap with about seven seasons on it was kind of an ideal trap. It had the right amount of saturation to it. The lobster seemed to just kind of take to them, rather than, say a new trap, which he found tended to scare them off. Having to use a new trap was something of a pain. Whenever you'd build a new one, you had to make the drive into town and get a new tag. And then you had to break it in a little. You'd tie it off to the curb of the wharf and lower it down to the bottom of the bullpen and leave it there for a couple of days, or even a week, if you preferred. Or, if you didn't have the time, you could just add more ballast to the traps when you set them. Herring'd fill old milk or oil jugs with concrete and put these in the traps, though they did take up a fair bit of room in the parlours. Anyway, you only left them in there for a few days. So Herring preferred to see about getting as much life as he possibly could out of each trap. They didn't have to look pretty. They just had to be tight enough to hold a lobster in.

Cephas Hicken came down to the wharf with a load of fresh traps. He tied them to the curb and threw them over. Each one floated. Cephas muttered to himself, trying not to attract notice. Herring said,

"You building a dock there, Cephas?" Cephas gave him the finger and hauled in his traps.

Gerry and he kept an eye on the weather each time they were in and out of the shed. Willy Lyon MacKenzie ambled by in his silver rig, the bed of it supporting a cage made out of two-by-fours and chicken wire, with which he transported his peacocks.

Herring asked him how the day was going.

"Oh, ya know, up and down like a hooker's skirt," said Willy Lyon, the movements of his weathered face inappreciable and mere, as economical as possible. He was a man whose every action indicated that he had spent a great deal of time pondering how he could save energy and time. His was the face of a man who knew that each action was a transaction with the future. The stoop of his shoulders, indeed, his whole posture and gait revealed the full understanding of that grand, boundless calculus just ever so underneath the surfaces of all things. He was likely the only fellow left in Kings County who operated a boat he had built himself.

His rig rolled on by and he called out, "Looks like a whore of a storm is coming," his voice fading as if it were a plane in a tender nosedive, a plane in love with its ruination.

Herring and Gerry stood in the bait shed among the traps and the trays, the ladder to the loft, and the few pocket and fillet blades, dull and rusty, tucked into studs beneath the little window, the concrete floor dirty with debris and hardened specks of gaspereau, the smell of the place vaguely aquatic, fusty, and yet with a kind of gelded tinge, and rolled up a bit of hash putty. Gerry got a half-litre bottle of pop, and they burned a little hole in the bottom and let the smoke fill the bottle, the curling snows of an unseen mountain peak, and they each sucked in as much as they could muster.

Outside, the first flakes were etching their way across the doorway.

Gerry pinched his eyes and cracked his neck forward. "Did ya hear that?" he asked. Herring put two fingers to his lips and wiped them clean of debris. He remained quiet. There was a faint sound, like the cries of an infant, colicky and stemmed. The two of them were both now quiet, old cows before a new gate. The cries flickered in intensity, as if a symptom of bad wiring and a trounced electrical panel. Their ears strained to pinpoint the location of whatever little thing was making such a noise. They spun, their hands out, enacting some idiotic and sacrificial dance only half remembered, and then, as if on cue, both of them sensed that the sound was coming from one of the traps near the back of the shed. With some measure of frenzy and agitation, they began moving traps, each man fancying himself a rescuer against the consignment of an avalanche.

Gerry, rather suddenly, dropped onto the floor. A tabby cat, with ripples of brown and veins of black, had found its way into one of the traps, and from the look of her had been there quite some time. Gerry set the trap on its flat and opened the trap, expecting some kind of fight or a hostile movement from the animal. The cat stared at them, weak and dumb, its eyes like plucks of beach glass. The snow was now lashing. Herring shuffled over as Gerry took the cat in his hands and lifted her out. "Must've been after mice," said Gerry, opening his jacket and tucking the cat into his chest, giving her his breath. "Poor thing." The cat ceased its whimpers and looked content to give itself over to Gerry. "You've a way with animals, don't ya?" Herring said. "It's too bad for my wallet that fish are allergic to you."

Herring loaded the injured traps into the back of the rig, leaving the tailgate down, while Gerry hopped into the cab to keep the tabby warm and sheltered. Herring suggested that Gerry spend the night at his place, as the storm looked like it was going to be a heavy thing.

They stopped at Keeping's to grab a couple of bags of storm chips and some cans of tuna for the cat. Otis was out from the kitchen, his apron about his waist and a bit of sweat on his forehead, sheltered by the overhang of his lifeless hair, and he gave them a wave. "That's some pussy ya got there, Gerry," he said. Gerry was stood at the edge of the counter, his back against the rack of chocolates and gums. Loretta, who was an odd fish herself, rolled her eyes at the profanities from behind the counter, then continued ringing Herring through. "Now, now, Otis, let's be clean," said Gerry. Otis came over and gave the head of the thing a few, stiff pats, as if pressing the buzzer on some game show.

"Well, there's a first for everything. No chloroform necessary, eh Gerry?"

"She is cute to be sure" said Gerry, his voice a song.

—

Gerry was surprised when he realized that Euna had left, and that she had probably left the house some weeks ago. Herring had lowered himself into the basement. The place looked rough, lacked a woman's touch. The rooms were cold and lonely. In short, it reminded him of his place, and this was more than a little depressing. He busied himself with tending to the cat, which meant that he stood in front of the kitchen sink, struggling to figure out how to use the can opener. Eventually, he ended up punching the lid until enough tuna was exposed that he could shovel it out of the can into a bowl. He'd made a brilliant mess of the counter, and his shirt was damp with juice. He set the tuna before the cat. The animal sniffed it, gave him his eyes, and then walked over to the chimney in the corner of the living room and laid down to rest and wait for the heat. Gerry wasn't too eager to bring it up, what was going on with Euna, but he did feel that, if he waited for a decent moment to do so, it was the proper, friendly thing to do.

They drank a few more bottles of Schooner, and Herring readied some spuds and set about throwing some steaks on the barbecue. He walked out into the darkness to fire up the machine, white streaking across the beam of his headlamp. Gerry stood and watched the corners of the windows fill with snow. They looked like little albino perogies. Herring came in, stamping off his boots, and loaded a plate with steaks for each of them and went back out. Gerry watched the glow of his lamp, its jerky movements, slicing and unpredictable, like an incensed bronco so used to its anger it was trying to buck a phantom rider, and its planked light struck him as painful and somehow tragic. His throat got thick and he felt a welling of emotion in his eyes.

Herring cleaved a bit of fat from the meat. The cat hopped up onto the table and the three of them ate quietly, listening to the howling of the winds, the soft granularity of snow mounting with a distinct haste. Gerry watched Herring's hands tremble, the fork in his left heaped with a serving of spuds. Sometimes it seemed like he wasn't going to be able to get the food into his mouth.

They polished off a case of Schooner listening to the hoedown on the radio. "I tell ya, I'm so drunk I couldn't lick a postage stamp," said Gerry. He had the spins and, his arms against those of the chair, he braced for the worst. He had but a fragile notion that there were actually walls and a proper house about him. He felt as if he was afloat in the universe. Herring brought him a glass of water. With every ounce in him, Gerry resisted the desire to ask after Euna.

Herring said that he was going upstairs to wash some clothes in the bathtub, adding that the washing machine had broken down.

Gerry took the stairs into the basement, loaded the stove, and lay down on the chesterfield by the workbench. The cat joined him a few moments later. "We'll see what kind of mouser you really are, eh," he said, stroking her chin. They rested together as the fire's heat worked its way from floor to floor, touching everything, warming each thing, the pens by the phone on the wall, the plastic remotes for the television, the drawstrings on the blinds, the dust on the blades of the ceiling fan. The wall hooks in the mudroom, discoloured by the salt water carried home in hats and clothes. The sticky notes in the lunch can that said, *I love you. Be safe. Have a great day.*

—

Herring mixed the ash and the milk in a two-quart measuring cup and poured some of the solution into a saucer. Gerry had managed to get at the guts of an old DVD player, and in less than an hour, the two of them were ready to begin the process of tattooing. Gerry rolled up the sleeve of his T-shirt and indicated that he would take Herring's design on the shoulder, next to the names of his parents, which his brother Randy had tattooed years ago when they were both doing a stint at Pictou Correctional. Gerry said that Herring should get some shine, that shine would help with his spins. Herring said he was officially out of shine, but he might have some wine that one of the Daley boys had made and passed around. "I'll have no part of that stuff. That's lunatic soup," said Gerry. "That stuff'll make you throw rocks at yer own porch." They chugged a few more Schooners, though Gerry was hesitant to do so. "Ink whatever you like," he said. "So long as it isn't a cock and balls. Make it something dignified. No swastikas, fer Chrissakes."

"Shut yer mouth, ya fool," said Herring. Gerry looked away when the blood seeped to the surface, yelping a little as the needle marked its movement, the line of its particular boundaries. Gerry could feel the sweat of the man's fingers on his own skin, the immense heat of the man, the stink of his breath as he leaned in and out, adjusting his perspective so that the images were as true as they could be, so close that the pores in his nose looked like chestnut divots that formed a kind of net, or cover, upon the rind of him. He was watching his friend, a truly impatient man, become patient and single-minded, and it shocked him that Herring had these qualities somewhere in his reservoir.

Herring drew on him the line of a little lobster boat. No bigger than a toonie. Admittedly, the ash and milk didn't do a terrific job, but he supposed it was a whole lot cheaper than getting some stranger in town to do it. And that he'd done a fitting job of illustrating was mutually recognized. Next to the hull, he had scribed the words *per mare*. Next to this he had placed a lobster trap, about the size of a loonie, and the words *per terram*. Gerry asked after what these things meant. Herring said that he'd let him figure that out on his own, but allowed that the words were Latin.

In the wee hours of the night, Gerry awoke on the chesterfield in the living room and felt the tenderness of his shoulder whimper out to him as he repositioned himself. The storm had passed and the sky was a pure void, as black as the tail of a grouse. He said, "My teeth are floating I gotta piss that bad." He walked himself to the kitchen and set a chair before him, climbed it and pissed into the sink, and then dumped a few chips into his hands. The crunch would help the hangover, he figured. There was a picture on the television stand of

Euna and the girls out on the boat, and he looked at it as if it were a vending machine treat that couldn't figure out how to fall. He liked being here, liked spending time with Herring, but there was always some bit of pain involved with the man, some comfort and then the pain, and this was something he hadn't ever thought of until just now. All of this mulling made him ache. He supposed that everyone did have a bit of suffering to them. This was life, the way of things, to be certain. He felt the cat move between his legs. In an old storage chest in the centre of the room he found a VHS tape with some porn on it and put it on. He walked back out to the kitchen and boiled the kettle, and then he sat, the tabby beside him, watching a man and a woman with fine skin and perfectly manicured hair have a bit of fun in the truck bay of what was supposed to be a fire hall. When he hit the bottom of his mug, Gerry realized that he was really quite bored with the whole thing. He found another tape, *Breakfast at Tiffany's*, and he ended up watching it from start to finish, while eating a bowl of instant noodles. He thought that Audrey Hepburn was just about as beautiful a human being as he could bear. He looked at the cat and ran his fingers down its neck and down its back. Gerry said, "Boy, these noodles look like little tapeworms. Speaking of which, if yer gonna be an outdoor cat, I spose we ought to check ya fer tapeworms." The cat closed its eyes to the blue light of the television, appearing to relish his touch. From where he was, he could hear the scraping of Herring's teeth.

# THREE

The rain had been coming down for just about twenty-four hours straight, and the world outside was a series of glossy ballasts, as the rain, the ice, and the snows settled into their truest form, a communion of solutions, routed and stricken, all things receding to their nethermost point. The wharf was flooded, taken, suppressed beneath a platform of inert fluids.

Herring and Gerry were in the basement repairing traps on a set of old bucks topped with a sheet of plywood. Herring had his jig up, too, from which he hung the traps while he worked on them. His grandfather had shown him how to do this. Herring poked his head out the cellar doors.

Gerry said, "Is it still raining?"

"Well, the puddles are still wet," said Herring.

The air compressor was going and his eighteen-gauge brad nailer was connected. There was a bit of sewing to do today, as well. The table saw was there if they needed it, too. Some fellows preferred softwoods, like spruce, for making their traps. Herring didn't like it, though, because the wood was too bright. He liked hemlock and oak and juniper. They had a couple of bows to bend today. To do this, he'd put a pot on the stove and from this a hose that brought the steam into a length of sewer pipe. He'd put his junks of wood in there and let them cook until they were ready to be bent. Years ago, he'd got into making back scratchers, thinking that this would be a profitable venture. He'd gotten pretty good at it, and after a while he had a pile of them that he couldn't get rid of.

Gerry, trying to be as precise as he could be, without really know-ing what he was supposed to be doing, held two strips of hemlock together with his right hand. He fired a one-inch nail, and it took a bounce through the grain and entered the flesh of his palm. When Herring pulled it out with an old pair of side cutters, Gerry said, "Jesus, that hurt so much I might remember not to do that again." The both of them looked down at the blood thumping out of Gerry's hand.

"Well, it's a ways from yer heart," said Herring. "Boy, the only tool you're good with is yer tomahawk." Gerry got so worked up, trying to attain a level of precision he just didn't have the training for, that his hands would shake with the pressure of it all. "We're not building watches here."

Gerry wrapped a measure of duct tape around his hand and seemed content to proceed as if nothing had happened at all. Herring watched the tape fall off of Gerry's hand as he tried to fire another nail where the other had foundered. There was blood on the handle. "What's the matter there, Gerry, you need a bit of hair on that hole?" Gerry jammed the trigger and the shot took. He winked at Herring, triumph blazing in the folds of his eyes. The air compressor roared, filling its bladder.

They worked for a while more, silently, and then Gerry said, "We need some more beer." Herring put down the nailer and turned off the compressor, bled the tank. The phone rang from upstairs and he hopped onto the platform and pulled himself up to the first floor. Rankin Jackson, out at Boatswain Point, a little speckle of a community but five minutes down the road from My Bonnie Harbour, was on the line. His boat hauler, Mantford MacKay, a man with all the contours of an iceberg to him, a man who had spent his life bound by a transitory covenant, one with a bad diet and clogged arteries for handmaids, and who now operated out of My Bonnie River and called the place home, had got the trailer stuck in the backyard trying to load his boat. Sheldon Brehaut had brought out his dozer to clear a path, but it too had got stuck for a while. Somehow or another he'd gotten it free and it had managed to pull the trailer out, back onto the road.

So Rankin was calling everybody he could think of, trying to get all hands on deck to haul the boat out to harder ground, old-fashioned style. "You free in about an hour?" he asked. Herring said that he was, that he would be right over.

"Bring a friend, if ya like," said Rankin, his voice a tranquil and moored contrivance, fit for the ecclesiastical heart.

As they walked out to the rig, Gerry asked Herring if he was all right to handle the thing.

"I drive better when I'm drunk," he said.

—

Rankin Jackson was a tiny fellow, had about as much meat on him as a bicycle. His back was bent like a question mark, and he had terrible arthritis in both knees, hobbling him like a flightless bird. His skin had to it the colour of raw milk and his eyes looked like they had been painted on. His moustache was a kind of stiff vellum. As a matter of fact, you couldn't help but assume that he was a dairy farmer. There didn't seem to be that knot of pride and vanity in him that most men got tangled in. Somehow this arrangement suggested the presence of cows. When Herring and Gerry arrived, there were enough rigs parked on both sides of the road to put a person in mind of a funeral. Mantford was smoking in the cab of his truck, the window down a wee bit. As Herring rounded the cab, he said, "I thought for sure we were here to pull ya out of the yard, Manny." Mantford sighed and worked away at his cigarette. There were around forty of them there, quite a commotion, and things, to Herring's mind, were mighty confused. Some of them nodded at him. There was the odd mumbled hello. Gerry, but a few paces behind, received a few hearty slaps on the back, and his big toothless smile made this little encounter slightly less excruciating for all involved. "Well, this operation is as confused as Father's Day in Georgetown," Herring said. One fellow, Billy Clow, was from Georgetown, and he had to be restrained a bit. Gerry was with Herring and he was from Georgetown, so the slight was allowed to pass. None of these boys were going to scrap because one fellow from

Georgetown was offended. They were here to be of assistance, not to get niggled.

Herring scanned the men. "Too many captains here, I spose, and not enough corks." The men whinged and moved their legs, enacting aimless and frivolous little configurations on the lawn. His evaluation of things was right. Herring made his way through the crowd to a length of rope that hadn't been taken up by anyone else. He got one of the young fellows to climb up on the boat and tie some more ropes. A bunch of the other boys tended to the pine pile cut-offs from when the wharf had been built, which was how they were going to move the boat. Her name was the *Jenny Lynn*, after Rankin's mother, and she was a very fine vessel.

The rain was still falling, tapping the PVC highliners of the assembled men with the mad consistency of roofers blasting their way through each new bundle laid before them. If ever your ear truly took hold of this class of bombardment, it was enough to drive a man off his rocker.

The men with ropes tied loop-knots into their ends, and Rankin, about twenty feet from the bow, rather pleased that the men were organizing themselves so, cupped his hands about his thin mouth and said, "Now, let's not get too horny here, all right, boys. Nice and gentle, if ya will." The men readied their grips on the lines. "On the count of three," said Rankin. When the keel came off its stands and hit the sod, the grass and the soil hissed as if it were an irritated chemistry. The men leaned real hard into their lines, some of their noses right close to the ground. A few of them spilled, wiped out, but quickly regained their footings so as to avoid being torpidly run over by the plow, its blade wheezing like the last breaths of King Saul. They hauled the *Jenny Lynn* over a number of piles, and then let her slow, to permit the boys in charge of the piles to move the ones now printed into the earth from the stern to the bow.

The wives brought out coffee and cherry balls left in their freezers from the holidays. Rankin made sure to directly thank every man, save Herring. And though it was still early in the day, and as if to fill the wound of this lack of expressed gratitude, Herring asked if anyone wanted to go for beers. A silence came over the assembly. Coffee cups steamed and teeth were prodded at by tongues. A few cigarettes tried to find flame, but failed. "Well, don't everyone say no all at once now," Herring said, and then he walked away, out to the road where his rig awaited him. Gerry stood where he was.

A pair of red hands pitched a miserable snowball at Herring as he got out by the ditch and it missed his right shoulder by about two yards, obliterating itself upon contact with the road. Herring got into his rig, and, as he wiped the condensation from the windshield with the side of his arm, he said, "Jesus fuck." He didn't know what on earth had come over him. And as he drove home, squinting through the small rectangle he had cleared upon the surface of the window, never considering that he could enlarge its scope in a number of simple ways, he used the nail of his index finger to pick out bits of walnut and cherry from the gaps in his teeth.

The men hung around the Jackson place for not too much longer. Conversations of the casual kind were, at this time, with only a few Saturdays to setting day, generally considered a trifling and shallow pursuit. If a man chattered, his mind was assumed to be uneasy. Quiet held primacy, and the sound of these fishermen, gathered as they were, and who understood what was before them, was a faint quiver, like a string line pulled thoroughly taut, compelled by the wind to speak of its tension. Their arms and their legs tingled to be rid of the Devil's work, of idleness. They had gathered to do their good deed in the hope that this amity would bestow them some store of luck and benevolence when out on the water. Jack MacLeod pointed at the curl of Gerry's nose and said, "You got one hell of a zit there." Gerry said, "I'm thinking that I'll let this one brew and get a good pop out of 'er."

—

Herring called the plant in the morning and spoke with the dispatcher.

"You got any spare mud riding around anywheres?" he said.

"How much you need?"

"Oh, a yard is all I'm after, I spose."

"And what time would you like it?"

"I'm not up to too much trouble today. Anytime works fer me."

"Okay. I'll see what I can do."

"Is Horace still driving?"

"Yeah, he's blessed us yet again with his presence."

"Well, if he's willing and able, would you mind sending him over?"

—

A mutt chased the concrete truck as it slowed to a halt on the road. The air brakes let out a great whimper and the wheels of the truck turned and it began to back down the drive. The mutt pursued for a few more yards, then grew disinterested and took off down the road towards the cove.

Herring had the doors open and a bunch of fish trays stacked, ready and waiting. He'd spent the day keeping the stove hot and putting swatches of felt paper in the traps under the ballast slats. He had a bolt of the felt paper up on the work bench and a little jig, which was only a piece of lath, set up to spare him measuring each piece. He ripped and he ripped and he listened to the crackle of the stove. He got into such a rhythm and then it was over. He made enough space on the floor to flip each trap so her belly was exposed.

Horace Trainor was a few years older than Herring. His face proclaimed a great, white beard, so lustrous and contoured it was as if he'd tacked the carcass of a gannet to his chin. He was from Melville but had married a fine woman from up west, whom he'd met at a kitchen party in town many years ago, and whose roots ran deep and would not be disturbed. And so, in the year that Angus MacLean became premier, he picked up and moved himself to her, for you couldn't truly blame him, because she was a dark-haired and very fine, slightly mysterious thing. And there and ever since, he'd fished the fall seasons out of Miminegash and drove truck back east for something to do when he had the time. Horace had strange, reserved eyes, the kind that are quietly overwrought because they have beheld cancer and its routing of a family. He had worn hands and stiffly bent fingers, and one too many holes in the elbows of his green sweater. He was rather neckless in that his head just kind of dissolved into a pair of shoulders. He didn't like commotion and yelling, and if a fellow on a crew, doing curbs in a new development or some such thing, began hollering at him, Horace would tumble out of the cab and take him aside and scoop him real close, so as to inform the offender of what was what, and then everything was usually copacetic.

Horace walked to the back of the rig, his steel toes scuffing the gravel. There was a pack of smokes in the stomach of his sweater, this little bulge of a rectangle.

Herring pointed at it and said, "Horace, you've got to chew your food."

Horace laughed. "I keep 'em there so's I 'member to smoke 'em."

They shook hands.

"A man with your name ought to have gotten into horses, eh there old-timer?"

Horace liberated the smokes. "Jesus, you'd think it's Pick-on-Horace Day down here in the harbour," he said. "Nope, ol' Horace here never had any truck with horses. The only truck I ever had was with trucks." And he slapped the ladder up to the drum.

"Where you coming from?"

Horace said, "Oh, they're pouring a wheelchair ramp there at the community centre. After this I gotta go and get another load and head out to see the McCarthy boys."

Horace turned out a bit of concrete at the top of the chute.

Herring said, "Give her a bit of a drink, huh?"

"I'm not sure how much I got left, eh," said Horace.

Herring brought Horace a cup of coffee, and they sat in some lawn chairs and watched the trees and listened to the winds, the drum of the truck turning and turning, and the whole machine rocking, bobbing on its many wheels, hopping from foot to foot as if it were a child who had to pee.

Horace said, "How many new traps going out?"

"I got twenty or thirty. Fifteen double-enders and fifteen a' them," said Herring, and he pointed over his shoulder with his thumb. "Big fishing this fall?"

Horace said, "I got fifty left-rights going out. Fuck. But I haven't got one trap I like. Started off, fella said he'd build me fifty traps. And I said, naw, and he said, yeah, I'm building 'em. I didn't know he couldn't build traps. He said I'll staple 'em."

"Yeah," said Herring.

"I never built a trap since my father passed away, but I cut all the heads anyway before he departed. His eyesight was going and everything," said Horace. He puffed on his smoke and inspected the grease embedded in his left hand. "It was just hard for me to go in the shop. Me and him was pretty close."

"Yeah," said Herring. The mutt came back down the road in the opposite direction. As it passed the barn, it stared into the cavity of the doors. The three of them all observing one another, jammed like keys in a frozen padlock.

"Time is, you know—" said Horace, his thoughts getting away from him. "Yeah, I had everybody in around workin' on them traps. The fella, he stapled them. So, then we had to re-nail 'em. We had to nail 'em. Then we had to— we took them, and when they built them they never even put the ballast slats on 'em. They just framed them and they fucking cut off all the sills. I had my sills like twenty-six inch and there's twenty-three-inch centres. They cut them all off, for fuck's sake. Now the bows are showing through the, through the—"

"Oh my fuck," said Herring.

"And then they went to rig heads. They made all the heads for a trap that was two inches shorter and tried putting 'em in it."

"Oh my good God. See, now, the only thing I had problems with. A little bit of lacing. Not too serious. The rest of the trap was built the way I had it. A little bit of lacing, a few holes."

"And then we got the heads all straightened out, okay? Nice head, everything. Gave fifteen of them to a fella and he said, Oh, them heads were too big. I had to cut three meshes off 'em. Now I got a trap that's this wide and inside it's that wide."

Herring laughed.

"I just had to take what I got, like, you know what I mean?" said Horace. "No, I was cutting heads for the last ten years. Dad's gone five years, but the last ten years I cut the heads. Not that his eyesight was real bad, but he'd go at 'er. But I learnt from him."

"Holy fuck," said Herring, "I couldn't cut a head. Jesus Christ, I start going and I eye 'er up, and if you hold 'er right together in a ball, I can get 'er."

"It's a different program," said Horace.

"And all I got going through my mind is, if I stretch this out around a wire and hook the wire up to a two-twenty, I can press a button, and zip."

"Yeah, two-twenty."

"I'd burn them all out. There it is," said Herring.

"The biggest thing is, I'm just gonna tell you now, is me and dad building traps and everything was good now. Lots of crew wants to come with me. And between me and you, I'm not cheap, but they all want cash.

"And, well, I may's well go and pay an extra fucking twenty dollars. But I'm going to build 'em next year. I like the guys that'll help me. They're good guys, you know what I mean. The biggest thing that was bothering me is my father just not being there. Just going into the shop all the time."

"And him not there."

"Yeah. This year was a better winter," said Horace, "and even though I spent more time in the shop. I'm not gonna tell you what I was doing. You know what I was doing. Drinking. But before I'd go in there I'd break down. This winter, maybe once or twice. There's a fella brought me a paddle, an oar, for my birthday. You prolly seen something like this before. But anyway, it had a picture of his boat on it and a bouquet of flowers setting in a pair of rubber boots and everything. And it was nice. Well, I kinda lost it, but it's five years."

"Yeah, that's nice."

"I'm only human and I ain't scared to say that I am. We were so close."

"Oh yeah."

"He'd want you in there, too, you know."

"Oh yeah, that's the way I look at it now, too."

"Yeah, he'd want you in there."

"Get at it, you lazy fuck, you. Don't be drinking 'cos I'm gone."

They stood up and Horace sprayed the chute with his hose. He backed the truck up to the trays and filled them up with what he had left. The concrete, this magical and obedient stuff, sliding from one vessel to another without complaint, as grey and as cheerless as a penitentiary. Herring thought of all of the walls in the world holding people in. And then, of course, he thought of all of the walls in the world holding people out. He tried to picture them and connect them all together in his mind. There was a bleak kind of honesty to this line of thinking.

Horace asked where he could wash out, and Herring told him to park beside the barn.

While Horace moved his truck, Herring took his tomato cans and began dipping these into the trays, packing them with concrete, his hands bare. He paid the burn no heed. Then he'd walk over to the traps and pour the concrete into the ballasts, and then he'd walk back to the trays and scoop some more. Each ballast was about two-and-a-half tomato cans. This process was heavy with walking. Just him and his thoughts. He stopped and had a splash of coffee and got a joint going.

Horace was at the doors. He gave Herring the ticket and said, "Anyway, we'll be talking."

"You have a good one," said Herring.

The truck rolled down to the road and disappeared. He looked at the work before him and tried not to let his mind become overwhelmed. Small strokes fell the mighty oaks, he said to himself. Another mutt ran by, headed towards the cove. He popped a Ronnie Milsap tape into his old stereo and hit play. The music warbled out, as if the stereo was on fire, but then it got going and sounded true.

—

Well, the truth of the matter was that Gerry was very much in love with one of the servers at Maid Marian's diner there, in town. He couldn't recall her name exactly, but he knew that it was exotic sounding. Colette or Claudine or Camille, though maybe it was just Daphne. She flustered him without her having to do anything, least of which recognizing that a man like Gerry even existed, or that he merited her attentions. Gerry had even written her a poem in which he had tried, in earnest, to express just exactly how she made him feel. How she elevated his heartbeat and made his pits damp. He could feel himself just roasting, cooking himself. She seemed to him like a kind of princess stolen from another century. She was the kind of woman that men would gladly go on crusades for or in whose name they'd start a war. He was torturing himself. Gerry knew, all the while, that a woman like her, any woman, hell, all women like her, ought to have no interest in a man such as he. She was so fine, so beautiful, that she made him feel ugly. And yet he couldn't stop thinking about her. When he had nothing on the go, when his mind was an aimless thing, she came to him, always, as if he were parked at the drive-in, watching the film of her grace and beauty. Herring had said that he should just try dipping his toe in the water, that he should just say something to her other than ordering from the menu, to feel her out, to see if there was any kind of potential. But there wasn't. Gerry knew.

He had been feeling confident that morning, though. His brother, Charley, had driven him into town for a dental appointment. He was getting a bridge put in on his upper teeth. When the procedure was over, and the dentist had walked him through how to care for the bridge, he rinsed his mouth out and walked down the hall to the washroom. After he locked the door, he stood and stared at the reflection of his mouth in the mirror, and the sight of him wasn't so much of a new man altogether, but of a newer version made so by virtue of fresher parts, so to speak. His new teeth seemed to be, like Colette, forever unaffected by time and deterioration. His eyes welled up, and he blinked tears onto his cheeks. The whole thing hadn't been cheap, but he had gone to see Lizzie Francis, one of the Abegweit councillors, in Morell, about getting some assistance. He said to her, "Listen, Ms. Francis, I got no problem going to the funeral home. They got a barrel of teeth, and somewheres in there is a set that'll fit me like white on rice." Lizzie recoiled at his suggestion. Hoped it was a joke. He told her that the worst part of having no teeth was that you couldn't really taste anything. And you had to cut up all your food into portions that could just be swallowed. In the end, the teeth had been worth the pity and the groveling.

After Gerry's appointment, Charley had been hungry and suggested they hit up the diner. Gerry said he was anxious about eating anything for a while, but agreed to go and just drink water. He remembered that he had the poem in an inside pocket. Maybe today's the day, he thought. The two of them stood shivering outside the front door and finished their cigs, the sun hesitant for any publicity and the winds howling down Brackley, from the north.

Charley flicked away his cigarette butt and reached for the door. "Jeez, Gerry, you look like a million bucks." Gerry smiled.

Well, it turned out that Colette wasn't working today, and all of a sudden Gerry lost hope. He couldn't hide his dejection. His brother pushed food into his gob like a man possessed, and Gerry sat opposite, pushing his glass around with his thumb. "Jeez, what's up? You look goddamn miserable," Charley said, taking a pause, his mouth full and about to get fuller. Gerry didn't want to talk about it. "Don't be a sook," Charley said. Gerry looked out the window. It was as if he'd totally forgotten that he'd just got new teeth, Charley said to their mother later that night. "That's Gerry's way. He's always been like that," she said. "I don't get it," said Charley. "I just don't even know."

—

He had the washing in and was feeling a little randy, so he went up and knocked on Sheila's door. He had with him a mickey of lemon gin. He had no affinity for it, but lemon gin was panty remover, tried and true. She was wearing those tight nylon and Lycra pants and a pair of white sneakers, and it was about all Gerry could do not to just rip her clothes off. They smoked a little pot and shot some gin, and then Sheila got up and put a Deana Carter record into the machine. When she turned off the lights, Gerry knew that the deal had been sealed. They started making out and then they were both peeling their clothes off. He kissed her thighs and then moved his head to her crotch and pushed the tip of his tongue into her vagina, drawing the whole of the alphabet into the folds about her clitoris. She tasted great, brackish and wet, and Gerry found that, for but a brief moment, he was overcome with the religiousness of the whole thing. Women were grand, he thought, trying to make sense of what had been, overall, quite an emotional day. The tides had been incredibly high the past two days, he thought. And then he got back to work.

—

"If I tore my back, I'd still work. If I broke my wrist, I spose I'd still try to work. There's not much that would keep me away, you see. That's just the way I am." They were working their way through a bottle of red wine. Gerry didn't really enjoy the taste of wine, but the warm radiance of it sure was hitting the mark. The lights were on. "I worked as a painter for a while there and I got to be real particular about the work that I was doing. If I seen that I'd missed a spot, I'd give the whole wall a new coat. I got so damn particular I made no damn money. And when I did, I'd be dancing with the door for an hour and a half with these folks. Old ones. Had to tell you their entire life story. And then you'd have to help them find their wallet or their purse. And blind as bats, all of 'em. The wall could be greener than envy and they'd say, Jeez, that white is perfect." Sheila laughed a bit. He could tell that she was starting to lose interest. It was getting late. "The worst job I ever had was cleaning pigeon shit out of the attic of St. Cuthbert's. It was terrible. So hot you could barely breathe and you were just covered in it. I got five dollars an hour and it took me three months." He poured her some more wine. "Nobody else would do it."

Sheila fetched a box of crackers from the cupboard and wrestled her hand inside.

"Here, I wrote you a poem," he said and passed her the crumpled sheet. Sheila seemed somewhat disturbed, but she received it anyway, straining to make sense of his penmanship. Once she'd understood what words were what, she couldn't make sense of the whole thing, the message of it. "What kinda man writes poetry?" she said, and as these words came out of her mouth, she knew that she'd hurt the man once and for all, perhaps for good, and she cursed the lack of decency in her heart. Gerry just looked away, and as he did so, she came to think that he'd been trying to tell her something, one single important thing.

—

The phone rang and Herring shot up from the chesterfield. Gerry was on the line. He was frantic, and when he didn't seem able to communicate the nature of the emergency, he just kept swearing. It was two-thirty in the morning. Gerry had left his bridge in the pocket of his pants and these had been put through the wash. "Can't this wait until the morning?" said Herring. Gerry didn't reply. It was a forty-minute drive to Georgetown. Herring replaced the phone, lowered himself into the basement and grabbed a pair of needle-nose pliers. He found the keys to his rig and as he opened the side door, the cat burst out and put for the fields. And the swiftness of its travel, frantic and more alive, like a kind of prison break, suggested to him that it wasn't interested in ever truly coming back.

There wasn't much room to operate between the agitator and the paddles, and it was painful leaning over as he was, but Herring took his time, tried to work as precisely as he could. The teeth, all five of them, were lodged into the holes in the tub, like buckshot into a deer, and, given how pristine they were, Herring was anxious about scraping them with his pliers. Gerry was holding a flashlight above Herring, though the shadows it created were more of a hindrance than a help. Herring tried his best not to be curt with the man. He would isolate one of the teeth and then he would wrap it with a rag and then, by placing a little block of wood under the jaws of the tool, he would leverage them out. They were in there pretty good, embedded and fit like strange little mortise-and-tenon joints. Gerry kept pestering him, asking after him how was it going. "Gerry, if yer in a hurry, yer in the wrong place," said Herring, his pants slid down below the gloomy crack of his bum. The teeth would come, even if he had to remove the whole damn drum.

And as he successfully retrieved a tooth from the wall of the drum, he realized, quite without any sentimentality or any prompting, that Gerry was as faithful a friend as he could be to a person such as he, and that it was precisely this faith in him that had him here, biting his lip at three-thirty in the morning, trying to be patient and genial. Strangely enough, prior to this little scene, he had never thought of Gerry as a friend. But now, the notion took a hold on him. He swallowed hard, yoked by the sense that something had opened in him, given him a kind of admittance. Yes, he was running on a drunken sleep, which was no sleep at all, that had been divided by the need of another, but somehow or another he felt quite awake.

When the ordeal was over, and Gerry could breathe a little lighter, the teeth back together in a bowl with their wire connector, he looked at Herring and said, "That was some hellish."

—

He was down in the cabin of the *M&M*, sitting with his thoughts, listening to the 350 tremble and drone in its wonderful dialect, when he heard his name being called. Euna had stepped over the coaming and was on the platform. She smiled at him and he smiled at her, and as she looked at the state of the boat, she said, "This used to be a better looking boat, huh."

"It's a bit like me in that way," said Herring. "You know charm when you see it, eh?"

"Listen, I'm going to—" and she stopped. "How are things coming? D'you think you're ready and done for the season?" Herring nodded his head. "Does the Pope wear a funny hat and shit in the woods?" he said. "Well, anyway, I'm all done worrying."

"Well, good then," and she hopped back to the wharf.

He walked back to the washboard where the waters were disrupted, churned by the prop, and he said, "Euna, I just don't know why I cut that hole in the floor." He looked to her and she looked to him, and she said, "Okay."

—

Whenever it was that he found himself at the culmination of a good bender, his skin would revolt, just as it had done with his father, turning crimson, as if the veins in him wanted to be free of all that liquor, to bound away, to seek after another bodily habitat, and these swatches would become scaly and painful ornaments that he could not be rid of. His father told him that tomato paste was the miracle cure. Then again, he also told his son that his acne would go away when he stopped worrying about it. Herring, like his father, would stock up on cans of tomato paste from Keeping's, and he would spend hours with the stuff on his head and his face, his elbows. This procedure created a hell of a mess. His family doctor, a fellow by the name of Newton MacDonald, who was older than Methuselah's goat and had a hunchback that had terrorized Herring as a young boy, had informed him that this was a rather strange breed of dermatitis. Newton then asked him if he'd eaten any venison from the mainland in the past year. He said no. And after this there had been a long, strange bit of silence in the examination room. Newton, it ought to be noted, didn't particularly enjoy seeing Herring all that often, either, because this fisherman invariably had a number of rather serious ailments, bones that had been broken and set poorly, if at all, hernias that were exacerbated by sheer ignorance, funguses that needlessly lingered, rotten teeth and exposed nerves, rashes that enacted considerable tissue damage and then degenerated, morphed into some other infinitely complex problem. It was utter neglect and dazzling stupidity. One time, when the girls were still infants, Euna had found Herring keeled over by the barn. Euna called Agnes in a right panic, and Newton, who happened to be out at the cove paying Agnes a visit, agreed to whip over. When he got there, he took a hose and sprayed the man. Revived, Herring had started up after him, chasing and cursing him, his vanity and his gall. When the tests came back they revealed that Herring had endured a seizure. "Just kind of a fluke, really," said Newton. He had wanted to sound reassuring.

He was sitting in the tub, shivering a little, covered in tomato paste, and he was casting his mind backward, to Euna. He was trying to identify the moment when he understood, or when he had sensed, that what had burgeoned between them was irreconcilable. He had been late for a Thanksgiving supper out at Agnes's place on the shore. His licence had been suspended for the second time, so he resorted to riding his Honda four-wheeler about. Somehow or another he missed the driveway and ditched the thing, and in the process, he broke his nose, tore something in his foot. The week after, he was laid up on the chesterfield, watching the idiot box with the girls, who were but five and six, and Euna said that she was going into Montague. When she got home about two hours later and was in the midst of preparing supper, he asked her if she had refilled his Tylenol 3s. She hadn't remembered to do so, and this was immediately odd to him, because Euna never forgot anything. But he hadn't made a fuss of it, hadn't made a scene. Sometime after this she quit her managerial position at the Kent store. It was a shame because she was well liked there. One night she said to him, as he was touching her under the sheets, his hands on either side of her stomach, trying to hold her together, as he saw it retrospectively, so as to see if she was in the mood, that she wanted to go back to school. For some reason, he felt that this was somehow an affront to him, to his role, felt that, quite in truth, she was being disobedient. It was as if she had said that she didn't think he was a man. No, that wasn't it at all. In her admission, he had sensed betrayal. And he snapped at her, not too, too harshly, but still a good snap, like what a wound-up tea towel can do in terms of damage. Well, she seemed to get scared by it all, by the changes that she thought she had foolishly desired, and by what she considered to be no concern for any person other than her own yearnings. Euna believed that personal desires were antithetical to good parenting. It was all she knew. And so, after this, she seemed to grow skittish. They stopped being intimate. And then Herring cut the hole in the floor of the living room, and she had moved in with her mother for a while, until she found a little house to rent near Belfast. This sequence, as he revisited it, had been something of a whirlwind. Weeks later he realized she had never really asked him what he wanted of life, and it was this lack that had been the thorn, so to speak. He wondered if his inability to say this to her had made him weak in her eyes. Maybe he didn't want to be a bloody fisherman. But, if it wasn't fishing, he didn't know what he would do with himself.

He ran a bit of water, waited for it to heat, and began cleansing himself of the red paste he was set in, the thick and clotted shanks of it running off of him like some fetal membrane.

—

Herring lowered himself into the basement and unlocked the gun cabinet. He set the recoil pad of the stock on the dirt and put his mouth over the muzzle. Just practice.

—

Bobby Sorry lived with his mother, Alberta, in a little place, just an intersection of dirt roads, really, called Iris, which still had a number of hippies who had congregated and hunkered down there back in the early seventies, who spurned the notion that they relinquish their call to arms. They were still fighting the good fight, but nobody really knew what this meant or what the good fight actually was, other than an excuse to permit all things to enter a state of true disrepair. Bobby was but a year or two north of fifty. He was a cousin of Gerry's. Everybody called him Stretch and Herring could never properly recall why he was named so. When he had asked Gerry, the answer was, "Oh, 'cos a long stretch of misery." The first time he'd been out on the water, Herring had watched the man inhale a handful of joints, almost pressing them into his mouth, such was his wildness. When they started picking the traps, Bobby just tossed everything he touched right back over. No grading, no eggs, nothing. Herring cut the engine and hollered at the man. "What are ya doing?" Bobby looked up from the thrash and struggle of the lobsters he was about to plunge his arms into, his eyes red and his face just as green as baby food. Like a deranged, and yet somehow festive, surgeon. He said, "What? We're sposed to keep 'em?"

The house they lived in was rotten, and it had no plumbing, which struck Herring as madness. There was no excuse for it in this day and age. He imagined the old woman having to use the shitter in the winter months. The poor old thing, scuffling across the snowdrifts without a morsel of food in her guts, muttering "glib, glib, glib" to herself. The cold and the wind just pulling the years off of her. About fifteen years before, Stretch had been married to a woman. They'd had a son, who, rumour had it, was either a cripple or mentally handi-capped, or something. They'd split and he refused to pay alimony, so he just never worked. He totally shut down, moved back in with his mother. This was the story Herring had heard. And, in truth, he'd never had the gumption to corroborate any of this. It wasn't his busi-ness, he reckoned, but something about this story really upset his stomach. Turning your back on your kid, to not work, was strange and unnatural. To Herring it seemed that the man had chosen to move from one prison cell to a much, much smaller one, and had, all the while, confused this downsizing, this recession, with enfolding the bosom of Liberty herself. Some people were like this, though. They had never experienced freedom, and the thought of it terrified them, ran them in the opposite direction altogether. This long stretch of misery, most of it self-inspired.

Stretch did under-the-table work with bees and blueberries, and he had another gig cutting cemetery lawns. He was a genius with bees. You'd get talking to him and he'd say things like one out of every three bites yer gonna take in yer life are directly related to bees, or, strawberries and corn are the only things that can exist without bees, or, how a reconnaissance bee will communicate to the others in the hive how far away a flower patch is by shaking its ass and flying in a figure-eight formation. And, all females have the potential to become the queen, but the differential is the royal jelly.

Herring walked up the path to the house and knocked on the door with his left kneecap. Stretch came and opened it, his skin the colour of porridge, his moustache like the steel wire potters use to cut clay. The place smelled of cigarettes and manure and mould. He had a slightly haunted look to his eyes, the loneliness and despair of a man who was thoroughly convinced that reasonable foreplay ought to involve pulling hair and smacking. Stretch was something of an indoor cat, and as such, Herring tried his utmost to keep him away from Euna and the girls. The floors were all decayed and crumbling, and it didn't take much imagination to notice the dirt of the basement. His mother was an incredible baker. Herring sat with them and had a biscuit with some butter. There was a hockey game on. Herring said that he just didn't get hockey, ya know. You do all this work for the puck and you get to the other end only to have the thing stolen from you. There's as much sense in hockey as a dog chasin' a car. Alberta and Stretch just looked at him, their brows as creased and rutted as a pair of mining camps. Herring said, "Wrestling. Now, there's a sport. I'd take Jake the Snake over Gretzky any day." Alberta asked him to make sure he dropped off a couple feeds of lobster, and Herring said he would. He made sure to smile at her as well as he could muster.

They drove around for a while, smoking shatter. Herring was thinking of making a trip into town to Mermaid Marine, but then he realized that the place was likely closed. He needed to get a few things. Herring's foot was heavy on the pedals, his steering fitful, and as he covered ground the two bags of sugar, the box of galvanized nails, his damaged copy of the Stright–MacKay catalogue, and a bunch of six-inch wooden rings for the traps fell from the seat to the floor and then shifted all about until they were trapped beneath the seats. Whenever Stretch got high, he'd start asking you a million little idiotic questions that you mostly didn't, and weren't ever going to, know the answers to. One time he'd asked Herring about what kind of anchor you'd need for a lobster boat. Herring had said, "I don't know. Something heavy, though, with a good bit of chain, I spose." Herring watched Stretch nod and pretend to run some calculations and ratios through his head. And then Stretch had said, "Well, a mortgage is a pretty good anchor. So's a woman, I spose. Just a pair of eternal anchors, them."

Herring told him what was what, asked him if he was good for setting day and the like. Stretch said he was good to go. They stopped at the house for some shine. Herring had incorrectly assumed that Stretch would stay in the rig. When he came downstairs, Stretch was standing in the living room. He said, "Boy, yer place is beginning to look just like mine."

—

"Jesus H. Christ, that is rugged stuff," said Herring, trying hard not to clamp his cheeks with his teeth. He had driven out to My Bonnie Harbour North, which was about twenty minutes southeast of Irish Montague, to visit Rupert Ellis. Sometimes you could make out North, the Clow wharf there, too, from Boatswain Point, but you had to know how to see through the Gordons and Herring Islands, whose beaches were legendary among the locals for their oysters. All his life Rupert had been notoriously fond of drink, just a famous gulper, one with an immense gift of gab, in addition to being a tall drink of a man, a veritable mammal of a human being. So people came to calling him The Bear. And then this became the full title, Rupert "the Bear" Ellis. Some of the boys with an ear for the music and meanings of words, the play of them, came to state that he, Rupert "the Bear" Ellis, was a drinker of barrels. It was also noted that, as he'd spent his days out in the tar sands, pulling barrels of oil from the earth, he was also a producer of barrels. Well, after these serendipities had been recorded, his full title had been abridged to the mononymous and utterly appropriate Barrels. Now retired, he had come home to live the good life, to relax and drink and try his hand at painting. His life was mostly a kind of stationary one. There was a confusion and a vague paralysis there that you couldn't help but pity, and as such he'd become gaunt in the way that some career alcoholics can be.

When Herring saw him, he said, "Jeez, Barrels, you're wasting away. Pretty soon ya'll just be a cock and some sneakers." Barrels was always in a celebratory mood, most especially when he drank, but it was exactly this quality that rendered him somewhat suspect, because, as Herring knew, a man could not sustain the energy of happiness by feigning it. He felt that no man or woman could trick a thing into existence. There was no permanence in this strategy. Herring had never thought of drinking as an act of happiness, hell, not even of joy nor love, but he had also never thought of drinking as the opposite, as sorrow nor desolation. No, he had always, it seemed to him, drank for something to do, as rote, a memorization. Drinking was just a way, a decent enough way, to pass the time. "What in tarnation is in this?" said Herring, staring at the mug in his hands, the black roil of it. Whatever the concoction was, it didn't seem keen to sit still, was a mess of bubbles.

"If I told you what was in it, you'd never forgive me," said Barrels, smiling a fine smile. His teeth were lovely things, and if you drank with Barrels, you got to see them quite often. Good teeth were hard to come by out in these parts and Herring didn't think that Barrels quite understood how stirring his teeth actually were. Gerry loathed to be in the man's company. Rupert Barrels had just been blessed with electrifying teeth. But, so had Gerry, if you thought about it. They, the two of them, were the yin and yang of odontology.

Herring always visited Barrels before the season began. Not only were these little visits just something that he liked to do, but he also felt compelled to come and talk nonsense. The thought of him out fishing not having spoken to the man vexed him. And so he came.

"You know, Herring, men like us, we're too honest to be millionaires," said Barrels. Herring didn't know what they were now supposed to be talking about. Barrels motioned for Herring to stand, and he ushered him into another room, adjacent to the kitchen. There was a canvas leaned against the wall, and Barrels asked him what he thought of it. Most of the canvas was a kind of vortex of greys and blues, and in the middle of this gyre was a touch of this whitish, pearl colour. "It looks like an airplane stuck in a cloud," said Herring, and he threw a bit more of the fellow's solution down his throat. Barrels rested his chin on the knuckles of his right hand. He said, "You know, when I was a young buck, I used to go with a girl that smelled like a Digby herring." A bit of a hush came between them. The drink in Herring's hand and guts began to feel like it was cast of iron. "I reckon Heaven smells just like a Digby herring." Herring still didn't know what they were supposed to be talking about. This felt a lot like trying to decipher the Bible.

—

He got pulled over just a few kilometres south of Irish Montague, on a winding stretch of Route 4 that made its way through a set of hills, just about his favourite section of road on the whole island, especially in fall, with the turning of the leaves all about, sensuous peaks and valleys, and, after he had slowed and stopped on the shoulder, he rolled down the window and lit a cig to help with his stomach, which felt like it might spasm out of him, just a sack of wolverines.

The officer came up to the window and she said, "Herring, I thought it was you. Did you hear about Randy?"

"Lillian, is that you?"

She set her hands on the door panel, at the bottom of the window. Lillian was Charley's wife, and Randy was Gerry's eldest brother. Randy had been ice fishing up west and he'd thrown back a quart of shine. His heart just stopped.

"Tragic," he said, looking at the nail polish on her fingers.

"You've got some bad breath there," she said. "I ought to make you spend the night in Sleepy Hollow."

He offered her a cigarette.

"You knew it was me when you pulled me over," he said. "Anyway, as far as I can tell, I pay my taxes, same as everybody else, and that means I own this half of the road as much as that half of the road."

They smoked together for a moment, looking down the illuminated road as if doing so would shorten not only the length of its transit, but the general direction of all things. The sky was uniformly black and the stars were out. The universe was expanding, all right. Lillian sighed. "Just keep it between the mustard and the mayo."

—

Gerry was pretty distraught when he opened the door. His face was red and sweaty and the place smelled like a locker room, in that the absence of soap was unmistakable. They sat at the rickety table for a few minutes so that Gerry could rightly collect himself. Herring made him a cheese sandwich, nervous that his guts would turn on him, given the expiration date on the slices in the refrigerator.

They drove for a while, just puttering, as if new parents trying to get an infant to sleep, chain smoking and listening to the radio, waiting for the sun to come up. Herring turned off the highway just before Wood Islands, and as he was passing Hooper's he saw Red John lugging buckets of molasses from his rig into the back entrance. "Wait just a minute," he said and cranked the wheel, scratching a U-ey over the pavement.

—

"Ya got me, ya bastards," said Red John, and they clinked their respective bottles of shine together, their backs leaned up against the many freezers in the mudroom. Red John said, "I've got boxes and boxes of this stuff in the basement. You gotta know alcoholics to move yer liquor. Good thing I know ya boys."

"That's some sun porch you've on you there," said Herring, patting John's paunch. John's face twitched at this wound. He tended to the disobedient hairs in his moustache, licking the side of his thick thumb and running a bit of dribble over the crowns of these whiskers. People were forever making fun of his body. He had three moles on his neck, just below the left ear, and the parity of their settings had a calibre of mathematical precision to them that was, quite frankly, pleasing to the eye. Some of the older fishermen were split over the matter of nomenclature. Half of them seemed to delight in calling them Larry, Curly, and Moe, while others, with more warmth and divinity, perhaps, referred to them as the Father, the Son, and the Holy Ghost. That three little growths on a man's neck should have such power, inspire such fervour and spirituality, even camaraderie, seemed a wholly logical thing to all and sundry. There was a Catholic, a man by the name of Danny McKearney, and he and his brother, Séamus, would come all the way down from Naufrage, like bloody pilgrims, before the lobster season began, to get a look at Red John's spots. This ritual of theirs was clockwork. Now, of course, they pretended to be just down to see the sights or to see a man in Pinette about some gear. Some of the locals would gather on the day and take great delight in observing the two brothers greet and chatter with Red John. Danny and Séamus were so polite, too, that they'd wait until John had accepted their payment for the fuel, before heading back to the rig, so that they could make the sign of the cross. Some people started to call him John the Apostle, but it didn't stick. He was just too red to be anything else. John had done his best to pretend that this whole song and dance wasn't actually occurring, that he was ignorant of the matter, but in truth you could tell it didn't quite sit right with him, that, when he was at home, and safe from the devilry of the world, it chewed at him, held precious sleep at bay.

"Pretty good glow off 'er," said Gerry. He looked at the liquid in his hands and scrutinized.

"Gerry, ya still tryin' to get around with that Georgetown licence of yers?" said John.

"Does a duck's boner drag weeds there, John?" said Gerry.

John held up a coffee mug and said, "You boys want some stay awake?" He went and filled up the machine with water and grounds. Herring burped into a closed fist and looked through the lace curtains, as the sunlight reared up the trunks of the spruce trees.

"I remember the first time they nabbed me for drinking and driving," said John. "I was in at The Black Girder there, in Cardigan. You boys remember that place?"

Gerry looked at Herring. "The ol' hug and slug."

"Their punch was shine and Tang. Well, anyway—"

"Souris has good shine," said Herring.

"Fort Augustus, too," Gerry said.

"Those wood apes up in Tignish have good stuff, as well," said Red John. "Anyway, I spent three weeks in jail and paid $1,500 in fines.

And the judge took my licence for three years. Those three weeks were some boring. I'd shower for a goddamn hour just to pass the time. We were so bored I seen a fella stick his own thumb up his arse just for something to do. And the worst of it was, nobody, I mean nobody, played cards."

"Was yer judge Mary Bell?" said Herring.

"Ya, the one and only." Red John walked to the threshold of the door and looked anxiously to the parking lot. "She's good at her job, though." He bent down and repaired his laces. "It's a shitty job, but someone's gotta do it. And she's a handsome woman." Herring told them about the first time his licence had been revoked. He spent the winter getting around on his four-wheeler. When the river froze, you could get to Boatswain Point in about twenty minutes. He said, "The ice so smooth you could slap a puck a mile or two."

Red John took off his coat and his toque and cracked his knuckles. He told them that back in the day, if you wanted to hide your shine, or anything, really, from the Mounties, you'd bury it in horse manure. Didn't matter what you put out there, it would never freeze. "You boys want that coffee?" he said. "It's strong stuff. I like to see my spoon stand up, huh." Red John said that they were welcome to hang out as long as they wanted. He had a day to get started, had to get the place ready for customers, pumps to open and shelves to stock and whatnot.

—

The time, for Red John, passed rather quickly. Willy Lyon MacKenzie pulled into the store around half-three and filled up his rig and a couple of jerry cans. He had a peahen in the back of his rig, and she was pacing, nervous. Herring had passed out in the truck, and Gerry was sitting outside, next to the ice freezer, shivering on an aluminum chair with yellow webbing, scraping mounds of heavenly hash into his mouth in an effort to sober himself up. On account of some harebrained superstition, he hadn't put his teeth back in, even though Herring had mended the prosthesis all back, soundly. As such, and with fewer obstacles between the tub of ice cream and the tub of his guts, the hash was going in at record speed. There was a field behind

Hooper's that ran down to the river, and for a while Red John had set Gerry up for hitting some balls. When he had brought out his bag of clubs and handed Gerry his three wood, Gerry had said, "Christ, I'm so drunk I forget which way I swing." Red John then said, "You should never forget which way ya swing, bud."

Gerry went over to Willy Lyon's rig and beheld the peahen, the blues and the greys and the greens, the crest somewhat white, the strange fan atop its head as if it were a target riddled with darts. "She's pretty, ain't she?" said Willy Lyon, directing the nozzle with a fair amount of precision into the mouth of his last can. The bird let out a squawk that put Gerry in mind of a turkey, a formless utterance that lacked any emotion or conviction. Gerry sensed that the fowl was reminding him to keep his distance. In truth, he was nervous of most exotic things. Colette, and now this peahen. Maybe he was mostly terrified of anything female. The colours on the hen were so vibrant, so refreshing, that Gerry felt like he was in some art gallery, spellbound by the painting of an ancient master. He saw Willy Lyon looking over at Herring's rig, the windows all steamed up like the plume of a kettle.

At the cash register, as they passed bills and coins between them, Red John told Willy Lyon that his hips were bothering him something fierce, and Willy Lyon said that what he did for aches and pains, like, if he got a charley horse in the leg, he'd rub Rawleigh's medicated gel on the bottoms of his feet before bed, then he'd put his socks on and go to sleep. "You can feel the tingle all the way up into yer thighs and that's how you know it's taking," said Willy Lyon. Red John said that his father used to put two herrings in his socks at night, and come morning the stink would be something, all right, but the pain would be gone.

—

Red John and Gerry were drinking coffee by the window, watching vehicles glister by, their transport like a kind of sales pitch, the proud revolution of some vastly intricate wedding ring, evoking in both of them the eerie sense that the movements before their eyes were on a loop, were controlled by some grander trickery. The winds began to shake the trees. A squall was moving in, and fast. "Why don't ya just drive him home there, Gerry? I won't tattle on ya." Gerry rubbed the tip of his nose and looked at Red John as if to test the trustworthiness of this claim. John set his cup down and crossed his hairy arms. "Just so ya know, I'm not operating a soup kitchen here." He coughed a bit to take the dryness out of his throat. "Y'boys owe me for the shine and the ice cream." Gerry went out to the rig and fetched Herring's wallet from its roost on the dashboard. Back in the store, he was thankful for the heat pump, blasting what it could, straining and gurgling like a drunkard in the act of congress. He handed Red John two twenties, but the man refused the offering, pushed Gerry's hand away. "I was just foolin' is all." And then, quick as a gannet snapping a mackerel out of the sea, he caught one of the twenties. "Fer the hash," he said.

—

It happened, as is the way of these things, quite fast, and in a manner that made it seem rather preordained, or fateful, if you like. The squalls of snow came in with incredible force and vigour. There was a violence and a chaos to the conduct of the snowfall, as if the clouds and the weather, the whole of the natural world, understood that on this day they just might be able to pulverize humanity with the softest of blows, with the perpetuity of flurries and flakes. Gerry had always been wary of machines. They made him nervous. He found that when he got flustered, the knowledge of what pedals and levers were designed to do just absented outright from his mind. He had pushed Herring over into the passenger seat of the burgundy rig. "Git over there, ya big lug," he said, as he pushed the man with straightened arms. Herring was a big fellow, after all. He snored a tad, but mostly he was silent, his head pitched forward somewhat awkwardly into the bulk, the escarpment, of him.

From Hooper's Gerry had turned left to head northeast along the shore road. Visibility was down to about fifty feet at this point, so it was a good thing they'd got going when they did. Gerry turned the radio right off, cranked the heat, and loosened his window. He needed to concentrate. They passed the Buddhist place there, which was on the left, and the cemetery in Little Sands, just past which was a tiny but steep dip in the land, with a gorge or valley on the right hand where the waters of the strait had been pulling away at the sandstones for just about time immemorial, and on the left side was another little dint, a glen that bore a crick along its belly, just before the winery there. Gerry felt the wheels go on him as they broached their descent, and the rig swerved to the right, to the ocean, and just as the side of the truck scraped the steel of the guardrail, there was Herring, foggily come alive, his arms and his legs instinctively stiffening for impact against any surface that would accept these gestures, and Gerry yanked the wheel hard to the left, and the rear of the truck gave a mighty wobble, as if they were riding the back of a giant fish, and, with a surprising lack of resistance from everything that had been put in place to prevent such things from occurring, the truck, briefly airborne, flipped onto its driver's side, its wheels spinning noiselessly, and everything quite still, the stomachs of the two men slammed high up into their chests, their mouths open with mute panic and their eyes white with dread.

The impact, no more in the grand scheme of things than a stubbed toe or an inconvenient eyelash, just a brief snap of plastics and metals, of welds fractured, was enough to shatter the layer of ice that had formed over the crick from the convergent sweeps of the opposing fields, and the water soon found its way into the cab. Herring was on top of Gerry, and he scrambled like a senseless thing, a dog on the highway that has just been clipped, spinning round and round in a summons for ultimate mercy, trying for the door, the treads of his boots punching and trampling Gerry, who was stuck under the wheel, soaked and frozen. For some reason, Herring couldn't find a way to get out. He would get near to the door but could not muster the strength and torque to open it, having engaged the handle. The wind and the snows, the strength of both together, sweeping down the valley, its momentum, had them entombed. Gerry's teeth were chattering. "Boy, I'm wetter than an otter's pocket," he said. Herring tried the door again. And then tried again. Each effort a more ruthless pulping than the last. "Jesus, Herring," said Gerry. "You'll make wine out of me yet." Herring, shaking with effort, let himself slide back down to where Gerry was. He'd lacerated the both of his hands somehow. There was only the sound of their breath, dimmed by the whistle of the storm, the windshield banked with snow. "What's next, crypt keeper?" said Gerry, and then the door opened and a number of strange faces peered down at them.

—

The young fellow by the name of Zhaxi patted his trimmed head and smiled at Gerry, and Gerry patted his own, closely shorn head. He had been given one of the monks' robes to wear while his own clothes dried. With his skin so tanned from a life in the sun, Gerry could have passed for a true Tibetan monk. In the summer months, garbed in sandals and shorts, Gerry loved nothing more than to take to the lawn with his whipper-snipper and trim what he could about the bushes and hedges and the trunks of trees, though this work had the appearance of penitence or self-flagellation. When the job was done, Gerry would sit where he could and drink a nice cool beer, and his legs would be scattered with blades of grass and blood, like a foot soldier from the Great War come through no man's land. People, Susan and the boys, his mother and his father, would say to him that he should just wear pants for Christ's sake, but Gerry loved the feel of it, the communion of agony and industry. These things, such as trimming the lawn, made him feel alive.

Venerable Mike sat with Herring on the cot as one of the students wrapped his wounds. "It was a good thing we were out walking," said Venerable Mike, noticing a bit of dirt on his glasses. He removed the modest equipment, just wire and glass, from his fine nose, and cleaned them with a portion of his currant-coloured robe. His skin was without blemish, as immaculate as Mary, downy and as natural as the moss upon the face of a rock. Timeless, really. Calm and kind, giving. Venerable Mike was a behemoth of a man, and wherever he went, for he was fond of walking great distances, he carried a giant staff made of hazel that had been stained to give it the look of an ancient oak. He was also a miracle worker with regard to chiropractic matters, could give a man his spine back to him in under five minutes. The fishermen loved him. He had a two-year backlog, such was his renown. "This is quite the place you have," said Herring. Venerable Mike smiled back at him, the kind of grin given to succour obvious statements and anxious bromides. They were in an outbuilding, a kind of gatehouse, with a pleasant wood stove, for the main facilities, the dormitories and the cafeterias. The storm continued and it was dark out.

Another of the boys, Pema, had brought them each a bowl of noodles. There was plenty of tea to be had, as well. His wounds wrapped, Herring thanked the boy and bowed his head a little in an offering of thanks, feeling like a fool all the while. He didn't know how to comport himself in such an environment. They may as well have been kidnapped by aliens.

"What do you do here? Nirvana and all that, eh." said Herring.

"Well, what is it that you do?" said Mike. Gerry stood, fussed vainly with his costume, and looking at Herring, put two fingers to his mouth. Herring passed him his cigarettes, and Gerry went outside for a puff, his boots still by the stove.

"I lobster," said Herring, scowling at the sheet of cold air allowed into the hut. "I'm a lobster fisher." Gerry's clothes dripped intermittently onto the iron of the stove, fizzling and sputtering, as if some queer sustenance could be fashioned from water and denim. Venerable Mike admired the darkness of the night and its ability to hold the energy of such a storm. He looked intently at the man opposite him, and Herring had a sense, brief and fleeting, that this man knew so well what he wanted to say that, in a way, it had already been said, that he was plucking something out of a world that cared not a whit for the future, or the past, or the present, a world where things were just as they were. A world where everything happened at once. "I would say that I am another you. I am a fisherman, too," said Mike, and he did not look away from the man, he stayed as he was, managing, as best he could, what he had uttered, tending to it, like a shepherd or a father to his son.

When the monks left, the two of them laid on their cots and stared at the rafters. Gerry wanted to apologize directly for the whole affair, but somehow or another Herring had communicated to him that this wasn't a necessity. This didn't mean that Gerry felt he was forgiven. Herring didn't work this way, you see. The man had a shocking propensity for tabulations, for keeping ledgers. He had the memory of an elephant.

"Boy, they sure do pay an arm and a leg just to figure out that we're all pretty much the same," said Herring.

"That one fella told me they have these two big books that takes like fifteen years to get through. And they have to be silent for eight months," said Gerry.

Herring said, "It's all pretty queer, if you ask me."

"Why are they here?" said Gerry.

"'Cos we give 'em cheap land and smile while they fuck us in the arse."

"Some of the boys say that they're actually samurais."

"That makes us just a bunch of Trojans, don't it?"

"I heard that all their groceries are brought over from Taiwan in shipping containers."

"If all you do is avoid pain and be happy, then how can you really appreciate pleasure?"

They felt their bodies sweat and Gerry closed his eyes and imagined that he was atop some mountain in Asia, so high that he could see heaven, all of the assembled venerated elders wrapped in joy and love, as if this paradise was simply on the other side of some atmospheric pane. He pictured meeting the Buddha, who was also Jesus, and everybody else, really, and he looked like the fellow from Nickelback and all he wanted to do was sell Gerry some drugs. Gerry started to crack up, but he kept it in, he kept this down. Somehow the two of them, Gerry and Herring, had locked into a competition to see who would break the silence first, but neither man spoke a word, unless you count snoring as a kind of drawn speech, a prorogation.

—

When she saw the placement and condition of the rig, Euna started to weep. "It's not as bad as it looks," said Herring. Gerry tried to find her a tissue in the pockets of his jacket, but while he was rummaging around, she produced one from a package of them that she kept in her purse. Gerry, from behind the two, cursed all of his little failures. "Well, I mean, it looks bad. Should we call a tow truck?" she said. Herring hummed and hawed and said, "Well, that'll get the cops involved, I spose, and I'd prefer to avoid them as much as possible." He worried that she would find this too much. He'd been clear, though. As clear as he could be. All he needed was the ride.

As they drove Gerry home to Georgetown, the car silent and dawdling behind the plow, which spread sand from its undercarriage as it made its way along the shore and down Norman's Road to My Bonnie River, Herring said, "The help of God is on the road," as if it were a recollection, a neglected verse from scripture, befitting such a series of events. Euna didn't know what to say to this, and, in the rearview mirror, it was abundantly clear that Gerry didn't know what to say either. She was just trying to control her anger, the more she got thinking about everything. She resisted the urge to remind the men that they both could be dead right now. Goddamn, he's frustrating, thought Euna. As fucking innocent as a little boy.

The CD in the stereo began skipping and Herring pulled it out. He inspected the disc, licked the back of it, and wiped it on the thigh of his jeans. When he put it back in, the thing played properly. Herring was rather impressed with himself. Euna said, "You licked that more than you ever licked me." And from the backseat Gerry giggled.

—

"You were never drinkin' last night, were you?" said Lillian.

"No, not to my recollection," said Herring. He pulled his jaw away from the phone and hocked a bit of phlegm, which he then swallowed, as pleasurable as an oyster.

"Well, listen, I'm going to send a constable over to yer place," said Lillian.

"Sounds good to me," said Herring.

"A little birdie told me that they seen yer rig in a field out in Little Sands. I'm just letting you know, eh?" she said.

He hung up and immediately called Joe McInnis. He nearly yelped with joy when Joe answered.

"Joe, Herring here."

"Well, well, well, brother, I've got to say this is a surprise," said Joe.

"Joe, I don't have much time, truth be told. What if I made you some breakfast?"

"Well, I just ate breakfast. I just ate breakfast in the comfort of my own home."

"Listen, Joe, I need you to do me a favour. I'm in a huge pickle here and I need to cook you breakfast. How quickly can you get here?"

"Hmmm, I'd be lying if I didn't say that this sounds fishy as fuck," said Joe.

"Can you bring yer rig?" said Herring.

"Oh, I think I see what's going on here. I'll be there in ten minutes," said Joe.

———

Herring had steak and eggs on the go when Joe pulled in with his truck. "Where's yer truck?" said Joe, as he came through the side door, knocking snow off onto the mat. But when the constable pulled down the drive and parked among the barns, putting the radio to his mouth, Joe said, "Oh, yeah, I see what's going on here. Most definitely." They watched the fellow in his car, Herring giving him a wave from the kitchen window, the archetype of domesticity and rectitude, while Joe hid from view, packing his belly with unnecessary food. The steak was pretty tasty, he would be the first to admit. The constable sat there and watched. This wasn't the first time this little show had been performed at this place. Both sides knew the score.

"Thank you so much, Joe," said Herring, when the constable had driven back up the lane.

"He'll be waiting for me down the way, I suspect," said Joe, accepting the toothpick Herring put in his hand. He scraped away at his teeth. "I think if we wait him out, Lillian'll give us a pass this once." And so, they sat and played a few matches of crib.

"Yer kinda running low on favours, there. How will you get yer rig out, I wonder?" said Joe.

"Well, it's in quite a spot," said Herring. "I imagine that I'll have to get Old Sellar Hume to help me."

"Good luck with that," said Joe. "Just try to lie low, you know? Don't make a scene, if you can avoid it." And then he said, "Fifteen-two, fifteen-four, fifteen-six, eight, nine, ten." He clapped his hands together. "That's the game."

—

"Hey, I know ya," said Hume. Herring had come down to the barn and set himself just inside the large doors. He had a case of Schooner in his arms, and he was wet and cold. Sellar had his leather apron on, treating a length of steel all aglow with its own forged sunrise, its own romance, soft and heartbreaking. He had his two-hundred-pound Chambersburg power hammer lively and humming, his wolf-jaw tongs nearby at his bench, and his mighty anvil chained to an elm stump just a decent lean away. His truck was parked in the barn. He dropped a few tools as he worked and cursed himself while they rattled about his feet. The old man halted what he was doing and marched over to shake Herring's hand. He said, "This is what we call percussive maintenance, huh." His hair was bountiful and slicked by a stiff, good comb, the grey of it like a sea trout, the lines of his face a spider's web, the latticework of grace and experience. His teeth were in decent shape, and he was fond of tending to his lips with these teeth, as if scratching an itch or sharpening a blade. Herring took his hand with little enthusiasm. "God, yer some misery, aren't ya? I can say that 'cos we're family," said Hume and gave Herring a wink. As a rule, Hume insisted that he was related to everybody on the island. "What a load of storms these past days, eh," said Hume.

During one of the winters of Herring's childhood, a particularly bleak time when his father had gone into the woods of New Brunswick to fell, Sellar had come out, three or four times a week, to visit on him, and he'd shown Herring how to roll a cigarette with one hand while you drove with the other and how to rim your pot with butter when boiling beets and how to get splinters out of a person's eye with a mollusk called an eyestone, which he kept wrapped in a silk handkerchief.

Herring relayed to him what had happened, and Hume said, "Well, ya sure can't fix stupid, but ya can smack it with a two-by-four." He looked back at the hammer, wiping the lavish amount of sweat on his face and neck with a rag he kept in his back pocket. "Just about every vehicle on this island needs rear struts," he said. Sellar took one of the beers. He looked at his watch, shrugged, and had a sip of beer. "Which is odd 'cos all they do is pave in the summer." Herring stepped to the side, as if to avoid the path of a phantom, and Sellar, watching him do this, make this little move, could not hide his puzzlement. "What is it they say?" said Sellar. "There's only the two seasons. Winter and construction." And he roared a little at his humour. "Well, even if it's only summer, the road to Hell is paved in summer and it's paved with good intentions, eh?"

"I'd say good intention and shitty compaction," said Herring.

"Yessiree. Between you and me and that fencepost over there, this Island has some of the most unfortunate roads in the country on it."

Sellar called in his collie and went to fire up the tractor.

"I'm not certain how we're gonna do this, but I spose we'll make the *Guardian*."

Euna and Herring drove up on Wednesday to the First Nation Chapel in Scotchfort for the funeral. They ended up parking next to Charley and Lillian, who were in uniform, and Herring found himself giving them both a hug, which unsettled them a little bit. They muttered to one another that he must be all over the pond drunk. The remaining McClellan children, Thomas, Catherine, Samuel, Thelda, Mary, Peggy, and Gerry, were all stood with their mother, Dolores, and their father,

Joseph, in the receiving line within the narthex, and all of them, except for Gerry and Mary, were in their campaign hats and red serges and breeches. It was quite a sight to behold, and the majesty of it reduced more than a few friends and relatives to utter tears. Chief Amy Francis was there, as were nearly all of the council members.

The sun was out, and its operation was noticeably indolent, but even in spite of this, there finally seemed to be the sentiment that winter was done for now. Perhaps this sense came from the birds or the tones of blue in the sky. Perhaps it was the movements of the winds, the emotion of the waters. Gerry was pretty drunk, and Peggy was doing her best to prop him up, but he had the speed wobbles, those juddered boulevards of a mangled nervous system. Herring gave him a hug and said, "You lowly fisherman, you. It's all right. It's all right." And Gerry's nose coursed and seeped like he had been taken by seasickness.

When Herring reached Dolores at the head of the line, she shook his hand said, "There's no money to be made in this place so you just mind yer manners." The venom in her voice was strong and it rattled him more than a little. He said, "Ah, but that's where you're wrong, Dolores. Don't forget that we're all here, stood in a church, and a Catholic one, at that. You've given away hard-earned money to the Vatican for the fantasy and magic of it all, and we all know it." Dolores said, "My God, you're a bastard," and immediately gave Euna her eyes, and this elusion, this wide and cunning berth she had sought away from him, was a condemnation. Euna and Dolores made small talk about this and that and Herring took a deep breath, walked away and had a piss.

After the ceremony, Euna went downstairs to seek out Susan and Robbie and Mickey and stood with them a while, trying to make them feel comfortable. Joseph came over and asked how his grandsons were doing. He made a couple of bad jokes and eventually got them to snicker somewhat audibly. Joseph had the longest of white hair, this great, gently sloping pompadour, like the fender of some gangster's sedan, that bolstered his good nature, his humour, which the majority of his kids had failed to inherit. Joseph said, "Jesus, I need a haircut. Soon enough I'm going to have to climb a tree just to take a shit." The boys were taller than both of their parents and they seemed, by their colouring, to be allergic to the outdoors. Joseph asked both Euna and Herring how the girls were, not knowing the situation. Joseph and Dolores were long separated themselves. Euna said that they were fine, that their studies were coming along nicely, and Herring had looked at her while she related this information, the look of a man who has some dim understanding that he has driven, perhaps irrevocably, the love and the goodness of women away, a herding beast who, having sent his stock over the cliffs, realizes that he has put himself out of business. Norman was there, too, as he had begun to see Susan on something of a regular basis. Herring whispered to Euna, "I guess Susan now likes her candy hard and white." Norman and Herring got to talking about this and that, neither of them knowing the other too, too well. Tommy joined them and said, "There was a fellow up west ice fishing. He was so hammered that when he went out to piss, he froze to death. Well, when the boys found him and brought him in, they hooked him up to a car battery and boosted him back to life." They got onto the subject of mussels, each man with two little triangles of sandwich to a hand, and Norman said, "Diving for mussels is just an ignorant job. And tryin' to swim in a straight line under water is just about the hardest thing to do. Fer some reason, I just keep wanting to turn left." Herring overheard Charley say to someone that Norman looked like that kinda guy who always had a runny, snotty nose when he was a kid. And then Norman got to talking about a fisherman from either Georgetown or Graham's Crick, a fellow who insisted on wearing flip-flops out at the wharf. Pretty cavalier. "Well, one day there he takes a sliver of creosote into his big toe. I don't know, maybe he was doing crab. Anyway, one night before bed, he takes his sock off and there was a thud when he threw the damn thing onto the floor. His toe had plumb rolled off," said Norman. He washed a bit of his sandwich down with a splash of coffee. "Poison," he said.

—

On the way home, the mood in Euna's car was gloomy, and Herring had a sense that she wanted to speak her mind and lay into him a tad. He prompted her as well as he could, not wanting to distract her too much from the driving, though route twenty-two was mostly straight from Pisquid to New Perth. She almost took out a raccoon in Maple Hill.

"What's up?" he said.

"You know," said Euna. "Why do you insist on being such a dick-head. Like, you've gotta make everything a confrontation. You've no problem pointing out the stupidity of others, and yet, who do you think you are? You cut a goddamn hole in our goddamn floor for no goddamn good reason, for Christ's sake. You create these huge fuck-ups, and yet you always come out of them sounding off like yer a goddamn prophet, like you've learned something profound, like you know everything." The veins in her neck were as taut as mooring lines at low tide. "If the stove was such a goddamn problem, why didn't we just move it to the first floor?" She'd spit a little during this last portion, and both of them had noticed. She wiped it from the steering wheel and focused on the road. There wasn't much in the way of conversation for the rest of the drive.

When she got him to the house, he said, "I've some socks that need to be darned. Would ya mind? I can bring them out to yer place." She said that this was fine, she didn't mind mending them.

"I'm going to arrange a meeting with you and Moses Standing," she said. "I want you to go and talk to him. Really, really talk to him, for me, please." Herring said that he would, and then he ran into the house to fetch his worn socks.

—

Every Thursday evening, at half-seven, there was an AA meeting in the basement of St. Mary's in Montague. Gerry was late, though he had showed up early, as he did whenever he was anxious about the thing he had to do or, as in this case, felt that he had to do. Sheila had given him a ride. He walked down to the station at the bottom of the hill and then walked back up, and in that brief amount of time, he had sucked back two cigarettes. There must have been about twenty men and women in the basement, which Gerry found rather surprising, and of this number, the only people Gerry didn't know were the three or four who had clearly driven some distance so as to remain as anonymous as possible. The lighting in the place was a series of those four-foot fluorescent bulbs, so strained with neglect that you could hear the electricity coming into them all the way from New Brunswick. There was coffee and cookies at a little table in the corner. Gerry waved at the fellows he knew and they all waved back. That there was no shame or stigma here, in this place, was obvious, and this put Gerry at ease a bit. He had on a pair of pants that he had rediscovered only that night, and the stitching in the seams around his crotch was irritating, to say the least. He wanted to get out of the things and burn them right then and there. People were seated casually at a number of tables, and for the first little while, different people, mostly those from town who had fine clothes and well-groomed hands, would get up to read. A fellow by the name of Archie Beck was the chairperson. He was a farmer from out in Iona and had been, for a time, a fine singer. He was probably ten years older than Gerry. He was a brute of a man, tall and heavyset, and he wore a pair of black braces over his green, plaid shirt. There was a littering of dander upon his collar and his breast. He had on a pair of outdated glasses, and he was mostly bald, save for some tussocks about his ears the colour of pecan, which resembled antlers stunted by some youthful malady.

The topic that night was courage. Beck informed those gathered that they were there to clean house, that the first three steps had been about trusting in God, that the last was to be about helping others. But, right now, they were to summon the courage to enact a moral inventory. Beck talked about honesty and open-mindedness and of a willingness, and said that this was the how of it all. They were to look at themselves and to make a moral inventory, searching and fearless, of what they truthfully saw. Gerry was overwhelmed by it, and, foolishly, he had not taken into account that this would be the case. Someone had slipped him a pen and a pad of paper, and he looked at both of these things as if they were foreign instruments, which they mostly were. Gerry hadn't thought about having to write anything longer than his signature since high school. And then he got to thinking that that was just about thirty years ago. What was morality, he thought. Were men like him supposed to know about these things? The time, from school to now, had just flown by, and no one had told him that he was supposed to be thinking about what was right and what was wrong. Now, to be sure, he knew when things were bad things and when things were good things, but so what? The news each night on *Compass* was mostly terrible, and it was mostly about how men and women seemed to be getting away with dishonest and often criminal undertakings, in what he thought was an awfully plain view. And, somewhat uniformly, all of these transgressions revolved around the almighty dollar. Then Gerry got to thinking about all of the drinks he'd had over the years. Forget the drugs, he told himself, and just focus on the drink. His eyes closed firmly, he laid them out before him on the wood of some infinite bar, and he counted all of them as well as he could, knowing that he was failing, that this was something near to futile. But he sensed that this imagery was important, maybe even critical. Out behind his physical body lay a trail, a vast path, and it was littered with bottles, and shame, and broken things, promises and friendships, he supposed, although he did wonder about these last two items, for he'd never had many friends. Was Herring a friend, he thought. People generally seemed to like him, but only superficially, and only because he was mostly harmless. He knew this about himself. He didn't like being this way. He didn't know how to stop. I don't want to do this, and I can't stop doing it. Something seized him, a tenuous but pleasant feeling, the likes of which he had yet to truly know, something like poetry, and he clutched the pen and scrawled on his little pad the phrase, *I am in hell.*

There it was. It was a frightening accomplishment.

*I am in a hell*, he scrawled again.

———

A fisherman by the name of Isaac Cahoon from Boatswain Point came hobbling up to Gerry in the parking lot, while he was waiting for Sheila. Gerry was more than a little frazzled, packed like a shopping cart with sensation, and he didn't want to be bothered all that much. Isaac had played junior hockey for a while, and the boys all called him Icon, which was a fine handle, but, according to Herring's estimation, it had given the lad only trouble, had given him a false set of security and of importance. Isaac thought he knew more than he did.

Isaac said, "When I was in a hockey fight I had this push-and-pull technique. You push and then kinda pull the fella into yer fist. I actually punch with my left. It's one of the few things that I do with my left. Punch and pull myself. I guess you could say I beat things with the left hand."

He let out a cackle.

Cahoon bummed a smoke from Gerry, and then he looked at Gerry, the desire for confrontation just purring off of him, and said, "Is Herring still putting his shoes in the freezer?" This detail was an intimate thing that only a few people ought to have known, but somehow or another, it had become common knowledge. For a fellow like Isaac to bring it up, here, and to Gerry, of all people, was beyond the pale. He was out of line. Gerry sucked on his cig and shrugged his shoulders. Overhead, the clouds ambled through the stars, discarnate boats upon the waters of a dream.

———

Moses Standing lived in a fine white house out on the hill in Caledonia. When Herring arrived, Moses was moving a wheelbarrow across the lawn with some pruning tools in its tray. He was younger than Herring, but only just, and had a soft and fey manner about him which people often confused, at their own peril, for something else, for a feebleness or infirmity, and this estimation of him was all the more odd considering that he had a prominent scar on his cheek, like the leather of an opened wallet. The mutilation had come from a car crash some years ago, while driving through Ingonish, there, in Cape Breton. A drunk driver had hit him coming from the other direction. For a while, it was all touch and go. Euna had come to know the man because her father had known his father, a fellow by the name of Pius Standing, who had travelled to Africa years ago, and she spoke of the son's good character to anyone that wanted to hear her judgment or philosophy regarding the nature of grit.

The trees had begun to bud, and the grass had been liberated enough to allow the wind to inflate it, swell it a bit. All things, animate and inanimate, were ready and willing ingredients in the great cook-up that was the summer. The sun was as industrious as ever, drying the soils and encouraging all the creatures of the forest to begin anew, to rejoin the symphony. The house was being aired out, relieved of its bleaker duties, so to speak.

"Boy, it's drier than a popcorn fart today," said Herring.

"Herring, I haven't seen you since Mary Compton's wake," said Moses. Mary, herself, had died in a car crash in early November of last year, not too far from here, on the way to Montague. "What's a-stir today, good sir?" he said, and Herring said he was none too bad.

They sat in the kitchen and Moses asked if he wanted to sip some whiskey. Herring thought about it for a second, could tell by the look on the man's face that this wasn't a loaded question, and then consented to the arrangement. Moses poured two shot glasses. "I like my whiskey Protestant and I like to shoot the stuff. I'm like a sea-gull. I just gulp 'er down. So, I guess that I can only handle Prods in small doses, which means you can't stay long." Herring waved these notions away with his hand, laughing with the man, and he felt that the gesture was as unnecessary as it was dramatic. His nerves were at him, but the whiskey, scant though it may be, would help. "Well, what would you like to talk about?" said Moses, after his amusement had lost its momentum, for he could tell that Herring had grown impatient. These fishermen, they're either as silent as the cosmos or as oratory as a volcano, thought Moses. "We're not here to debate doctrine. Just tell me how you're doing."

Herring brought a hand up and stroked his chin, and he said, "Lobstering is just a game of chance, you know. You've gotta attack the fish."

"But the hauls have been good these past years, eh?" said Moses.

"Yes, yes, I've been very lucky to have a little left over," said Herring. "But, you know, you gotta take yer good years with yer bad. I know what it's like to haul eight hundred pounds of lobster one day and twenty-eight pounds the next." Herring squinted his eyes. "Nine times out of ten, when you think you know what a lobster is doing, it'll do the exact opposite. Hell, if we knew anything about lobster, we'd have none left. No one seems to remember the seasons when you were happy just to have enough to break even. To pay yer fuel and yer wharf fee and yer hired man, yer insurance, and then have a little left over. Everyone's living on credit and buying these huge boats. They don't know what's coming because they haven't fished the years where there's nothing. And fer fifty days a year. Fifty days. And that's it. That's not working. And you can't be the little fella these days. No. No way, José. You gotta love the big fella. Snuggle right up to him."

"Well, it seems to me like these are all things that you know about. So, then, what is it? What is it really?"

"Something has happened, you know what I mean?" Herring said, splashing a bit more whiskey down his throat. "You know, scrap that. Everything has happened."

Moses was more than mystified by what Herring was saying, but at the same time, something impressed him about the man. Perhaps it was the sincerity in his very inarticulateness, that there was something diligent and sober in his soul, and that his mind was trying to cast after these things, trying to haul them to the surface with the best tools he had at the moment. This metaphor wasn't lost on him, and he told Herring so. "You have a reputation, you know?" said

Moses, and then he got up and raided the refrigerator, preparing a little plate of cheese and crackers. "You like mustard pickles?" he asked, attending to his work.

Herring said, "Fishermen are a strange people. But they're a good bunch, too. Sometimes, I sit in the house and I drink and I get to talking to myself, which worries me a great bit. I'm out in the world and it just seems to me that everything is just eating everything." Herring took a deep breath and helped himself to the water from the tap. "There's a noise to all of this eating that's kinda hidden and I'm convinced that I can hear it, eh. It's quiet, but when you catch it, it's the loudest thing a person could ever imagine."

Moses had a pinch of cheese and a sip of his whiskey. "Survival of the fittest, huh," he said.

"Yes, something like that." Herring scraped at his chin. "Morals, is that the word I want?"

"I'm not sure," said Moses. "Ethics are out in the world and morals are in you."

"Some people, their morals are looser than the balls on a goose. Yer talking to them, a man you've known yer entire life, shooting the breeze, and then you realize that the man right across from you would cut yer throat right there if he could get away with it."

Moses leaned back a little and digested what he could.

"There used to be twelve types of fish here. Now there's one. The hake is all gone. Herring, too. Fishing'll be dead in about a decade. And what's else, you know, I have no peace in me, at all. I mean, none, no peace. And I just feel like every day, every goddamn day of my life it's been kill or be killed. Kill or be killed. And it just doesn't have to be this way, eh, does it?" said Herring.

"There's a kind of a grim romance to fishing, isn't there?" said Moses. And he added, "But doesn't each man rob as much as he is robbed? I think what I'm trying to say is that there has to be a balance, huh. There has to be a balance in your mind and in your actions."

Herring nodded, and he got to tapping the toe of his left boot upon the floor. "I mean, at no point did I sign up for any of this. Any of this bullshit, eh. I wouldn't have built the world the way it is and I can't do a goddamn thing to change it. I just have to sit here and jump through fucking hoops. Hoop after fucking hoop."

"What about you and Euna?" said Moses.

"What about us?" said Herring.

"Well, from what I gather, it's—"

Herring feebly cracked the table with his knuckles, as if knocking on the door of an elderly person at suppertime, not keen on the disturbance, but there to make sure they took their medicine.

"With all due respect there, Moses, as a representative of an organization that doesn't have to pay any property taxes, in addition to one that does a pretty good job of harbouring kiddie fiddlers, I'm not sure that you've the high ground to tell me anything about anything," he said.

Moses adjusted his legs, rubbed his left calf. "There's something holy and even sublime about the discontent you have," he said. "It's a start, a movement toward something, isn't it?"

Herring looked at his scar, the caramel ridge of it, and then he moved upwards, to his eyes. Herring said, "Do ya like tomalley?" and Moses said that he did. Good, said Herring, and he handed him a little mason jar of it. "I made that myself." A layer of silence was hung and stretched between them. They looked at the world around them. They looked at things of no consequence. They looked at harmless things. Herring said, "Lobster is the only fishing in the world a fella can leave harbour and not know what he's gonna get for it. The Chinese there waiting to see how much is landed before they set their price." He stood and said, "I'd better go before I get a job doing whatever it is that ya do." He shook Moses's hand. "You know, I don't know what the hell I'm going on about," he said, and then he left, insisting that Moses did not need to see him to the door. Moses sat at the table and spread the paste onto a cracker with his knife, and then he listened for the roar of Herring's burgundy rig, looking like it had all four wheels in the grave.

The visit had been as if the wildness from outside had ventured in and took a seat at his table, as if the wilderness had paid a social call to the ordered household of man and had left, finding the whole rubric wanting. The lobster mash was delicious, certainly, but he knew, too, that with high enough doses, with elevated exposures, tomalley could warp the mind, could disable a man.

# FOUR

Herring slept fitfully, and dreams visited him in which he built a house with no remarkable features to it, near some kind of flood plain. And then the inevitable happened. You could feel it hanging in the air like a giant, indiscernible gull. A flood arrived and everything had to be built anew. The same but somehow just ever so different, like a man who finds himself in a nightmare of dating a twin whom he suddenly cannot tell apart from the other. When he finally got around to moving into the place, some years later, it seemed, a condominium had been built right outside his front door, obstructing his view, whose beauty and serenity, its remove, had been the bloody impetus to build there in the first place. He had moved in with a prostitute, or, if she wasn't this, then their arrangement clearly involved the transaction of sex for money, mutual love was clearly never a possibility, only to find that there was a man already in the place, claiming squatter's rights, and not only that, but the squatter would sneak in from some indefinite hiding place within the bones of the place when Herring wasn't there and make a cuckold out of him.

When he awoke from the dream, he was in bed, but placed at such an unsettling and suspicious angle, Herring felt as though he had been violated by something, not so much a physical body, but something deeper and larger, an abstraction or some principle, and he felt that he had been left to float, abandoned, and that the bed was a kind of makeshift raft and the ceiling of the room was the stars and everything was dark and malevolent. For the remainder of the day, he would be unable to shake this portentous feeling.

He went to the sink and ran the faucet, cupping the water with both hands, and he snorted as much of it as he could up into his sinuses and then he blew with all of his might, producing wattles of green and yellow mucous that resembled the liver and pancreas and roe of the lobster. He helped himself to a bottle of beer and a bit of hash and went out to take stock of the truck. Getting into the rig, post-accident, required that Herring use the passenger side door, and once the engine got going, the truck dragged its guts like a prisoner would a ball and chain. But it ran, and at the moment that would do.

He stopped by the garage in My Bonnie Harbour to see Fletcher Jordan. Fletcher's mother had broken her femur on the stairs two days after Christmas. She did the books and answered the phone, sold eggs and sauerkraut, had an English bulldog at her side named Chaldon. She had sewn a little vest that went over his broad shoulders. She walked around with the cane her eldest boy had used while he had been dying.

"Boy, she's been rode hard," said Fletcher, looking at the damage, bending down here and there while he circled the rig. "I mean, short of ya buying another, I could tidy up what I can, just so's yer not a death trap." Fletcher quoted him five hundred bucks and was keen to reinforce the generous nature of this appraisal. Fletcher said, "There's only two things I can't weld back together. The crack of dawn and a woman's heart." Big Arbot Herring rolled by triumphantly like the first person to ever ride a bicycle. Herring said that he'd think about it and get back to him.

When he got back to the house, he grabbed a few more beers and walked out behind the house and sat himself down on the turf and, for the day was clear and without wind, stared across at Pictou, the indigo of its scale, its very shape majestic and that of the wraith. Uncanny, really, he thought. He felt that he was in the world of fairies and sprites, that the border between reality and fantasy was marked right through his own body.

Euna and the girls woke him up from his slumber, and, as he stood, he felt the dampness on his back and his legs and the cold in his bones. He gave them a wave. He hadn't seen Marcelina and Marceline since the funeral, and even then, it had been only very briefly, at Agnes's place. They looked chipper and pleased to be there, for now. "You ladies haven't lost yer freckles, I see," he said, and they rolled their eyes at him. The two of them looked like a tourism advertisement. They wanted to run down to the shore, and he told them to mind the stairs, for they were getting old, and said he would prepare them some bacon and eggs, if they liked, and as they ran down the path, he said, "Well, this is a surprise."

Euna pressed her palms into her hips and said, "I'm going into town to go shopping with my sisters and I thought that you might like to spend the day with the girls."

He said that was lovely of her. "Thank you," he said.

Euna drove off and he stood, watching and listening, nervous that they were out of his sight. He knew not to infringe on their independence, so he resolved to go rassle up some food for the three of them. He set the oven to its lowest temperature and fired up the propane burner, brewed some coffee and set about frying bacon, keeping an eye on the shore through the kitchen window whenever he could spare the attention.

He splashed some shine into his coffee to help with the cobwebs, put the television on, and then went outside and hit the air horn.

"Where's Murphy, dad?" said Marceline.

"She's hanging out with Uncle Gerry. He's pretty lonely these days. You girls don't drink coffee, do you?" he said.

Marcelina wrinkled her nose. "No, dad, we don't."

"Yer loss," he said. "It'll put hair on yer chests."

"Why would we want that?" said Marceline.

"Well, how are all the boys going to find you attractive."

"You must be lonely, too, dad," said Marcelina.

The girls tucked into their meal with full ardour. Herring was satisfied with the level of pleasantries they had been able to exchange. Customarily, his daughters were brief, favouring abridged conversations with their father, most especially since the divide, which was still raw between all of them, a rift that was understood to be a pit of snakes. He looked at Marceline and said, "Now then, which one are ya? Marcelina?" She smacked him on the arm and then realized that he was bandaged there. Her eyes welled with tears, and he patted the back of her hand to indicate that everything was all right, that no injury had been done by her that he hadn't already done to himself. She'd never liked injuries or blood, was afraid to truly know what a person was made up of, the warm guts of each of them, preferring ignorance, for now. And this was fine. Marcelina, on the other hand, had no problems negotiating all of the liquors and secretions of the body, the corporeal, organic miscellany that was life.

Mostly, he missed all of the little things, the tactile and delicate things that only girls could offer a father such as he. He was a lowly thing, he thought. To have them here was sweet and touching, and Euna's generosity moved him, but it was also a bitter thing, for their grace and candour, their simplicity, which all had a kind of expiration date on them, was a stark reminder of how much of a bastard he had become. There would come a day, most certainly, when he would look at them and contemplate whether they'd become commonplace and ordinary, like him, or whether there was a bit of the transcendent in them. As a father, he felt that he had outright failed to nourish the spirit in them. These were crucial years. A person was, in essence, wholly formed by the time they were eight or nine. He had been anxious to never subtract qualities from them, or to suppress their strengths and their weaknesses, the things that were encoded in each of his daughters, these pieces of him, imposed features, but, yes, he felt that he never added to them, either. He hadn't encouraged them enough. He hadn't shown them that failures could lead to successes because he didn't believe this was the case. No, he knew, deep down, he truly believed that failures only led to more failures.

He gave them orange juice and poured them some tea when the kettle had boiled, insisting that they drink it. "Yer gran said that tea was very important in the grooming of any respectable person. You have to hold yer cup with both hands, like so," he said, and he showed them what he meant. "'Cos, when you drink tea, you should drink tea, and do nothing else."

He reminded them of the pet crow they'd had when they were younger. "Do you remember you used to play games with it?" he said. They nodded and laughed, the food entering their mouths at a torrent. "You had a little stone that was flashy in the sun and you would hide it from the crow," he said. "The crow would find it and he'd hide it on you two and then you'd find it. Well, one day the crow took the stone and dropped it down the chimney, and that was that," he said.

—

He had been in the basement tending to his traps, for the girls had made it understood that they didn't need to be entertained by him, that they were going next door to the Glovers' place to visit their friend Marcy. Well, he'd snuck a few more bottles of beer into his gut and had promptly fallen asleep again. The commotion, the screaming and the heavy, almost metallic footfalls, the sounds of glass shattering and of wood breaking, woke him up, and running up the stairs, using them for the first time since he'd cut the hole in the floor, he came up into the kitchen to find the walls streaked with blood and shit, mad steaming globs of it, everywhere. The sliding doors that opened onto the little back porch had been reduced to pieces, though some shards remained in place, crooked razors of glass, the fingers of witches. Off in the distance he could see a pony, its mouse dun streaked with red, galloping in a northerly direction, for the trees. The girls were tangled among the kitchen chairs, hysterical, shrieking as if they were possessed. He removed their hands from their faces and made sure they knew it was him. He spoke calmly and kissed them both on the heads. He said there was nothing to worry about. He said he needed to go after the pony.

He went to the basement and retrieved his lever-action out of the cabinet and grabbed a junk of rope. In the barn he fired up his four-wheeler and took off down the lane and onto the trail that rimmed the field.

When he got to the edge of the forest, he dismounted and turned off the machine. There wasn't room enough to navigate the machine through the trunks, so he settled for walking. The wind was from the north, and aside from the odd nuthatch or waxwing and the scrape of branches, he couldn't hear much else. Once he had penetrated the trees, he moved laterally, from east to west and back again, hoping to pick up the trail of blood, and once he'd located the trail of scarlet, he followed this.

The highland pony hadn't got much further into the forest than Herring was now. In the dim light afforded by the canopy, it was wedged between two young red pines. Its breathing rasped, solemn and stark, and from some distance, he could both hear and feel the beat of its heart synchronizing in a way with the pulse of his. As he approached the animal, he saw a number of significant lacerations, and its belly was essentially opened, hemorrhaging blood at a staggering pace. He ran a hand over its mane and buckled his knees so that he could meet the animal's eyes. Herring felt his own heartbeat quicken. He realized that his nostrils were releasing a near steady stream of liquids.

He raised the rifle, worked the lever, and fired into its head. The body went limp, though it could not collapse, held as it was by the red pines, a beauty of a pony between chopsticks, a monument to some miserable and unheralded notion. Herring sat some yards from the pony and vibrated, noting the blood dropping from its sheath. He closed his eyes and the dread came up in him, eager for his company, to be entertained.

—

He dragged the dead pony behind the Honda as slowly as possible, so that its head and legs didn't snap and buckle with such cruelty, so that the thing could retain some smidge of dignity. The thing was already dead. He didn't need to exaggerate the devastation of its physical form. He did the same with fish, any fish, even the dirt in the traps. If a thing was injured, he had a duty to end its suffering. This was a principle of his that he clung to, would not deviate from, for he knew that if he gave but an inch in this regard, he would become a monster in his own eyes, as lowly and wretched as any degenerate.

He parked behind the house and went in the side door. The girls were cleaning up as best they could. Marcelina, her head wrapped in a tea towel to keep the smell at bay, was trying to clean up the feces with a shovel and some toilet paper. Marceline had a bucket of soapy water on the go and was wiping the walls. They ran over to him and he held the both of them. They began to sob and it broke him a little. He said, "It's all right about the mess. Let's get you cleaned up."

He took them to the Whites' farm, which was situated to the west. Cindy opened the door and tried to censor her look of distress and horror. She ushered the shivering girls in and Herring asked her if she wouldn't mind running them a bath and getting some food into their bellies. Her sister, Elsie, came out from the kitchen and, sensing what was going on, ushered the girls into the kitchen. Herring told Cindy a bit of what had happened, his voice quiet. She looked at the man and took his hands in hers.

"Just go do what you need to do," she said. "I'll look after the girls." Herring walked down the porch steps. It would be getting dark soon, and he saw the lights of Emerson White's tractor flicker on, down near the bluffs.

—

Chessel Glover paced the floor of his kitchen, his hands locked behind his back. He looked like a prisoner devising an elaborate scheme for revenge, one that would take years to enact, one that would permanently disrupt entire sectors of civilization. Selina sat with Herring at the table, the wood stove next to her, their foreheads brilliant with sweat. She was quiet, as was her way, but she was tense, reading the body language of both men. Chessel was upset, but torn as to how to correctly respond to all of this. "Walk me through this again," he said. "Yer girls came over lookin' for Marcy. They find that she's not home. They go to the barn and take Reuben out. They walk Reuben, without my consent or Selina's, back to yer place. They decide that bringing him into the house is a good idea. Then, Reuben spooks, and—"

"What's done is done, Chessel," said Herring. He walked the man outside and showed him the body of the pony, laid out on a tarpaulin.

Chessel knelt down by the animal and said, "Jesus Christ." He stood with crispness, the bones in him cracking. "Are the girls okay?" Herring said that he thought they were, that they were at the Whites', with Cindy and Elsie. "Reuben didn't suffer too much, did he?" Herring shook his head.

"And where were you while all of this was going on?" said Chessel, but he already knew the gist. He wasn't an idiot, he knew his neighbour.

"I'm pretty tight for money right now," said Herring, one foot on the grass, one foot on the lowermost step, only noticing right then that the knees of his canvas pants were greased with blood.

Chessel knelt back down and put his right hand on the poll and then the muzzle of Reuben. He said, "Such a handsome fella you are, Reuben. Yeah, you are."

"I'm not certain what to do," said Herring, his throat dry and difficult to move. He licked his lips and plunged his hands into his pockets.

Chessel stood and turned away from the pony. He stooped a bit and brushed his own knees off, noting the state of Herring's knees, as well. "My father always used to say that the first rule of investing was don't put any money into anything that eats hay, you know?" said Chessel. He removed his cap and scratched the back of his head, his hair curled into a holy predicament, glossy with sweat. "But Reuben was an investment, you see. So, the matter is simple. You owe me for the pony, and that's a God's fact." Herring lit a cig with shaky hands. "I want five hundred for Reuben," said Chessel. The both of them understood how tacky and vulgar it was to haggle so near a dead thing.

"Can I write ya a cheque?" said Herring.

Chessel placed a hand inside the ceiling of his upturned cap and moved about in there, searchingly. "Well, no. No, you can't. Yer cheques, and forgive my language, are like big tits."

Herring shifted the weight of his hips and said, "Huh?"

"They bounce," said Chessel, returning the cap to his head. He invited Herring to sit on the steps with him, and the two of them sat there, as still as grotesques warding off corrupt spirits.

"I'm sorry about all of this," said Herring. Repairs on the rig would just have to wait.

"I'm sorry, too," said Chessel, using his tongue to press out his cheek, as if punching a hole in leather to mark some irremediable weight loss.

—

Emerson was on his porch, smoking his pipe and observing the stars and the waning crescent of the moon. He watched Herring come down the drive on his four-wheeler, and as Herring was dismounting, he met him and took the man, with urgency, by the elbow, as if he were indisposed, wounded by gunfire. He showed Herring in, who refused the possibility of digesting any food, and then led the man upstairs to the spare bedroom where the girls were sleeping. Herring stood in the doorway and looked at his daughters, smelling of soap and of considerate, unruffled dreams, the light from the wall sconce warm upon a single side of his face. As they receded, Emerson's footfalls were the lightest things, like a curfew had been broken and a punishment were being evaded. Herring stepped into the room and removed his coat. He laid down on the hand-loomed rug, bunching up his coat so that he could place his head on it, and then, after listening to the syncopated exhalations of both of his girls, the odd twitching of a leg within the sheets, he slept.

—

The day that Euna's father died, her mother, who had always been something of a passionate smoker, quit the habit for good. The house that Agnes still lived in out at the cove had once belonged to the Harris family, in particular, Spurgeon Harris, who had been the lighthouse keeper out at Cape Bear until the government decided to automate. A few years after this, Spurgeon accidentally drowned, so this was around 1963 or 1964. Joe Sr., in fairly short order, raised the money to buy the homestead and proposed to Agnes. Spurgeon's wife, Della, and the children moved to Boston. They needed a change of scenery to get over the loss of such a fine, hardworking man. Della said that if she had to stare out at the same waters that had swallowed her husband for one more week, well, she'd sooner go stark mad. The widows of drowned men sometimes did go mad, especially in olden days, having to be so nigh the sea that it was, in a way, like sleeping with the enemy. And so, the sale was enacted rather quickly. When Joe and Agnes married and had moved in, she realized that this would be the only house that she would ever live in, and, indeed, this came to be the case. She loved it, the carmine of its exterior like a giant adobe of lipstick, the windows and the pine floors, the pantry and the cellar doors.

Agnes had a bit of the crone to her, and a fellow could be forgiven for thinking that, if she wasn't the spirit of some wolfhound, then she was a wolfhound that had learned to walk on its hind legs and had shorn itself of its hair by rolling among the stones. Her hair was sturdily parted down the middle, and this crisp separation, the line of her exposed scalp like a bead of cream, bequeathed a single blade of grey to each side of her face. She wore glasses, which made her seem more human, but when these were removed, which was seldom, reserved for sleeping or in moments of great solemnity, the thinness in her face often gave people the impression that she was in pursuit, on an interminable hunt for a singular kind of stag, one that held a number of secrets about the nature of reality. As a rule, she ate well and drank a pot of coffee, black, every day. From June to October she swam in the waters of the strait, sometimes going as far as High Bank or Cape Bear, after which she would hike up to the road and walk home, that is, until somebody picked her up and gave her a ride. To give Agnes a ride home, especially among the fishermen, was something of an honour, for it was believed that the very sight of her brought a man good luck, ushered the lobsters back out, away from the shoaler waters. She had never been a pretty woman, and as a result, people took her quite seriously.

When Joe died and Herring brought him back to her, Agnes noticed that Euna had set her eyes on the hapless fisherman in a way that suggested Euna did not yet know that the matter was already something of a foregone conclusion. There was something about grief and love, deep down, in the shadowy places that most people did not have the courage to investigate, that revealed the nature of their union. Sort of like links in a chain. The two were wedded, and more often than not, these qualities would root themselves in people, and thusly bring these people together. Agnes had seen this in her own life more often than she cared to admit. It was a funny little trick, and when you noticed it, you found yourself believing in fate.

Euna had just returned home from Vancouver, where she had worked as a dance instructor for the better part of ten years. Agnes remembered how, at Joe's wake, Euna fussed over Herring's clothes, and how she had stood so near to him during all of it, in a way that spoke of how physical and unshaped, how callow their attraction was. She knew, too, that it was a mutual affair. Agnes didn't know, in truth, what to make of Herring. He struck her as odd, as unusually quiet, with a manner not quite shy, but a symptom of something else, something untamed, and perhaps even despicable. But she had tried, as was her way, to come to like the man, and she had succeeded to a creditable degree.

Since Joe died, Herring usually came out to visit Agnes once a month or so. He would arrive unannounced and they would sometimes sit outside, depending upon the weather, and talk aimlessly. She had learned to let him mostly direct their wanderings and tried not to resent him his desire to talk. She knew he enjoyed doing so, that speaking to her softened him in a wholesome way. After a while, she came to realize that the man was difficult to pin down, that he was as slippery as his namesake, as indeed his father had been. She believed she understood the man, because she believed she had understood his father. Herring's father had been a remarkably limited man. A man driven by an animal need for public commotion. A man who would say anything, spin any yarn, just to keep his inner self guarded, untouched by the world. If you asked him what day his birthday was he would say that the truth of the matter was that he'd never been born, and for a brief moment, by the tone and gravity of his voice, you would have believed him. And though she would never know this, while they chatted Herring thought often of his father, of him on the drunk, rambling about moments from the past as if liquor had moved him back through time, revealing that even though Agnes's family was dirt poor, she had a different pair of shoes for each day of school, and his voice would be hot with confusion and anger and desire, going on about how eccentric and unnecessarily conceited these shoes had been. His father saying, "There is no such thing as time. Only heat."

Agnes and Herring were sipping iced tea. The day was hot and the winds were kicking a wee bit, the flies were out. She'd spent the morning opening the windows and getting the screens on, beating rugs, doing laundry and hanging all of it out on the line. Herring had yet to get talking, and Agnes was trying her best not to get irritated with him. He was keeping her from her work, though. "I heard some talk that they're thinking of pushing setting day back. The weather's sposed to be bad," she said. Herring nodded. Agnes considered mentioning the hole in the floor or the business with Chessel and his pony but decided against raising these topics. She didn't want to put him on the defensive. She thought about her daughter and him. She did want Euna to be happy, and she wanted this man to be happy, truly. She hoped they might repair whatever it was that had come between them and return to that former place, but she knew such things rarely happened. The losses of love were about as sensible to her as the triumphs of love, and this was as far as she could get in this regard.

"Years ago, when they were building the fish plant, a gull impaled itself on a lightning rod. We sat all day and just watched it flap itself to death," said Agnes. "The next day the damn thing was gone and we never quite figured out what became of it."

Joe drove down the lane, parked his rig next to Herring's, two burgundy things, one nearly dead and the other quite alive, and carried a plastic cooler over to them. "Hello there, mother," he said.

"Hello there, sonny," said Agnes.

"Herring," said Joe.

"Joe," said Herring.

Forty-eight feet. So, roughly speaking, a buoy, eight fathoms, a trap, eight fathoms, a trap, eight fathoms, a trap. The *M&M* could handle a load of 102 traps. So, that meant that each trip out to their grounds was seventeen dumps. Their last trip was only eleven dumps, with two dumps having seven traps to it. Herring had everything mapped out on a sheet of plywood, twenty inches by twenty inches. He spent a great deal of time over the winter months preparing his routes for setting day. He would lean the plywood up on the workbench in the basement and come back to it, revising his thoughts very much like a painter might. He worked in pencil until he felt that the route was flawless, and then he cemented it by tracing over his lines and strokes with a permanent marker. If his hand trembled, or if a detail wasn't as clear as it ought to be, he would start all over on a fresh square of ply, of which he had ten or so stacked up against the foundation. The slightest of errors could make or break him. He had come to know this as something of a certainty. Forty-six north, sixty-two west. The meridian that went to the Shetland Islands, to lands with volcanoes and penguins and the wrecks of old whalers and sealers. Everyone else had made the switch to the GPS plotters. Herring had one installed but then welshed on this. He told Gerry that he refused the technology on principle, but as to what that principle was, no one quite knew. As much as he hated to do so, the man had to embrace this technology. And as Gerry pointed out, the boat had a depth finder, didn't it? Principles were important, to be sure, but there was no point to them if a person was not consistent. Herring insisted that he liked being able to feel where he was and to know that this feeling could actually be verified upon a map. That a map was a tablet and that a tablet should exist in physical form, to be held and seen to connect man with his past, his ancestors. Not just a scramble of ones and zeroes. Fishing ought to require thought, because your thinking separated you from every other fisherman out there. Gerry had sensed that this was an excuse, and a poor one, at that, for some deeper atavistic fears or insecurities, had wanted to mention that having the plotter made for shorter days, especially if you needed to move gear. They spent what felt like weeks sailing around, blind as bats, really, when you thought about it, looking for buoys. A few years before, they'd been all the way out in Pigeon, looking for two dumps that Herring had misplaced, and they'd run out of diesel. It was pretty late in the day, and no one would come out to tow him in. So they had to wait for the tide to push them into shore. This took the whole night. Gerry splayed out for most of it on the roof of the *M&M*, real baked after only a few meagre toots, watching the sky darken. So high he couldn't feel the wind and the cold. Near to when the moon was at its zenith, he saw himself reach out and grab a handful of stars as if they were grains of sand. He put these in the pocket of his shirt, and in the morning he spilled them out onto the washboard as if he were a reckoner of such things, as if these were the ultimate proof of an exponential law. He marvelled over them. Stayed close to them, for they required protection. One of the boys from the Annandale wharf took pity on them, this ghostly ship drifting aimlessly, pathetic and wounded, as if torn from battle, and sailed out a jerry can to Herring before he ran aground. The captain of this vessel, asleep in his bunk, shivering from the cold, and his cork, his hired man with the strange eyes and the toothless mouth. The pair of them returned from the abyss. Marked. After this incident, Gerry had hoped that Herring would come, of his own volition, to see the error of his ways with regard to the plotter, but unfortunately, this had yet to occur.

Gerry was dragging his feet, and Herring could tell that he wasn't in good form. The 11 and 23 dumps were always the sevens. He watched Gerry double-dip the first 23 buoy to a stack of only six traps and he went over and smacked him on the back of the head. "McClellan, what in fuck?" he said. "Yer drivin' me foolish." He pointed to the buoy and then he pointed to the plywood that he'd tacked to the shiplap. Immediately, Gerry was already more flustered than he usually was, and he stumbled a bit, the heel of his boot caught in the rope. Gerry righted himself, took a hearty breath, and offered him a cig. "Okay, okay, let's have a little powwow here," said Herring. "Gerry, you need to slow down, otherwise you'll work yerself out of a job."

# FIVE

On Wednesday night, Herring and Gerry went into the Legion in Montague to play pool in the local league. As they were walking up to the door, Herring said, "Gerry, you've got to take yer hat off."

"I hate going to the Legion," said Gerry.

Gerry called it The Wrinkle Ranch. The old ladies loved him, and when he danced with them, he had a forceful pair of hips, so they tended to take their teeth out. Gerry would always offer to put them in his shirt pocket while they danced, and then he'd smile and reveal his own lack of teeth, which was awfully charming and self-deprecating. And when the dance ended, he always made sure to slap them on the buttocks. Later, he'd say to the boys, as if to explain himself, that they, too, had been young and beautiful once. He'd say, you know, we're all headed in the same direction. It's folly to pretend otherwise. But nobody really paid much attention to this.

The beers were three dollars a bottle, shots were a dollar seventy-five, and the place was crammed. The entrance was at the back of the building, and one had to walk down a rather precarious and steep set of stairs. At the bottom, the bar was on the right, and the juke-box, which was permanently free of charge, was on the left. A group of young women, who were mostly blond and from Cardigan, were sat at the bar. The tables, two for pool and two for snooker, had just been treated to new bumpers and wool over the holidays, and the balls were running fast. There were little machines mounted on the walls next to each table, and you fed these quarters to keep the lights on. On a bulkhead by the jukebox were a series of photographs of local

men who had served in the military. Herring's second cousin, Little
Arbot Herring had his photograph up there. By the washrooms lurked
a trinity of electronic slot machines. As Herring and Gerry walked up
to the bar, a group of people, led by Deborah MacLeod, were trying to
pick the lock on the door of the women's washroom. Somebody had
trapped themselves in there.

Herring ordered four beers and two pickled eggs. A fellow came
to the bar and asked for a knob of ice. Annie Campbell lifted up her
shirt and showed Gerry a tattoo that said *eros* next to a little arrow.
He caught a little bit of side boob and smiled at her. She was home
from Mount Allison, where she was in the final year of her psychology
degree. She said that Eros was the father of psychology. Gerry downed
his egg and patted her on the shoulder, wished her good luck with her
studies.

Herring asked the bartender, Edith, for his cue, and she handed
the case to him. Back in the day, he used to play nine-ball at Dooly's
on Kent Street there, just about twice a week during the off-season,
well before he and Euna got together. He learned quite a bit and had
represented the Legion a few times when the districts assembled in
town to establish who would represent the province. He didn't like
Edith one whit, and she felt pretty much the same about him. The
year before, on Gerry's birthday, Herring got rather cut and started
knocking over chairs and dropping bottles on the floor. Edith had
refused to serve him another beer. He went over to Georgie Graham,
who was set at the bar, asked him to order another beer. Georgie
ordered the beer and gave it to Herring. Edith watched all of this
go down, tried to hide her displeasure at the pantomime before her.
Herring looked at her, trying to roll her, thin her out, lessen and break
the woman. He wobbled a bit in the way that the drunk do, one step
forward, with intent, and three steps to the side, as if attempting to
shake off a horny dog, and he dropped the bottle to the tiles where it
shattered and spumed. Edith had said, "Get out, Herring." He put his
hands up in confused protestation. He was a paying customer. "Get
the fuck out, Herring," she had said, and he'd leaned over the bar as

best he could and said, "Worst bartender ever." But secretly he liked Edith, despite her faults, which, he considered, were many. She wore them without a care in the world. She had mustard. One day he would tell her. One day he would say, "Goddammit, Edith, yer a hell of a headache, but you have some grit to you."

Soup was there, sitting by the wall in his flannel coat and a pair of greasy jeans. His picture was up on the wall, too. He'd had a four-year streak of winning the league not too long ago. Soup didn't play too much anymore, but he came just for something to do. He was talking to Billy Miller about seeing Rush open for Nazareth back in the day. "They were so loud," he said, "I got home and couldn't hear, hell, I couldn't talk right for four days. The wife's never had it so good since." He looked over to the bar, keeping an eye on his great-niece. With a few more rounds into some of these fellas, they'd be on her like stink on a monkey.

Dunbar Gillis came down the stairs and a great hush fell over the place. The man avoided eye contact, went right to the coat tree, hung his jacket, and then marched through the crowd to where Gerry and Herring stood.

"Dunbar," said Herring.

"Herring. Gerry," said Dunbar, adjusting the collar of his shirt.

"Ya missed a button there, Dunbar," said Gerry, pointing at the man's gut. Herring passed him a beer and indicated that he ought to throw it right down the hatch so as to make things a little less unbearable. This was a volatile situation.

Herring played against one of the old timers. An Acadian fellow by the name of Carmine, who had a birthmark on his head and face that was the colour of ink. Herring broke and then Carmine ran the table. Carmine looked at his cue before he sank the nine ball and said, "This thing's more crooked than a politician." Herring didn't like that he wasn't shooting well. Historically, he had always been something of a slow starter, but tonight felt a little different, a little more calamitous.

Billy Clow and Jack MacLeod came down the stairs and ordered drinks, talking briefly to the fellows at the bar, and then they came over to the tables. About thirty years ago, aboard the school bus, Jack MacLeod had taken the both of Herring's thumbs and yanked on them, dislocating them with almost no effort. In all of those years, Herring had yet to get back at the man. Jack looked at Herring and said, "There ya are, lookin' like a bucket of scrunched arseholes."

Herring said, "Hey Billy, ya know why gulls fly upside down over Georgetown?"

"Why's that?" said Billy.

Herring said, "Because even they know that Georgetown's not worth shitting on."

Billy Clow said, "Jeez, I've never heard that one before. Those are some sneakers you've on there, Gerry." Everyone looked at Gerry's Velcro shoes.

"Went to a party in high school and had my sneakers stolen. Went to a party the next night and had another pair stolen. Mom sent me to school in these Velcro shoes and I wore them till I finished. I think my girlfriend broke up with me 'cos of these very shoes," said Gerry.

"They sound like bad luck," said Billy.

"Well, I spose bad luck's better than no luck," said Gerry.

"That's about the way of it," said Billy, and then he looked at Dunbar Gillis, daggers in his eyes. "Speakin' of bad luck. You've some nerve showing yer face here," he said. The league players halted their games. The lights went out over the tables, and no one made a move to put a new quarter in. Dunbar Gillis scanned the room, tightening his mouth as he sorted out a response. Herring set down his bottle and leaned in, between the men, separating them like the blade of a knife.

"We're not looking for trouble there, Billy," he said.

Billy said, "I'm as calm as a kitten's fart."

Herring looked at Deborah and said to Jack, "Why don't ya take the ol' blister home and slam the guts outta her. That'll put yer mind right." Jack blushed, started to twitch.

"Why don't you and Chingachgook hit the road," said Jack.

Soup said, "It's all fun and games till someone loses an eye, boys. Then it's a sport."

Billy looked at Jack and at Soup, at the players around their tables. "I gotta get a drink of water. I'm as dry as a boot," he said.

Gerry said, "How 'bout a round of the little brown fellas on me." And with this, everybody relaxed.

—

The executive director of the PEI Fishermen's Association had an early morning conference call with representatives from the Department of Fisheries and Oceans. Everyone in attendance agreed, after consulting with the latest forecasts, that setting day was to be pushed to Friday. Word was put out.

—

Herring went down to the wharf. The winds were brutal and high, about forty-five knots. The surf outside of the bullpen was severe, and the spray, dark nets of it, so abundant and heavy, it was like some paste that held the heavens and the seas together, had abrogated visibility. He stood on the platform and rocked with the boat, and then he put a hole in a garbage bag and slid it over his shoulders like a kind of cape. He rubbed tomato paste into his scalp and experienced a vision of Reuben. Upon his knees, he put his head over the sheerline, as if he were a prisoner beneath the guillotine, the spray meeting and soaking the back of him.

—

Gerry was up at Sheila's drinking a few beers while she worked on her taxes. The woman was passionate about doing her taxes. She did them every year. Spread all of her papers and receipts and documents out on the kitchen table for a few days. Her tax booklet and her calculator at the ready. A heap of pencils at the elbow and a wastebasket near to foot. Coffee just bubbling and frothing, black and permanent, in the kitchen.

Gerry said, "Boy, you know, if you were an accountant in Houston you could call yer business Taxes in Texas."

Sheila groaned and lightly smacked her forehead. She said, "How 'bout just Texas Taxes?"

"Darn, that's way better," said Gerry.

They were listening to some Gordon Lightfoot records. Gerry had been trying to pay attention to the lyrics. There was a sadness there, or a darkness, that he hadn't ever noticed before. He thought, bloody hell, this is a sad, sad man. The guitar bits sounded so happy, too. He hadn't ever thought that something happy, or at least pleasant, could also be hard and damaged, at the same time. Maybe he was a bit like a Lightfoot tune.

Herring showed up unannounced and said, "We're going for ice." Sheila gave Gerry the look. They were supposed to be hanging out, even if that meant him watching her rummage through an infinite series of calculations. Sheila said, "Go on, git." She had tried to sound playful, pretended to swat at Gerry's ass as though she were a mother scolding her child.

They drove down to Machon's and pulled between the buildings. A few forklifts were buzzing around. Herring got out and walked over to the large, blue tanks. A fellow by the name of Yves emerged from the barn doors with a net in his hands. His face was red and he had a fat neck. There were blood and guts all over his oils. Herring asked him what he had for bait and Yves removed the lids from the tanks. There was fresh redfish and gaspereau. Herring hummed and hawed.

He said, "What do you mean, fresh?"

Yves said, "Fresh."

"Well, when was it caught?" Yves looked at the crew of workers in the dim light by the scales, smoking and watching, silent, like weary animals in a barn, waiting for summer days.

"I'd say the day before yesterday."

"Where's it from?"

"None of it's from the Island, if that's what yer asking."

They had frozen mackerel, too. It was from New Brunswick. Herring said he'd have a hundred and fifty pounds each of redfish and gaspereau, and a tray of mackerel. The crew took their nets and dipped them into the brown waters and brought them up thronged with bait. These giant spoons of red and silver. Herring and Gerry watched them weigh the trays. Yves recorded everything in a soggy notepad. They threw these five trays into the back of Herring's rig, and then Yves gave a wave and turned away from the winds coming down the channel. All about him the world was a wall of stacked trays and dented panels of corrugated steel. The boys around here weren't too keen with their brakes. Every rig dangling its front and back bumpers like ruined limbs. Some of the guys were wandering down to the rocks. Something down there was causing a commotion.

They drove across the road to the barns. People were all over the place, milling about in the parking lot. There was a fair bit of excitement. The reefer trucks were all lined up and ready to go. A young fellow with a well-manicured beard and hoops in his ears and a beak of a nose came over to the rig and asked what he could do for them.

He opened the double doors to the silo, and there it was, this colossal pack of ice that just seemed so unreal, as if it were carved out of soap and somehow made to seem more vast and mighty than it actually was by a rather easy tampering of slant. You could feel the cold of it bite at you, demand your attention. This was always breathtaking for the both of them, this going for ice another little ritual of theirs. Only minutes before they had been other men, other people. And now, here they were, wayfarers of a sort who had come out of the wilderness to this little bit of land at the edge of the sea so that they could witness this mountain of ice, held in captivity. The sight shocked the mind and the feeling lingered with them, as it always did, for a day or two. This mammoth of ice. A forklift picked up a dumping bin and drove into the silo where it then charged the face a few times, scraping at its body to calve enough ice away. The operator then drove over to the back of Herring's rig and dumped the ice over the trays of bait. The rubber of the tires sinking nearly to the rims.

They drove down to the wharf, the overburdened truck leaking water and blood, and layered the ice and bait in a couple of tanks until they were right full. A few shovels of ice, a few of bait. Herring said that he might drive up to Mount Stewart to get some crab. The guy up there said that he could give him a deal that'd be worth the fuel he burned. Herring didn't know if the rig would make it, is all. And then he said, "Sposed to thunder tonight. The lobster'll be on the move."

—

After his peacekeeping stint in Egypt, Little Arbot Herring had been a history teacher in Montague. He'd written a few books about boat building and sailing and had even managed to get them published. He had a new book out and was doing a talk in at Holland College. Herring drove in to Georgetown and crushed a few beers with Gerry, watching the Islanders game. Gerry had always been an Islanders fan. He scratched his cheek and said, "The Battle of Hastings is about the only thing that I remember from school. 1066." He had a snap of Schooner. "I've only read three books in my whole life. One was *Charlie and the Chocolate Factory* and I can't remember the other two."

They drove the back roads to town, the rig just a blur and a hum. Gerry had found a bit of electrical tape in the passenger door, and he leaned over and slapped it over the check-engine light. "There, that's fixed," he said. "I had a rig in the '90s with brakes on her that rubbed and squealed. I drove her till the noises stopped and I said to myself, 'There, that's her all fixed up.' The brakes were gone on her, though, no doubt about it. So, after herring fishing I had to drive real gentle on the railroad tracks to get home from the Harbour."

The darkness of the sky began to lessen as they drew nearer to town. Gerry said, "That's some light pollution up there. Like a heavenly candle near the Devil's arsehole." He rubbed his nose. "One time a Junior Burger I had fell down one of the vents. You couldn't have the heat on or the damn thing would cook, and my God, the smell of it was something I'll never forget. Smelled worse than a baby's diaper. I just about froze to death driving that winter. We had to take the whole dash off just to find the damn thing."

The college auditorium was filled nearly to capacity, mostly with grey hairs and the various and amalgamated smells of stale airs and bodies, tartan tams, and garish felted wool coats that reached with a direct confidence to the floor. Lots of crossed knees and hiking boots and a sea of tea-stained teeth, indubitable and guileless, as only the truly old can pretend to be.

Gerry and Herring quietly set themselves at the back of the hall, tried not to make a scene, for they were acutely out of place, imposters. But as out of place as they were, that they were even there was somehow reassuring to everyone. Like a kind of counterweight, so to speak.

The lights were dimmed, and you could almost hear their exhausted filaments praise the Lord. A woman came onto the stage in jeans and a turtleneck that were both the same hue of black. She was either a librarian or a bookseller. She spoke a few introductory words and the audience then clapped.

Gerry was anxious and visibly overheated, the line of his hair glistening as if it were a burst water main. He didn't want to remove his sweater, lest he make a greater scene of things. This was going to be torture. He heaved in a serious breath and tucked his hands into his armpits.

Arbot Herring followed the bookseller's path in front of the audience, dressed exactly as he had when teaching, a cardigan and a tie, loafers, and pants just a few fingers too short, his ankles clicking as he walked. His hair was white in the way that only those previously cursed with red hair can be, the frost borne out by a kind of transposed oxidization. He read a passage from his new work, which was called *The Weight of Twenty Atlantics*. It was a memoir about his building a sloop, a Nordic folk boat, and sailing it from Boatswain Point to the Azores and then, using the trade winds, back to America. The book covered a decade of his life. To Herring's mind, there seemed to be a great deal of philosophizing. Little Arbot was a rickety fellow, teeny and light, but with a rage just ever so slightly beneath, a rage whose life's work had been that of domestication, so to speak, of tapping into its mystery and rendering it into a more palatable expression. That of the ceaseless tinkerer whose trade was mostly the superfluous. This rage, as incomprehensible as it was, served as the man's anchor. It was the rage that all Herring men seemed to hold within them, stark and forsaken, driving them to drink or to preach. Each Herring either took to guzzling with enthusiasim or lecturing with gusto. The two would not mix. You were either the one or the other. And this rage assumed that it knew best. Presumptuous bastards, the lot of them. Towards the end, Arbot looked up from his pages and ad libbed for a bit,about a fellow by the name of Pascal, spirals of metaphysical thoughts within other abstract spirals. Dizzying.

After the reading, Arbot cut through the crowd and shook Herring's and Gerry's hands with a surprising vigour, which emanated from the scalded muscle of him. He patted them on the back and gave a fierce smile. Arbot said, "Let's go for a tipple, there, boys." They went out to the lot, where his car foundered under what must have been all of his earthly possessions. He climbed into the rig and shuffled through the garbage. Arbot was a man who lived his life worrying about the end of all things. From protons to language to consciousness. The creases near his eyes suggested that he found the world too bright.

They went to the Olde Dublin and sipped Scotch whisky at the bar, while a group of unreasonably tall musicians tuned their instruments. Arbot asked Herring and Gerry how they were doing. Gerry said, "Oh, ya know me. I'd get lost in a shoebox."

"Feast or famine," said Herring.

Arbot looked down the bar at a rowdy bunch of middle-aged women. They talked about women for a while. Gerry mentioned Sheila and the woman at Maid Marian's. He talked about Susan, too. Herring didn't say word one about Euna. Arbot mentioned that after the Middle East and prior to teaching he'd operated a dump truck to make ends meet. He said there'd be some trucks in the quarries that would just be beat all to hell. Some fellow would come along and think to put a new coat of paint on her and sell it, sell it for quite a price. "But, you see, underneath, it's still the same ol' truck." Arbot shrugged and then said, "It's handy having a woman's touch. Without it we'd surely be dead."

They moved to vodka. The band got into their set. Gerry walked over to the group of women and said, "So, which one of ya is taking me home?" More drinks were consumed. They dispersed to smoke cigarettes and order more drinks. Coming back in, Herring heard Gerry tell some women that in high school they'd called him the tuna can 'cos he was three inches thick and chock full of protein. A few pints later, the three of them met at the urinals and were happily surprised by this little coincidence. Arbot asked after Big Arbot. They were second cousins. "I'd say he drank the price of two farms," he said. "He was some good hockey player, but boy, was he a professional drinker."

Gerry bumped into a younger fellow on the dance floor, and an untidy fight ensued. The crowd moved and swung like water eddying about a boulder. They drank more and more, till their throats were glistened and full, and then Gerry started taking his jeans off. He folded them up real nice and set them on something of a little ledge. Then he took his shirt off and folded this up and set it atop his jeans. He continued until he was standing there, on the little dance floor, his arms crossed and his eyes as still as plumb bobs, naked. The bouncer, a guy by the name of Toe Tag, rushed over and started pressing his clothes back onto him.

"Gerry," he said. "What on earth are ya doing?"

Gerry wobbled a bit and said, "I'm just really hot, is all."

Toe Tag threw them out while professing just how sorry he was to do so. Gerry said that it was okay, that he didn't want to be bad for business. He shook the man's hand and then stumbled down the stairs to the sidewalk.

Arbot said, "Liquor sure has caused a whole lot of problems, but it's also solved a bunch, too."

Beneath an obsidian page of a sky, the three of them shuffled over Queen Street for a time. Nothing was much open and the stoplights swayed. They talked about the passing of Wes the Cat, an infamous petty criminal in town, who had somewhere near two hundred convictions to his name. Arbot told them about a kleptomaniac priest who had lived near him. Every time he went into town he came home with something from the shops. If he'd taken from their store, the owners would get in touch with the deacon to arrange a suitable time to drive out to the rectory and bring back what had been taken. They walked down to the wharf and watched the dredging that was going on out on the barges, the lights on the bridge uncommon and few. Arbot said that he'd always liked them, Herring and Gerry, in a manner that emphasized how far they'd fallen, and then he disappeared around a corner.

—

Leverett MacNeil was up in the loft of his shed passing traps to his teenage son, Lowell. They were working quickly, keeping warm. The skies were dirty, and the rains upon the horizon were all wrath and poverty, their shadowed sweep like the sixth seal of Revelation. Herring was out checking his lines. His hands crossed over his chest and nestled into his pits, he walked over to their rig. Lowell's hands were chalky things and his veins blue striations, as hostile as bad ideas. He gave the young fella a hand with the traps. Leverett climbed down the ladder and shook Herring's hand. "Boy, those things are heavy. Just wreck yer back, huh."

Herring said, "Yer cutting washers with yer arsehole." Herring mentioned that the birds had been flying low that morning, and both men agreed the weather was going to be dangerous.

Leverett said, "I used to keep fifty-pound bags of bait in my freezers, but these got to be too heavy for me. So, I got forty-pound bags of bait and put 'em in. These got to be too heavy, so I got thirty-pound bags. Then these got to be too much, so I got twenty-pound bags. No matter how you slice it, a ton is still a ton. At this rate, I'll have no need for all those freezers. My back'll live but I'll not be much for lobster."

Herring said next year he was going to buy three thousand pounds of redfish and gaspereau, and that way he could sell to who he liked.

Out at the breakwater, a few of the boys had set traps over. They parked their rigs in a vain attempt to hide this fact from everybody. Herring and Leverett watched them haul up a few, hand over hand, knees bent, the traps right thick with lobster.

"The first thing the Navy divers who went down after Swissair 111 said when they got back to the surface was they were never going to eat lobster again," said Herring.

Leverett said, "Yup, that sounds about right to me."

Leverett asked him if he'd heard about the lighthouse. Herring said he hadn't. Leverett said that out at the cape, the ice had pushed the lighthouse in about a quarter of a mile. "When I seen it there it was just lyin' on its side like a baby in a crib and the ice was all gone. It was as if it knew I was comin' out and wanted to fool me."

Herring slapped Leverett's son on the back and said that he needed to eat more. Lowell was all gangle and tall, damn tall. Herring said, "Yer a piece of spaghetti." His read on the boy was that he was an overwrought thing, snooty and rather superior. Lowell, like his father, knew everything about everything. They were just born so. It was a kind of magical quality. And if they spoke to you, you felt it was because it was their moral and ethical duty as good Christians to help you elevate yourself toward the highest good.

"The only thing with four legs that he wouldn't eat are the dinner table and the chairs," said Leverett.

Herring wished them both well and returned to his berth. Lowell had the look of a person who was suspicious of both life and friendships, of these things bringing about anxious condemnation. The birthright that pronounces trust as the ultimate liability. Herring watched the boy follow his father, like a dumb animal, a pet. Adjusting his glasses every few steps or so, as if doing so might reverse the order of all things. The differings between the two were thoroughly eerie. The milkman must've been quite a charmer, he thought. And then he thought that you don't see fathers and sons like you used to. Men seemed to have lost interest in showing their boys how important their hands are in figuring out the way of the world. Or perhaps it was true that boys had lost interest in what the experiences of their fathers might amount to. A dog makes sense of the world through its sense of smell. How a boy touches things, how he handles tools and other people, himself, too, will mostly determine his understanding of the world. Seeing a man and his son in such proximity, with such closeness, was now strange and odd. This display of kinship seemed like a punishment or a lack of trust.

—

He drove out to the cape because he had nothing to do. The truck wobbled like an injured dog, the wipers upon his windshield frenetic with the rain, duelling metronomes gone haywire. The deferential stalks of marram grass in the sands, made crooked by the wind. Mad, beckoning fingers. Through some small and strange miracle, he found an orange in the glovebox. That wasn't black with rot. He parked at the end of Rebecca's Lane, careful not to sink the truck, and bit into the rind of the orange. He placed both of his hands onto it, as if about to turn a laundered sock inside out, and hooked the nails of his thumbs where he could.

He walked out against the wind to the lighthouse, on its side like a captured rook. One could see all the way up through the tower to the cupola. There was something unguarded and truly fragile about this vantage. Herring sensed that he was taking in the whole alimentary canal of another world, of spirit and symbol before or after civilization. A place ever so, between the general order of things.

On the way back to the rig he thought about Euna's suggesting he go and see a psychiatrist. That perhaps something like valium might help him, his mind. He lit a joint and listened to the rain pester the hood as if it were an infinite series of playfellows tapping the grand shoulder of friendship with some inscrutable request.

—

Herring stopped at Keeping's and loaded his arms with bread and eggs and bacon, windshield fluid and the newspaper.

Otis said, "Where there's a will there's a way."

"No, where there's a will, there's a family in ruin over money," said Herring.

—

Just after supper on the Thursday, Herring had Gerry and Stretch in the rig with him, and when they pulled onto the wharf, Eben Daley waved at them. He walked over, his mouth stretched wide, chewing on a length of black licorice as if he were being repeatedly punched in the head, the lines about his eyes deep and resonant trenches, as if recovering from a mysterious fright, his black and white collie, Wolf, beside him. You could try to pet the dog, but he'd just let out a howl and scamper away, as if he'd been beaten his entire life.

Eben observed the rig and said, "Those are some dents you've there."

Herring said, "They're beauty marks. They're supposed to add character."

"I hear the new models have heaters in the tailgate to keep yer hands warm in the cold while ya push the damn thing home. Jeez, Herring, ya got a litter of men in there."

When he walked away, Herring said, "Every which way he looks, he walks into money. And when it comes to his money, he don't focus on what he has. It's all about what he's going to have. He told me once that he eats broth all winter just to keep costs down."

They retrieved the tanks from the bait shed and drove them over to the traps. Herring hooked the battery up to the charger and ran the orange extension cord to the plugs up on the wharf. Stretch and Gerry pulled the trays of redfish and gaspereau and mackerel out. Stretch hacked at the block of layered ice and frozen redfish. When a fish was free, he would hold it by the nose and begin to fillet it with the bread-knife Herring had given him. Two slices, each side of the fish, and just enough of a cut for the lobsters to smell. Herring didn't put the knife to his gaspereau. He just folded them on the spikes. Gerry cut each mackerel into threes and stuffed these into bait bags. Gerry would pass down the first buoy, and Herring would walk it over to the corner of the deck and start coiling the rope. Stretch baited the traps, topping each spike off with a redfish driven through the eye.

When Stretch took one of the spiny dorsal fins into his hands he would say, "Cocksucker." Come morning, he'd be lucky if he could open his hands without crying. "I'd have more fun running my hands over a table saw." Stretch's diet out on the boat was always beer and shatter and handfuls of acetaminophen.

Gerry would put in some ballast and pass the trap to Herring, who would lug it over the deck. When one trap was particularly heavy, Gerry would say, "These traps sure are soggy," and then Stretch would say, "Not fit fer a dog." This banter was repeated quite often. With the six traps set on the deck of the boat, Herring would measure out half a fathom and tuck this bit of rope into the net of the trap. He did this to indicate that this trap was the final one in the dump. And then he'd tuck the buoy into the parlour of the trap. It was slow work and hard on the arms and wrists. There was no point rushing. Every so often they'd stop. Stretch had all of these little alcohol testers. Tequila and bourbon and whiskey and rum. He called them spark plugs, and they'd gulp these down.

The gulls were moving from the sandbar to the bullpen in this great formation that was as wide as creation. Some of the fellows would tie tarps down over their traps to keep the birds from getting at their bait.

Stretch said, "There was this fisherman and he was too busy to see the birth of his son. When he finally got to the hospital and spoke to the doctor, he asked him if the baby had cried. The doctor said, yeah, the baby had just wailed and wailed and wailed. More so than any other baby he'd ever delivered. The fella said, Well, by Christ, I guess he's gonna be a fisherman."

They stacked some more, then took a break. Herring had a technique for stacking the traps that he called the pyramid. Each trap, as you layered up vertically, would kind of hook into the next. There was some measure of stability to this, which was what you needed for a setting day, especially if there was a bit of a roll to the water. They watched the other crews work. Herring said, "I should have hired some Mexicans to help." Stretch had a bread bag full of baloney sand-wiches. He offered one to Herring.

"You want a horsecock sandwich?"

Herring ate one and washed it down with a beer. He said, "Now, remember, tomorrow, don't take yer feet off the bottom of the boat. If ya feel a coiling taking, just let it run its course. Don't jump."

The three of them, seventeen dumps stacked in the back of the boat, their work completed, hopped into the truck and drove to the west side of the wharf and pulled around behind the line of bait sheds. They watched the sun disappear behind the channel that ran to My Bonnie River, relaxed and exhausted in their seats, their fingers pinching their cigarettes against the warm panels of the mangled rig. Stretch asked about saltwater boils.

Herring said, "Javex is good for 'em. Like, ya just scratch the top off and splash a little bleach on 'er."

Gerry said, "I heard that breast milk is good for cuts and stuff. If ya rub it on it'll heal it."

"You ever wonder why breasts are so attractive?" said Stretch.

Gerry said, "Anything bigger than a handful is too much, I find."

Herring had a pull of beer. "Sposed to be flat cam tomorrow."

"Man, the mosquitoes are the worst they've been in forty-five years, I'd say."

"We need some DEET."

"I thought that stuff was illegal."

"Only over thirty per cent, I thought."

"Kent Bell had a can of mosquito juice on his fridge out in the workshop. Sat there for nearly twenty years and melted itself right through, into his freezer. I seen it."

"We need the DEET they used in Vietnam."

"Yeah, I'd happily rub myself in napalm to keep the bloodsuckers away."

"I heard that if ya set a Big Mac out for a year it won't take no mould."

"You know, the amount of people who eat tripe in the world might surprise ya."

The glug of their throats and the satisfied breaths that come when hard work seems far behind. Herring put his hand over Euna's bar of soap in the pocket of his jacket. He traced its form and then he ran a finger through his Murphy hairs. He said, "Well, we're 1-800-get-the-fuck-outta-here, boys."

—

The both of them were up just after two. Sheila heard his alarm going off through the floor, and she stumbled into her clothes and walked outside, down the steps to Gerry's apartment, and gave him the tuna sandwiches and chocolate oatmeal cookies she had prepared the night before. Leaned against the edge of his door, Gerry was groggily poking a finger into his bridge, as if it refused to fit right. He pulled a heavy sweater over his head and a pair of worn denims up from the floor and over his thermals. He thanked her for the treats, and she gave him an awkward thing of a hug. His nerves were in him like he was a ware-house of baby rattles. She knew that today was a big day. Always a bit of an upset. Nerve-racking.

He had no belt. He wrapped a length of twine around his waist and knotted it as tightly as he could. Sheila watched the pants sag and yawn. Gerry didn't have much of an ass anyway.

—

Herring had gone to bed rather early, around half-nine, and he had woken at just after one in the morning. The room was dark, and from beside the bed he retrieved the square of plywood, etched with the lay of his traps, and stared at it in the beggarly light. His tablet. He wanted it to speak to him with plainness and clarity, devoid of nostalgia, free of delusion. He wanted it to tell him of what was to come, to prophecy and lay bare his future. If there was anything out there, on the waters or in the waters, waiting for him. A force that would be, if not indifferent to him, then against him. Herring moved his arms across the textile of the duvet and gently stubbed his fingers against something in the corner. He stood himself and scratched his ass, unbuttoned the duvet and pushed his arm into the envelope of the fabric and brought forth a wooden clothespin. Euna. Herring ambled to the bathroom and sat to piss, one hand over the back of his neck, his toes curled, trying to grip the wood of the floor as if not doing so meant a great fall. He was bloody terrified.

—

They were one of the first crews there, and the only lights, those of the standards and the trucks, a gathering of illuminating cones, some stood tall and thin and haunted, others laid on their sides, well-fed glows, fattened beams. Feast or famine, all right. The long caravan of fishermen in their rigs would soon be coming over the gentle hill that led into the harbour, this procession an isolated tendril of dormant adrenaline, a muscular tongue that ushered men from the land to the sea, from their beds in the early hours to about dinnertime, provided all went well, such that the afternoon could be napped away.

The unwritten order was that the boats were to be let out of the bullpen from south to north and east to west. Lately, which is to say, for the last decade, the men had democratically come to a uniform and binding agreement that Willy Lyon MacKenzie and his older brother, Louis, and the *Maranatha* were to be let out first due to his seniority. When presented with the notion, Willy Lyon had blushed and refused. But Joe and Slippy Dick Hume had insisted. It was just the right thing to do. "Things ought to be done this way," said Dick. Willy Lyon had consented to the arrangement, though it made him embarrassed and more than a little nervous, all of those young bucks staring at him, waiting on him. The canary down the mine, he thought. He came to see that it wasn't too much of a cross to bear. Though, without fail, every few years someone shirked this knowledge, their uncollected oath to the system, usually a younger fellow full of piss and vinegar, and gunned it hard for the waters, bashing hulls and creating quite a wake, and this turncoat would receive a small beating upon his return to harbour. Just a few shots to the face while he was held. Nothing that would disfigure. Nothing that wouldn't heal up. The men all knew, from experience, that to allow any transgression, no matter the size, was to allow a confession that their world was a Sodom.

Herring climbed slowly over the load of traps and into the cabin. He fired up the engine and unplugged the extension cord. Gerry pulled it in and coiled it on the shroud. Stretch stood up on the load of traps, real high up there, and smoked a big joint, just staring at everything. His Thermos of coffee and his bag of sandwiches tucked into an armpit. Leverett and Lowell came over and wished them good luck. Joe was barking orders at his hand, young Isaac Cahoon, who was a frenetic thing of a young man. He just bounced, and bounced lamely, all over the traps of the *NHL Joe*. He'd better be careful or he's gonna bait himself, thought Herring.

About five or six years ago, Herring had tried a season selling to a buyer for the live markets out of Maine, which was really just the Chicago mob, and he had taken Cahoon on to help with banding. The lobster out of Nova Scotia were generally larger than those from the Island. And so, as he could not understand why a mainlander would branch out, especially to him, Herring was more than a little wary of this arrangement. He'd been bitten in the ass before, trying to be greedy. Gerry noted that Herring had been a mess of nerves that whole season. He was grinding his teeth so hard while he slept that he gave himself a black eye. Though the season had gone mostly well, he spent more than he was comfortable spending. During the second week of May, Cahoon had come to him to ask for an advance against his wages. Said he needed to fix something on his car. Herring was getting tired of having to transport both Gerry and Cahoon around. He figured the advance was in his best interest, would save him down the line.

On the last day of the season, with a few lobsters in the pot in the bait shed and one of two cases of beer already on the go, the three of them drinking recklessly on the platform of the *M&M*, Herring had asked the young fella for his advance back. Cahoon said he didn't have it. Herring dropped the subject for a while. Busied himself tidying ropes of their knots and loading them into the back of his rig, where the water from them began to release, working their way down through the body of the rig, dripping onto the wharf, marrying with veins of oils, both refined and unrefined, as if all of this was the grease from some animal joint being cooked, being slowly and deliberately roasted.

But Gerry knew he was standing in observance of a truly explosive situation, and he felt awfully helpless as to how he might remedy all of it. The divide between the two had been growing ever since the loan had been granted. Herring had begun to catalogue all of the little things, minor deceits and tiny overdues soon became grand thefts, an elaborate and calculated series of slights and reproaches. The orchestrations of a major chicanery. Each day saw Herring sail them out to the grounds, all the while muttering to himself that the boy was nothing more than a snake in the grass. "A supergrass," he had said. And Gerry would have to talk him down over and over.

"Let it go, Herring. Let it go," he said.

So, on that last day of the season, the day right before Canada Day, it all came to a head. Herring said, "Cahoon, yer not worth a pinch of coon shit." More beer was consumed. Herring egging Cahoon on, downing a series of cans in quick succession as if to say c'mon, boy. C'mon ya weasel. Be a man. Be a fucking man. "Forget 'Icon.' I'm gonna start calling ya 'eye-coon.'" Cahoon foolishly tried to keep pace with the slinging of insults. Again, Herring asked him for the principal. The two of them on the deck of the boat. Again, Cahoon said he didn't have it, and anyways, it had only been $120. What was this in the grand scheme of things? Herring was practically vibrating, an outboard poorly mounted to its transom. He whacked the boy with his fist and Cahoon stumbled over some gear and slipped to his knees, one leg bending and snapping in an unnatural fashion. Cahoon righted himself, his mouth a band of agony. Stiffened by adrenaline and loosened by drink. Herring was at him, dragged him up onto the wharf, sat on his chest, hammering him while the boy flailed his arms in a poor defence. The other fishermen halted what they were doing and watched. No one made a move to intervene.

Herring decided the matter was finally settled when he felt the third finger on his right hand break. He and Gerry burst open a few lobsters and put these down the hatch. Cahoon was still laying among the heap of ropes, this whimpering, bleached thing in the sun. Gerry gave Herring a look of disdain, for he wasn't impressed, but he knew better than to say anything. Herring showed him his broken finger and said, "You ever try to wipe yer arse with yer other hand? It's not easy, let me tell you."

Cahoon brushed himself off, walked to the breakwater, climbed down the boulders to the brine and cleaned his face while oyster shells and various lures stared up at him. Herring took the man to the hospital to get stitched up. He sat in the waiting room and then drove him home. When he pulled up to Cahoon's apartment in Irish Montague, he'd raised his fist and said, "Cause," and then he pointed at Cahoon's stitches, the black twine in his cheeks, and said, "Effect," as if all of this trouble were simply a lesson in physics.

Now, the tide was going down fast. The sky as dark as a raven's wing. The harbour was filling up. People were everywhere. The other men started firing up their engines, a great and ancient cacophony, Hannibal's elephants before the Alps, unsure but steadfast. The loud grind and propulsion of commitment in the face of sense. Sheldon Dawe and his sons, in the *Dump 'n Chase*, did a hasty spin about the bullpen, unfurling a fine wake. The men aboard the *Pleasure Seeker*, Jimmy Beck and his boys, gave out a bright hurrah and splashed rum down their throats, as did Howard MacNeil and his crew on the *Tide 'n Knots*. Eben Daley, aboard the *Strait 'n Narrow*, just shook his head. Down the wharf, Jack and Deborah MacLeod were tending to their boat, the *Jack & Deborah*, named after their kids. As doubly vain as it was unwarranted. Leverett and Lowell in the *My Bonnie Harbour*, clean and well tended to. Everything just by the book and above board.

Euna and Agnes and the girls had driven out to the end of the wharf, joining the other wives and families. Herring waved at the girls and they waved back. Euna turned her head. He had set his bar of soap and his Murphy hair by the wheel. His totems of what was real and true. He saw Rankin Jackson on the *Jenny Lynn* and waved at him. Rankin waved back, then pulled a bare foot out from his rubber boot, bent back down and retrieved its sock. His foot as white as a milk bottle.

Nary a man had come to blows this season. This was taken as a good thing, a sign of how the men would prosper this season, for the mood was fine and noble. A parable of talent. A blameless and unblemished setting day for all and one. Another good-luck charm was Gerry getting shit on by a gull, but that had yet to happen.

Two boats from My Bonnie River came scuttling up the channel. From the bullpen, there were no indications other than their lights and the faint hum of their engines. They were beating the Harbour boys to the grounds. "Crafty sons-a-bitches," said Joe. Isaac said, "Don't hate the player. Hate the game."

The sun began to rise. A shag came to the surface with a fish in its mouth and looked around at the commotion.

Donald MacPherson, a squat and thickly man, in his kilt and his piper's plaid and his feather bonnet, his socks tucked into his rubbers, stood out at the breakwater with his bagpipes and began playing "The Skye Boat Song" over and over. It took a few notes for him to get the bag and the lungs all warmed up, but then he got going. His stubby fingers red and distraught with chill upon the canter.

Willy Lyon and Louis on the *Maranatha* made the run to open waters, giving all the people waiting a bunch of waves, their skinny arms raised to the heavens as if they were the relatives of some monarch. Billy Clow, sailing the *Chasin' Tail*, was the next boat out of the harbour.

Herring said, "Now, remember, no bananas and no whistling. You'll whistle up a storm. Oh, and you can't say pig. The minute you say pig, we're breaking down."

Stretch managed the ropes and then climbed over the wall of traps to stand next to Herring in the wheelhouse. Herring said, "We leave our problems at the wharf." They set out at nine knots for Pigeon, a good pace, real steady, an hour-and-a-half sail directly east into what would become the rising sun, the line of the horizon like the edge of an overturned mug of beer. Herring said, "There's no water coming in the scuppers, is there?" Stretch investigated half-heartedly. It was tough to see what was what through all of the traps. He shook his head. Herring said, "Stretch, poke your head in the hatch there and tell me if there's any water in the bilge, eh." Stretch knelt down on the cabin floor, lifted the door, and took a gander. He said, "She's as dry as the manger." And as he closed the hatch, he looked at it for a real moment and then he said, "Everywheres you are there's a hole in the floor, eh."

Once past the cape, the waves increased, and there was a great spray all about. A bit of wet snow began to fall in a dawdling manner, a release of powdered milk. "Like a slow kick in the balls," said Gerry, sat on the tall load of traps, shrugging away from their touch, though Herring didn't hear him over the din of the engine and the slap of the sea. Stretch said, "So much for flat cam. You should see about replacing Boomer Gallant at the ol' weather desk, eh."

The hull began cutting the tops from the waves, shuddering and bolting from one curl to the next at a ferocious pace, as if the boat were a great disk of sandstone pitched from the shore by a greater hand. Stretch watched Gerry struggle to light a cigarette, hunched over, hiding the lighter and the smoke from the winds, and once he got this going, a bit of snow and water extinguished it almost immediately. He tried the cigarette again, but it was righteously soaked. Flicked it over the side. He retrieved another and managed to give it flame, hunched over like a mad thing, only to have it soaked, yet again. Gerry tried another one and even managed to get a decent haul out of her, his nostrils releasing little torrents of smoke, but then he was again sheened with the wet. He flapped his arms in helplessness and defeat. "You've baptised yer cigarettes there, Gerry," said Stretch. A few gulls were chasing them, battling the spindrift, too, but then they gave up and turned for home, back to the channel. Stretch stood next to Herring and started hauling on a joint, that silvery look of the shoal in his eyes. He said, "Do ya have a wind meter on the boat?"

"Nopers."

"Funny, 'cos they got 'em on tractors."

"That's 'cos they spray chemicals. I just spray spray," said Herring.

When they got to Pigeon, Herring slowed the boat down, cut the throttle, and put the boat in neutral. This line here that he was about to fish was beyond the line that constituted the Eastern Bank, which you weren't supposed to fish past, though as far as he could tell, this was only an unspoken rule, and one that nothing truly significant swung on. But Herring did fish past it, for his father had shown him this line, and his father's father had shown him this line, too. So, that it had been passed down from Herring to Herring, long before any talk of boundaries existed, was his justification for continuing to do so. Besides, nobody was going to come all the way out here and give him hell. He was out here for a reason. To get away from all the other fellows. He said, "All right, boys. Here we go. If anything happens, you just holler at me and I'll throw 'er in reverse. Make sure you've got yer knives handy." He handed each man a life jacket and insisted that they buckle up, if only for the day. "Gerry, do you want your tomahawk?" Gerry gave him the finger. You could see the factories in Georgetown and the windmills up at North Lake, these stubborn and barren sentinels, auditing the outer record of the planet. The Island this muted and humble sweep of land. To behold it so stirred something in a person, soothed you. You could feel yourself grow. The sky and the earth and the waters, and whatever lay within each of these tiers. Man was in constant communication with these things, and out here, to be reminded of this was lovely, reassuring. This acknowledgement was like an embrace that you could relish even as you outgrew its influence. Everything, all things, were fermenting.

Stretch climbed up and over the traps, the snot hanging out of his nostrils like the strings on a Newton's cradle. Herring checked his compass and his watch as Gerry and Stretch set a dump on the stern washboard. They set with the falling tide, from west to east. Herring sailed northeast for a minute or two and then revved the throttle three times in quick succession. This was the cue. Gerry would throw a buoy and push the first trap over, and then he and Stretch would stand away, which was virtually impossible at this point, staring down at the deck as the ropes came alive, their eyes tracking this giant bed of serpents, slithering and crazed, pure corporal menace, as if they were a kind of savage people who had been chased into the trees. Last season, a rope had snagged around Gerry's boot, where he stood between the third and fourth traps of the dump, and before he knew what was what, it had leapt up to his knee. He started yelling at Herring as his knee, which was carrying the weight of three traps trying to sink to the bottom, punched into the transom, the rope cinched around the cap of his knee and the soft flesh on the back of his leg. Herring got the boat going in reverse and this served to relieve the pressure on his leg. Herring yelled at him to cut the rope, but Gerry didn't like doing this, so he waited for his moment, then slid the loop down and over his rubber. They kept going and Gerry took a few deep breaths. His nerves just shot. His hands a mess of trembles. He hobbled about for the first few weeks, a raw band of flesh across the back of his leg. So the urgency of this notion gave both men headaches that felt like blades put through their skulls.

Herring yelled for the number and Gerry answered, and Herring wrote this down in his notebook. Herring said, "Are they sinking?" and Gerry and Stretch watched the traps. They seemed to want to float, were fighting their fate, the corners of the traps a few fingers above the churning waters, and then they surrendered, disappeared, this strange line of caskets that would hit the rocks and mud and send the flounder and lumpfish and seals back, a great gesticulation of flinches. Gerry yelled that yeah, they were sinking, sinking like curling rocks.

As they dumped, a gull landed on the uppermost row of traps and was giving Gerry the evil eye. Gerry let him be, for he thought he remembered this particular one, the ragged, coal-coloured wing and the darker leg, like he'd been halfway dipped in oil, though it took everything in him not to pitch a buoy at it or grab for the gaff and swing. Stretch threw it the odd mackerel, and it ate with an air of superiority. This gull would stay with them for the day.

They set seven dumps in the mud that divided Pigeon from the Eastern Bank, and then they sailed west and placed four more in Crow Bank. They sailed to the bluffs and set the remaining six, three at the Giant's Thumb and three at the Tits, a pair of conical rocks that looked like breasts on the depth finder. Every morning at 7:20 someone played "Barbie Girl" by Aqua over the radio. And then, invariably, some other fellow came on to say grow the fuck up, buddy, keep the radio clear. Occasionally, Lillie McDonald, a captain out of Graham's Crick, came on the radio, and Herring would listen to her voice as she talked to the other boys from the wharf. It was a lovely thing of speech, seductive and warm, like a fire or a glass of whiskey. He loved her for her voice, whoever this woman was, these sentences unfurling as if they were tinsel about an evergreen, all pulse and shimmer.

When they came back into the bullpen for their second load, they'd been out on the waters for just over three hours. Stretch and Gerry hopped up onto the wharf and started baiting and setting weights again. There was no wind in the harbour, and Herring could feel his arms burn with the gleaming of the sun. Some of the wives were down at the wharf, helping with baiting traps. Stretch scrutinized each one. Herring, from the deck, heard him mutter to no one in particular, "I'd lick her, no problem. And I wouldn't even ask her to take her pants off."

Herring said, "Jeez, yer some vulgar."

"I can turn it on when need be. Hell, I could talk the pants off a nun," said Stretch.

Sailing out through the cut in the breakwater, Miles Mackenzie yelled at Gerry to take that fucking jacket off. Gerry sheepishly removed his PFD.

...s they headed out to the bluffs just off Poverty Beach, to set another eleven dumps, the sun reached its apex. Later in the season, when the weather improved, a woman would come out and sunbathe in the nude. Both Herring and Gerry enjoyed fishing when she was about. Her skin wonderful and bronze, like something removed from a pharaoh's tomb. From here, they sailed west again, and set another six at Rat Bank. Herring was awful particular about where his traps went. He knew what he was looking for on the bottom. The other difficulty he had was navigating all of the other fishermen's dumps. So, as most crews were wrapping up for the day, there was the *M&M*, sailing northeast and southwest, its captain trying as best he could to find that sweetest of spots. Gerry looked at Stretch and said, "It's like trying to find the G-spot." The third trip had them place another six dumps out at the Bluffs, and the remaining five they sailed up the crick to My Bonnie River and set in the mussel mud. The lobsters down here were colossal, but the meat wasn't very good, unfit. Herring fished down here to increase his poundage, and he only fished these ones every other day, for a kind of double haul.

About four in the afternoon, Herring insisted that they sail back out to Rat Bank and pull some traps. He wanted some lobster for supper. Leaned up against the wheelhouse, Stretch was snoring, his toque off-kilter and his skinny torso slouched against a balloon, a life jacket under his arse, a joint fizzling out between his fingers.

All went well for the fishermen of My Bonnie Harbour. No engines broke down and no one became hopelessly tangled up in their gear such that they had to get on the radio and ask for a tow back to the bullpen. This congregation of men returned from their boats to their trucks, staggering and shuffling, their bones bent and pining for their mattresses, as if drunk on the spirit of the sea.

Three trips in and out. Forty-five dumps. Two hundred and seventy-two traps. Sixty boats, bobbing out on the water, dropping wood and cement and rope and bait every eight fathoms, to the bottom, expiations to forces well beyond the governance of man, as the sun rose behind the wall of clouds and the tide receded, the gentle scrape of its blade the sign of its submission. Things, all things, all masses, were being pulled toward one another in the unhurried and unmoved competition, this strangest of frolics, that was the natural world.

After they hauled a dump and set aside ten pounds of canners in a yellow bucket, Herring sailed farther east for a few moments, then cut the engine. "Back in the day it was nothing to just sit out here and have a two-hour confab," said Herring. There was no one else out near them, and so, for as long as they wanted, it was just the sounds of things as they were without interference. The gales were diminishing. The waters were being smoothed out by some unseen spatula. "See, flat cam." You could almost see the foghorn out at the cape. "The groaner," said Herring, pointing. There was the orange and black buoy for the Brooks shoal, bobbing, riddled with shit. Gerry said that he had to drain the vein. He stood, wobbling on the transom next to the faithful gull, and pissed into the wake. Already there were jellyfish in the water. "Must be gettin' real warm," said Gerry. They watched a flock of gulls chasing a school of silversides into one of the coves.

Gerry and Herring smoked a bit of hash and had a few smiles of shine, so they got to feeling bleary. The both of them let go, as best they could, of all the anxieties fastened up in their bodies, their bone and muscle. Herring wanted to ask Gerry about how he was doing, where his thoughts were with his brother Randy since his death, but something held his words in, the same feeling that had haunted and trailed him his whole life. Anyway, Stretch was there, pretending to sleep, which is what he did when he wanted a bit of gossip to take home with him. It was none of his business. And it was at this moment that Herring felt, truly felt, not only the distance between him and Gerry, but also his distance from everyone, each beautiful person, in his life, as truly and utterly natural. If he didn't fight, he would lose these things. He would lose his friends, if he hadn't already. This was the way of it. And if he was alone again, living in isolation, as was

...bit, as he had done with Euna and the girls, for when they had truly needed him, he had always been elsewhere, on another floor, out fishing, or out drinking, he risked a break with reality that might never be reinstated, that was irreparable. With Euna and the girls he had wanted companionship, people to share the good times and the bad times. A true and real companionship, and yet he had never fostered its growth. He had only discouraged it, despite himself, his desire. When he ought to have tended to it, to have embraced it, he had turned himself from it and walked away. Let Euna and the girls do the work. They would've done it if they had really loved him. And if things fell apart, which they had, then it was their fault. Walking away meant that he wasn't covered in the dust of blame and liability.

"Yer not fishing if you don't have some liquor with you," said Herring. "You want to do any jigging?"

Gerry shook his head. "A hook'll catch everything but a fish," he said.

"I've got a chest of drawers at the house full of socks, some without their mate, some with holes in 'em," said Herring.

Gerry said, "I save those for when I run out of shit tickets."

They laughed together and hauled on the hash.

Herring said, "When I was younger there were only two things I loved. My rig and my socks." Gerry turned down the final offering of shine. Herring looked at the bottle and then put it away. Gerry asked him if he remembered coming across the bags of cocaine floating in the waters out at Pigeon. Herring nodded. "God, that was years and years ago. We were practically babies." Gerry said that he often wondered how different their lives would have been had they taken some. Herring said, "That's an easy one. The Hells Angels would have found us and we'd be dead." Gerry said, "That first shower after fishing is always the worst. Spinning and rolling, just dizzy with the sea in you, in your mind. Your bones wanting to be rid of it."

The gull that was on the washboard was suddenly landed upon by another gull, and for a number of minutes the two fishermen watched these gulls atop one another, pairs of beholders, their fatalistic tolerance, acrobats in search of a festival.

On the way back to the harbour, Gerry ran the hose from the Jabsco and cleaned the deck off as best he could. Herring said, "My feet are gettin' sore already. That's not a good sign." Gerry climbed down into the cabin and sat by the stove, red hot.

—

Peggy, Tommy, Sam, Gerry, and Sheila were at The Muffler in Irish Montague slugging a few drinks into themselves. For a Friday night, it was awful quiet, so quiet that if one truly cared, it might inspire suspicion. Gerry was nervous Sheila might say something that would make a poor impression on his brothers and sister. He was fidgety as hell, kept running the palm of his right hand over his freshly shorn head. Sheila had shaved it just that afternoon. She'd done a nifty job all right, everyone thought so. Gerry said, "When Sheila finished she said that my head was gonna be pretty aerodynamic and I said no, no, Sheila, it's going to be *hairo*-dynamic."

Norman and Susan came through the door about an hour into the evening. Their coats were wet with the rains, which were silky and tapering. Outside, the branches quavered, rising and falling like the arms of carpenters toenailing joists. Susan ordered a dirty gin martini and Norman ordered a Caesar with gin, and then they joined the party. When it was served, Gerry admired the light within the martini. It looked like a piece of moss preserved in formaldehyde. When things were quiet, he could hear the ice in their drinks crack.

Tommy started talking about fishing octopus out west, some place near Vancouver Island. It wasn't clear to anyone if his talk was first-person experience or a second-hand filch. You'd swim down in your gear, he said, and try to find their burrows. Then you'd determine which end of the burrow was the highest. Then you'd go to this entrance and place some ammonia into the hole and as quickly as you could, you'd swim to the other one and wait for them to come darting out. They put up a good fight when they're on you. Tommy balled his fists and punched the air in front of him. "They'll bash at yer mask and yer regulator on the way up to the surface. If you keep at it this way, you can catch about three of 'em a day," he said.

Sheila said that this sounded terrible.

"It's gotta be better than mussels," said Norman. "Mussels are ignorant as hell." The skin of his nose was a bit red, and this red was spilling a coral patch onto his cheeks. Gerry was looking at it. Norman pointed at his face and said, "Rosacea. The sun." And then he said, "If yer doing mussels, you gotta learn to shit at home, otherwise yer going in a five-gallon bucket with a junk of plywood to kinda hide behind. The boys on the boat'll talk just so yer not too nervous about the sound of yer splash."

Susan flagged the server and ordered a round of tequila shots.

Sheila asked Peggy how she was doing. Peggy replied that she was doing okay. The change in the weather was nice. Sam said, "Yeah, I dated a black woman years ago, huh. I liked her a lot. Used to call her and she'd say, Oh, I'm just so sad."

The shots arrived. Susan said, "God is great. God is neat. Let's get fucked up," and everyone drank. "That'd float a goddamn horseshoe," said Gerry, grimacing, wiping his mouth with the back of his sleeve. "Where's the lemon? Isn't there sposed to be a lemon?"

"Anne Murray stood on the back of Gene MacLellan. Didn't even have the decency to come to his funeral when he died, eh," said Tommy. "Snowbird" was on the radio. "Springhill, Nova Scotia," he said, as if it were phrase that could reveal hidden treasure. "There's a Springhill up west."

Norman said, "Women are like tornadoes. They come in all wet and wild and they leave with the house and the truck." Susan rolled her eyes.

Gerry said, "There's three types of women, as far as I can tell. There's moaners, screamers, and grunters. And there are the ones who don't say jack. Just sit there like warm apple pie."

Peggy looked at him. "Yer driveway never quite met the road, did it?"

"My father used to say," said Norman, "ya treat the whores like queens and the queens like whores and the rest'll take care of itself." Susan punched him on the shoulder and Norman bopped her right back.

"There's this fella," said Sam, "he's a bachelor, kinda down on his luck, eh, at the beach, going for a walk, and he scuffs his toe against something hard in the sand. He scratches out a lamp and he says to himself, could be a genie in there. Well, he gives the thing a rub and sure enough, out comes a genie. The genie says what he always says, I'll grant you one wish. And this fella says that he's awful tired of being alone. I'd like you to make me irresistible to women, he says. And the genie says to him, okay, are you sure about this? And the fella says, yeah, I'm sure. And presto, the fella turns into a credit card."

Everybody had a laugh. Susan looked at Gerry and he looked right back at her.

Sheila said there was an eagle's nest just outside of Georgetown just full of dog collars, like a kinda pet cemetery.

Gerry said, "Herring told me he seen scallops up west so big they're like dinner plates."

Norman said, "Fuck Herring. What does he know?"

Gerry said, "Scalloping is terrible, terrible work. Yer just clawing rock all day long and yer wrists from the shucking, my god."

Peggy and Gerry went out for a smoke after the second round of shots, this time Florida Tracksuits. The night was mostly still. Peggy's posture was immaculate. Gerry noticed he was all hunched over, as if one leg was shorter than the other by the length of a shin. Peggy asked him if he remembered ol' Ricky Arsenault.

Gerry said, "Naw."

"He got burnt in a house fire about twenty years ago. I guess he finally got a new nose. I seen him the other day and didn't recognize him. He used to have just two holes and a bit of a point," said Peggy.

You could hear four-wheelers off in the distance and voices down at the docks.

Peggy looked at her brother and said, "Listen, don't go gettin' all fucked up over Randy, okay?"

Peggy tilted a wee bit and ran the palms of her hands down the length of her thighs, smoothing out her denims. "Randy was kind of a scumbag anyway, huh."

Gerry crushed another dart and walked around on the deck. He could still feel the lobster tails sweeping and kicking against him, impenitent things, cradled, as if he were about to enfetter them, the stainless banders threatening in his other hand.

# SIX

It was always choppy till you passed the cape, and then the rolling began. As they motored out, there had been so many cormorants that the channel had been a wall of black, this moving thing that you could feel from miles away, like the silhouettes of a dream.

Herring had picked Stretch and Gerry up early, and they'd come down to set the boat up for fishing. They put six tanks on the deck and counted out trays to hold their lobster and cut bait. The deck was a bit of a mess. Herring said, "We're going to have to snug this place up." They put their oils on and Herring got the stove with a bit of flame. Stretch filled two tanks with redfish and gaspereau and then fired up the Jabsco and soaked them in water so that they would thaw enough to handle. They smoked a bit of hash, and then they cut her ropes and set these on the walers. Gerry pulled up the balloons and fastened them to the railings over the wheelhouse, and then he sat up on the roof and watched the surf spread, created and ploughed so by the hull, as white and new and as carefree for authority as any Galilean or Lutheran proposition, a razor drawn across the back of a leviathan, the scribe of something that would change everything, reduce and eliminate all complexity, if only man could properly divine what it foretold.

Stretch said, "How long does it take to sail to Wood Islands?"

"About an hour and a half. Thereabouts."

"Yeah, I guess that's right, because you have to sail around the cape, eh."

"Well, how else are you gonna get there?"

"No, well, I just mean that the cape is longer than it looks. How long to Souris?"

"About two and a half."

The black of the sky before them began to lighten.

Their first blue-and-white buoy was only half a nautical mile away. Port Hood was in the background, to the southeast. Herring pointed and said, "If you head straight, you'll sail right into a coal mine."

Gerry said, "I think the Rankins are from Port Hood, huh."

"I thought they're from Mabou," said Herring.

Stretch made a face when he heard this. Then he said, "Boy, that Heather'd look good with her feet up by her ears. Years ago, I had a chance to date her."

Gerry tucked the gaff into his armpit and adjusted his bibs. His hands were red and cracked, and Sheila had put udder cream on them this morning and then slid rubber gloves over. His toque was pushed back from his hairline, glistening and dripping with brine, two chocks of spittle rucked into the turnings of his mouth. Herring looked at him. He had a big old shit-eating grin on his face. The air was lovely and still, the gulls overhead a taciturn crown of white, their shadows upon the boat like marionettes. Stretch looked like he was going to ask another question, so Herring said, "Always gaff yer buoys with the tide."

Gerry leaned over the sheer-line and gaffed the buoy, wrapped the line around the pin and roller and down through the wheel of the hauler, and then he set the gaff against the steel handle of the sliding door. He knew when they were approaching a buoy because Herring would take his gloves from the ledge by the window and squish them on. Herring took the M&M out of gear and flicked the electric clutch on, and Gerry walked the buoy to the back of the boat as Herring, one hand on the clutch lever, waiting for the knot to come up and over the pin and roller, hauled up the first trap. Gerry set the number-3 buoy on the washboard and coiled the rope up near it. When Herring saw the knot from backline to snood, he slowed the hauler down, lowered the hydraulics, put the hook on the snood, and pulled her in. He looked over to the rocks of Cape Breton. Herring said, "At some places in Cape Breton the rocks are so steep they lobster right from the shore."

Gerry said, "Some good overhead there, eh."

Stretch was always keen to get into your personal space, and Herring could feel him itching to go and get his clumsy hands on something. Herring said, "Careful of the hauler. Don't put yer hand between the pin and the hauler. Fella up west got caught and lost his hand past the wrist."

It was a nice day. A lovely Saturday. Things were going good. Herring was happy. He knew it. So he just slowed it down and everything was smooth. A trap would come up through the sea, silently and without any commotion, as if this displacement was the natural order of things, the ash from their cigarettes flaked out on the surface of the water, like the seasoning on some infinite soup, and he would catch the knot and slow her down, turn her back off, stop her. The traps were teeming with lobster.

Stretch said, "Christ, they're more stuffed than a slave ship."

Herring picked the traps, fetching the lobster by the body or by clasping their arms together, checking for spawn, and if he had time, he would remove some of the dirt. If you held them by their arms too long, a lobster would drop its arms right off its body so that it could increase its chances of getting free. He'd turn each one over and say, "Dirty arse. Dirty arse. Dirty whore. Too small. Too small. Canner. Canner. Market." If they had spawn, over they went. Gerry and Herring made sure to turn and drop the spawners so that they hit shell first so as to not disrupt the eggs, but Stretch paid no mind to this kind of thing, no matter how many times you told him otherwise. The markets went into a wooden box with some lengths of six-inch PVC pipe in them. There was a bucket of rubber bands in this box, too. The canners to be measured went into another tray lined with SM insulation. Herring wanted them to rest on something comfortable, hated the crunch of them fighting one another, tearing their arms off.

Stretch just pitched them in like they were fastballs. Herring said, "Bobby, never throw a lobster. Always set them. They're no good to me without their arms."

Gerry would run the trap down the washboard, clean the remaining dirt, and bait them. Stretch would then turn and set himself at the tanks, measuring the canners and banding the markets, a cigarette in his mouth. Herring said, "Now, 'member, any close ones, you leave to me. I'm not overly interested in losing my license 'cos yer not certain." Stretch would nod his head, his eyes with that unsettling, faraway look to them.

Herring swore to God that Stretch took the same number of steps in the boat every day. He had an amount, and neither would he go over this, nor would he go under. Herring wanted to know what the bloody number was. Whatever it was, it held the key to the whole material world, he was certain of this.

When he got a rhythm going, Gerry was faster than hell. Like he was trying to out-hustle the Devil. Fishing was a different kind of work. You were there, right there, beside one another, shuffling over the deck, bending your knees with the roll of the waves. You could smell each other's breath, the salt on your sleeves, the fish guts on your chins, and the sleep in your eyes. The blood from the cuts and wounds on your forearms, the dull odour of cramped hands in wet gloves. There was an intimacy to this environment that could feel more delicate, more tender, than that of a marriage. You learned to hate a man for truly silly reasons, for his lack of sleep the night before, which was to say, his fondness for beer during the game that went into overtime, for the direction of his thoughts and the inclination of his speech, the zits in the bend of his jaw and the hairs in his nose, the stained teeth and the creases on his neck. And since this type of fishing was so repetitive, and since your mind thought of everything in terms of movements and how to reduce them, you learned to hate a man for his unnecessary steps, the gait of his heels, for his elbows and the way he held the tools in his hands. The murmur in his throat and the click of his neck. You praised the Lord when adjustments were made, when remedies were considered. When a manoeuvre in the system was eliminated, you wanted to hug the fellow. This was truly a kind of domestic life, out here, on the waters.

The boat rocked tediously this way and that, gentle in its obliging, but still somewhat bothersome. As he beetled about in the scrimmage of turning from trap to trays, Gerry said, "Boy, you sure work every muscle out here. As soon as yer knees go bent, they're straight again."

"Yeah, even yer asshole gets a workout," said Stretch.

On the rougher days, Herring would say, "It could always be worse. You could be out here without a boat."

There was a lumpfish in the third trap and Gerry leaned back over the rail and stuck it to the side of the hull, its lips like motionless slugs and its underside the colour of a dog's tongue. Herring saw him do this and gave him the thumbs-up, hauled up another trap, and then another. The washboard was nearly full. There wasn't too much dirt in the first dump. Some sea urchins and rock eels, too. Crabs scuttling here and there. They were trickier to get out, and if they clamped onto you, they'd draw blood, no problem. The only way to get them off was to smash them against any surface you desired, so long as this surface did not give. Crab made good bait, as well, but they had to be dead. So, you'd cup one in the palm of your hand and smash its head a few times against the corner post of the trap you were baiting, and then you'd hammer its shell down over the spike, its legs kicking gently, treading the air.

A couple of puffing johnnies here and there. Herring said, "Watch out, Johnnie Blowfish."

Gerry saved the johnnies, put the knife to them, and stuck them on the bait toggle in the kitchen. They fished well, but Herring didn't like killing them.

Gerry said, "I had a friend who drank himself to death. We called him Johnnie Beerbottle."

If the bait was good, they kept it, but mostly for the first six weeks, the gaspereau, being a softer fish, would be ravaged, just picked to the bone by the lobster.

The redfish were a good bait. They were hard to chew on, hard to pull apart, and this seemed to keep the lobster coming, luring more and more into the traps. And their spikes kept the seals at bay. Herring hated using mackerel because the seals absolutely loved it. There was one of them that followed him around the whole time he was out in Pigeon. The thing just gorged itself on mackerel. And when you got into the Bluffs, there was what seemed to be a whole family of them, just waiting for their free meal. Stretch asked him about this and Herring said, "Seals'll open yer traps and just take yer bait. I'm not kidding. They're smarter than a dog and cute as all get-out."

"I put some plugs in a seal when I was young and the poor thing bled and howled for two hours," said Gerry.

Stretch said, "You try skinning a dead seal. It can't be done. But a live seal'll just roll out of its pelt." He hocked some phlegm over the side of the boat. "I was on a plane with a lady from Ontario who was out with Paul McCartney protesting the seal hunt there, a few years back, and I was thinking to myself, that's all good and well, but my grandfather used to feed us on seal meat over the winters. We were too poor to eat anything else."

The tide had pulled them in quite a distance, so Herring sailed back to where the dump had been set, straightened the boat out, and revved the throttle three times. Gerry threw his buoy and pushed his first trap, his eyes downward, watching the rope whip past, over the stern, and when the line to the snood came alive, he pushed again, sending the whole string back down to the bottom. Two or three miles away, a boat began to grow larger. The Higginbothams had a few strings out here, too. Herring said that, back in the day, some fellas would just poke holes in tuna cans and use this for bait. "I guess they thought they were being spartan and clever," he said, then sailed for the next buoy.

Gerry opened his lunch pail, compelled one of Sheila's tuna sandwiches into his mouth, had a swig of coffee and a crumbling oatmeal cookie. He could feel the sun on his neck. Burning. He'd be browner than shit, the end of a good week of sun. Herring didn't tan. He just got a darker shade of red. Gerry fetched another gauge and gave Stretch a hand measuring and banding. He checked each lobster again for spawn, turning them, inspecting the flappy bits beneath the tail, and then put the gauge to them, from the eye socket to the carapace, the back of the shell there. If they were too tiny, over the side they went. Stretch would measure one, and if it was tiny he'd throw it over his shoulder, and more often than not, the poor creature would slam into the wall of the cabin just under the awning. Between dumps he spent a fair chunk of time picking these battered fellows up and dropping them overboard. Herring would call out, asking for the numbers. Stretch, without fail, would always say, "Seven canners. Seven markets." This was his mantra, and it was inexorable.

Back in the '90s, before the stocks fell to critical levels, Herring's father had a licence for herring. He'd lobster in the mornings, then go out in the evenings for Pictou Island with all the other fellows. It was a city of lights out there on the waters. Talk about chaos. Fifty boats all cramped into the space of a bowling alley. And beneath this clutter, as though in a distorted mirror, the tuna and whales jockeyed for their plots, feasting on the herring that they could catch. Some guys over north had a spring run of herring. They'd go and put their bait nets out in the early, early morning, haul these nets, shake out the herring, and then they'd have their own fresh bait for the day. He remembered his father talking to Billy Miller, from the River, saying that herring doesn't work good on the Fishermen's Bank because it used to be a big herring spawning ground. "The lobster, it's like they're almost sick of it," he said. "They want something new, you know what I mean? Something a little different."

Herring said, "You boys see the next buoy?" Stretch and Gerry scanned the waters. Herring lessened the throttle and looked at the coordinates on his sheet of plywood. "When I was working for my bona fides, I fished with Kent Bell, and if you pointed out a buoy to him, he'd lose his mind."

They hauled the next dump. Stretch sang a little ditty. He said, "Oh, she burped and she farted and she shit on the floor, and the gas from her ass blew the knob off the door."

Gerry said, "Eight and eight is sixteen, rub yer nose in kerosene and wipe it off with ice cream." He had a pull of beer. "We used to sing that when we were littler." And again, Stretch had seven canners and seven markets.

Herring said, "Let's get outta here. The Higginbothams are watching us."

They sailed to Crow Bank and hauled.

Stretch asked Herring about fishing up west. Herring said the tides were bigger, but that's about it. The fishing is pretty much the same.

Gerry's wrists, from handling the gaspereau, were covered in scales. In late June, with the heat, it was as if these scales were trying to fuse or graft so as to heal some trauma. You could feel them on you, burning off their former energies. There was just something about this sight that always struck him as miraculous. He would say the word, miracle, over and over in his head whenever he looked down in observance of this insignificant coupling. Man and beast, of different planes, united. Nothing short of a miracle. His eyes would well with tears, and he wondered if he was going crazy. He thought of his mother and his father. He thought of his spirit, if that's what you wanted to call it, though even he wasn't sure that it was truly a thing, and how it had come from them, and how, despite everything that had happened to him, it didn't seem to want to give up on him, just yet.

Off in the distance, another boat appeared.

Herring said, "Young McCarthy is the best fisherman out here. When the lobster are down, everybody, even the old boys, watch him to see what he does, and then they follow suit." In previous years, if the weather was supposed to be rough, Herring would call McCarthy in the wee hours and say, "You weren't sleeping, were ya?" And then he'd ask him if he was going out that day, or what he was doing. McCarthy always obliged Herring, which was saying something, because he had no truck obliging most anybody else. One time,

Herring had called to interrogate him. It was about quarter-three in the morning. Gerry was sat at the kitchen table, drinking coffee, Euna and the girls up in their beds, the rain in just a terrible mood, smattering in every drift and carriage under creation. Herring hung up and looked to Gerry. "Can't trust a word that man says. Oh fuck, I despise rain." He had poured himself another cup of joe and looked out the windows. He adjusted his denims a tad, pulling them up. "Godforsaken bare-arsed sou'westers."

Stretch asked a bunch of questions, afraid of the silence. He asked if the lobster seem to prefer colder waters, and why did he use certain bait here and not there. Herring told him about his theory that the lobster prefer colder waters, that this colder water keeps them from moving, that it sort of blankets them and keeps them dormant. In shoaler and warmer waters, the lobster were more aggressive and irritable. If you were going to get bit and chomped by them, it was most likely to be out at the Bluffs in June. Herring said that, generally, the best fishing was in slack water, when the tide had come out all the way and was deciding when to come back in. The lobster were more curious and able to do as they pleased without the current as an influence. Everything just kind of dangling there in a kind of universal suspension, all the things from the surface to the bottom.

Herring said, "The mud on the bottom near Wood Islands, ya put a trap there, it'll catch lobster. You do that near the crick, nothing." And then he said, "The mud there has been that mud since there were dinosaurs." He talked about sand fleas, how to squeeze your bait bags, and how to cut your white-backs and black-backs.

They watched some blackfish playing in the waters, their forms precise and rigid, plunging and reappearing as if they were water mills of a sort.

Herring said, "We used to call sea urchins 'whore's eggs.' We put them in all the gardens in the Harbour and Boatswain Point and the River, till the fishermen figured they'd fished 'em all. The ladies just loved us for it. They'd bring you iced tea to thank you and you'd get a good look at their legs. God, women have fine getaway sticks. Back in those days, everybody took the time to help each other out, you know."

Stretch had his sevens and sevens.

The ropes that came out of the waters were already thick with bloodsuckers, and the odd trap would have a mound of jellyfish served on it, its saucer wobbling, aloof and institutional. When the ropes were put in the hauler and the clutch got going, there would be this red spray everywhere, on your face and your arms and all over the deck, like an operating tent in some theatre of war. The bloodsuckers burned something awful, like they were acid. The hauler itself appearing as if it were a bronze shield covered in veins and arteries liberated from the bodies of enemies. And Herring standing right next to this, his face just splayed currant like some demented butcher, blinking so as to keep them out of his eyes. His mouth as tense as a mutinous desire. "Just hateful," he said. "Just hateful."

Stretch said, "The last girl I went with was legally blind. She was albino and only had twenty per cent vision."

Herring said, "Yup, that sounds like something you'd pull in."

Some of the lids had been damaged on the bottom. Herring walked into the cabin and brought out his ring pliers and his peanut butter jar of ties and hog-tied them back together, bent them as well as he could, the cuffs of his oil pants dragging on the deck, ragged and torn.

They got their first window lobster and Herring was overjoyed. He went for the gauge and measured her carapace himself, and, once assured that this was a proper window, he held her by the claws and kissed her on the head. They passed her around, admiring how light she was for such a large creature, and then Herring took her back. He said, "Go and get pregnant, you lovely thing, you." And he dropped her over the side, the three of them watching her descend into the murk and darkness.

Stretch got bit by a few lobsters during the course of the day. Hell, they all did. The worst one, by far, was a crusher right on the end of his thumb, just bearing down on his nail. He held the thing in front of him, this heavy market dangling there, pulsing on his thumb, his eyes shedding tears, his face just a twist of red. Stretch said, "Oh, fences." Herring and Gerry watched him, wondering why he didn't just smash the cursed thing and be rid of the entire spectacle, the pain. Herring didn't tell him that if you grabbed its pincher claw, toyed with this one, they'd usually let go of the other. When the thing finally let go and he'd put the lobster in the PVC to be banded, Stretch walked to the back of the boat and set himself by the buoy and the coil of rope. He pulled his hood up and over his head and lit a cigarette and stared out at the horizon. There was blood coming out from under the nail of his thumb, which was as purple and alien as an embryo. Gerry came over to take stock of the damage and said, "You need some maiden oil on that." He winked and slapped Stretch on the back.

Stretch had the Jabsco going, hosing down the bait bags. Herring told him to make sure they were good and clean. He couldn't abide maggots. "Soon as I see 'em, I throw right up." During herring season, if you didn't wash the trays out properly on the Thursday, there'd be a line of maggots on the ceiling of the cabin come Sunday, trying to make their way to the stove where it's warmer. Some captains fished herring in their slippers, they kept the place that clean. You had to keep the cabin free of scales. If you got scales on you, you gotta get back out on the deck and take yer oils off, pronto. He remembered his father telling him about herring fishing with the Gaels. They wore cotton gloves that would just fill up with maggots and when they took their meals they'd all sit on the deck of the boat and glug their penny wheeps and eat cheese sandwiches. This gathering of red and black tresses discussing and interpreting the aikers and the keethins, the signs they saw out on the waters. These betrayals. And they never took their gloves off. When it was near dawn, they'd all yell dhachaidh at the captain and he'd have to turn the boat for harbour right then and there or he'd have a real problem on his hands.

Gerry had a mackerel in his hands. Herring said, "I'll give you twenty bucks to eat him." Gerry twisted it into halves with his fists and then bit the head off.

Herring said, "You won't be kissing any women with that gob tonight."

Gerry lobbed the tail up into the air. A gannet snatched it, scarfed it down, and headed for the nearest buoy.

When they were hauling the last dump out near the Bluffs, at Giant's Thumb, the trays brimming with lobster, some of them not so confused or submissive, biting at one another, this undulating russet mass, heaving like a trapped wave, it was Gerry who saw that they were bringing in another back line, that they were underneath Jack MacLeod's string. Herring stepped back to where Gerry was and leaned over, his nose a few inches from the water, with his sleeves rolled up and his hands buried in the waters. Herring enacted a quick scan at their surroundings. He saw MacLeod's pink and brown buoys. This wasn't a slip up or a pulling of the tide. The man was well onto Herring's plot.

Herring said, "That miserable cocksucker."

"Should I cut it?" said Gerry.

Herring said, "No, no, no. We're not getting into that kinda business just yet." The both of them removed their gloves, and Stretch went down to use the shitter.

Herring said, "Bobby, no paper towels, eh. I just fixed 'er."

Herring got down with Gerry, their guts hooked around the washboard like repentants, and Gerry passed him MacLeod's rope. Gerry then passed him a bit of their back line, which Herring took in his left hand. Gerry, also clutching their line with his left, cut it with his right hand, passed it over the other line, and then threw a quick reef knot into it. As he worked, he said, "Right over left. Left over right." He cinched her real good.

Herring said, "I'm gonna start callin' him Cock MacLeod, 'cos every time I look down, he's there, just like my cock."

Static came over the radio. A swarm of bees. And then other voices came over the radio, captains announcing that they were heading back to the harbour. "It's been a large day, for certain," said Willy Lyon MacKenzie.

Herring looked at Gerry. The water lapping at the hull. Gerry said, "Something needs to be done."

Herring nodded. The man was right. He said, "It's a queer thing, ain't it." He pulled a bit of his sweater out from the neck of his jacket and wiped his nose with this. "Let's have a beer, boys. I'm as dry as a wooden idol."

As they sailed in for the wharf, Gerry stood at the back of the boat emptying the trays of rotten bait into the waters. The gulls, this fellowship of starved curlicues, dropping into the waters at a remarkable frequency, their wings out, scraping the winds, an elegant coordination of violence.

—

"Ya want some gaspro?"

Rotten Rick worked for the Arsenault Brothers from up west. He had a spot down at the wharf with a crane and a forklift, a scale, and a reefer truck. There were Arsenault brothers in virtually every avenue of the Island economy, from plumbing to wedding DJs to drywall to catering to life coaches. Stretch and Gerry tied the boat to the wharf and Herring hopped up to look at what he had to offer. He could see Kemp Reilly's truck, the Higher Tides decal and the phone number on the box, over on the west side of the bullpen, the rickety platform made out of two-by-sixes and held together by poorly driven nails and stripped screws. That meant that they could see him, too. It was a free country and he wasn't legally bound to sell only to Kemp, but still, he felt poorly about testing the marketplace in such a brazen, impudent fashion. He didn't like spreading himself too thinly, either. There weren't any secrets down here. Every crew knew the score and only pretended not to know to mostly make things a little easier on themselves. Rick's man, a squat, dense fellow with a balding head and a look to him that suggested he had grown up east of the Ural Mountains, opened up the back of the truck, and Herring poked his head in.

He said, "I've seen fresher bait at Angie's." Rick came shuffling down to the back of the truck. Herring looked at Rick's neck tattoo, the lines of it as green as an American dollar, either a figurehead or an angel, with ridiculously large breasts and feathery wings, and below this, the stiffness of his leather jacket, his wilted jeans, and his brightly coloured sneakers. "Rick, what do you know about bait?"

Rick said, "I know you put it in a tray with some ice." His voice cylindrical and of a singular quality, like a dead man's last breath hurled through a clarinet.

Herring laughed and fetched a gaspereau. He pulled the gill covers out with his thumbs and gave the filaments a sniff. "See, it should be red in there, and it's not."

"I can give ya a nickel more per pound for markets, and ya don't have to band 'em."

Herring said, "God, you must be doing well this year. Let me think about it. What's the story with her?"

Rick said, "Huh?"

Herring pointed at his neck.

Rick said, "Angela, my wife. She took cancer over the winter and was gone in just about six weeks."

"Jesus Christ," said Herring, his hands on his hips. He shifted his weight and felt the box wobble on her axles.

"Yup," said Rick, "the last thing that went was her taste. The final couple of days I just rubbed her lips with ice cubes, there, to keep 'em from drying out."

Rick and Herring finished their business, and as the *M&M* rumbled over to the other side of the wharf, Herring said, "He's some terrible nice guy." Stretch had a swig of beer and said that tonight he was splitting a hive.

Kemp wasn't down at the wharf, but he had a young fellow doing ice and bait, and a woman of about thirty named Evelyn, who had fished a season with Jack MacLeod. Herring looked at her. She had dark hair and a ball cap on, and she was quite beautiful. Her arms and legs were strong. They had to be because of all the shit she'd had to wade through, he reckoned. She looked to be in something of a mood today, the cigarette in her mouth on a steady pulse. The fronts of her rubbers slapping her shins as she walked from the cab of the truck to the crane. She had three kids by three different men.

Stretch and Gerry got the trays ready and did their best not to gawk at her. Markets first, then canners. Gerry thought that it must be tough being her, sometimes, to have all these boneheads staring at you, thinking that maybe they would be the one to win her heart once and for all, to remind a large population of men, by virtue of her mere presence down at this wharf, that maybe they had been younger and more passionate and better looking, less ravaged by time. But there was something about the look of her that made you feel alive, too, and you'd be a fool to ignore this notion. Men were awful simple things. He wondered how much she was able to laugh.

Stretch saw her sometimes at the grocery store in Irish Montague. She drove this little red Pontiac Vibe, and whenever he saw her in it, he would say, "She likes her vibrator, I reckon."

Gerry said, "I'd love to take her to pound town."

Herring asked Evelyn where Kemp was.

Evelyn said, "Oh, Kemp's making the rounds. We're up at the Crick and Launching and Naufrage this year."

"Well, it's nice to see that the big fellas haven't run you off just yet."

He got his trays of ice and bait, and then Evelyn handed him his slip. He looked at the trailers lined up in the grasses alongside Wharf Lane and said, "Hard to believe there's half a million worth of lobster in each of those."

—

Herring filled himself a glass of water from the tap and turned around, sharply and swiftly, as if he were about to announce something dramatic to a room filled with people, leaning the small of his back into the edge of the counter. But there was no one there. Just him and his thoughts, as strange and recklessly timid as they were, as he knew them to be. The wind had picked up, and he could hear its current running against the cedar shingles, making it seem as if the house he stood within was an insubstantial tool, a comb to arrange the interminable hairs of some beautiful and mythical creature in repose.

He went to the phone and removed the receiver from its cradle, and as he did so, he felt a kind of surge, as organic as it was inorganic, the orchestrated swell and escalation of all of the articles in his body, the rush of his plasma in him, like a storm shaking the contents of a harbour, the same flowing that had always told him his body knew something his head did not. In the moment, he scrambled with dimness to realize, to understand, that he had already, perhaps even long ago, committed to doing something that, quite simply, could not be undone. A newborn mountain goat trying to scale a meagre height in the path of some unknown avalanche. Panic. Herring punched the numbers in.

"Hello." The voice was leaden, dwindled with irritation, expectant.

"Hello, Jack," said Herring, his thoughts racing, his voice dry.

"Herring."

"What are you up to?"

"Oh, ya know me. Smokin' darts and breakin' lobster hearts."

"Listen, Jack, I'd like to come out sometime to see you about some things."

"Like what?"

"Are you free tonight?"

"Nope."

Herring thought he could hear the footsteps of someone quite near to Jack. Murmured and indistinct sounds, the odd, trebled whistle of inhalation through a pair of hefty nostrils, the way these things arrived within Herring's ear gave him the sense that the room at the other end of the line was full of other people. Perhaps he had called in the midst of a birthday celebration or just a good old-fashioned kitchen party.

"Tomorrow?"

He heard some fingers rasp through a bit of neck beard. He heard nail meet skin.

"After church. I'll be around, I spose."

"I'll see you then," Herring said, then crisply hung up. He raised his hands to his face, his fingers fanned out before him with drama and revelation, and while he marvelled at the droplets of sweat balanced upon their ridges, the sparkle of them, each crease alight, he trembled at how very alien his own flesh and desires could be.

The chains clinked and jangled his descent into the basement. He loaded the stove with more wood, then pulled himself back up to the first floor, this modest, humourless ceremony of his. He sat a case of beer and a bottle of whiskey on the kitchen table, a lifeless and rather barren guest opposite him, and he remained still for a long time, feeling his armpits sweat and his feet sweat with the rising temperature in the house. Through the windows the world was a sheet of darkness, hung as if a part of the Almighty's washing.

Herring drank only water that night, as a kind of test of his resolve. Four glasses, in something of a rapid succession. He wanted to see what it would feel like to stop drinking. He walked himself to the chesterfield after midnight, the swig of his guts loud, a frenzied and hydrous affair. He could see the case and the bottle on the table, mute and stupid, but all the while calling out to him, taunting him, like bullies on the playground. These voices in his head that had been there since the beginning. Since he had come into this strange world. And though he wished mercifully for a great bout of sleep, hardly any of it was visited upon him.

—

Jack MacLeod lived out at the cape, just five minutes down the road from the Jacksons. He'd fished out of Boatswain Point for most of his life, but after some undefined bit of trouble, the fellows down there had asked him to see about fishing from the Harbour. The boys who fished out of the Point liked to refer to themselves as caped crusaders. If you were out of My Bonnie, you were a harbour hero. Rightfully, Jack MacLeod could call himself neither.

The brilliance of the sun threatened to quickly abolish the mere bit of snow that had fallen during the night. With the window down, the air was calm and gentle, and it spoke to Herring of the warmer weather to come, the changing of the seasons, the flowers and crops that would grow, the birds that would sing, the mosquitoes that would swarm. The road before him was dark and slick, as stiff as a truncheon.

The Church of Christ lot was full when Herring drove by. Gulls lined up on the ridgeline. The roof spilled with white, as if a cloud had been folded over it. He spotted MacLeod's rig, a Chevrolet the colour of a tortilla, and contemplated going in, being cheeky, poking the bear a tad, but he thought that to do so would be foolish, too disruptive. Though he assumed, quite rightly, that he had been seen by a number of the parishioners through the windows. Reverend Colbert wasn't the most captivating of speakers. His presence and his notions about the metaphysical had about as much authority as a pair of stockings drying out on the line. During sermons, most of the congregation sat and watched the road into the Point for their entertainment, and each time a vehicle passed, usually only once or twice per service, a considerable fuss was made in each member's mind as to the nature of the travellers' business. And, as was the way of things, and given the nature of Jack MacLeod's tongue, word was getting around, passed from pew to pew, with all the mayhem and clatter of telepathists. Herrings had no call out this way, unless it was the assemblage of nuisance. Besides, if he did make an appearance, he knew that people would assume, not unlike the last time he had entered the church doors to denounce God, that he was on the drink again.

He tapped a bit of ash off his cigarette and realized that he didn't know what he was doing, didn't know what his angle was or ought to be, with Jack. What was his leverage?

He drove out to the lighthouse and got out of the rig and walked for half a kilometre. The rig was just about dead. Fletcher Jordan said he could get some more miles out of it for five hundred. Chessel Glover wanted five hundred for Reuben. A thousand bucks, right there. He was behind on his money for Euna and Marcelina and Marceline. He had enough, as of today, to buy a week's worth of fuel and to pay Gerry for the week. He was so nervous, he started to shake. He wobbled a bit and set his arse into the sand. Life was crushing him into smithereens, and he had too much pride and not enough friends to ask for help. He lit another smoke and tallied up how long he could last, but his mind scrambled on him and he arrived at no figure.

There were still measures of snow and ice left on the beach, like the dice of a vast series of abandoned games of chance. Years ago, this place had actually been an apple orchard, but the water and the winds had conspired to pull the earth away, back to the depths, those neglected spaces where humans could not see. Where all was the cold and dark gunge of restoration.

He looked out at the waters, their curls. How indifferent they seemed to him. It felt as if he'd spent his whole life bobbing up and down on currents of indifference. What if he robbed a bank? What if he checked himself into a mental hospital? What if he blew his brains out? The way he saw it, lobster fishing was, and had always been, a bit of a crapshoot. He stood up and brushed the seat of his denims off. You had to take your bad years with your good years. What else could one do? God wasn't going to come down from Heaven and bail him out of all of this.

—

Jack spent his horizontal hours in a split-level house at the end of MacLeod Lane. The bottom half was red brick and the top was white vinyl siding, heavily worn by the winds. The front door was yellow. His garage door was aquamarine, and on the front of the house was a new deck that had yet to be stained. From the road, you could tell that the deck was poorly constructed, which is to say, you could tell that the deck was built by fishermen. In the back corner of the lot, down a gradual slope, a group of snowmobiles and four-wheelers sat, exposed and disregarded. A bulky dog lay in the sun, chained to a tree stump, near an old Pontiac sedan up on blocks. Two wooden punts were up on bucks, waiting for a fresh coat. An old washing machine scowled next to a tin watering can. Back where the grasses grew taller and the birches canted was a pile of tuna heads, starched and brown, as if they had been mummified. The chimney was puffing with some energy, and Herring noticed the curtains of the front window quiver as he pulled in the drive. The engine of Jack's truck was still humming and dripping, and there were about fifty empty bottles of Cheez Whiz in the bed of the rig. The MacLeods were about as religious as the dog was free to roam. Herring couldn't remember exactly when, but some years ago, on the day after a season had ended, while most of the fellows were venturing out on their two-week drunk, smashing bottles of Russian Prince and firing golf balls out into the channel from behind the bait sheds, Jack had taken some lobsters and put them in a lock-tight tray and tied this to the rope going from the curb of the wharf to the hauler post of the *M&M*. He left them there, floating, and then he called the DFO. Herring didn't know what to tell the officer who was writing him the ticket. All he could think to say was, "Well, they're not mine." The officer had replied, "Well, they're tied to your boat." And Herring had said "Yup, but anybody could have done that, eh. I mean, this isn't exactly the Lindbergh baby here, c'mon. Ya gonna run any forensics back to the lab? Check for fingerprints or hair?" The officer's neck had flushed red. Herring hadn't done himself any favours.

Jack was bent over, taking off his boots, when the door opened and cranked him in the ass. He swore, said, "Jesus, what's the matter? You can't knock?"

"I knew you were home, Jack, and you knew I was here," said Herring. "Just so you know, Cheez Whiz is one chemical away from plastic."

He insisted that Deborah sit at the table with them. This was a fishing matter, and, seeing as he fished with his wife, this involved her, too.

Jack was a tiny little fellow that put many a person in mind of a dwarf from some commonplace fantasy series. He was about the same age as Herring, though both the plenitude of wrinkles on his face and the trampled, smoggy quality of his voice suggested that he was on the verge of receiving his pension. He looked and sounded like an old Victorian farmhouse being razed to the ground. Years ago, when they were building the Link, he had taken a holiday to the Dominican Republic with some buddies and proceeded to get wrecked on cocaine. Deborah hadn't been invited. Somehow, he got his hands on a four-wheeler and ran over a villager's chickens. He spent a few nights in jail.

"With them blackies," he said, "you know the ones I'm talkin' about. Right from the fuckin' jungle." Proclaimed it something of a minor miracle that he'd lived through this ordeal. When he wasn't talking or eating, he was always humming some strange tune, some song with the words "shakin' all over," but not the song by the Guess Who, and he walked around as if he had a frozen turd down the leg of his pants.

"So, what seems to be the trouble, Herring?" said Jack, trying to sound like a Mafia don, picking away at a jar of olives, tucking each one into the embrace of his tongue as he waited for a response. Deborah was stirring a cup of tea and seemed content to do so until the rapture.

"Well, Jack, this is the third year in a row that you've set yer gear on my grounds. And not by a little bit or even accidentally," Herring said. "And, if I can read a calendar correctly, it's not later in the season, either, when everyone's cramming their gear for lobsters."

Jack looked at Deborah and she looked back at him. In the background, their kids slinked from one room to another.

"Huh," said Jack.

"What's right is right, Jack," said Herring. "What's right was right before we were here and what's right will be right when we're gone. Right is right."

Deborah scoffed and Herring could feel the anger shoot its way up through him. He put his hands in his lap. Jack noticed Herring's neck ripple and blush.

"Listen here, let's call a spade a spade and a Chevy a Chevy, okay?" said Jack, extending his arms over the table with what he considered to be diplomacy. "Nobody likes you, Herring. Yer a halfwit. Go and complain all ya want. Tattle, if ya want. 'Cos I've got news for you, ol' friend, no one's going to listen to you."

"Reality check," said Deborah, as if she'd just won a game of cards named so. "We're lookin' out fer ya."

"Yer word's no good any more out here," said Jack.

"With all due respect, Deborah," said Herring, "you couldn't exactly roll a tire down a hill."

Deborah wrinkled her brow and creaked back in the chair.

None of them were thinking of it, but in this place, they were less than fifty days away from the longest day of the year, from midsummer.

"What's wrong, Debbie? Don't like getting yer nails dirty? Everyone knows yer whole miserable family fishes from the radio. That's gonna come to an end soon enough."

"Anyways, that's enough of that," said Jack. "And if ya cut my lines I'll cut yer throat."

"I wouldn't piss on either of you hobbits if you were on fire," said Herring. He stood up and walked for the door.

"Well, it's like my mother always said. Go fuck yerself," said Jack.

—

Christ, that went over like a lead balloon, thought Herring, hovering over the propane stove as it hawked and spluttered fat and butter out at him. He preferred to barbecue his steaks outside on the grill, but he'd run out of propane in his twenty-pound tanks, so he was cooking his steak in a skillet, which for him felt like a sin. He also didn't know how much propane was left in the five-hundred-gallon tank, and it had been sometime since the fuel company had topped him up. His account hadn't been in good standing for what felt like years, and every time he saw the truck drive by he'd wave and the fellow behind the wheel wouldn't even nod at him.

Herring was alone and he could feel the cold air coming through the hole in the house where the line ran from the tank to the stove. He'd never gotten around to patching the darn thing. It would only take a warmer day with no breeze and a few spurts of spray foam expansion. Hell, some of the houses in the Harbour and the River were practically built entirely of spray foam. Euna complained and complained so much that she couldn't cook in her socks she took to preparing meals in her winter boots. He shook some salt and pepper out of their shakers and looked at the sheet of plywood and Tuck Tape where the sliding doors used to be, noticed some blood that he hadn't before, low on a cupboard door. There was a knock and some muffled talking. He turned the flame down and put a pot lid over the skillet.

Gerry and Red John were at the door and he let them in. Red John said there had been the thinnest layer of ice on the river this morning. Red John had a cousin down in Rhode Island who had sent him up a thousand hits of acid. One time he went into town and sold some of it at Colonel Gray, out by the soccer pitch, for twenty bucks a pop. He bought himself a stereo with the proceeds. Came back the next day and made enough to buy himself a set of really good speakers. Red John's best friend owned the bike shop in town there, and they'd get all fucked up on whatever and ride penny farthings as far as they could get. "It was quite a sight, huh." Rather miraculously, Red John was able to manage a unicycle, his body just fierce with convulsions, as if in need of an exorcism. "It had a little shock absorber on the post there so yer bones wouldn't shake too much," he said.

Red John and Gerry were already pretty wrecked on mushrooms they'd got from the Brudenell golf course back in the fall. Red John had dried the stems and made some kind of a tea from this, which was barely palatable. Gerry had gone hunting for mushrooms down in the cow pastures at Orwell Corner. He said, "Ya gotta watch it because the little white fellas are totally lethal. I think they call 'em destroying angels. Something like that, anyways." Red John got onto the topic of oysters, insisting that the best oysters on the island were in the Brudenell River.

"Just git a bag down with ya at low tide and be careful to not take too, too many," he said. "Oysters taste like their rivers and the Brudenell is the best-tasting river." And then he said, "Off island, every oyster is from goddamn Malpeque, which isn't true. I don't git it. I mean, I git it, but I also don't really git it."

Gerry said, "Do you think there's more doors or more wheels in the world?"

Red John looked into the nothingness before him as if the results of a paternity test had just been announced over a loudspeaker.

Herring needed to catch up, so he proposed that he snort some of the purple microdot. Red John gleefully chopped it up for him at the kitchen table, and then Herring sucked it up his nose. Red John said he'd never seen anybody do this before. The novelty made his eyes sparkle. The high hit Herring almost instantaneously and he ran outside, leaned over by the foundation, and vomited profusely into the grasses.

He walked back to the door, but then suddenly he felt himself lifted, caught from above, and conveyed to town, to the parkade on Queen as if he were an article of clothing at the cleaners. He was being chased up the levels. He was running and crinkling, wrapped in a plastic sheath, pumping his arms as fast as he could, but his rate of propulsion wasn't exactly impressive. He was moving at an unremarkable pace, and he wondered why he was running at all. His head was sweaty and his heart was slithering in him like an eel in a barrel. He wasn't dreaming and he didn't know where Euna's bar of soap had gone. He wasn't sure where he actually was. The asphalt was turning into a kind of taffy-like substance, boiled and stretched beneath him, and behind there were a number of shadowy figures. They were out for blood. His blood. All of this felt real to him. He had to keep going. As he ascended to each new level, he would cast a glance behind him to verify if the figures were still following. With every peek, there they were. He got to the highest level, wholly exposed to the elements, the sun up in the sky with an eyelid drawn over it, and he quickly realized that in order to escape he was going to have to jump from the line of Jersey barriers across to the roof of the Tim Hortons on Kent. He went to the edge and sized up the distance. The difference in height was severe. If he managed to jump out far enough, he didn't know whether he'd survive the descent. The figures were there, they'd caught him, were closing in. This was it. He paced out what felt like a suitable runway and hit the thrusters. And as he propelled himself off the edge of the parkade, he knew, with a great smack of clarity, that he had fallen short of his goal. He was plunging. And then he was driving on a back road and the sun was setting and Gerry was there, smoking and wiping his sweaty face, and Red John was in the back, cracking his knuckles and eating cereal out of a box.

They drove to the drive-in at Brackley to watch the *Iron Man*

the night drinking and smoking hash, listening to classic rock on the station from Pictou. When "Bad Bad Boy" by Haywire came on, Herring said, "The greatest band from the greatest place on earth."

Gerry was so obliterated he felt as if he'd travelled into another world altogether, pushed by some force through a preposterous kind of ring or hoop that had just materialized out of the air. Shoved out like the turd in his drawers, though each time he felt certain it was there and pulled his pants away from his belly, it wasn't. Gerry McClellan and the Adventure of the Phantom Turd, he thought. Mostly he fought tooth and nail to keep his eyes open. His eyelids felt like dumbbells. He was getting a real workout in. A memory floated out of the dimness and landed before him with such ease and clarity, it was as if it wasn't a memory at all, but what he was enacting in the present, and so he went with this for as long as it wanted to last. In high school, the two of them had done a boatload of ecstasy and then stolen, or if you like, borrowed, some four-wheelers that had been parked outside of Keeping's, for a bit of a joyride. They weren't out for too long before the cops were chasing them. Herring cut off the main road, through some bush, and before either knew it, they were riding through a great bank of potato fields, on the way out to the cove. There was a wire fence running across a culvert that led to the shore road and Herring hit it first. It just about took his head clean off. The four-wheeler shot out from under him and made the road, where the handlebars got all twisted on it and it drove down the road for a while before it moved rather softly, like a child set before a playground, into the opposing ditch, driving through the field of soy before its wheels got tangled. Gerry slowed right down and ran over to Herring. He was bleeding pretty bad, lost just a desperate pile of blood. Gerry didn't know if something was broken or if he was dying. Sometimes the smallest of injuries can bleed the most. When the cops arrived, they said that this was lesson enough for the both of them. Gerry swore off engines for a while, not getting his driver's licence until he was twenty-one, a lateness that was virtually unheard of on the island, a juvenile fright that burdened a great many of his friends and relatives. But once he'd finally gotten his licence, he proceeded to lose it but three weeks later, driving stone drunk. In truth, he'd never had a legitimate licence for more than thirty-six months. He'd just gone right off the Georgetown road and driven about the length of two football fields into the woods. The officers had a hundred-foot tape and they paced it all out. At his sentencing, the judge told him he'd gone 309 feet. "It's nothing short of a miracle that you're even here, fit to stand before me," she'd said down to him.

The whipping of the tarp against the hull woke Gerry up. He had been dreaming of his brothers and sisters, and in the dream they had felt so real and so close that when he awoke he was already weeping because they could not be touched. He crawled past Herring out the door. He wrestled the tarp down and rolled it up, drew a rope around it, and then threw a bowline around the handle of a bucket, lowering it into the thrusting waters, and brought some up with which to wash the sweat from his face. The sky was as dark as outer space, but keen to lighten, and there were a few lights on at the fish plant. He guessed that the Mexicans and Chinese knuckle-pickers would be getting off the night shift soon. He pissed off the stern, then got out of the wind, ate some chips, and sucked down some orange soda. The weather was bad and he felt worse.

Gerry untied the ropes after Herring fired up the engine. That great gurgle of combustion, the churn of water, the spurt and slice and the smoke. The fenders stained black, this smudge on green timbers that indicated the tidal range. He turned the lights on, and the mist was as fine and as pressed as a veil. His head felt like it had as much sense in it as a cinder block.

They'd left just as the other fishermen began to arrive at the wharf. Gerry said, "What about Stretch?" Herring didn't respond. Gerry wanted to remind him that today was a double haul, which meant that if it was only him picking and baiting and measuring and banding, well, he was going to be right slammed. He thought better of speaking his mind. As they passed the breakwater, the full force of the winds struck the *M&M*. The waves were cascading from east to west like mad razors. Herring said, "Goddamn bare-arsed nor'easters." Herring looked infirm and sickly behind the wheel, kept asking, "Where's the red buoy? Where's the red buoy?" and Gerry, crumpled by the washboard, glugging soda and shivering, could barely think straight. They were doing twelve knots, just hammering through the waves. Everything in the cabin was on the floor. Screwdrivers and gauges and bottles. This way and that way. Explosions and debris. Water cascading over the boat. They may as well have been sailing through the atmosphere. The tanks groaning and sliding about the deck like sinners mortifying their flesh. A gaff was caught by the wind and snorted up into the sky. Herring's knees bent as if he were a knockoff Atlas. Before him, the wipers just a tangle of stutters. Gerry didn't know how he was going to get the bait thawed out, let alone do anything else. A handful of cigarettes floated upon the water that had collected in the back of the boat, calm and indifferent. Years back, they'd had a good piss-up at the wharf, and this deckhand, young and green as all get-out, well, they found him in the morning, splayed out on the deck, covered in blood and beer and vomit. Herring had looked him over and said to Gerry, "That there's the working definition of scudgie." Gerry thought Herring looked worse now than that boy had. He looked scudgie all right. As if he were a cow about to be exploded by some hurtling train. Gerry said, "It's some feathery out there." Herring motioned for Gerry to come and take the wheel for him, and he did. "'Member, if anything happens, just head west. You'll bump into somebody eventually." Herring grabbed his stomach, said, "I've a bit of the springtime splash," and showed Gerry where to point the bow, the windshield splattered by the sea. The boat heaved upon the waves, as large and imposing as a disregarded cork. Gerry could feel the propeller yielding, the quiver of the skeg, and he clutched the wheel with everything he had.

The emergency call had come over the radio around quarter to five in the morning. Leverett and Lowell MacNeil were the first to reach the *M&M*, just a forlorn shadow of incurvation bobbing among the waves, the man on the deck a gyrating wheel of spittle and sweat. The joggle of madness and the clouds so low you could touch them. Behind them the great darkness. Linen out to dry on the line. To see Gerry so distraught had made Leverett shake. Gerry's face red, his body throbbing. A whole man reduced to a spasm of flesh, howling and blubbering, a suture come undone in a pot of boiling water. Leverett had never seen a person in such a state of agony. He thought the man must be high on drugs or something. Other boats began to arrive at the scene, casting their spotlights to the waters.

When they got back to the wharf, Leverett told Lowell to stay on the deck of their boat and to keep busy, make sure the bait and ice didn't spoil, and Leverett tried to be of service as best he could. He stopped each rig as it came down to the wharf and told every fisherman, every cork, what was what. He thought that to keep the lines of communication clear and concise was paramount. Strange tales had a habit of taking root in such situations, and when they did, people tended to set out in asinine directions, chasing their own shadows. By nine a.m., reporters from the television and newspapers had arrived.

Gerry spent a few hours under a warm blanket in the back of an ambulance down at the wharf. He pleaded with the paramedics, two classmates from Montague, to let him stay so that he could apologize to Herring when they brought him in. Gerry had required a heavy dose of sedatives to calm him, and whenever he woke up, the paramedics gave him water to drink.

By afternoon, the fishermen who had joined the search decided that, due to the storm front, they had to try attending to their traps. A few hundred pounds, at the very least, just to break even. Most of them felt terrible doing so, but what could they do? Their faces could not hide how upsetting the whole thing was. The helicopter from CFB Greenwood decided to call it, as well, and headed back to Charlottetown to refuel. The ceiling was just too low. *Cape Mercy*, the coast guard cutter out of Souris, operated by Corporal Garfield McHerron, put in a few more hours of searching, before it tied up at the wharf and took fuel from the tanks. From the start, McHerron thought the situation was hopeless, but he had kept this to himself. The volunteers from the My Bonnie River fire department, six men split between two inflatable outboards, agreed that the waves were too much for them and came in for the night. To the gulls high up, the waters hadn't been so animated in a long time. It was like olden days, when the men had surrounded a harpooned whale with their boats, eager to finish it with a final lance and a great display of blood forced from its lungs, a fountain that would coat the tired whalers and briefly warm them, energize and further obsess them.

—

For some reason or another, Euna was one of the last people to hear about what had happened. The girls had got on the bus for school at quarter past eight. She walked back down the lane and sat herself at the kitchen table. Bored, she made coffee and slathered some butter onto a slice of sourdough bread. She worried, very briefly, that she was too inactive, that her body was going to pot. She pinched her stomach, and what a handful it was. She watched the alders through the window tremble in the wind. They had a little running joke where whenever Herring saw one he'd holler, "Respect yer alders." The rain was getting to be a nasty affair. A yellow finch flitted about in her rose bushes. The starlings usually came around supper to pick through the garden.

Deeper in the forests that surrounded the property were mounds of snow, untouched by the sun, which would remain until the end of June, and which she would visit in secret and think, snow, in June! And then the phone rang.

She was too much in shock to drive. She felt that she was floating high above. She called her mother, who picked her up right away. The first person they were able to talk to was Joe. He gave Euna a hug and filled her in on what was happening as they walked up the wharf, her mother and brother on either side of her and everyone just looking at them as if they were the second coming. Joe said not to worry, that he and Isaac would haul in Herring's traps. And when they passed the ambulance with Gerry in it, she didn't even notice him. She didn't know what to do. Didn't know what she could do. She sat herself on the curb and stared out at the lights of the boats on the horizon. All was chaos and omens.

—

Minnie Carver, a reporter with the CBC program *Compass*, and her cameraman, Grant Gallant, had driven through the morning rush-hour squeeze from Charlottetown, Grant smoking as he drove through the hills around Caledonia, for which he had no fondness. After the morning's tumult, as if the whole of Kings County had converged upon My Bonnie Harbour, just a mad barrage of folk walking purposelessly about, the two of them had a quick lunch at Keeping's, where Otis, recognizing Minnie from the television, came out and asked after them what was going on down at the wharf, to which she could offer no reply and said as much. It had been too miserable to film anything, and nobody wanted to talk much to the media. Eventually, she and Grant and other reporters, from the *Guardian* and the *Eastern Graphic*, met with Major Rosalie Bernard, spokesperson with Joint Rescue, around half-three. They were in the lunch room of the fish plant, sitting at a long plastic table. The major blinked quite a bit as she spoke. There was dog hair on her pants. She said that, as of three o'clock, no clothing had been located, which was atypical of such circumstances, that they did not know if he was wearing his PFD. The search area, at present, was nebulous. The water was four degrees Celsius. She said that, based on all available models, a man of Herring's build could remain functional for about ninety minutes. That he could survive for one hundred and eighty minutes, give or take. "Yes, we are well past these limits, but we will continue to hope for the best," she said, and then she thanked them for their time.

Minnie and Grant went back to the wharf found a suitable spot to set up the camera. The wind was still a bit too much, but there wasn't anywhere else to go. She rehearsed her lines and then Grant counted down, hit record. They reviewed what footage they had and sent it off to the station. Their executive producer, Mary Dixon, asked them to hang around for a live feed at six. A fisher by the name of Jack MacLeod, who had been the first to unload his lobster, offered to go to Keeping's and get them some clam chowder and biscuits. Minnie gave him a twenty-dollar bill, but Jack refused it. He drove off in a truck laden with bottles of Pepsi and never returned. The workers from the fish plant stood outside and watched. The last time there had been this much excitement was when Dunbar Gillis had killed Slippy Dick. A trio of forklifts drove the trays of lobsters from the wharf to the plant. Occasionally, they would hit a bump and spill a bit of ice. A stream of brown water trailed out of the overhead doors of the plant and worked its way into the rocks and boulders around the bullpen. The smell of this water was beyond rank. Three older fishermen stood around talking, blowing their noses into their handkerchiefs and waxing philosophic with hushed voices. Their names were Willy Lyon and Louis and Eben. Their teeth were yellow and few. Grant asked them if they would consent to going on camera. With voices so timid and accents so heavy that it took Grant a minute to precisely sort out what they had said, they declined. Minnie thought that a great many of them were drunk. Herring's mate, Gerry, wasn't available either. No one knew what he knew, what may have happened. They had rushed him into the hospital in Irish Montague about an hour ago, and apparently, the poor fellow had soiled himself in the ambulance. The harbourmaster, Joe McInnis, was also a fisherman, as well as the brother-in-law of the victim, but he declined to comment. The missing man's wife, Euna, and her mother were still out at the end of the wharf, sitting in an idling truck. Minnie didn't feel like bothering her today, or anybody, really, for a picture of her husband. Utter despondence was the best description of the wharf at My Bonnie Harbour. Gloom and doom.

—

Grant found them a room at the Bonnie Harbour Motel, on the Mill Road, just off the river, and they spent the night here. They were the only guests and the rooms were pink. They heated up some frozen pastas in the microwave and finished a bottle of port between them. Grant spoke to his girlfriend on the phone, pacing on the gravel of the parking lot. Across the road in a field were a number of wooden herring decks and scallop dredges, rusted and dripping rain. Minnie thought they were sombre things, vaguely medieval. The damage these things wreak is just irreversible. It's a miracle anything is bloody left out there.

Minnie turned off the television and listened to the sounds of the geese on the shore, honking and bleating their disgust at the varied and threatening shadows robbing them of their respite. These fishermen were awful tight-lipped, she thought. Grant snored a little while he slept.

—

Over the course of the evening, Major Bernard received phone calls from the maritime search and rescue coordinators, ensuring her that arrangements for a fixed-wing aircraft from St. John's to join the search the next morning were concrete and ratified. They estimated that they had about sixty vessels lined up to assist the next day. This number included fishermen from My Bonnie Harbour, My Bonnie River, Boatswain Point, Wood Islands, Grahams Crick, and Georgetown. Fishermen and police along the coast of Cape Breton had been contacted, as well. The forecast for Tuesday was lots of sun and little to no wind. She knew what the science had to say about all of this. In such cases, nature was often the prevailing spokesperson.

—

Marcelina and Marceline spent the night with their grandmother and their uncle. Something was up, but as to what it was, no one seemed interested in telling them. Lying in the bed they had been given, they talked for a while and arrived at a feeling that it had something to do with their father and their mother. They had a vague feeling that this was a big event. "A calamity," said Marceline, trying it on stiffly like a new pair of shoes eager to give blisters.

—

Euna drove back out to the wharf and covered herself with a sleeping bag. She sat and thought, replaying the whole of her life with the man who had disappeared. There was lots of pain and anguish within their memories, for sure, but there were joys aplenty, too. And there were the girls. Their beautiful girls. If he was alive, she resolved to forgive him everything, every trespass. The drugs and the drink. The pornography. The hole in the floor. The debts. The wrecked cars. Everything. She didn't sleep until daybreak, when the sun lulled and enchanted her. Agnes got the girls off to school and brought her daughter home. She made her tea and toast, but Euna said that she had no appetite. She went into her parents' bedroom and slept until the girls got home from school. Agnes knew heartbreak when she saw it. When she looked at her daughter she saw herself the day that her husband had died. Such a grief just comes in and pulverizes a person. There's nothing to be done about this, no remedy. Only time and a bit of grace could release the afflicted.

—

The sunrise that morning was a beautiful, amber gradient. Quite serene and comprehensive, as if the world had been rendered a fresco upon some magnificent plaster globe. Chessel Glover and Emerson White did what they could. They walked the beaches that morning with their dogs, one a terrier, the other a spaniel, their noses down, sniffing the great tapestries of Irish moss. The only thing they found was a dead seal, stripped of half of its flesh from the waist up. "I imagine Herring'll look the same right about now," said Chessel. It was a grim observation, one that gave him no pleasure at all. Emerson kept walking so as to not throw up.

—

The *Guardian* ran the story on the front page and continued it on the second page, where, down near the bottom, they had a small black-and-white photograph of Herring standing next to a halibut held by rope to a crane. Minnie wondered how they'd got it, but wasn't bitter about it. She had no notion of how old it may have been. He was a big fellow. His face was large and thick, his skin weathered, the veins in his arms thick and distended like beef hocks. His nose was well shaped while his eyes were somewhat upset, or troubled looking. On his left forearm was what appeared to be a terribly rendered tattoo. He wore a ball cap, pushed back a little. He was probably just north of two hundred pounds. Minnie sensed that he was an unremarkable man with a lot of darkness in him. She felt confident with this assessment. She knew character.

She and Grant drove down to the wharf to see what was going on, and all around was that quiet feeling, that thin film of unknowing.

—

Gerry woke up and his whole body ached like it never had before, felt like he'd been hit by a Mack truck. He sat up, because he had to piss, and realized he was tethered to an IV machine by a PICC line just below the knuckles of his left hand. He was in a hospital gown, and his clothes were in a clear plastic bag on a green chair by the wall. His rubber boots and his wallet were there, too. He ripped out the line, and his blood started spewing every which way, and when he had set his bare feet onto the smooth floor beneath the gurney, he slipped on his own blood and crashed to the floor, rattling his head off the aluminium bed rails. Two nurses with clipboards, one male, one female, pulled the hanging screen back and one of them said, "Jesus," and the other said, "Git 'em up."

—

Joe gathered all of the fishermen around the little port authority building before they headed out that morning. He introduced Corporal McHerron and Major Bernard to those assembled and said that each crew, for the foreseeable future, was to volunteer as many hours as physically and financially possible. That they were here to support the rescue efforts in any way possible. But he understood that they had their own fishing to complete. Joe asked if anyone would be willing to haul in Herring's traps today. No one raised a hand. The men were solemn, dejected. Not a one had anticipated that this was how the season would be going. At least they weren't angry yet. Joe put his hands on his hips, looked out past the men to the wharf where Herring's burgundy rig sat, as patient and loyal as a dog, and said, "All right, Ike and I'll see to them." Isaac grumbled, but got on with things, loading up the *NHL Joe* with bait. The harder he worked, the quicker the day went. As the men turned and headed to their boats, Joe said, "And, please, for Christ's sake, wear yer PFDs."

—

The helicopter came from the west, a red-and-white reptile in the sky, a toothless and wingless symbol of ingenuity and hubris, a kind of omniscient thing. Soon, the fixed-wing was up there, too. Everything was quite loud. Minnie watched a man by the name of Norman back his fifteen-foot skiff down the slip. He worked by himself to unmoor the boat. Grant walked over, set his tripod up, and she asked for an interview. Norman dragged his feet while he walked and his nose leaked at a steady rate. He had a thin moustache and a bit of a belly underneath his Metallica tee. He was wearing a coast guard jacket that was unclipped. Grant turned the camera on. Norman asked them where he ought to start. Minnie told him to explain, as best he could, what it was that he knew.

He puffed on his cigarette and looked out at the channel. He said, "That's why she's called Mother Nature, eh. A man wouldn't do that. Anyways, ya don't want to be talkin' to me. I'm a fart smeller. I'm not smart." Minnie persisted, and asked him what he knew about the missing person. Norman produced a bag of chocolates and a bottle of pop. "Herring was some character. A brother to dragons and a companion to owls, huh. One time I seen him hit a man with a Greco submarine. Anyway, karma is about the only thing I believe in. So, I'd say whatever came to him, he had it comin'." He looked at his skiff, popped a few more lumps of chocolate into his gob, and said, "It'll be a miracle if I don't get the diabetes by the time I'm done here. She's a good boat, but she kinda porpoises." He raised a hand and moved it as if it were flowing against some resistant force that wasn't there. "My grandfather built her."

—

Out at the end of the wharf, Moses was with Euna and Agnes, Marcelina and Marceline, close to Herring's rig. The girls found out what had happened at school that morning, and the both of them just kind of crumbled. The principal had called Agnes to see if she could pick them up from school. He told her they were inconsolable. Most of the boats had disappeared from view, out past the cartilage that was the little sandbank off the cape. There wasn't much to be said. A touch and some hope, optimism, were the only offerings, and they were fine things, indeed. Moses looked to the steel pans of the breakwater to determine if the tide was coming or going. It was going.

Little Arbot Herring showed up and introduced himself to Moses. He had a Tupperware container with some fresh banana bread, speckled heavily with chocolate chips. The six of them passed the slices around and ate them until they were gone. Moses was left holding the plastic tub. Arbot hugged the women and the girls, not with much spirit, but with convention, as if there were a great many issues between them. Like enemies, once bitter, now resigned after a lengthy stalemate. Arbot looked out at the rising sun and blubbered a little, and then he took the container from Moses. "If I don't bring home the Tupperware, Joyce will divorce me. I swear, it's like gold," he said.

—

At noon, a joint statement from Percy Clouston, the president of the Fishermen's Association, Preston Millar, the president of the Southern Kings and Queen Fishermen's Association, and Horatio Kennedy, the vice-president of Southern, was released. "Our thoughts and prayers go out to the missing's family and to the entire community of My Bonnie Harbour." Sitting in the van while Grant smoked outside, Minnie received a phone call from Blanche Hicken, the press secretary for Mayburn MacIntosh, the rather eccentric minister of Fisheries, Oceans and the Canadian Coast Guard. She told Minnie that when a person is lost in this industry, it effects all of us. Minnie had her repeat what she had said and she wrote it down. "Thanks, Blanche," said Minnie.

Down at the end of the wharf, she observed Joe carrying garbage bags off of the *M&M*. He threw them into the back of his truck, which was the same colour and in about the same condition as the truck that belonged to the missing individual. She noticed that out here, about half of the trucks seemed to be brand new, obnoxious monsters, and the other half were tired things that made the pack mules of the Chilkoot Pass look handsome and vibrant.

—

The first boat back from searching and hauling was the *Alice Partridge*, owned by Atwood LeLacheur and his crew of Tony and Dave Poole, who were cousins from Pooles Corner. LeLacheur agreed to speak to the *Eastern Graphic* and *Guardian* reporters, along with Minnie and Grant, but he refused to be put on television. "That thing'll take me soul, as sure as the day is long," he said. Grant was beyond frustrated, he didn't like the bedlam of it all, and he went to take a look at the horses near Wharf Lane. Atwood was a few short years from turning seventy. No single item upon his person seemed to fit him well, being either slightly too big or slightly too small, and what's more, he didn't seem to care a whit. He was a remarkably tiny man, spry and simple and God-fearing. He knew the positions of all the constellations and all of the satellites up in the sky. The reporters all wanted Atwood to speak about Herring, who he was, what were his interests, so that people could get a sense of him.

"Well, ya can write what ya like for yer gossip sheet," he said. "Herring was a bigger man. Now, ya take me, for example, I've seen more meat on a shadow. I believe in exercise, huh. Anyway, everyone knew Herring, and he was about as warm as a stepmother's breath. He was, like his father, very fond of the drink. The last time I seen him he was all-over-the-place drunk. My heart just breaks for his wife. I believe he had two daughters. Anyway, like I said, everyone knew him and ya never want to see something like this happen. He's fished these waters for over twenty years."

"Did Mr. Herring know how to swim?" Minnie asked.

Atwood itched an elbow. He said, "Well, I don't really know. Anyway, I don't think most of us can swim, and even if we could, it wouldn't be of much good when the water is as cold as it is. I swim 'bout as good as a horse-drawn cart. Last year I caught a lobster with Malpeque tags on 'er. That thing travelled well over three hundred kilometres. Maybe he was just tryin' to get home, too. Who knows, eh? Granted, the tide prolly did most of the work, but that's still a hell of a distance. Things move real fast in the water. Sometimes the way of the crow isn't as fast as we think, huh." He put a pair of binoculars to his face and stared out at the waters.

———

Percy Clouston, Preston Millar, and Horatio Kennedy all travelled together to come and see what was going on. Out on the wharf, upon witnessing the search efforts, Horatio looked at his colleagues, and, as if they were all in an elevator whose cables had snapped, he said, "This is quite something."

At supper, McHerron and Bernard had no news to report.

———

On Wednesday, Gerry was moved from Kings County Memorial to Hillsborough Hospital, the mental health centre, in town. Joseph, Gerry's father, called Susan and told her what was going on. Susan brought Robbie and Mickey to the hospital to visit with Gerry. He was unresponsive, stared at the backs of his hands the entire time. Susan just about fell apart watching him. There was nothing to him, no feeling that he gave off. It was like he was being waked. Dolores and Joseph arrived and took the boys out for some lunch. Susan stayed. She closed her eyes for a bit because the lights were hurting them. The doctors said that he had refused to eat, wouldn't accept any medication. She tried to hold his hand as she relayed to him that pills would help him get better, that he had to get better, but he pulled away from her like an animal that had just been beaten senseless.

—

A fellow in a pair of sunglasses and a black beret came down to the wharf. Grant said, "Hey, yer Cian Collings, the painter." Collings smiled. He looked like a European, was totally out of place here. He spent half of the year in central Italy with his partner, a woman from a village by the name of Casperia. Collings asked what was going on. Grant filled him in, and then he admired the man's shoes, like polished licorices. Cian told him a story about some French guy who had a lobster for a pet, walked him around at the end of a ribbon. He said that the lobster knew the secrets of the world. "Jesus," said Grant. Cian said, "Yeah, he ended up hanging himself in a cellar." Grant said, "That sounds about right."

—

Euna went to see a medium in Wood Islands. She was nervous and the woman's home had a kind of strange odour to it, as if something had just given birth or had just died a few hours before. When she sat in the chair opposite the woman, she sat on her hands. The woman looked at the picture of Herring for a number of minutes. She put a can of Pepsi to her lips and then scratched a pen across a brown leather notebook. She said, "I can't sugar-coat it for ya. This man is dead."

—

Sheila hadn't seen Gerry in a few days, and she was starting to get real nervous. She called in sick to work on Thursday morning, coughed a little to sell it. And then she spent the day watching soap operas in her nightgown. The turkey sandwiches that she'd made for Gerry on Monday evening were still in the fridge.

—

Major Bernard returned to Halifax. Corporal McHerron felt that things were hopeless. He took sleeping pills and emptied a pint of rum. He had yet to sleep since his engagement here began.

—

On Friday, the investigation was still deemed an active search, but the helicopter had been sent back to CFB Greenwood, the fixed-wing had returned to St. John's, and the cutter sailed east, to Souris. Kings County RCMP had assumed the lead role, further coordinating efforts from East Point to Wood Islands. Lillian drove her cruiser out to the bullpen at the crack of dawn, and then she took the shore road through Boatswain Point and, her foot entirely off the gas pedal, rolled all the way to Wood Islands, her neck turned to the left, watching the glimmering waters of the strait. Media coverage waned. The CBC, the *Guardian*, the *Eastern Graphic*, and the *Chronicle Herald*, out of Halifax, all decided to drop the story. For some reason, likely a miscommunication, the *Summerside Journal Pioneer* ran an obituary. As to who had submitted the write-up, which offered no first name for the departed and was the definition of terseness, it seemed the author desired to remain anonymous. The winning ticket of $11,804 for the Rotary Gold Mine was drawn, and for the first time in its history, no winner came forward to collect the winnings.

—

Joe and Isaac checked Herring's traps. He was on track to have had a good and profitable season, firmly in the black. On Saturday, they hauled up his traps, as well, but they returned them to the bottom without bait. They'd haul a few dumps home on the washboard when they were able to. At present, Joe didn't have room on the deck for both his and Herring's lobster and all his traps and ropes and buoys. The *NHL Joe* was liable to sink. "Let the lobsters come and go as they please," said Joe, as the empty traps descended. Isaac nodded. He had wanted to cut the heads right out of the traps. Buoys, too. Just saw them right up and let them float to Poverty.

—

The Sunday was Mother's Day. Euna and the girls picked daffodils out at her mother's place in the late morning, and then they all made zucchini bread after a lunch of grilled cheese sandwiches and tomato soup. The clouds rolled in from over Cape Breton and a bit of rain began to fall. The rest of the day was dreary. The girls read by the stove in the living room, while Euna and Agnes sat drinking coffee at the table in the kitchen. Agnes tried to remember the name of the plumber that used to come around while Joe was still alive. "He spoke so slowly and with such long breaks between his sentences, you could grab some shut-eye," she said. "He never did anything too, too fast in his whole life. But boy, could he tell a story. And he loved to gossip. The two of them would just laugh and laugh." Euna made no effort to talk. Agnes looked at her nails and decided after all that she liked their colour.

# SEVEN

Willy Lyon MacKenzie didn't believe in electricity all that much, and as a result, his home was as illuminated and as warmed as it could be by candles and the stove. As such, it was about as hospitable as a cave and not much easier on the eyes. He had hung a propane lantern over the table, but he found it too bright, and he didn't like to waste the propane. In general, he didn't like waste. He'd been born and lived in the farmhouse his entire life and he knew it so well, all of its dimensions and all of its curiosa that, if pressed, he understood the impossibility of describing the place with any accuracy. To do so would be like trying to describe air to a person. In the stairs to the cellar he had installed a little sneaky drawer. You found the knobs and pulled it out, and within the wood of it he had embedded and laminated photographs of naked ladies fondling their breasts and genitals. His younger brother, Louis, lived with him, and during the summer months, the man insisted on sleeping out on the porch, though the mosquitoes were generally so horrific, Willy Lyon didn't know how the man had any flesh left on him. On some of his lonelier nights, especially in the summer when it was too hot to sleep, even after walking down to the shore and going for a dip in the water, or standing out on the lawn to receive the night rains, he would walk the stairs and pull out the secret drawer and look at the women. About a decade ago, in the winter, he and Louis had driven to Montréal to visit their youngest brother, Kenneth, who was in commercial litigation, and on one of the buses, as it shuddered and jerked through the streets, a younger woman had brushed up against his skin, and he had, quite unexpectedly, wept openly and without shame while Louis and Kenneth looked elsewhere, confused and uncertain. For him, this hadn't been a moment of weakness, but the opposite. A moment of revelation, if you will, in which he had been given some understanding about the true human cost of renouncement. Kenneth had taken them to a jazz club and it had been a truly beautiful night. Two fishermen and their brother, in a warm city in those islands on the cold St. Lawrence, being serenaded by a saxophone and an upright bass and the drums, the way they played their notes not like they were leaving a trail, but rather pursuing something that was infinite, chasing that which would never surrender. And all of it this strange and baffling language that reached into one's soul like a struck match put to tinder.

The night was as opaque and formless as the shadow of a lung, and Willy Lyon and Louis were drinking their shine. Occasionally, a rig would rip past, down the shore road, its engine a great muscle. The gentle pound of the surf down at the beach like that of a foot on the pedal of a sewing machine in some distant room. A stitch constantly being torn and fastened, torn and fastened. These things of the Island sang in their languages, too, but nothing had ever quite compared to that night of music with his brothers.

The house, their clothes, their skin, everything, lingered of fish. Willy Lyon had come in from delivering crickets to his peacocks. They had the Gospel of Matthew opened on the table before them, their eyes squinted, nearly blind with doctrine, and Willy Lyon, his head just a kind of whir, was thinking about Peter and Andrew, about Jesus saying, "Come, follow me, and I will make you fishers of men." It had been exactly a week since Herring had gone overboard, and the search had been entirely abandoned. He hadn't known the man, and what he had heard greatly troubled him. There were mutterings that the man got what he deserved, that something of this nature had been a long time coming. Nevertheless, this wasn't sitting well with him. It wasn't the Christian thing to do, to forsake the forsaken. His own lack of searching had been troubling him. His mind wouldn't allow him to think of what, exactly, there was out there left to find, but whatever the state of the man, he ought to be found, at the very least so that his family could have some closure. It's what he would want if, God forbid, he went over.

—

Tuesday morning was foul, just a mackerel sky, so Willy Lyon and Louis daubed Vaseline on their cheeks and fetched their oil gear from above the stove. Willy Lyon caught Joe at his boat and asked gently if he might be able to speak to everybody about the state of things. Joe said that it was no problem, though they'd have to wait for most of the fellas to get down to the wharf. Willy Lyon and Louis were on the *Maranatha* getting their bait organized for the day. The water had a terrible chop and the rain was coming down, hard and slanted, real bothersome. And then the thought of having to talk to everybody, to stand and ask for their attention, the audacity of it, scared Willy Lyon so, that he ran back over to Joe and told him to disregard his earlier request. "No problem, Willy," said Joe, frowning a little. Isaac, his hand, made a little noise, a titter. Willy Lyon performed his bow-kneed shuffle back to the boat, feeling like a righteous fool, but confident that he had spared himself a greater embarrassment. The age he had attained could command some respect, but his voice was something else entirely. He didn't have the gift of gab that others, such as Joe, had. Willy Lyon was no preacher. He was no politician of the soul. He had convictions, but he knew from limited experience that he could not persuade others, especially fishermen, who cared little for most things beyond their noses, of the weight and urgency of upholding the civil laws of the Deuteronomic code. He beheld his shortcomings with understanding. He knew about moral inventories. He didn't like vanity, and speaking in front of others was immodest. He felt like he had trespassed himself.

—

Willy Lyon and Louis were first out of the bullpen. From behind, Joe had come over the radio. "Hey, ya MacKenzies be careful out there, huh," said Joe. Willy Lyon said, "We will," and his voice had been dour and bad-tempered.

The rain had turned to snow, and the waves were rough, absolute things. They were hauling with the wind and the tide, in an east–west direction, the nose of the boat cutting through the wind, cascading with the waves. They had six or seven dumps left to haul, and Louis had the traps on the washboard, emptied and ready to be sent down. Willy Lyon was waiting, getting his timing on the waves so that he could turn a 180 to starboard and catch the surf. Willy Lyon cranked the wheel and hit the throttle and just as the boat was perpendicular, a wall of water crashed over the side and threw Louis and the traps across to the other side of the platform. In an instant, there was about a foot of water in the boat and Louis was working quietly to free himself of the rope and traps. The water slid back out of the scuppers. "Okay, we're done, Willy," said Louis, after the dump was reset. He was shivering pretty bad. Willy Lyon said, "Yeah, maybe we should call it quits." He had enough trays to break even for the day. And besides, everyone else had called it.

The *Maranatha* was about four miles from the harbour. The boat was heaving and Willy Lyon was spilling his tea all over the wheel and his oils. This puddle of bronze around his boots like an embryo trying for culture in a Petri dish. He said, "You rollin' cocksucker." They were sailing fast, cruising at nine knots, high up, surging with the crests. Louis was looking, somewhat absentmindedly, off to the starboard. He could see Barrels's place, in My Bonnie Harbour North, the chimney boiling, and beyond, the plunge of the treeline, ample with grace, as clear and legible as a bar of music. And then, through the gobbets of snow, a head in the water, a bit of torso, stiff and rounded like a sandstone vestige. He looked again, thinking the cold and wet were playing tricks on him, but it certainly was not a buoy. Louis yelled at Willy Lyon, startled him. Willy Lyon looked to where his brother was pointing. "By Christ," he said. Willy Lyon waited for a plodding breaker to crest and curl and then plunge so that he could spin the boat.

They hauled him from the current. Getting him into the boat felt about the same as trying to catch a waterfall in a wheelbarrow. His pants were all shredded. His boots were gone. And his skin, both stretched as taut as cheesecloth drawn over a jug and as distended and rotten as a parsnip uncovered in winter, bore the stigma of sharks. He lay on the deck for a short time, as imperturbable as a bead of snot. They moved to help him but he put up his hands and gave them the stop signs. He'd been in the water for eight days. The boat rolled with the waves. Herring looked at his toes, hocked a bit of phlegm from his mouth and then gave the brothers the thumbs up. He was ready. Willy Lyon and Louis helped him up and shuffled him down to the cabin where they stripped him of his clothes and dressed him with a few spares they stored in the cabin. His wounds were disturbing, and though they handled him clumsily, bumping him with steps and cupboard doors and their arms and legs, the man did not complain.

Louis kept him by the stove and Willy Lyon radioed in that they had Herring. The first one to respond was Joe McInnis and he said, "Like the fish?" and Willy Lyon said, "No, like the man."

Louis rummaged around for some food and produced a sleeve of saltines. His fingers were so wet and cold that he had to cut the plastic wrapping with a knife. He passed them over and said, "Here, eat something so I know that you're not a spirit." The man grumbled something in response, his eyes just these strange chinks. Louis counted the days on his fingers. And then he counted the days again. He stared out the windows of the cabin. He scratched his neck and had a long haul of tea. "The dead have risen," he said, and the big man by the stove stuffed into ill-fitting clothes said, "Yes, I spose it's been a long time coming." Louis took a small pot of boiling water off the top of the stove and made the fellow a mug of tea. They listened to the water dash against the hull, illuminated by the glow from the meagre light of the stove. Louis said, "Well, was it worth the wait?"

When they sidled up to the wharf, and Louis threw the lines of the *Maranatha* to Joe, Herring said, "I think I left the stove on." With a rather striking nimbleness, as if entirely liberated from physical concerns, he stepped from the washboard to the curb and said, "I'm going home." Joe, who had rushed back to harbour to assist, just about fell over, started dry heaving with the shock, stumbling a bit like a

drunkard. Joe's hands were trembling, his muscles burned and weak.
Isaac went to steady his captain, but he wasn't of much use, because
once he started to think that Joe was going to vomit, Isaac began to
retch. They made quite the pair. It wasn't the first time two boys down
at the wharf had been sick at the same moment. Willy Lyon and Louis
just stood as still as carved figureheads, watching Herring almost kind
of float to his truck. He turned the engine, which went off with a bang,
and drove away in a cloud of dusky smoke like it had all been a well-
rehearsed magic trick.

—

The ambulance caught up with him as he turned down his drive. He
got out of the rig, shooed the two paramedics away, and walked into
the house. He took the lid off of the skillet and picked up the steak.
"Jesus, it's as hard as a whalebone." And though it was sputtering and
coughing, the propane was still going. "About time I buy stock in Irv-
ing," he said.

Herring cracked some windows and began rummaging through the
refrigerator. He let the paramedics in. They insisted that he come with
them to the hospital. Herring said, "Listen, check my vitals. I'm okay."
They checked his vitals. He was right. Again, they insisted that he
come. "Well, at least let me have something to eat and a hot shower."
He made corned beef hash and some coffee. The paramedics declined
the hash, but did accept the coffee. The three of them sat at the table.
The one paramedic said, "You can relax. Yer food's not gonna run away
on you."

"The Island is a good place to live if you like salt," Herring said,
between greedy mouthfuls.

As he showered, the paramedics sat and picked through a newspaper that was at least two weeks old.

The water gurgled out of the tap and it took a while for the warm
water to get up to the top floor. He stood under this and smiled, pissed
into the drain, put shampoo into his hands, and, as he went to lather
up his hair, he realized that he had gone completely bald. Ha, what a
swindle, he thought. When the soap got into the wounds on his legs

and arms, he winced a great deal. His feet looked malformed and over-cooked. The water that went down the drain was the blues and greens of a shipwreck.

—

Herring insisted that they stop at Brehaut's and get some more food on the way into town. They went in, too, as if following a prisoner, and he ordered a cheeseburger and a chocolate milkshake. The few people set on the pew by the ice cream freezer all stared at him, their mouths open. Herring looked at them and said, "Careful there, Phyllis and Tom, you'll take some flies." As they got back into the ambulance, Big Arbot came rolling by. He waved at them, and, seeing Herring, his mouth dropped and he nearly rode off the bridge. Herring said, "Now that I'm back from the dead, it's good to see that I still get the same reaction. Some things never change, huh."

From here on out, word would spread quickly.

He finished his meal from the gurney and then smacked his forehead. "Oh dear," he said. "I've should have introduced myself. I'm Herring." He extended his hand to both of them. "It's nice to have someone to talk to."

—

Lillian and Charley, of all people, were the first who actually got to see him and speak with him. She was in to see about some uterine polyps and Lillian's best friend, Margaret, was a nurse at the hospital. They bumped into Margaret at the front doors, and she told them what she knew.

Herring was in an intensive-care bay, thumbing with bandaged hands through a gossip magazine. He was bald in a manner that brought to mind chemotherapy. His arms and his legs were extensively wrapped, too. He seemed in good spirits. "Jesus, Herring," said Charley. "How are you?" Lillian had a hand over her mouth and seemed incapable, at present, of speech. Charley helped her into one of the chairs. Herring said, "Well, I'm doing none too bad. A lotta stitches. Fallin' overboard is a right good way to quit smoking." His teeth were as yellow as they'd ever been. He set the magazine down by his right hip, closed his mouth, and looked out the window at the tops of the poplar trees. "They have a way of fluttering, don't they, huh?" he said. "I wonder if there are any woodpeckers out there." Herring splashed some apple juice down his throat and looked back at the both of them, his eyes moving from Lillian to Charley, slowly and studiously, an adagio that made all three of them truly feel the spaces between them, like an empty lure dragged, spinning through the depths, back to its spool. "I'm mostly sleeping," he said.

To Lillian and Charley, the man looked somehow both older and younger. From where Lillian was sitting, his legs, the flesh on them, appeared stiff and brittle, like the strangest of vinyl offcuts swept together on the floor of some factory. She didn't think that she'd ever seen such a sight, so as to how she was thinking this, she didn't rightly know. Herring saw her admiring his legs, and he said, "It's a ways from my heart." To Charley, the man had an appropriate number of wrinkles for a fisherman, but there was a kind of texture to his skin that made him seem younger. There was a freshness to him. He was like a fresh thing, a field of slop and mud and manure renewed by the rains.

"Leigh White was this young fella that I used to take out fishing. Dunbar Gillis was his uncle. You guys know Dunbar. Big boy was Leigh, tall and gruff. A bloody Scots pine. Always seemed to me to hate fishing. You'd ask him how he was doing, and it wasn't until you were coming back in, a few miles from home, that he'd finally get around to saying how it was that he was doing. People always said, too, that he was a miserable fool. That he hated everything and everyone. Nobody liked the boy. Least of all his parents. Well, I knew all of this, and yet I still felt the need to hire the boy. At the end of two months I really did feel that he hated fishing, but I seen little things that made me understand that he was just starting to come into himself. He was real gentle with everything. The traps, the bait, the lobsters. He didn't like to see them fighting, tearing their claws off, you know. This process was going to take a hell of a long time, but it was there, huh. The road was being laid out. Anyway, it turns out that he was just really, really shy," said Herring. He blinked, and then said, "I ought to have gotten to know him better," and the ring of these words reminded Lillian of being in a room with lawyers and siblings and this strangest of debates emerging with regard to the last will and testament of her father, of confusion and grief and then a nugget of understanding, that in some sense, this was the way of the world. Charley was put in mind of being somewhere when he had been much younger, perhaps the mainland, perhaps Whycocomagh, and of walking up a steep, dirt road to a spring, a thread of water seeping through a cleft in a great escarpment.

In all of his years, Charley had never heard the man speak so much. He didn't tell Lillian, as they made their way home along the highway, but he felt that the man in the hospital with the bandages wasn't Herring at all, but an imposter. Lillian wondered why the man hadn't asked after Gerry. She also wondered why she hadn't thought to bring him up. These thoughts upset her quite a bit, and she turned her face away from her husband so he might not see her cry and worry.

Laid out on the bed, Herring could still feel the waters around him, its swirl, its boundless drift, the peaceful risings and fallings that lived without record. The vast and gentle throb of an entire planet, beheld by him, and him alone. A spare part. A kind of last man. A finger on an artery waiting for a pulse.

—

The premier, Robert Ghiz, came, along with Percy Clouston, Preston Millar, and Horatio Kennedy, to pay Herring a visit a few hours later. Minnie Carver and Grant Gallant showed up, as well. Minnie was impatient, and she irritated a number of nurses and doctors in getting to the man. Herring consented to being filmed. Grant hit record, and Mr. Ghiz introduced himself and placed his left palm on Herring's shoulder. Polished and sincere. "This is quite a story. Quite a story, indeed. I don't think something like this has ever happened before. You're very lucky to be alive," said Mr. Ghiz. Herring grinned a little. Mr. Ghiz said, "If you don't mind me asking, how on earth were you able to survive?" Herring said, "Well, the truth is, I was high on acid." Herring offered a broader, more triumphant smile to those in attendance. Mr. Ghiz blushed noticeably and tucked his hands into themselves behind his back. "Quite a story," he said.

Percy Clouston said, "Man's insanity is heaven's sense."

"Yeah, we'll have to start calling you Pip, I spose," said Mr. Millar.

Herring scrunched his face. The members of the PEIFA admired the numerous medical appurtenances of the bay. Horatio ran a hand over the curtain and appeared impressed by its ability to hang with such vitality. This drapery was so sufficient and so pleasant. Their conservatism, their preconceptions, had been revealed with all the jangle and ease of a nerve exposed in a cracked tooth. Grant saw this often with political folk. How easy it was for them to stand before their illusions, to converse with the mirage. These men all left quite hastily. Herring said, "I'd rather pick garbage than be a politician."

Grant stopped recording and Minnie sat herself next to the fisherman. Grant moved the tripod, levelled it, gave her the thumbs up. She spoke into the black foam of her microphone and said, "How do you think you were able to survive for so long, eight days, in fact, in such conditions?" The microphone in her hand moved toward him and settled, hovering over his chest like a strange kind of bird caught in the long hallway between thought and action. "Well, as I mentioned, I was high on acid. I spose that when I fell in, I was still, like, my brain still thought I was on the boat, or what have ya, and that I wasn't in danger, you know. Anyway, I sensed that everything was upside down, that the air had become water and the water air. It was like a womb and I was just minding my own business," he said. "I wasn't thinking about time or how cold or how wet it was 'cos I really wasn't concerned about these things, huh."

The patient on the other side of the curtain coughed and shifted their body. Minnie looked at Herring, his blue eyes, and the bridge of his nose between them, felt like they had the force of a barge or a tugboat down the stilled, acquiescent waters of a canal, that silent channel from the soul to the heart.

"It was nice not to be goddamn bothered by anybody. Jesus, it was the first vacation I've ever had," he said. Grant tried to suppress a laugh. Herring pointed at him. "See," he said. "He knows. He knows what I'm talking about." He looked at Grant, this young kid, and just beneath, as if throughout his bones, he remembered the profound joy of being young, of not knowing the number and nature of what the road would bring. The slenderness of taking everything for granted. Herring said, "Three minutes with no air. Three days with no water. Three weeks with no food. Staying alive is just three threes. I just had to outlast them threes. Prove 'em wrong. What the fuck is a number, anyhow. There's no spirit in 'em." And then he said, "Please don't put this up on television. Besides, it's none of yer business how I conduct myself, dead or alive."

A week before, Minnie had intuited, by virtue of the trouble in his eyes, that there was an immense darkness in this man. But these things were no longer there, if in fact they'd ever been there at all. No, instead, she saw lightness and something near to harmony, as if the coin of life had merely been flipped in the hand of some god.

Minnie found herself intrigued by the man in the bandages. She wanted to see if she might devour him. She wanted to know if the man could swim. Surely the man had grabbed onto something, a buoy, perhaps. There was no shame in admitting even this. He'd still lived through quite an ordeal. No one would take this away from him. She also knew that Mary was going to be furious. They'd wasted a great deal of time for nothing.

—

He considered calling Gerry or Joe, even Euna, but something held him back. He thought the most important thing he could do was to avoid bothering anybody, least of all for a bloody ride home. But also, the idea of seeing somebody real familiar was somehow upsetting. He knew the decent thing to do would be to call Gerry and make sure his friend was doing okay, reassure him that he didn't need to blame himself for what had happened. He knew that this course of action was right and true and perfectly simple, and yet he didn't call. In him, in the very centre of who he was, in some essential grain, there was a desire for Gerry to suffer. He recognized this as it was, this want, and it scared him. There was a great deal of darkness in him and this idea, his comprehension of it, somehow eased his own pain, but for a moment. This was all the more odd, given that Gerry was not responsible in any sense for what had happened that morning, and if the world were as it ought to be, both of them would know it.

Specialists of every kind examined him. He was even taken down to speak with a psychiatrist, but nothing much came of this meeting. The fellow seemed a sullen, aggravated kind of human, awful keen to avoid eye contact. After forty minutes of holding his tongue, Herring said, "This is a righteous waste of my time, mister." A man and a woman showed up, stating that they were lawyers from some association whose name sounded as if they'd just made it up in the hallway before entering, wanting to talk to him about disability claims or some such nonsense. Herring found them boring, smiled and nodded as they spoke in quiet and placid tones. "Money, money, money," he said. "Is this all ya goddamn people think about? Always looking for another teat to suck on, eh." Neither of them said a word. "Well, there's no money to be had outta me. I'm as dry as something that's really dry." The man and the woman blinked and wrinkled their faces. "Respectfully, I'd like the both of you to leave, please." They left.

He got to thinking that what had happened to him really had occurred. That he'd lived through a rather astounding experience. That this wasn't some silly dream. The dream of a coward. He had survived. He was still among the living. And, after all of this, after everything, it was odd, maybe even a little tragic, that he should have no one to pick him up.

In the end, he happened to cross paths with Dunbar Gillis in the bathroom right by the stairs. Herring had been out for a walk, to see how his legs felt under him, and a great wave of nausea had braced against him. Dunbar Gillis was wearing his flannel jacket and a pair of oily jeans, his work boots dragging like cans behind a wedding car. He was in to see a doctor regarding some spots on his lungs, and said that if Herring waited, he'd gladly drive him home. "Jesus," said Herring. "I was just talking about you and Leigh."

And as the rig hurtled down the highway toward the hills of Caledonia, Dunbar drinking shine from a little flask he kept tucked between his legs, staring at the road before him with the kind of blankness that comes when a person is trying to comprehend the things that are, mostly, beyond the realm of sense, Herring had a vision of himself, alone, in the house. His mind scanned the place as if it were merely a set of architectural plans, locating all of the stashed liquor and drugs, circling them with a red marker as if to say danger. He pictured himself awake in the wee hours, pacing the floors, splashing drink down his throat out of utter boredom and loneliness, and an immense feeling of dread basted him. "Hey, you have a pony, don't you?" he said. Dunbar nodded with the slightest of movements.

When he got home, Herring hobbled around for a while, his mind restless. The house smelled stale, the air in it damp as a washcloth. He was hungry but he didn't feel like eating anything. His loss of appetite likely had to do with the antibiotics the doctors had him on. He found the bottle of lunatic soup that the Daley boys had made, and he poured himself a hearty glass of this. He stood a chair on the porch and sat, facing the waters, watching the robins and the blackbirds scouring the grasses for worms, flicking tufts of dried grass here and there like grain harvesters of old. He fell asleep and only woke up because he was cold and shivering. His lips coated with thickened spit. Night had fallen and he hadn't touched the wine. He left the chair and the glass where they were, and as he opened the door to walk inside, the brown-and-black tabby materialized, shot up the stairs and across the boards of the porch and snuck inside. Herring lowered himself and the cat into the basement, and he loaded the stove with kindling and wood. Once the fire got going, the cat returned from the darker depths of the house and nestled up to the bricks about the stove. Herring imagined that the damn thing had shit someplace. He'd deal with this in the morning. Perched, the animal looked at Herring while he warmed up some mackerel taken from the freezer. He cut this into portions and laid them before the cat. "Just so you know, mackerel is the skunk of the sea," he said. The cat ate quickly and with very little noise,

oceans had been pulled and the world leaked out into space, like a cracked egg or the spit-up marble of a toddler.

—

He made coffee. There wasn't much in the way of food in the house. The sun was out and the sky was without a single cloud. He peeled some potatoes, slowly and methodically, for his hands were hurting him, and boiled these on the stove, praying that the propane would endure for him, mashed them with a fork, salted them, and then sat at the table and ended his hunger as best he could. He got some mackerel out and prepared it for the cat, who came out when he set the bowl near the stove. He slowly climbed the stairs to the bathroom and turned on the tap. The water was red with clay. He brushed his teeth. His piss, the colour of butterscotch.

—

Euna drove down the lane. Herring was in the little barn, sharpening the teeth on his chainsaw blade, though the teeth were in pretty good nick. He topped it up with oil and mix, spilled only a little onto the broken concrete of the floor. He let her walk to the house before he emerged from the barn. "I'm over here," he said.

As she came closer he could feel her, as if her physical self was but the nucleus of some larger structure, dynamic and filamentary and wholly unseen, but a funnel for a larger organ. She hugged him and blubbered a bit on his shoulder. He let her take a moment or two to compose herself.

She still had her winter tires on. "Running a little late, eh?" he said, his hands on his hips. She said, "Well, you're always the one to do it for me." He said, "I'll do it if ya make some lemonade." She grinned at him. "Pop 'er," he said, walking around to the back of the car.

He changed the tires, bagging and storing her winters in the barn, and then he said, "I'm going to take it for a test drive." She was in the kitchen, doing some dishes for him. She'd brought him some things to eat. Chicken thighs and bread and pasta and cans of soup. A bag of Granny Smiths. She said, "Where's Murphy?" and this question had that solid and thin sound to it that answers already perceived and known can have. A tennis ball in suspension between two swinging racquets. He took her by the small of the back and walked her out to the century oak and showed her the bit of concrete. They were still and without talk. He felt her shake a little and he let his tears come down, made no move to shield himself, his pain. Herring walked Euna back to the house and sat her down and made her a cup of peppermint tea. He drove to the cemetery in My Bonnie Harbour, down by the waters, and he found the headstone.

Joseph "Junior" McInnis Sr.
November 15, 1937
May 10, 1998
MacAonghais a-rithist

There were some saffron crocuses coming up through the grasses and a great majority of the older headstones had toppled. "Strange times, Joe. Strange times, indeed. Again and again and fucking again, Joe," he said, and then he drove home. He wanted to see his daughters.

—

When he picked the girls up, Agnes didn't say much. Heck, she didn't say word one to him from the porch. Joe was out in the fields messing about with the girls, and when Herring's rig had come down the lane, rolling and coughing like something with distemper, he saw the girls running in from the bluffs down near the shore. Agnes just kind of stood herself on the porch. He noticed she was shaking a little, in the way that some women can, so that you don't know if they're about to burst with anger or collapse with fear. Euna had a smidge of this in her. All he could think to do was stay out of her way, to not poke the bear, so to speak. He said hello, gave her a wave. Joe stayed where he was, in the higher grasses around the outbuildings. He said hello and gave Joe a wave, too. Joe just lit a cig and stood there, his head wrapped in a scarf of smoke, with a look on his face like he was trying to figure out how much time was required to untangle two gillnets.

He and the girls headed into Montague and stopped at the buffalo park near the Buddhist place. They pulled into the parking lot, and they walked over to the fence. The buffalo herd was out, and there were even a couple of calves. It was strange to see them here, on the Island, he supposed. But they probably didn't know any better themselves. He thought that they'd been a gift from the bigwigs in Alberta some years ago. They walked ever so slowly, with their mouths to the grasses below, these strange, dark beasts, incapable of hiding their sluggishness and fatigue, indifferent to the strange creatures who lined up on the other side of the fence to observe them, as if there was a kind of lesson to be understood from the spectacle. In the adjacent field, a tractor was hauling a trailer, spreading manure.

Marceline said, "They're bison."

"Huh?" said Herring.

"They're bison. They're not buffalo. I guess there never were any buffalo out west," she said.

"Well, my word. The damn park is named after them," said Herring. "How'd they get that wrong, I wonder."

Marcelina said, "Yeah, why is it named wrong?"

"I don't rightly know. Maybe 'cos we get things wrong and it's easier to keep on pretending," he said.

"Like Green Gables?" said Marceline.

"What do you mean?"

"Well, it's from a story that was never real and then someone built a house after it and now people come from all over to visit it," she said.

Herring thought about this for a moment or two. "Yeah, you're onto something there, I spose."

Herring saw the monks walking the fence at the opposite end of the pen. The ground was elevated here, and their procession walked the line of a hill. He remembered that they had assumed control of the buffaloes. He watched them for a while, and eventually he spotted Venerable Mike. Herring gave a mighty wave from the tips of his toes, his shirt coming untucked so that his daughters could see his chafed and bandaged skin as it was. Venerable Mike stopped and leaned forward, trying to make out who was waving at them. The monks all waved back, then continued on.

"You ladies want some ice cream?" said Herring, and he realized that they were staring at him the same way he had looked to his own departed father at everlasting rest in his coffin.

"You girls know how the ice cream man takes a poop?" he said. They tried to move their heads, their faces stunned and blank. Herring put his arms out and wiggled his hips like he was swinging a hula hoop. Marceline grunted as if she was going to vomit, and Marcelina, seeing this, started cackling with laughter. Then Herring started howling, too. Marceline watched the two of them for a moment or two. She laughed, but only after she understood that it was okay to join in, that nothing bad was going to happen. They went to the dairy bar and ate hot-fudge sundaes. The girls even got cherries on top.

# EIGHT

Joe dropped by to give Herring his redfish and cash. Herring was out in front of the house trying to repair a century oak that had been cracked by lightning a few years prior. He had mixed up concrete in a barrow and was carrying buckets up a ladder to a hole in the shattered trunk, where the limbs all diverged, about eight feet off the ground. He'd rigged up a come-along and some straps, and this was doing a decent enough job of supporting the limbs. Joe walked over, snapped a beer open, and held the ladder with his feet. "Damn thing was rotten before the lightning got to it," said Herring. Joe adjusted his crotch, admired the bandages on the man. Herring looked whiter than he'd ever been, like a bucket of cheese curds, like he'd been unwell, had battled some strange virus and lost a ton of weight in doing so. His bald head was unsettling, made Joe's stomach agitate a tad. He had to look away. The sweep and curl of the wind in the boughs of the hemlocks by the road.

"Well, in about thirty years that's going to put somebody's chainsaw through hell," he said.

Herring climbed down and wiped his nose with the bandage on his left arm. "Yeah, I spose," he said, and troweled some more concrete into his bucket. "It's the *tree* that matters right now, Joe." It was the edge in the man's voice that Joe noted. He liked this, felt this venom was a well-considered thing, and that he could make sense of it also seemed like an indication that he, himself, wasn't in danger of becoming too much of an asshole just yet. Herring had always had jam, but somewhere along the line, it had all seeped out of him. He knew about the troubles with Jack MacLeod, and he knew about the business with Cahoon. He knew a bit about him and Euna, the hole in the floor. He knew about the shoes in the freezer, too. Jesus, the man struck him as helpless. Just a landslide. But he was thinking, too, about how debilitated he'd been down at the wharf when Herring had come in. He'd never been so useless before, and this falter had embarrassed him a great deal. He pictured himself, bent over and swaying, and this image burned hot.

His father had always said that the Herrings were mostly decent men. The grandfather, Spargo Herring, had come home from the war a communist. "When he wasn't fishing and building houses, he was trying to convert ya." Spargo's mind had latched onto the notion of Utopias, of heaven on earth, and thereafter it was all his tongue could offer. People began to consider the man unreasonable and dogmatic, which, given the general religiosity of the affronted, was saying something. That was when things began to buckle and deform. Virtues grew to become sins. And, consequently, all of his kids had become drinkers. It was this, among other qualities, that mostly turned their friends and neighbours against them for good. The Herrings had, at one time, something like revolution in their blood, said Joe Sr. "At least for a little while, anyways." A man that could survive as long as he had at sea had jam, all right. "Ya have to give 'im that much," said Atwood to Willy Lyon and Louis and Joe one night at a ceilidh down at the community centre. "His sins have been cleansed, eh."

Joe offered him a beer. Herring declined. "You think you'll come finish the season?" said Joe. Herring shrugged. "I should get back on 'er, I know, but I've got the fear in me," he said. "I feel like a fart in a mitten, you know." Joe told him that there were four or five dumps of his still out there, that he hadn't been able to find them. "No bother. I imagine Miles or Jack are just picking them right clean," said Herring. "Anyway, Jack always said he wanted two fleets."

Joe drove his rig over to the side of the house, the wheels crunching through the stiff grasses, and began handing him the boxes of bait, and Herring would take them and walk down the cellar steps and disappear into the darkness. When the truck was empty and Joe had watched Herring count his money, Joe said, "Listen, Herring, I'd like to say something to ya." Herring tucked the money back into its envelope and folded it in half twice. "I've— Well, ya see, there's been— I've been thinking about things, and— Well, shit, I'm strugglin' here." He was flustered as hell, but he stood himself still, tried to order the words in his mind. Herring's knees were dirty with soil. The man positively radiated patience. "Anyway, I can't find the angle to come at this correctly."

Herring said, "I can lend you a protractor, if you like." They smiled together. Herring could tell that he had flustered the man. He'd created an opening by which to terrorize the fellow, but he let it alone.

Joe said, "I'd be lyin' if I said I hadn't rehearsed all of this a couple of times. I wanted to apologize for my conduct, my behaviour, over the years. There's a distance between us that I allowed to grow. I thought poorly of you. I spoke ill of you. I'm not sure if I can patch this up, or if you even want to patch things up, but, man to man, I'm sorry for not treating you better. We're family." He could feel the urge to keep going, to keep running with the momentum he'd built for himself. His heart was pounding. He kept his mouth shut, felt his jaw crunch and pop. He was tight all over. Herring put his arm on Joe's shoulder. "Thanks," he said. "There was a lot in there. But thanks for saying what you did." He went into the house and came out with a bottle of the Daleys' wine. Joe took it, had a sense that the man was done drinking for good, that he was turning some grand page, once and for all. He had to be honest. The thought moved him. Herring said, "We'll just have to see what happens."

As Joe drove down the shore road, wrath and fury against Herring arose and pestered his innards like someone at the door during an election. My God, he was grey and white. We'll have to start calling him the silver darling, Joe thought. And then he remembered when they were kids, jumping from ice floe to ice floe like scalded cats, in the drifts of winter, Joe going home every hour or so to change his socks and pants. Watching in awe as Herring, who was older by a few years, hopped the ice flawlessly. With the grace of a gymnast.

—

Euna had a cut-and-colour appointment in Irish Montague. Her stylist, Josie Bell, she'd known pretty much her whole life. Josie hadn't slept particularly well the night before, so she wasn't in the mood for talk just yet. She began putting the foils in, combing and wiggling Euna's hair. She brushed on the highlights. The shop was quiet. The two of them breathed quietly and listened to the radio. Euna had her eyes closed and was on the verge of dozing off. About an hour later, Josie removed the foils, rinsed, and toned, and as she was shampooing, Josie realized that Euna's hair felt different, that it felt faint and alien, like she was reading mail sent for a previous resident, or like her toes were brushing against brown algae. Flesh and focus. Yes, Euna's hair had fundamentally changed, and though she didn't tell her, she knew that the woman was with child.

—

Herring slept in, which was unusual for him, a sign, perhaps, that something outside of his understanding might be happening to him. Like an experiment was being run on him. He was frightened for a little bit, still and groggy and idle in the bed like a trailer abandoned at the side of a road. He got up and slowly pulled his clothes onto his body, the light in the room cool and bare in a way that reminded him of his youth and of being in love, the pleasure of waking next to another human who has accepted you and embraced you into a very sacred place. How potent this feeling of love was. His memory of it built by lines, horizontal and upward, like the movements of paint layered upon a hull, forming a sculpture.

He thought about the medicine, the painkillers, thought about not taking the stuff. He called the hospital about seeing that useless psychiatrist, but when he got through, he asked the receptionist if he might be able to speak to a woman instead. She'd see what she could do. When Herring hung up, he threw his bicycle in the back of his rig and drove into the Harbour to visit Fletcher Jordan.

Fletcher was busy, his legs sticking out from beneath a rusted grey sedan, a squirm of the knees every so often like he was in a wrestling match, fighting the pin. Adam Buell was in the shop, talking to Fletcher's mother, gesturing in big sweeps with real dried, nearly prehistoric hands. His eyes were always kind of wet, as if he'd just had some nose hairs pulled out. Adam liked to talk so that everybody could hear. He said, "Well, they caught me for stealing. I'm going to the sin bin. Now, if this cheque bounces, call the missus. She'll come in and settle it with cash for ya."

Fletcher's mother asked Herring how he was getting along. Herring said, "Oh, you know, none too bad." His mother said, "You probably don't remember this, but when you were born, I made you a snowsuit." Her bulldog, Chaldon, groaned from his bed under the wall of timing belts. She patted his fat head.

They were going to have to wait on parts. Why didn't he take the truck home and bring it back in? Herring said, "No, I'd prefer to leave it here with ya." Herring went to the rig and heaved the bicycle out. "You'll look like the Invisible Man on that thing," she said. Her leg was doing much better. "It's amazing what these doctors can do nowadays." She adjusted her glasses. There was an old fellow in the parking lot that she didn't seem to recognize. "I might get my hips replaced just for the fun of it," she said. Herring purchased a carton of eggs from her. "You'll lose these, for certain, on that rickety bike of yours. I'll drop them off later this evening," she said. And with that, he rode off, up the hill, standing on the pedals, his neck taut, choked, held by a phantom leash, wafers of blood rising up through his bandages where the stitches had failed.

The air was cooler today, and when he got home his skin was red and his shirt soaked. His lungs were on fire, and he leaned over and collapsed with the bike, and as his body contracted, the whole of it pulling for more air, he began to laugh. From her window, Selina Glover watched the man struggle down the road and fall over. She thought that he must have lost his mind. Chessel, the almanac in his hands, said, "Well, at least he's drunk on a bicycle and not in his damn rig."

Fletcher's mother drove out in her truck with the eggs around supper. Herring thanked her, walked with her to the old garden, marked by lupines and quinces and hawthorns, asked her about English cucumbers. She said, "Oh, they're thirsty things. They like rich soil, so compost'll be yer friend. It's a good time of year for them 'cos the soil is warm. Keep them about three feet apart, you know, and you gotta pinch 'em after six leaves so they'll spread out for you." They were quiet for a moment, enjoying the cooler air as it moved inland, combing the grasses and ushering the mice in the fields back to their burrows. The light airs of curfew. She observed the poise of the waters and envisioned him out there, as he had been, abandoned and isolated. "Oh, I see a bit of green tinge on the poplars there," she said. "Poplars are always the first ones to get new leaves in the spring."

"Lucky fellas," said Herring. He looked to her, her skin brown, like newspapers on a chair, faded by the sun. She has suffered so very much, he thought. Like all of us. She seemed so full of grace, in the same way that birds just always seemed to be perfectly and freshly composed when you saw them, as if God had just released them into creation.

"What put you in mind of cucumbers?" she asked.

Herring nodded his head. "I don't rightly know," he said. "I want some chomp in my life, I spose."

The cat emerged from the fields and joined them as they walked back. It walked under her truck and basked in the warmth of the engine. Herring shooed the thing away, and it ran to the back door of the house with a contemptuous glare, while Fletcher's mother drove away. If the cat hung around any longer, he supposed he was going to have to give the thing a name. Best to let the girls name her.

He ran a hot bath with a spurt of dish soap and sat himself in the suds, relishing the heat, his feet rested on the spout, marking the steel with breaths of heat.

—

Joe called to tell him that Miles Mackenzie was down at the wharf, pushing his traps over.

Joe said, "I'm sitting here in my rig watching him. It would be nothing at all for me to go over and throw him in, eh. There'd be two hits. Me hitting him and him hitting the water."

Herring declined the offer and thanked him for the call. He fetched his bicycle and began the ride to the wharf. He thought, jeez, by the time I get there on this thing, Miles'll be all done his work, anyway. He rode slowly and with reverence in the dark, couldn't see but ten or twelve feet in front of him, wary of holes or cracks that might throw him. There were few sounds. The world a kind of chamber. Hell, maybe Miles is doing me a favour.

The lights were on at the wharf, and the sky beyond it was just pitch black. The lack of balance to this spectacle, the luminous and the spectral, was frightening, placed a murmur in your ear that made you dizzy. The lines of the wharf like teeth, and the waters and the sky beyond a complete void, made him feel as if he were a scream perched on a tongue, staring out at where it was compelled to go, in love with its fate. That great slither before one thing, born of darkness, was cascaded into a mightier vessel, the cup of all things that bore yet other darkness.

And there Miles was, pulling on a mickey of dark rum, agitated and sweating, dragging Herring's traps by their bridles over the concrete deck to the curb and pushing them into the waters of the bullpen, the sound of every speechless trap hitting the water like a dull blade hacking at a suspended hide. Scrape and hack and glug. And glug. Scrape and hack and glug. Herring watched a few more traps fall. Damn, that's an awful pile of money. He felt no urge to confront the man and he understood this. Either the man would tire and give up, or he would continue until they were all gone. Herring pushed the bicycle ahead with his foot and turned for home.

It sounded as if the world had been put between the jaws of a vise, so heavy and consistent were the rains that woke him just after midnight. His head lay only about a yard from the roof. He'd never heard such an intensity before, and he worried that the roof might burst, had a vision of the rafters being thrusted, fractured apart, of the house filling with water like an overturned vessel. He got up and scoured each storey to ensure that, in fact, no breach had occurred. A bandaged man in only his underwear. Some eccentric, misplaced ghoul looking for a family to haunt.

He stood and looked at the trees and the plants outside, bent over like the stricken nails of an unsighted carpenter. As helpless as babes. He fell asleep on the chesterfield watching *Breakfast at Tiffany's*, the cat curled up next to him, and in the light of the morning everything seemed as it had been the day before. Everything, viewed from afar, was resilient, undamaged. All things within the dominion of Providence.

As if drawn by a kind of protean magnet, Herring found the bag of acid that Red John had left fallen behind the chesterfield. He set it on the table next to the case of beer and whiskey. He felt assaulted, besieged on every side. The medieval castle of some Saxon fable. Hold on, he thought. The day was overcast, the lawn an emerald green. Don't freak out. Be methodical. Small strokes fell the mighty oak. He found his calculator in the drawer beside the oven and reckoned, roughly, that with no income, he could stretch his money until September, at which point he'd have to get back onto the hamster wheel before the damage was irreparable. At the very least, he had a couple of weeks to figure this thing out.

He baked some blueberry muffins, and by the time he was done, the sun had appeared through the clouds. Before he shoved off on his bicycle, he put a hand down to the puddles in the lane. The water was hot, like the tongue of a dog.

It took him about forty minutes of regular pedalling to get to Boatswain Point. The limbs of the trees dribbled linkages of water upon him as he went, the cream-coloured bulrushes huddled upon the bases of the trees like spun confections. The bogs on either side of the road were rotund from the storm. A few trucks passed by, some hauling trailers of timber, some hauling scraps of metal and cabinetry. One of them had lengths of pine, wharf piles, tied down with ropes. The tires so burdened they were nearly flat. People were always stealing material from the wharves. They allowed themselves to filch because it was in such a state of disrepair. The water would reclaim these things if they didn't. May as well be practical about it. Every once and a while he passed through a dense cloud of insects, could feel them flitter about his nostrils. A speck would be caught and then take up real estate in the corner of his eye like an inadvertent thumb over the lens of a camera.

—

The Gillis farmhouse was set well back from the road, down a winding lane paved with crushed blue basalt trucked in years ago from Nova Scotia. The house, quaint and unassuming and set into a cleared field that contained a paddock and a barn of honest proportion, displayed some signs of considerable rot about the chimney stack and the gables. Some time ago, a few years north of a decade, when he and Dunbar had been a little thinner around the waist and closer to what you might call friends, Herring had come over to help him put down shingles, for the pitch was steep and Dunbar wasn't the ablest being on his feet. He'd got Dunbar to park his tractor on the west side of the house, and then he tied a length of rope to the tractor's axle. The other end he draped over the ridge and, with it cinched around his waist, worked on the eastern valleys. When it came time to install the western valleys, he hollered down to Dunbar, who fired up the tractor and drove it around to the east side of the house, all the while still connected to Herring, as if he were a sort of puppeteer. Herring hadn't been here since, he thought, and it was strange. They'd fallen out one day at the wharf. Someone had a radio going and there were pints of rum and shine being passed from fisher to fisher as if they were sandbags needed to dam the flow of some surging river. One fellow had passed around tabs of acid. It was sunny and dry and windless, and the gulls and flies were everywhere. He couldn't recall exactly how, but somehow or another he and Dunbar had gotten real messed up on acid and proceeded to start a punch-up over whether or not the name of the band who had written "What's Up?" was named 4 Non Blondes or Concrete Blonde.

Dunbar didn't seem to be around. His rig, which had a bed cap, was set by the barn. Herring took the path down to the shore, and as he reached the crest of the slope, where the lines of the waters grew less imprecise and harder, more marked, where the distinction between light and shadow came to be an academic idiom, he heard the humming of a tune, a plaintive strand of words about some faraway mountains, and there was Dunbar, walking with his pony, Stanislaus, who was, with handsome ease, dragging a load of Irish moss. "Good little tune there, eh," said Herring. Dunbar gave him a hearty hello. He seemed happy around Stanislaus. Being half-cut helped, too.

Herring said, "I couldn't carry a tune in a goddamn bucket."

Dunbar laughed, and Herring knew then and for certain that the man was drunk, because he never laughed.

Dunbar said that he used the moss to make little batches of ice cream, tinctures, too, that kept the body in health. Herring was surprised by this information. This hobby struck him as fey, too delicate for a man such as Dunbar Gillis. Herring attributed it to boredom and a lack of friends. Dunbar said, "Sometimes when I eat too much sugar I feel a tingle in my toes at night." And then he said, "Founder of feet in horses is just like diabetes." His trial was sometime in August. He had pleaded not guilty, which meant the Supreme Court. Dunbar said that he had one count against the Canada Shipping Act and one of criminal negligence causing death. Herring produced the muffins and the hundred hits of acid in their bag. "You know Red John, huh?" he said. Dunbar said that he did. "These are his, I spose, but I think it's fair to say that he's forgotten about them. And even if he hasn't, I don't think he'd mind knowing that you've them."

Dunbar was a little mystified. "Aw, g'way. By Christ, what am I to do with these?"

Herring said, "Well, take 'em if you like. Just don't snort the darn things or you'll get soaked like I did." Dunbar held the bag up and scrutinized the contents.

"The muffins are to say thank you for the ride, just so you know," said Herring.

They got a fire going out at the pit, and they stood around the flames as darkness fell, the lines of their faces rendered queer and alien, these creases of skin alive and bred by the coruscations as if braids of rope made to stand, like stalks of infertility, soulless, resurrected without purpose.

Rope is of no use if it cannot knot. He and Euna had tied a knot.

They ate the muffins and had some ice cream. Dunbar splashed some shine down his throat and loaded more wood into the fire. Stanislaus watched, his eyes black ditches. The fire spat at the men its staccato bursts of harmless rage.

"I've got a colony of rats living in the barn," said Dunbar. "Some nights I come out and just hide up in the rafters and you can see 'em, as big as dogs, their eyes just twinklin' in the dark. Wherever there's feed there's rats, eh. Came out in the morning one time and they'd even tipped over one of my feed mixers. The damn thing's the size of a refrigerator. I get traps from Cardigan Feed and I've got it down so that I'm killing about forty to fifty of 'em every night."

Herring said, "Jesus, that's quite a battle."

"Ya wanna burn some rats with me?" said Dunbar.

"No, I'm good for now," Herring said. "How's Leigh doing?"

"I don't know. I haven't talked to him in years," said Gillis. His voice was as calm and as straight as a piece of lumber floating down a river. Resigned. He said, "I'm beginnin' to see that it's easier bein' dead."

Herring said, "My psoriasis was so bad last year I thought about putting a bullet into my head." And immediately, he felt as if he'd given too much away, and the thought stung him a great deal. He didn't enjoy the sensation of such talk. Such disclosures felt as if he had become his own butcher, had cleaved a hunk of his own flesh, and in a moment of thorough vulnerability, had then offered this to the man, the confidant, before him.

Herring tried to split some logs, but found that his body was aching, could feel the pain jolt through him. Dunbar watched him set the axe into the stump and walk back to the light. From the darkness, a bird called out, and this sounded like a knife being pulled out of a drawer.

Dunbar said, "I used to work with this fellow from China Point. Joey Beers, was his name, except that we all called him Shockie. Didn't matter what he was doing, he was gonna get electrocuted. You could be fishin' the Greek River or clearing trees on the Fox River, and wham, electrocuted. It was coming for him, huh. He just kinda resigned himself to this fact. One time, we were framing houses in town there and Shockie gets the fucks put to him. I got into the ambulance with him and all the way to the hospital he kept getting jolted. Now, somehow or another, the current had got caught in his steel toes. Electricity does strange things, eh." Dunbar rubbed his face. "What I done changed the wharf. Changed the wharf forever."

Herring said, "Every harbour is different."

Dunbar stumbled into the barn and returned with a sack of dead rats. "Now, yer sure ya don't wanna?"

As he rode home in the dark, Herring had a foreboding of a truck coming over the last rise to strike him, mangle him dead, spread him into the ditches like seed. He was certain. But no trucks came at all. He rode on, in silence and in dread, wondering, alarmed that he could have been so convinced. The sound of the cranks and the rubber tires, the music of his own faith turned against him.

—

Wallace and Ruth Gray came out to visit him. He didn't know them too well. They were notorious Bible-thumpers, and their presence could be more than a little unpleasant. If you entered into conversation with them, you noticed immediately that they were always talking at you. They didn't like to share the tiller, so to speak. Where they were headed was always back to God. And so, the moment he got talking to them at the door, Herring wished that he was all-over-the-pond drunk. People could tolerate swallowing God better if they were also swallowing drink. The Grays had a son who was finishing his NHL career, after having won a couple of Cups with the Detroit Red Wings. He'd brought the Cup home to My Bonnie Harbour, and when Herring refused to drink beer from it, he'd said, "Yer the only fella who's ever refused to drink out of this thing." He'd even married a Hollywood actress, if you could believe it. As far as anyone could tell, he'd mostly turned his back on his parents. The couple also had a grown daughter named Nettie, a few years younger than Herring, and she'd married a fellow from My Bonnie River by the name of Hedley Moore. There was some trouble there, but as to its precise nature Herring didn't know, and didn't care to know. They had another son, Benjamin, but he'd had some manner of emotional problems and wasn't really seen all that much. Nettie, like both their sons, hadn't been around in a long while, though she did work at the library in My Bonnie River, and it was this distance, this inexplicable wedge between parent and child that had consumed and drained the vitality out of all of them. Herring felt for them. The matter of sons and daughters had been a trial for them, you could just see it in their eyes, the haunted plague of their own undoing that the both of them held within their hearts. God had judged their parenting and found them wanting. This verdict had very nearly defeated them.

Herring made them tea and served them some misshapen muffins. He watched them look the place over, the plywood in the door, the strange cat, the hole in the floor of the living room. Wallace and Ruth were probably near seventy and about the same height. They dressed conservatively, in blues and greys, which is to say that they likely shopped together, and their voices were always soft, like the sound of people gathered lying in a meadow for some ritual of the seasons, blessing crops, or whatnot. People like Wallace and Ruth were easily made to be the butt of jokes, and they knew it as well as anybody. Still, they persisted, quietly and with an unwavering assurance.

Ruth put her elbows on her knees and looked at Herring. "I'd like you to know that we prayed for you each and every day that you were out there," she said. "We prayed for the Lord to inspire vigilance, that He visit you in your storm, your moment of need." She produced her Bible and opened it. Ruth began to talk about Paul's letters to Timothy, about praying for kings, about how God desired each man to be saved, because Jesus was a kind of ransom so that each of us may have freedom. About the importance of not giving up. The three of them sipped quietly. Wallace smiled while he chewed his muffin. Herring found that he appreciated them for being here, saying what they were. There was no frustration or anger in him. He noted a bit of smugness, as if he should be more appreciative that their prayers had saved him, but he let this go, for he understood it.

"When I was out there, in the water, I thought about what Father Standing had told me about this fella named Saint Anthony. How he went to Rimini there, in Italy, to preach, and how all the heretics told him to shove off, you know. About how he went to the shoreline and began preaching to the waters and the fish started showing up, just droves of fish," said Herring.

Wallace said, "Well, that's lovely. Just lovely. But we believe, essentially, that God's grace touches everyone. That He elected you to fall into those waters and that His grace alone saved you."

Herring said, "I just imagined that I was like Anthony, standing around, and that if you talked for long enough, someone was bound, like the fish, to show up. And so, I talked, and the fish showed up. I seen them." And then, he swallowed roughly a number of times, as if he was having difficulty breathing. Wallace moved as if to help him dislodge the muffin in his throat. Herring kept him back with his forearm. "It's okay, Wally. I'm not choking here," he said. Herring stood up from the table and walked upstairs to the bathroom for a respite, to hide his tears. He held his Murphy hairs in his palm, and then he set this back on the sill of the window. The soft blaze of the world, all things draped under that ivory colour, the white of absolutism and kings. He was struck by the notion that there was so much in him that he felt he could share with people, that quite suddenly there were things he felt he could speak of with some accuracy. He realized, in that moment, staring at his own mug in the mirror, his face as red and wet as a plate of lobster, that he had learned something of value. He couldn't quite put a name to it, but it was beginning to make itself known to him. All he had to do was pull it from the murk and bring it into the light of day, so to speak. He also realized that what he had just admitted to Wallace and Ruth had been a kind of betrayal. He was trying to tell them the truth. Hell, he wanted to tell them the truth. But when his mind reached for the words to express himself as he had truly been, he ended up fabricating things, but not in an evil, or corrupt way. He wondered if he should tell them more of what he was thinking, of what he had thought out there, frozen stiff, a bottle in search of a message. Would he have to share each beggarly lie after beggarly lie until he was able to admit a greater truth? If he shared these things, would they mean anything to those that listen? Didn't they have to earn his trust? And would this sharing somehow weaken him? He'd never figured out how to be around other people. He was always thinking that they wanted something from him or that they wanted to hurt him. Everything was a transaction. He knew this was the ultimate way of things. There was no escaping this notion.

He went back down, and the three of them talked for quite some time. Herring didn't know doctrine the way they did, and he wasn't in the mood for debate. He didn't say that prayer was a bunch of baloney. He didn't want to hurt their feelings. He listened to what they were saying, but most of it truly confused him, dazed his mind, and he felt the way that he felt in high school. He felt dumb, as if he were there to be made to feel dumb. But he remained content that they had done this thing, that they had thought of him when he had been lost. At the very least, they were, in their own way, trying to be kind. And anyway, the business of telling others what it was that you actually believed was immensely difficult. He was pleased that Wally and Ruth were still interesting in trying.

He said, "You know, we get things so wrong, but we keep going, don't we?" and they had all agreed that this was true and fundamental.

When they left, he drank a few glasses of cool water. In all of his various folds he had grown sweaty and damp. His muscles were exhausted by impractical tensions. He and the cat went for a walk, and when they got back to the house, Herring realized that he had been visited by God out in the waters, a god that he didn't believe in. He looked at the cat and, raising his hands, said, "It's queer, eh. What a damn pickle."

—

Herring was set near the hole in the floor, making a list in a little notepad. To do this properly, he was going to have to tear the entire floor up. He'd cut through a bunch of the floor joists, and so he was going to need four lengths of two-by-ten to sister them. He reckoned that he would put down oak on top of the sheathing. He could call a lumber mill in Montague for prices. He had about two hundred square feet before him. He would have to patch the plaster of the ceiling, too, and he wasn't good with this kind of stuff at all. This was going to be a pricey affair. He still had to replace the sliding doors, as well. It was all starting to feel a bit overwhelming. He made some coffee and turned on the radio. Iraqi troops were moving to take back control of Baghdad while Clinton and Obama were vying for leadership of the Democratic Party.

He wound out the hoist by clamping onto it with a pair of channel locks, and then he set about removing the skirting boards with an ancient hammer and a nifty little ten-inch pry bar. As he was doing this, the phone rang. It was a nurse from Kings County Memorial. He had missed his appointment to have his bandages changed. Herring asked if he might be able to get in that afternoon. The nurse said that this would work. Any time around supper would be dandy.

He removed the skirting boards, stacking them out on the porch. He pulled a few floorboards up to see how it would go, then used his circular saw to segment them into lengths that the stove could manage. It was going to be a haul, all right. There must be about a million nails in these things. "Some hellish," he said to the cat. "But we'll be warm for a month come winter." He ate an apple and picked the skin out of his teeth. He fed the cat some mackerel and wondered if Dunbar Gillis would mind giving him a ride into the hospital. Even if he refused, it was an excuse to see him, spend some time with the man. He'd sensed a devastating kind of loneliness, one that had rooted itself quite firmly within the guts of the fellow.

—

He caught a ride with Joe, who just happened to be passing through. Joe said, "I seen a weasel down at the wharf the other day." "You mean Miles Mackenzie?" said Herring. "He was hiding under the stringer. I heard he was jumping onto boats, trying for food. You never want to corner a weasel. He'll rip yer throat right out." A road crew was patching holes out on the way to Montague and they came to a rest by a young woman in an orange vest holding a stop sign attached to a length of grey, polybutylene pipe. From around the bend in the road there was some hooting and hollering going on. Obviously, there was some kind of hold up. Joe and Herring got out of the rig and walked over to the shoulder where there were some machines sitting, burning fuel and emitting this great wave of heat. On the roller was an old fellow named Randall Reid. He wore a toque and a pair of aviators, and he smoked tobacco in a pipe. A great shroud of smoke enfolded him in its cerements, and Randall expelled a great gob of phlegm. "A few tears for Stephen Harper," he said, looking at his wet handiwork on the ground. Joe asked him what on earth he was doing back at work. Randall said that he'd come out of retirement because he was bored of driving his wife to the mall. There was more to life than just filling bags and emptying wallets. But he didn't have the heart to tell her what he really thought of it all. He puffed on his pipe, sliding his lips over the bit and clamping the stem between his teeth, making the smallest of ticks, like an idea clicking into place. "So, I guess that says a lot about me," he said. "Boy, I'd hate to be working a lute or a shovel. It's gotta be forty degrees round that bend there by the arse of those trucks. One of the boys up there has paved his way through nineteen years and two heart attacks. Only last week he got into a punch-up with a fella on a Harley who couldn't bear the wait. He has this aluminum lute and his hands are just green from it. Not even diesel will take it off. There's even a fella up there with a goddamn face tattoo, if you can believe that."

Farther down the road, a crew of convicts was pushing brooms, cleaning the shoulders of the road, and farther still was another pair of fellows from Sleepy Hollow, ridding the ditches of empty mickeys and beer bottles. One of these fellows, the older of the two, whenever he found an old cigarette butt in the grasses, he'd put it to his lips and see if he could get a bit of flame going to it because you just never knew until you tried. About every other mile or so there was an old mailbox in the grasses, shattered and unremembered, put there by the winter plows. Some of them even had a bit of mail still in them.

Joe dropped Herring off at the doors of the red brick hospital and said that he'd be back through in an hour or so to fetch him. Herring said, "It's no bother, Joe. I can just put the ol' thumb out on Main Street there." Joe pretended to smack him. "Fool, I'll be back for ya," he said.

A nurse with reddish hair and a thick pair of glasses asked him to take off his splash pants and put on the little gown that had been laid out for him on the bed. She changed his bandages quite methodically and with great care and gentleness. She said that his wounds looked good. "It must've been quite a thing that you've went through," she said.

Joe must have forgotten about him because he never came back around, and so Herring had to walk down to the drag and put his thumb out, just like the old days.

—

Stanislaus was standing guard at the barn when Herring cycled down the lane. The horse had a rather strange carriage to it, an agitation like you'd see in repentant drunkards staggering home, a desire for immediate abstinence, a burning need to undo what has just been enacted. A reversal of fortune. Herring tried for the doors, but the horse advanced, eyes ablaze and nostrils flaring, teeth bared and ready to chomp. How had it gotten free of its paddock? Herring stumbled and landed poorly onto the grasses, and he felt a bolt of pain come alive in him. The pony stepped over. Herring's nerves trembled in him as he made for the barn. He opened the doors and a great sea of rats scurried for the darkness, hissing and chattering. He could smell shit and poison and brine and the decay of it all nearly made his guts empty. He fought this sensation as best he could, navigating his way through a widespread succession of fish trays, each one loaded to the brim with Irish moss. Each one titanic and darkly glistening, the batteries of some alien device. He found the light switch and pushed it upward. His eyes readjusted to the light and his ankles throbbed with discomfort. Dunbar Gillis, in his greasy denims and his stained flannel jacket, was dangling from a length of rope cinched over a beam, a puddle of urine and excrement beneath. A wooden chair upon its side. His pupils so hardened with dilation that his eyes were like something created by a glassblower, his tongue rigid in the world, a coral pizzle. Herring found a ladder and cut the man down, the only noise his own laboured and fitful breathing and the blade of the knife murmuring through the fibres. Stanislaus poked his head in and watched. Behind him, outside, everything was still. Dunbar's body coiled upon the dirt like a pastry. Herring rolled him onto his back and locked his fists together and beat upon the man's chest until these blows sounded toneless, without vibration. He was sweating at an incredible rate, and an acrid smell wafted up from his clothing. His head was buzzing, and he had to brace himself from falling over.

He ran into the house and called for the ambulance and then ran back out to the barn. Just a daub of panic.

Some feet from the body, a nail fixed a piece of paper to a post. Herring took this down. Dunbar's handwriting was a chain of jejune hacks, a runic inscription. The note said that he hoped that Herring would be the one reading this, that he could give Stanislaus to Chessel

Glover as a way to replace Reuben. He thought Chessel would treat him better anyway. There was a line that said, "Whatever you do, do not get in touch with Sally, my sister," and there was thick pen mark under this to highlight its import. Herring could have his rig, too, if he liked. Everything else was to go to Dunbar's nephew, Leigh. It was the right thing to do. Herring was to call his brother-in-law, Garfield, and Leigh whenever he had a moment to spare, though it wasn't of the utmost importance. "I suspect people were kind of waiting for this to happen," he wrote "Well, in a way, so was I."

A yard or two from Dunbar's boots was the bag of acid that Herring had brought only the other day, plastic and barren.

—

Sheila had her head in her hands. With his words, Herring was pushing and prodding her as best he could. They were at her place, in Georgetown, and it was dark out. She said Gerry had been in a bad way. "He's fucked up all the time. He looks like death warmed over," she said. She couldn't get through to him. Herring reached across the table and took her hands away from her face. He looked at her and she looked away, briefly, and then she looked back. And then, there wasn't too much more to say, he reckoned. His intensity, his adamance, had initially scared her.

"I seen him drinking fucking Lysol, for Christ's sake," she said.

Herring winced. This had gotten nasty. He was angry with the family. They preferred to act as if nothing was the matter with Gerry, to stick their heads in the sand. All of this had been going on far too long. But maybe this wasn't the case, and they didn't really know what he knew. Herring thought Gerry'd probably gone over to the other side to fish with Hiram Macrae, which is what he always did when he felt that he'd fucked up a certain situation too much.

"He always had guts of steel," said Herring. He gave Sheila a hug and the feel of her, the touch of a woman in her hoodie and sweatpants, just about split him.

—

In the morning, Herring threw a pad and a sleeping bag in the back of Dunbar's rig and locked the hatch, and though it was still dark out when Herring picked up Leigh, Leigh saw the bag and got anxious. He didn't like to be away from home for too long. He had all of his little routines. Herring told him not to worry. At most, they'd only be the day.

On the way to the first ferry at Wood Islands, Herring and Leigh passed Venerable Mike walking with his mighty staff of hazel along the shoulder of the shore road. With a honk and a quick crank of the wheel, Herring pulled over and opened his door. He hopped out and gave Venerable Mike a fine wave. The monk squinted a bit, for Herring was directly in the light of the sun and, understanding who it was, gave him a wave back, his teeth bared with joy, white and polished, fresh cream in a beaker.

"So, you've a new truck, eh?" said Venerable Mike, taking the man's hand.

"Well, it's a tad complicated. How are ya?" said Herring. He shook the monk's hand carefully.

"Very fine," said Venerable Mike. "And you?"

"I'm getting there, I spose," said Herring. "Still breathing, anyway."

"Fishermen always drift home, don't they? It's a lovely day," said Venerable Mike, looking down the road for signs of any traffic that might ruin the serenity of their little moment together. There wasn't any, and this pleased him. Mike looked at Leigh, asleep in the cab. Leigh's knuckles were remarkably hairy things. Up top he was going bald. It was as if his arms were plastic conduits and some electrician was pulling his hair through, leaving them exposed as they were upon his hands so as to allow further wiring, further connections. "I know him. He's been coming to meditation classes. Leigh, right?" Herring nodded. Venerable Mike curved his arms out and puffed his cheeks to indicate that Leigh was a hulk of a thing, and then he planted his staff into the dirt and studied its shadow. He moved the staff, and the shadow moved. A heron flew up from the shore, its silhouette like a shard cast from a potter's kiln. Venerable Mike looked at Herring's bandages and the stark baldness of the man's head. Little pills of white were starting to come back in disparate splotches, like a map of some former world. Mike ran a hand over his own head. The crown was without its former colonization.

"I'm struggling to remain eminent, but yours is looking like it'll be a full pasture again. Any tips?" said Venerable Mike.

"No, not really. Well, potatoes make good french fries, I spose," said Herring. "We're as smooth as spuds. But anyway, the bald and the beautiful."

They laughed. Venerable Mike leaned on his staff as if to test its flexibility.

"Well, I'd best be going," said the monk.

"Enjoy the day," said Herring.

The monks were building another residence up in Heatherdale, and a story had been circulating that a bunch of them would sneak into the construction trailers at night and on the weekends and use the laptops to just gorge themselves on pornography. The head honcho for the general contractor, the fellow who signed all the cheques, so you knew the stories were at least slightly legitimate, had come in early on a Monday morning and found a young monk asleep at the wheel, so to speak. These monks were a strange lot. They were always waving at you and they seemed eerily content, no matter the day or the hour. Herring was suspicious of happiness. Always had been. He wasn't so certain it was actually a thing. There were stories, too, about the nuns in Irish Montague and Brudenell having indiscriminate sex with local fellows. Stories about younger monks and nuns, just kids, really, who'd paid an arm and a leg to travel across the world to live in neglect and depravity. These things made the mind reel. And here was Venerable Mike, beatific, just going with the flow. You never wondered about the demons he had in him, mostly because his very presence made you worry so damn much about the demons that you may or may not have in you.

In the gravel lay a June bug the colour of soldered copper, over on its back, its little legs articulating methodically into the skies above it, either a strange kind of drunken celebration or the movements of a priest exorcising some devil. He must have made his way up from the fields. Herring turned him over and sent him on his way. "There ya go, little fella," he said. "There's trees on the other side." Venerable Mike had slowed his stride and was watching this, and then he turned crisply, like a flag about to be folded for storage, and marched on. Herring hopped back into the rig and turned the key. The engine grumbled into existence, an unhinged and demented dog needlessly guarding its bowl, and Herring rolled past the monk. The both of them shared another wave. You could feel the heat rising, as if they were all in a pot on some stove.

Rosella Herring worked the toll booth, and when she saw Herring she said, "Jesus, you're still alive, are you?"

Herring said, "That's what they tell me, I spose."

Rosella was a little old spinster, and she shook all the time, as if she had an earthquake for a shadow. She was stuck in a turtleneck that she'd likely knitted herself sometime in the early days of the Cold War. She said, "And you're alive enough to leave the Island, are you?"

Herring nodded and waited for his change.

"Well," said Rosella, "don't feel that this round-trip ticket is legally binding, eh. Maybe there's a pile of drugs that you could move into on the mainland. They got them igloos way up north. It could be like that, what."

The ferryman directed them where to park. Leigh said he was happy to stay in the rig and sleep. Herring said that you can't do that, you have to get out of your vehicle, and gave the lad a motivational shove. "You know, this thing used to be just riddled with mice," said Leigh. "My mother was terrified of mice. Would scream like a li'l girl if she seen one runnin' about. We always had bags of birdseed in the house and the mice would get in 'em and just eat themselves these tunnels. We had a mouse die on the back lip of our wood stove and it rotted and turned to dust so that ya could blow on it like a dande-lion." The two of them wandered up to the restaurant and ordered two Islander breakfasts. The toast was kept in pairs on paper plates in one of those glass displays that rotated and was supposed to look appetizing. The fellow behind the counter, who had too much energy given the hour, reached in to fetch Herring his white toast, and he fumbled the plate and dropped the bread onto the floor. The fellow said, "I guess that toast is toast."

They got a table by the window and watched the other commuters populate the seating area. The sky was the colour of a peach and the waters reflecting this rind, these reds and yellows, as calm and cool as hot rolled steel.

You could tell the truckers by the general shapes of their bodies because they were all as big as haystacks. But as to what everyone else did, you just kind of had to guess. One fellow was reading from the collected works of Shakespeare, moving one finger under the words, like an ox plowing a field. Leigh assumed that every couple, regardless of age, were American tourists. He'd look at one couple and say "tourist," look to another and say "tourist." "What the hell are they doing here anyway?" he said. Leigh kind of talked like a typewriter. So, this got old fast. There were a number of families taking their sons and daughters to hockey and ringette tournaments. They all had a uniform level of anxiety to them. Marcelina and Marceline enjoyed things like soccer and piano, but their sense of themselves wasn't as invested in the results of the game. Herring liked this about them. It was a sign of maturity, he thought, and though he never told Euna this, it impressed him as much as it also scared the hell out of him. Euna worried that they weren't being properly socialized, which was also likely the case. "They need to learn about how to lose and how to win," she said. Herring thought that they were learning these things just by watching their parents dance around the truth of things, and this made him nervous. He didn't enjoy the feeling that his children, who were still quite young, were so able and so willing to quietly condemn him. The imbalance of it made him wobble. But maybe what seemed to him to be judgment in their eyes was something else entirely. He didn't know. Maybe he should just ask them. Euna was right, though. They did need to learn how to have fun with people their age. They needed to learn to work with others. Growing up was about having a bit of slack on the leash, about being an idiot for as long as others could bear it. When they had all lived together, like a family, Herring had often thought about the day when all of their periods would synchronize. Up until they left he had lived in terror of this event. Now he missed this fear, and this realization struck him hard in his guts.

Through the glass, the sun was hot on their necks and their faces. The lobster boats out on the waters were like peppercorns spread upon a tablecloth.

—

The seasons that Gerry had lobstered out of Pictou, he worked for a fellow by the name of Hiram Macrae, who hailed from a little place called Lismore and drove a rig with a wooden bed on it. The first time Herring had met him, in the parking lot of St. Mary's Church there, Hiram said, "Just so's ya know, the best lobster in the world is caught right here, in Lismore," and he pointed at the ground beneath his feet to emphasize this point. "Some eye-talian fella once said the three greatest wonders of the world are the pubic hair of a blond woman, the clean taste of an orange, and lobster." Hiram tucked some chew into his mouth and wobbled his ankles. "This, my friend, is the real Holy Trinity." Herring said, "Well, I've had all three, so I guess I'm doing pretty okay."

Hiram had been contracted by the council to help them get back on their feet with the lobster. They'd had a series of bad seasons, and they wanted some guidance with methods and gear and whatnot. Someone must have believed that Hiram knew what he was doing well enough to convey this knowledge to others, but the relative afford-ability of his services was likely the more decisive factor. When Hiram first showed up at Pictou Landing, he deduced fairly quickly that the pulp mill pouring wastewater into the river upstream, to the west, was contaminating the water. It wasn't rocket science. The water was black and looked in some spots to be boiling. He figured it took about an hour for this stuff to reach the straits. He didn't say anything about it. Anyway, who was he gonna tell? Who was gonna listen to him? The Natives seemed to know what was up, but they were pretty tight-lipped about everything. Sometimes he'd flick a butt over the rail, and he could swear that he heard a little puff of an explosion. He was a little nervous, truth be told. Getting burned had always scared the bejesus out of him. He was straightforwardly and as a matter of principle against cremations. After a few days, though, he stopped worrying about it. At the end of the day, fishing in boiled and contaminated waters didn't seem all that strange, compared to other stuff. Anyway, it only took the council a few weeks to realize that they'd found a dud, that what separates one man from the next is often just a matter of luck and resources and efficiencies. Hiram had never considered things like organization and productivity. He fished for a living. Efficiency was about the same to him as a hammer to a barber.

—

Herring took the 106 to the 104, and then at Sutherland's Corner he took the shore road to Lismore. Leigh slept pretty much the whole drive, so quiet at some points that Herring worried his heart had given out on him, and he'd reach over and squeeze the man's nose. Leigh would let out a holler and snap awake and Herring would say, "Just making sure yer still breathing, is all." And Leigh, seeing the reason in this, would promptly doze off yet again. This grew to be a kind of game. The boy slept like a goddamn teenager in a bedroom with no light.

Herring drove down to the wharf and parked near the fish plant. Boats were being unloaded and the generators at the plant were emitting their high and thin whimpers, sounding like a barn full of pregnant cows.

Hiram stepped off the transom of his boat, the *Barely Legal*, and said to Herring, "It's a fair day out there. Some good spurts. Broke the eye of a bunch of schools of herring out there. They just slide off the hull like yer driving through a cornfield." Heads were turned, uneasily watching the new fellows. Nearby, the crane operator lit a joint. He had a little burner hooked up to a propane tank, and he was boiling a bunch of lobsters. Discarded bottle caps lay all about, pushed by treads into the sands that gathered in the cracks of the asphalt.

Sensing that maybe a fight was brewing, a few other fishermen gathered, about fifteen of them, all lined up like babushka dolls. "And now look who's here, back from the dead." Hiram offered Herring a handshake. Herring let the arm dangle. Hiram's mouth like worms in a pot of soil. He admired the bandages of the Islander, and then he looked at Leigh. Hiram's own deckhand, an older fellow who had the musk on him of a bachelor long unacquainted with the finer details of carnal knowledge, stood beside him, hands hung at his side like punctured bags of milk. Two sets of two, sizing each other up. Hiram said, "Would ya look at this gommie. Hands on 'im like a bundle of bananas." Leigh shuffled forward, barrelled his chest, and Hiram backed right up, his rubbers smacking the bones of his legs as if a rug was being beaten, his hands up in a demonstration of his peacemongering. "Woah, woah, woah, there, big fella. I'm just pokin' about," said Hiram. "Calm yer hormones." Leigh looked crazier than shit, his face a gasoline fire upon a wintry field. "We're just a regular bunch of gorillas down at the wharf here, ain't we?" The crane operator chuckled, motioned for his joint to be returned to him. Herring asked him where Gerry was. "Shit, Gerry took on a fish infection a while back. I drove him to the hospital in New Glasgow. Aberdeen. Haven't seen 'im since. I spose he's in Pictou. He was pretty useless." Realizing that no blows would be had, most of the fishermen returned to their boats, silent things defeated by the unremitting boredom before them. Herring looked at Hiram's deckhand and said, "Is this true?" The man said that this was the case, though he looked about as aware of exactitudes as a skunk in a hall of mirrors. "I seen him there the other day. Fingers so swollen all his nails come right off."

Herring and Leigh walked back to the rig. Some of the fishermen were standing by it, uncomfortably close. They were itching for a fight. One of them said, "You Island boys gawon back home where men are men and sheep are nervous." Leigh moved this fellow from the door of the truck like he was adjusting a clothespin on the line. "Where I'm from we do three things well. Fuck, fight, and fish. And before I do any of these, I'm gonna need ya to buy me dinner first," he said.

The fellow looked dejectedly at his boots. "Them's the rules, bud. Chin up."

Not even five minutes down the road, Leigh was back to sleeping.

—

A number of dogs were running around the Landing wharf, weaving about the trucks, stopping to investigate wheels, to sniff and urinate on hubcaps. Scratched and worn cube vans were getting loaded up with lobster, the engines of the forklifts strained, their exhausts emitting horizontal teardrops of smoke, and gulls were walking about the pavement as if they were looking for the light switch in a dark room. A rumpled fellow sat on a lifeless motorcycle, his face confused, flicking at the cover on his tachometer with the nail of his middle finger. Off in the distance, a truck engine ran rich and burst like a rifle discharging, the sound reverberating in strange squeezes that put one in mind of a jellyfish propelling itself through the water. Men milled about in oil gear, adjusting their braces, smoking feverishly, crushing beers with abandon, their sweaters and hats as wrinkled as the skin of their faces. There was money in the air. The wharf was a magnificent and sumptuous teat, and these men had come to partake of it, to beguile and seduce it. Some were better than others, and usually the condition of their truck indicated how well they allured. The air was dry and bantam storms whirled to and fro, breaking, as soft as a lover's breath. There were a few picnic tables by the curb of the wharf with little tins at their feet stuck with cigarette butts in a way that made them look like porcupines. Men sat at some of these, arms riddled with tattoos, inhaling shatter from between serrated knives. Everywhere was peeling paint and flies, steel sheets and steel bars, everything rusted and hot to the touch, rope and plastics piled haphazardly here and there.

Gerry was seated at one of these picnic tables, his feet balanced on their toes, as if he was dangled. His hands were bandaged. There were two plastic bags full of clothes next to him. He was wearing sweat-pants and a collared tee. The hair about his ears damp and greasy, these scoops of tar.

Herring and Leigh got out of the rig and walked abreast down the wharf. Men stopped what they were doing and looked at them. Leigh tightened his hands into fists and kept his gaze straight ahead. Herring could feel his knees go a bit weak. He was petrified, but he kept on walking, marching forward. "Don't make eye contact," he said.

Herring took Gerry by the armpits, and Leigh managed his feet in an untrained army carry. Gerry had pissed himself quite consider-ably and his clothes dripped from the low of his back. Leigh paid the wet no mind. They left the bags of clothes. Some change and a few other trinkets fell out of his pockets as they shuffled back to the truck. They didn't stop. Their muscles were screaming, their faces red and anguished. Leigh was pushing the pace, going full bore, and Herring was anxious that he'd trip over himself, this or one of the gulls, hust-ling as they were. The men at the wharf watched. Leigh let the man's feet down and opened the latch on the cap, then he dropped the tail-gate, and they slid Gerry onto the sleeping bag as best they could. His face was sweaty, and dried slobber was crusted onto his cheeks. Gerry said, "Are we even yet?" They turned him on his side, and then they drove off, casting the gulls into the sky, unsure whether the truck was a hearse or an ambulance.

—

Just as they were slowing down to get in line for the ferry, the car behind them starting honking. Herring and Leigh both turned to look out the back window of the cab. Gerry was leaning over the tailgate, his body governed by spasms that pulled him in and out as if he were an accordion. Leigh slid the window open. "You all right?" he said. "I don't know what's worse," said Herring, "puking or shitting." Gerry wiped vomit from his mouth and patted at the tears upon his red cheeks. "Don't be growling at me," he said.

# NINE

Herring had been really nervous about going back to the wharf. He figured some of the boys would take him as bad luck. He didn't want to be a distraction. But nobody seemed to mind all that much. There was a languid kind of pace to this wharf, very much like a passenger watching a landscape scream by from the back seat of some vehicle. The sun was out and the waters were as still as sapphire. The air smelled of rotting fish and bleach. He and Gerry sat themselves a few yards from the crane, in a pair of white plastic chairs whose legs were so rickety it felt as if they were sitting on picnic cutlery. There was a picnic table there, too, and something of a communal barbecue. Jack MacLeod had just craned his lobster off and was fiddling with the hauler. "Some day, eh?" said Jack. He had a thumbnail in his mouth. He was thinking about something. "The winds are southerly, so the hauls aren't too good. The lobster don't seem to like it. Nobody's gettin' their quota," he said. Deborah stood with her hands down her bibs, looking up at the man on the wharf from behind a pair of fancy sunglasses. On the ground there were flies on thick white ropes like infinite grubs, and blue banding elastics here and there, the odd lobster claw, stiff and yellow like a dog treat. The boats creaking against their mooring buoys and fenders like bored students in ancient desks. Young fellows were loading their jet skis at the slip, their girlfriends nearby in bathing suits and cut-off jeans. Gerry just kind of sat there, smoking as best he could through his bandages. Herring said, "Yeah, it's gorgeous all right." He could see the *M&M* from where they were sat. It looked like an old friend after the airing of some intense grievances. It looked like a kind of political prisoner. Herring could feel his heart break in him, but he sat where he was. Leverett and Lowell came over and said hello, stood nearby for a while.

Leverett said, "What do ya call a cow with no legs?"

"I dunno," said Herring.

"Ground beef."

Gerry giggled.

Leverett said, "What do ya call a dog with no legs?"

Herring said, "I dunno."

Leverett said, "It don't matter. He ain't gonna come anyway," and laughed heartily.

Over the course of the day, nearly every fisherman at the Harbour came over to say hello. Willy Lyon and Louis MacKenzie, bashful and so quiet that Herring could barely make out what they were saying to him. He thanked them for being patient, for saving him. He couldn't figure out what else to say to them to make things right. He needed a bit more time to find the proper script. They seemed kind of embarrassed that they'd been the ones to pull him in. He saw Sheldon Dawe, Jimmy Beck, Howard MacNeil, Eben Daley, Rankin Jackson, and Clarence Clements. Clarence told them a story about getting his strawberries ready, about falling into some mud.

He said, "I was covered. Just covered from arsehole to appetite, huh."

Even Billy Clow came over and said that it was good to see him and Gerry again.

"You boys sure have been put through the wringer," said Billy, gawking at the two of them. "You two are so wrapped up you'll be walking like a pair of Egyptians." Then he said, "Boy, I was so drunk the other night down at Fish Alley, I was barely able to drive home."

When Billy left, Jimmy Beck said, "If that fella hauled up gear that had no lobster in it, he's gonna raise all kinds-a-hell on the radio, saying that somebody else already hauled his gear, because there's no way he's stupid enough to put his traps where there are no fish."

Eben Daley said, "Yeah, the first bit of fog rolls in and he's haulin' yer gear anyway."

"Rum rager, that one."

"Yeah, more like the Rum Ranger."

"The numbers are dying down. I'm all ones and zeroes."

"Well, we had a pretty good year, I'd say. You can't catch 'em twice."

"It's easy on the rubber bands, that's fer sure."

"Boy, the amount of hours I spent out there hauling dumps, all the while staring at the bottom of the tray."

"I'd say we need to make smaller trays."

"Any man that wouldn't fish for a market a dump is an idiot."

"They say we're crazy fer comin' out and fishin' all day fer two trays, but if ya threw fifteen hundred dollars on the floor, who wouldn't pick that up?"

"I'd root through yer foreskin for a market, I swear to Christ."

"You look like yer in a mood."

"I'm always in a good mood, what are ya talkin' about? And if I'm not, I got something to remedy it and it rhymes with mare-ah-wanna."

"From Pugwash to Antigonish, they're gettin' a dollar more for markets and canners than us."

"In Pubnico they're getting three dollars more than everybody else."

"I heard we're getting the shaft because they're saying they paid too much for snow crab."

"Ignorant. That's the only word for it."

A young fellow and his girlfriend had been hired by the port authority to put another layer of paint on the curb of the wharf. The type of yellow you'd see on a taxicab. They worked sheepishly nearby, their eyes downward, apologetic. Rankin said, "You git any of that on my boat and I'll sue ya into yer grave." The boy just blushed and walked over to the east side of the bullpen. Rankin snorted, shook his head, as if this boy and his girlfriend represented the total sum of all that was wrong with the world. Herring said, "Charming as ever, eh Rankin?"

Leigh White drove over, said that he was tinkering about on Dunbar's boat, the *Pair-a-Dice*, that he wasn't really sure what he was going to do about the rest of the season. Maybe the three of them could ride it out together, he said. Herring said the best he could do today was to think about it.

Leigh said, "That's fine by me. I'm just kinda wingin' it, seein' what'll stick." And then Leigh said, "Boy, there's so many barnacles on 'er, it's like dragging a shag carpet up river jus' tryin' to git anywheres."

Herring said, "If you do go out, 'member, when everyone else is running around, hauling gear all over the Bank, you walk. You walk."

Joe McInnis and Isaac Cahoon came over and offered them some beers. Herring said that he was good. Gerry just looked away, real quiet. Joe thought this was a little hoity-toity, but oh, well. They looked pretty terrible.

"Well, fellas, ya looked good from far, but yer far from good," said Joe.

They played a couple of hands of poker while Joe cooked some lobster with saltwater in a steel pot. Cooking lobster in unsalted water was tantamount to sacrilege, and each man offered his endorsement of this as fact with a nod of the head or a grunt that came gently from the bottom of the throat.

"Leave me some fresh canners, there Joe, so I can cook 'em myself," said Herring.

Joe said, "Diesel went up almost a penny overnight." Gerry was swilling down his orange pop so fast his eyes were leaking. Joe said, "Careful Gerry, you'll turn into a Popsicle."

Gerry won every game.

Isaac said, "Gerry, you've a goddamn horseshoe up yer arse." He gave Gerry what remained of his pack of smokes.

Joe had a cutting board and a hammer, and he bust open the lobster as best he could. They ate a bit of lobster and sat there like some peanut gallery, watching the boys pull up to the tank and refuel. Joe said, "I knew this guy who could catch bats with his hands. He was from the Big Smoke, and he'd catch one or two at night just standing out on his deck. When he wasn't playing hockey, he had a little side gig, building and selling houses for the bats, too. One time we went to a strip joint in the city there, and there was this black midget goin' 'round, slapping all the girls on their arses, trying to tuck bills into their butt cheeks. They'd just pat him on the head. The place was in the midst of renovations. They had all these shoring jacks up, and the pipes in the ceiling were all exposed. When the girls were dancing, ya could hear the shitter flush. There was a Christmas tree all lit up on the stage, too. Around the back of the place ya could get breakfast, if ya liked. And out on the street, later, this fella comes up to me, real drunk, and says that the last word in yule-issies was yes. I told him that sounded about right, but I never knew what he was on about. Oh, well." He yawned, his mouth a cavern. Even he seemed a tad bored.

Joe left Herring with ten pounds of lobster. Isaac patted Herring on the shoulder. "It was good seein' ya," he said, and they drove off. Some carpenters had built a new shack for the port authority. Nearby was a garbage bin the size of a swimming pool, full of crows picking for food, squawking at one another. Leigh said, "They call 'em a murder of crows." Herring said, "A parliament of owls. I like that one." "A bunch of hummingbirds is called a brilliance." Gerry said, "What do they call a bunch of starlings?" Herring said, "I don't know." Gerry said, "How about a shitload of starlings."

A while later, Gerry started to moan. The pain was pretty bad, and he'd left his antibiotics and painkillers at home. Leigh said that he had to drive into Irish Montague anyway, so he could take Gerry home. Herring said, "Gerry, make sure you take yer medication. And make sure you see Sheila. She needs some time with you." Gerry rolled his eyes and waved him off, said, "Yeah, yeah, yeah."

Herring didn't know what was going on with Susan and the boys. Sheila could be trusted to stay close. He'd talked to her, told her what was what.

Leigh and Gerry left, and Herring sat for another hour or so, feeling the sun on his arms and his neck, listening to the clatter from the fish plant, the jangle of forklifts, and the sound of trucks rolling slowly. A man could do just about anything if he had a bit of sun on him. It just brought you alive.

A battered rig was in the middle of the lot, its hood up. Two young fellows were staring into the engine as if trying to communicate with someone who had plunged down a well. Rotten Rick walked by.

One of the boys turned from the truck and said, "Can we get a boost?"

"Sure. What are ya climbing?" said Rotten Rick.

Kemp Reilly, who wore his cap real sloppily and had the strangest set of knuckle tattoos, in that from both faraway and up close they looked like some half-remembered Chinese characters, arrived, and once he'd parked his rig, he doddered over to shoot the breeze, his gait as buckled and skewed as an oaken carriage wheel. He was there to check the books for the day, wanted to know what the scoop was.

Evelyn's red Pontiac was a few steps from the staging, and she had coaxed one of the boys, Lorne Harris, to take a gander at one of her lug nut studs. She'd taken her car in to have a tire changed, and one of the mechanics had broken a lug.

"That's the second time this has happened," she said.

Lorne said, "Well, ya fool me twice. I'd say they like having you come back all the time."

Evelyn said, "The dirty cocksuckers."

Kemp said, "Jeez, the wharf is starting to look like a garage." He put a toothpick in his mouth and walked over to the picnic table where Herring was sitting.

Lorne jacked up the front of the car and got down on his knees. He took the tire off, and then the caliper, the bracket, and the rotor. A can of Liquid Wrench by his side. Evelyn had her shorts and her rubbers on, her hair impossibly long, her tanned legs slathered with floral tattoos. She smoked while Lorne worked, the trucks and forklifts kicking up dust. That fine, symbiont powder of flesh and soil, rendered so by fishermen and gulls and the elements, eternally roaming for ears and eyes and nostrils to alight on, and coating every cab of every rig and every sock in every boot, working its way into every pair of underwear and every bathtub, sleeping in warm beds with linen and pillows, to be there when romance bloomed and children were conceived or when fate called and loved ones departed.

"What's yer plan there, sensei?" said Kemp, shifting his toothpick from the right corner to the left corner of his mouth in a manner that was slightly feminine, as if he were shutting the zipper on a clutch purse. His eyes the colour of gherkins and eyebrows that looked like little moustaches, his hair soft and tapered as if it were morning sunlight.

Herring said, "Jeez, Kemp, I'm still in the business of trying to sort everything out."

"No shame in that game, bud," said Kemp. "Little by little, like the cat eating a herring." Kemp adjusted his pants, pulling the seat of them over his skinny buttocks. He asked Herring why he'd never used his herring as bait. "I had good Canso herring."

Herring said, "The thing about herring is that it's either good or bad, but it can't be clean, it's gotta be dirty, just a mess of oil and guts for it to be of any use, eh."

"Yeah, 'member back in the day, when you could see the flash of 'em in the waters? It was like the sea was on fire." And then Kemp blinked and scrunched his face as if bopped on the nose. He said, "The whole world is changing just too damn fast, what. Ya stop for one sec and you can just feel it on you."

Kemp hugged the man and then stepped quickly away, like a kid who doesn't want to be seen getting dropped off at school by his mother. "We've always had a good thing going here, huh." Kemp looked at his watch. He ought to be on the road. "Listen," he said. "Stay outta trouble. But if you do get into trouble, call me and I'll give you a hand. If ya wanna drive truck for a while, just say the word, huh. I can throw Gerry work, too, so's ya know. Hey, there's always the oil sands, too." Kemp left.

Cephas Hicken, who had been allergic to T-shirts his entire life, pulled up at the wharf and dumped a tray of red lobster shells into the waters. They stayed close to the fenders, bobbing with a kind of hollow conviction, like buoys of dissent. "The gulls'll pick 'em," he said and waved, the braces on his pants taut, over a torso that appeared to be composed of strands of chewed bubble gum all stitched together. He looked like a character from the Old Testament. "Get outta here, Cephas," said Herring. "You'll scare the tourists." Cephas told him to go fuck himself.

Herring called over to Lorne, who was sweating and muttering to himself. "You gettin' 'er fixed up?" Lorne said, "Oh, I'm gettin' fixed on becoming agitated." He'd bit off a little more than he could chew.

"How can I repay ya?" said Evelyn. Lorne shrugged his shoulders while he wiped his hands and his knees with a tiny rag. "You can come home with me, if you like," she said.

Lorne blushed. "If I went home with you, I'd have no home to go home to after."

Evelyn said, "I'm going skinny dipping. You're welcome to come and watch."

Lorne said, "Let's just agree that this is my good deed for the day, huh." Evelyn walked over to the beach, and Lorne stood there in the parking lot, watching her, admiring the reel and tumble of that long, long ponytail, his hand on his heart as if he was both pledging allegiance and taking a heart attack.

Herring thought about the garden, tried to visualize how he wanted it to look when it was all done. He watched, for a time, a crow taking a bath in a puddle of dirty water. He was dozing off a little, when he felt a presence behind him. An elegant blond woman was then sitting next to him. She was Minnie Carver from the television. She smelled of fine perfume.

She said, "You haven't moved all day."

He said, "They'll have to start callin' me benchmark."

And that was about all it took, really.

He drove her into The Muffler, and they were out on the patio, and the both of them were just slugging drinks back. The waitress would come and Herring would think no, no, no, goddamn you, you have no resolve you bloody fool, no principles to you, and he would say, "Oh sure. Another one," and he would throw it down the hatch, as did Minnie. She seemed to have no problem keeping up with him. Minnie asked him how the fishing was going, but he didn't really answer her. She said, "I've always been scared of the water. Must be the Macdonald in me."

He felt like a king among men for about twenty minutes there, because people were looking at him, this lowly fisherman with a beautiful woman, whom everyone knew, at his table, the face of the goddamn Island news. Maybe he was finally winning. Maybe all of his suffering had led him to this moment. He got to thinking. Besides Euna, he'd never really known the beauty of women. Minnie's was intoxicating. He realized this very quickly. Her beauty was a kind of settlement, a kind of non-disclosure agreement. God was saying, "Listen, we can't go on like this, dragging each other through the mud. It's too hard on the wallet. Let's settle." This voice was the way of things, thought Herring. This kind of justice was how the rich and powerful dealt with the annoyances of peasants like him, right? Maybe Minnie, as rough as this sounded, was a kind of hush money, a bribe, put before him. He was tired. So fucking tired. He'd take it. Her skin was so impeccable and her eyes so bright and fierce. He watched her and she seemed, against reason, to come even more alive, more articulate, the drunker she got. Her fingers were nearly immaculate, and the colour of her nail polish just about made his knees shudder. He was sweaty with nerves. And then it was quite dark out, and they were smoking. He knew that he didn't want to be smoking. And yet, still, this desire not to let her down, not to disappoint this total goddamn stranger. The stars were out and the mosquitoes were becoming less noticeable. Minnie sure could talk, he thought. Sometimes he didn't really know what on earth she was gabbing on about. She carried herself so well, was so refined a thing. He thought, I would fight a war for this woman.

Herring pointed up into the sky. "You see that light there?" he said. "That's the *International Space Station*. It circles the earth every ninety minutes." Minnie hugged herself against the cold as she followed his finger. He brought her to his side, scooped her close.

He shouldn't have driven, but he did. He was making a great number of unforced errors tonight, and the little voice in his head sure was good at harping on him, reminding him of this fact. They got back to his situation in one piece, thankfully. Minnie sat at the kitchen table and he poured her a shot of shine. "This stuff's from up near Souris," he said. "Now be careful." He offered her some scallops, but she said scallops didn't like her. He said, "A feed of lobster it is." Herring put some salt water into a large pot on the barbecue and boiled the lobsters Joe had left him. The night was still. He stood at the sink with Minnie and showed her how to get the meat out of them. How you twist the legs and the claws off. How you pull the tail off and cut this in half with a good knife. "Keep yer fingers on top of the knife or you'll lose 'em," he said, crunching the blade through its shell. He showed her how to remove the roe and wedge your thumb down between the shell and the flesh. Showed her how to look for the artery and get this out. Showed her the anus just to gross her out a little. Minnie had another pull of shine. She was stood beside him, and the smell of her, of her perfume, distracted him. He found a crappy nutcracker in the drawer and showed her how to bust the shell on its claws, how to bend the knuckles and pick out the flesh. "See, you go this way, and then you go this way."

"Jeez," she said. "Aren't you tired of lobster?"

He got some hot dog buns and buttered them and toasted these in a skillet. He said, "I wonder who the first person to eat a lobster was? Like, how did that go down, exactly? Did a lobster wash up and someone thought, well, heck, I spose I could try eating that thing? How'd they ever get at the meat?"

Minnie frowned. "You sound like you're stoned."

He said, "You know, it wasn't too long ago, you couldn't get anybody to buy lobster. People used it as fertilizer in their gardens.

Farmers would put it out on their rows. Eighty per cent of the market nowadays is cruise ships and casinos. The way I see it, lobster is just something people eat to distract them from the fact that they're pissing their wages away."

They sat and ate. She was smiling. She seemed happy. There were bits of lobster in her upper teeth. He didn't say anything. He was happy. He said, "Lobster sammies are the best with fog."

"Huh? What the hell is fog?" said Minnie.

"Always asking the tough, hard-hitting questions, eh?" She snorted, and Herring fell deeper in love. He thought about her question for a moment and said, "Oh, you know, it's bread that's mostly white and kinda not really anything. It's not really there." And then she leaned over and kissed him so hard, with such vigour, he thought his teeth were going to be pulled loose.

The lights were off, and they fumbled about for a while. He couldn't really seem to recall how a bra worked, so eventually she had to take over, and she seemed more than a little flustered by his clumsiness. They bumped foreheads. He didn't want to tell her that his arms and legs still hurt pretty bad. He didn't want to tell her how bad he actually was at this kind of stuff. Sex had always kind of scared him. Euna had picked up on this instantly, and she was always so kind and tender. That was her way with these kinds of things. Minnie was aggressive and messy, which unsettled him a little, seeing as she was so put together elsewhere. He'd wanted a bit of romance. Perhaps the both of them were too drunk for romance. He didn't know if he was going to get hard. She started biting him and scratching at his back, and it hurt real bad. He kept her at length as gently as he could manage. He lumbered over her, and she grabbed and swatted at his crotch. They fucked for a little, but neither of them were having any fun with it. She was wriggling beneath him like a fish out of water. Her breath struck him as unpleasant and laboured, and he was pretty sure his smelled like the dog's breakfast, as well. He kissed her again but could not equal her energy. They had come together to build a machine of love, he supposed. A complicated design that they drew forth from themselves in an act of faith and trust. They were racing down a kind of steep hill and, unknown to either, this engine had pedals to it that were spinning as fast as its design would allow. Both of them reached for these levers, the steel of it only wrecking their shins. And then came the matter of steering, and neither of them were in the mood for this kind of fight, this kind of effort.

Minnie passed out, and he pulled the sheets over her body. He watched her form, white contours in the darkness, the slow heave of her breasts. He went downstairs and drank some water. The cat came out and weaved between his legs. He wondered how Minnie would be in the morning. Would she be timid? "Well, she'll definitely be praying to the porcelain god," he said, the cat staring up at him. He fetched it some mackerel, and then they slept together on the chesterfield. He snored and ground his teeth, his stomach rumbling with too many combinations of drink. The cat stretched, got comfortable and real warm.

—

As the sun began to rise, he heard the cooings of a mourning dove. He put coffee on and scrambled some eggs. He could hear movement from upstairs. He was nervous, didn't know how this was going to play out.

Minnie came down and sat at the table. He gave her water and coffee and served her eggs and toast. She said, "It looks like a crime scene in yer bathroom."

"Yeah, that was the last reporter I brought home," he said. "It's only tomato paste." They ate together, but mostly avoided one another's eyes. The cruel scrape of cutlery and the link of teeth.

He said, "Listen, if yer free for the day, maybe you'd like to hang out?"

Minnie set down her fork and helped a piece of egg along into her mouth, patting the course of her lips with her fingers like she was testing a wall for studs. She was chewing and thinking. She looked at him and then glanced out the window by the sink. Her face tightened and grew stern. "Just take me to my car," she said.

They drove to the Harbour. Herring listened to the radio and Minnie stared out the window. There were fellows under the bridge catching gudgeons. Herring gave them a wave. He said, "Do you know how people got to waving?" Minnie grumbled. "Well, it was the easiest way to show that yer hand was free of a weapon, that you weren't going to try and kill each other just yet." Minnie said, "How illuminating." Herring felt himself clam right up. They drove by Keeping's and saw Big Arbot Herring's bicycle outside. Inside, he was sat at the window in his high-visibility vest, one hand in his pocket, splashing coffee down his fat throat. The Mexicans had their shoes up on the roof of the garage next to Keeping's to dry in the sun. The tongues all wrenched out, so that more light could get in.

Minnie said, "Are you sooking?"

"Nope."

"Listen, I'm sorry about last night and—"

"You know what?" said Herring. "Don't. Don't finish yer fuckin' thought."

By the time they drove down Wharf Lane, both of them felt like they had lived an entire life.

As he parked Dunbar's rig, Minnie practically detonated out the door. Joe McInnis was standing at the back of his truck, leaned over into the bed, a smoke in one hand and a beer in the other. He was talking to Tony and Dave Poole. Atwood LeLacheur was there, too, with his border collie, Martin. Tony and Dave called the dog The Great Martini. Tony was talking about a captain he'd worked for back in the day. He said, "Always had the little, white halos under his nose. Ya know me, I've always said that you can do cocaine or you can fish, but you can't do both."

Herring could feel them watching. He walked over to the slip. A flounder appeared out of the depths and climbed its way over the lip of concrete, slithering through the algae, warming itself in the thinner waters. Easy pickings for even the dumbest of gulls. Tony and Dave rolled by in their truck, the window down. Tony said, "The best way to git over a woman, eh, is to git under another." Dave said, "You gotta slay some dragons to git to the princess, huh." Tony said, "I'd say she's seen more cock ends than weekends."

—

The lumber mill in Montague called to say that he would have his oak by Friday afternoon, the latest. "The wood is some nice. Boy, yer just gonna fall in love with it," said the fellow. "Like walking around with moccasins on yer feet all the time 'cos it's so soft, except that it's a hardwood. Anyway." He fed the cat some more mackerel, and then the cat went out and laid in the sun. He threw his bicycle into the back of the truck and drove to Leigh's place. Leigh had just pulled in and had a number of documents in his grubby hands.

Herring said, "How goes?"

Leigh looked defeated, held up the sheaf. He said, "Boy, the hoops ya gotta jump through to get some lobster outta the water is unreal. Our lawyer is a decent enough fella, but I tell you, by the time I get this all sorted out, it'll be landing day anyhow. I've had diarrhea for a week, the stress has been so terrible."

"They have you dancin' a set, huh?" said Herring. He threw him the keys to Dunbar's rig. "I appreciate you lettin' me borrow this thing for as long as you did. It meant a lot."

Leigh didn't brighten all that much.

"Cheer up, buttercup. You can't let money get you down," said Herring. He pulled his bicycle out of the truck. He said, "Here once lied the ghost of Gerry McClellan." Herring threw a leg over the saddle and rolled off.

—

Fletcher Jordan came out to the parking lot and shook his hand. He told Herring that he was just about as red and sweaty as a stallion's boner. They looked at the truck.

Fletcher said, "Well, I did what I could as honestly as I could. Lipstick on a pig, really."

Herring said, "You know, Fletcher, all women are crazy. It's just how much crazy can you live with."

Fletcher nodded, looked over his shoulder to ensure that his mother was out of earshot. He said, "The next woman I date, I'm just gonna go right to the medicine cabinet and see what kind of crazy I'm dealing with."

Herring paid in cash and refused his change. Fletcher insisted that he take his change.

His mother said, "God does love himself a cheerful giver. How are you getting along with the garden there?" Herring winced a little, said he hadn't got there yet. He'd kind of forgotten about it and was agitated by the thought. Fletcher's mother flapped her hand. "Oh, no bother. These things aren't a race, you know." She mentioned that Glendon and Darling Acorn, who had a baby girl, named Treasure, had also just adopted a boy. His name was Amos. They were having a little party in a couple of days. It was also their anniversary. "Bring the girls," she said. Herring walked to his truck. Fletcher's mother called out the door, "Don't be a stranger, you hear. Don't be a fixture either." Herring laughed. He drove off. The truck looked about as right as a run-over foot. Fletcher was just hoping that the man didn't get pulled over. That truck wouldn't pass a safety. His mother said, "I bet you that rig of his is getting about a mile to the gallon."

—

Next morning, a whole fog had come over the island. You could feel the cold push in well before. Herring was out hacking at roots in the garden with his pick axe and his shovel. His stomach was sweaty and it showed through his shirt, and then he had goose pimples from the cold. His mind bored as all get-out. The brume approached like the slowest and gentlest of Biblical floods, and it occurred to him that this was the human condition. Things were obscured and revealed, and then obscured again, and man was a cold thing with poor vision, which stumbled through everything, good and evil, as best it could. The birds in the trees were making one hell of a ruckus. He was lonely, so he took a drive.

When Herring arrived in Georgetown it was late morning, and Gerry and Sheila were smoking shatter and watching television. He sat with them and watched them interact with one another, and they seemed relaxed and comfortable. They were building their own little language together, smacking it between them like a game of tennis, and it made him envious. Sheila was a fine thing, he thought. Had a hell of a pair of getaway sticks on her. She was a good egg, good for the heart, good for everyone, he supposed. She had a fine bit of love in her, all under the surface there, and he guessed that she was able to communicate this well to the people she chose to give access to. There was an immense and graceful power to this. Power. Nobody really prepared you for it, did they? High school had been useless. This was the truth. And it seemed as if you were only punished all the more for demonstrating your knowledge about this fact. And then, nearly everything was a kind of transaction, too. Some people just knew how to play the game that they wanted to play. Maybe he was reading too much into things. Maybe she was as quietly troubled as everyone else.

She asked him if he wanted some shatter. Herring didn't really think. His hand was out before him, and he had a little puff, of which he avoided inhaling as best he could. The taste was lovely and warm, and it seemed that the body registered it in each cell and pore and neuron, a substance that engaged you with true completeness, like an introduction to rum, or religion, and he wondered how long he'd keep doing this kind of thing. Would getting fucked up ever truly bore him, such that he'd be absolutely put off the whole idea, once and for all?

They hung around until *The Bold and the Beautiful* came on, and then he and Gerry drove back to the house and worked out at the garden for a while. Herring ran the shovel and Gerry pushed the barrow, dumping roots and weeds at the side of the barn. Gerry was annoyed. It felt a little like Herring and Sheila were competing for his time and attention. They drank pogey pop out of a two-litre bottle and did their best to ignore the blackflies and mosquitoes. The fog had receded and overhead the sun was trying to get through the clouds. It wasn't too hot, wasn't too cold. Good weather for slinging dirt.

Herring made them tuna sandwiches and tea, and then they started loading up the truck with the mess they had removed. Gerry couldn't get leather gloves over his bandages, so Herring loaded most of it. He would place his hands on the roots and drag them so that they pinched a bit of the other stuff, and then he'd throw it into the back of his truck, while little gusts of wind blew dirt into his mouth and face. Gerry drank pop and talked about Pictou Island, about the hippies over there. People left keys in cars and you could just take one if you needed it, though sometimes people grabbed the wrong car.

"How are you sposed to know which one is which?" said Herring.

Gerry said, "I don't know."

Herring groused a little. "Sounds like a terrible idea."

"I dunno. Sounds pretty good to me." Gerry had this tone in his voice that Herring knew about. Its sound was calm and patient, almost exhausted, but there was an immense poise, or certainty, right beneath it.

Herring was about halfway through the pile. He was getting tired, so he switched to the shovel. After a few loads, he saw something moving, and it took a moment for his brain to recognize the three baby moles, stretched and confused, their little paws slowly trying for purchase. Herring had cut one of them in half, and he started to panic, all hunched over, his movements wild and stilted, his eyes registering everything before him as just more and more severed moles. Gerry came over and blocked, got in front of him. "It's okay. It's okay. You didn't mean it," he said, leaning over. He took each one and tucked them into the dirt by the wall of the barn. Herring disappeared into the house. He splashed some water on his face and took a dozen or so deep, deep breaths.

When he came back out, they got into the cab together and headed to Machon's Point where everybody too cheap to go to the depot near My Bonnie River dumped their waste. On the drive in, Gerry said, "I heard that before a mole eats a worm, he pulls him through his paws like he's skinning an eel, to get the dirt outta them so the meat isn't tainted. 'Cos, if yer going to eat something, you don't wanna be eating what he was eating too. And they have this shit in their mouths that paralyzes the worms, so the moles can keep the worms all in one spot for a later date."

Herring said, "Jesus, they're little psychopaths."

"Yeah," said Gerry. "It'd be some hellish to be a worm."

—

In the barn he had a couple lengths of white pine trunks, each about three feet long and about eighteen-inches in diameter, and he brought them outside. He set up a pair of bucks and bridged their distance with an old, beat-up sheet of three-quarter plywood. He got his small chainsaw out, the one with the sixteen-inch bar, and took a pencil to the pine and sketched out, quite roughly, what he was going to do. He went inside and made a jug of lemonade. The cat joined him by the barn. "Measure twice, cut five times, eh?" he said, and then fired up the saw. The cat darted away as the engine blared. He hit the safety with the back of his right hand, and the teeth began to rotate. He carved a little set of toadstools and just left them real nice and rough. They were charming, even a little folksy, he thought. There were wood chips floating in his lemonade, but he drank it anyway. And then he smoothed out the bits that he had missed, that needed to go, with the tip of the blade. He had a can of white paint and a can of red paint, and he painted the stalks white and the caps red. He'd come back to put white spots on the caps.

—

On the bridge in My Bonnie Harbour, a bunch of Mexicans were smoking and fishing and generally minding their own business. They were drinking from a flask and some bottles, but they weren't really hiding this too well. Herring joined them, hung his head over the railing, and beheld the jellyfish in the waters. The Mexicans were quiet. They were looking at Herring. Herring said, "What do you call a Mexican goaltender with no legs?" They continued to stare at him. One of them shifted his weight. Another adjusted his crotch. "Grassy ass," said Herring. The Mexicans watched him for a few more moments, and then they just shrugged, went back to fishing. One of them sparked up a joint and sucked in, coughing strenuously. It was passed around. At one point, it seemed like all of them were hacking. They offered it to Herring, but he just shook his head. A few vehicles rolled by. People were getting ice cream at Brehaut's, big white cones that dripped and wilted beneath the sun. Herring clasped his fingers together and began twiddling his thumbs. Then he stopped. He wasn't the type of fellow to twiddle. He looked up. If the whole of creation was beneath the sun, what was the sun beneath, he thought. He supposed this was a dumb idea, but he liked the way he saw it in his mind, like an architect dreaming of a building, of the carpenters who would come to honour and serve these dreams, like ants who come out of the forests in search of sugar in the fields, who would raise walls and roll joists for floor diaphragms, so that people, families, could be safe and sheltered and warm, and so that things would be right and wouldn't fall down. Carpenter ants.

The Mexican boys had something heavy on their line. They were surprised by its weight. You could see the excitement in their eyes. The rod was bent right over, at just about the point where it ought to shatter. They reeled and they reeled. Whatever it was, it wasn't going quietly. For a few moments, it was quite the commotion. People came over from Brehaut's and watched. And then the thing burst through the surface, and some creature was hopelessly entangled in their line, hanging dumbly as if it were a shipwreck, and began dripping as it was elevated. The bottom of the harbour was just sludge, but the thing in their line wasn't even that dirty. When they'd cut all their lines they found that they'd caught a lobster. One of the Mexican boys held it out before him, his hands about its leg segments. They were all smiling and hooting and hollering. The damn thing had a span on it the size of an eagle. A few people in the crowd clapped. It was quite a sight. Herring went over and said, photograph-ee-ah. He took their picture. They all looked so vital, bristling with the thing of life. That look when man conquers yet another animal.

—

Over the course of the night, the air got real muggy, the house filled up with heat. Herring got up and opened the windows. He listened to the chorus of frogs down by the river. The moon was bright and he cupped its light in his hands and then let it go. One moment it had been in his hands, the next back to the floor.

In the morning he picked up Gerry, and they grabbed some coffee and donuts from Robin's. Gerry asked if he wouldn't mind stopping at Keeping's on the way through. The drive was mostly uneventful. Each of them was thinking about something, letting things wander comfortably. When they got to Keeping's, Gerry grabbed some scratch tickets and then went back to the freezer to see about some beers. Otis was in there, unloading cans from an ancient-looking trolley.

Gerry said, "Nice and cool in here."

Otis smiled and said, "Be a shame if one of these beers happened to open itself."

Big Arbot Herring was sitting at the window with a cup of coffee in his pudgy hands, waiting for someone to come over and talk to him. Herring ambled over. They watched a fat crow waddle through the field across the road.

Big Arbot said, "Diesel went up another penny again last night."

"We're getting the pinch, all right."

"We've always been getting the pinch."

"Jesus, Arbot, the amount you drink yer gonna be riding yer goddamn bicycle till you die, for Christ's sake," said Herring.

He pictured himself walking away as he would have done in the past, troubled well out of measurement to the interaction they'd just shared, shaking his head as if he, and he only, knew the program by which to better the world. But he stayed where he was and sorted through the mess in his head, hoping that Arbot wouldn't move either so he could figure out how to make his peace and get on with the day. Herring said, "Jeez, I'm sorry for being snippy there, Arbot." Big Arbot grumbled to himself, his hand shaky with the coffee. Herring went to the cash register and said, "I'm paying for his next cup." The cashier, a teenage girl with a cupcake tattoo by her wrist, couldn't understand that he didn't have anything to pay for, that he was paying for something in the future.

She said, "Holy jumpins, I don't think that's ever been done here before."

As they drove out to his situation, Gerry said, "You ever notice how the steel bit on a seat belt is a perfect bottle opener?"

The flatbed from the mill showed up just before noon, and the driver, a younger fellow, insisted that he get his lunch break. So Gerry and Herring unloaded the thing by hand, carrying the lengths of oak up onto the deck. Herring had also ordered a sheet of plywood and some sixteen-foot SPF two-by-twelves. Herring was mostly pleased with the look of the wood. One time he'd been at the lumber yard, sorting through lengths for something decent enough to use. Finally, an old fart had wandered over and said, "Ya've got to take what ya can get. Ya can't be sortin' like ya are."

Herring had looked at the fellow as if he had two heads. "I'm buying it. I'll pick out what I goddamn please."

"But that means the next fella'll be getting' bad wood."

"As I see it, that's yer problem. If we did this right, nobody would be getting crap wood."

The old fart said, "As I see it, mister wonderful, it's a matter of proportional dispensation," and licked his lips like he was eyeing up a T-bone steak.

Herring said, "Well there, piker, it sounds to me like ya got yer PhD in bullshit from the back of a cereal box."

He wasn't too fussy about this kind of stuff anymore. They had a whole pile of work before them, and he was anxious to get it done. He and Gerry sistered the ruined joists and patched the hole as best they could. They even put down wood glue. Herring opened the windows in the living room, and because his hands still hurt whenever he bumped them, he got Gerry to man the broom and run the chop saw. Whenever the cat showed up, Gerry stopped what he was doing and fussed over it. He got the cat to chase after his tape measure for a while, and it sounded like faraway thunder fighting with a steel-drum factory. He took note of how many beers Gerry was into, feeling edgy and unsure of what to do, here. The last thing he wanted to do was give the man hell or scold him. He knew that he'd lose him for certain, if he succumbed to these urges.

The windows did little to let in an honest breeze, and they sweated a great deal as the floor went down, Herring on his hands and knees with a rubber mallet and his brad nailer. His back was stiffer than hell. Gerry pushed the broom while he waited for measurements, a pencil tucked into his cap. He said, "Boy, I'm just about croakin'." He took off his shirt and used it to wipe his face.

The place was as near to spotless as Herring could have imagined. "Look at you go, Cinderella," he said.

Gerry gave a big smile. "I just love sweepin'," he said. "I take care of ya."

Herring drank cold coffee as they worked, and it made his teeth feel as if they'd been set in concrete and lowered into the ground, but he kept slugging away at it because he figured it kept him sharp. A guy he worked for back in the day told him that drinking hot coffee on a hot day actually served to cool the body down. This idea didn't make a great deal of sense to him, but here he was, not really trying the idea out, drinking cold coffee on a really humid day. Gerry was gabbing on, talking about nearly everything under the sun. He said, "You know, I got my sex ed from a nun. She drew a picture on the board of a dick and a vagina, and that was that."

Herring said, "Do you know why they call 'em nuns?"

Gerry shrugged.

"'Cos they don't get none," said Herring, and Gerry laughed so hard he snorted.

After a few hours of measuring, Herring's mind was exhausted. "Jesus, I feel like a goddamn auctioneer with all these numbers in my head," he said.

They took a break outside and Gerry destroyed a couple of smokes. Emerson White rolled by on his tractor. Chessel was working on something at his place. You could hear a drill going and the odd curse.

Chessel was always cutting and banging. He had about fifty projects on the go and never seemed to get any closer to finishing any of them. Like a fellow bailing out his skiff, not realizing that the plugs are out of her.

Euna and the girls showed up. They were over the moon to see Gerry, leaning against the handle of his broom as he was, in the corner of the room. "Uncle Gerry," they screamed and gave him big hugs as he raised his hands so that they didn't smack his fingers. Marcelina and Marceline asked him about his teeth and he blushed, and then they hugged their father and asked what they could do to help. They were intrigued by what was going on, by all of the trinkets set here and there. To them, these things were all another language that belonged to some other world. Herring showed them how to fire the nailer and where to put the gun. He let each of them have a squeeze, and they both closed their eyes and held their breath just before they fired off a nail. The floor was getting there. They wanted to know about the chop saw, but Gerry told them that they could only watch, that it was a bit too dangerous just now.

Euna, her eyes beaming with something like pride, watched Herring, his hair white and emerging in its strange little patterns, all bunched up on the floor like he was trying to hide in a suitcase, and she said, "Well, I'm floored." They laughed, him first and then her. Gerry joined in, too. The girls were playing with the cat, which mostly meant chasing the poor thing this way and that. They wanted to know its name and were bewildered that Herring hadn't christened it. To do so would have been to claim it as his own, to declare a kind of jurisdiction, that yet another life was within his dominion, and he didn't like the thought of this. Herring felt that there was a newness about, pointed and alive, as if his body had finally caught up with his mind, or vice versa, as if only now he was registering that on the other side of all these years of risk and stupidity and danger he had been rewarded, or more accurately, gifted with, not only a bit more of life, but a bit more of what seemed to be a fresh life. This feeling registered deep within, down with his shifting, dynamic cells. All around him and this little family he had tried to build, and this final friendship with Gerry, was a kind of new place, small and modest, and in this tiny ensuing he saw that life was everywhere, that life was each person's marrow. He felt his life more and time less. He thought of his father and considered that maybe he had been right when he said there was no time and only heat. These bodies and minds that he loved in this room, these hearts and imaginations, laying a floor in the heat that had rolled in over the Island.

Euna said goodbye to the girls and left. Gerry and Herring worked well into the night. He ordered a pizza from the campground restaurant, The Picnic Table, and drove out to fetch it. The four of them wolfed it down like wild jackals. The girls stayed up as late as they could manage, but they were both asleep at the table when the floor was all done, just after midnight, surrounded by cups of tea and pizza crusts and cards and Balderdash. Herring was terrible at the game. He could lie like a rug in real life, but when it came to faking it so as to win a board game, he just wasn't able to summon the same faculties.

He and Gerry carried the girls to bed. They'd do the skirting boards in the morning. Gerry was yawning, his mouth as wide as a harbour. He looked at the floor. Everything was quiet and the house had a faint buzz to it, hanging there, near the shoulders like a cloak. He said, "Boy, ya could just about walk on that."

Herring said, "You'd think we knew what we were doing."

"We could go into business. Herring and McClellan," said Gerry. "H&M."

Gerry insisted on sleeping in the basement. Said that ever since the accident, he couldn't bear to sleep above ground, for some reason, that the very thought of having to do so made him nauseous.

Herring woke up a few hours later, soaked in sweat. He walked downstairs and turned on the light, so that he could admire their handiwork in the living room. The fellow from the lumber mill had been right. He did love it. From beneath the new floor came the familiar, muffled clatter of wood being loaded into the stove and then Gerry talking to the cat, repeating over and over that it had just been yet another large day, a large day, my word. Herring listened to the patter of the June bugs against the windows as if they were spat gobs of saliva and plugs of chew. He hit the lights.

—

They had pizza crusts for breakfast. He made sure Gerry took his antibiotics and painkillers, and then they replaced the skirting boards, while the girls prepared sandwiches. He and Gerry loaded the canoe and a couple of hard rakes into the truck and packed the cooler, and they drove down to Boatswain Point and put the canoe in by the lighthouse that had been dragged back to its foundation. The nearly infinite tufts of marram grass bristled in the wind like streamers, somehow humble and noble at the same time.

Herring felt anxious about getting back out onto the waters. His temper grew short. He had no desire to be snappy, but he felt as tight as a hamstring. He made sure the girls had applied their sunscreen and put their life jackets on. They got the canoe into the waters and loaded her up, Gerry in the bow, the girls in the middle, and Herring at the stern. The sun was out and the sky was a light blue, a sheet of periwinkle. The water was dark and had a bit of chop to it. And jellyfish everywhere. Herring told the girls to watch the direction of the grasses at the bottom of the channel. From these you could tell if the tide was falling or rising.

They headed north for Herring Island.

About halfway across the channel, near the sandbar infested with gulls and terns and shags, Herring was staring absentmindedly to his port side when something caught his eye. There appeared to be a great dip in the surface of the water, a singular incongruence, not so much as if there was a hole or even a kind of puncture in the water, but as if the weight of the atmosphere was being plunged downward in this solitary spot, like a dipstick, or sailors performing soundings with a great stick in a sea that was just a basket of woolen blankets. He watched this valley deepen, entranced by its descent. The waters within this trough enacted a slow gradient from azure to charcoal. He had a sense that there was a great pressure to it, that he was like an ant watching humans knuckling down to play a game of marbles. Things had been hit in a way that suggested everything was rotating. He saw himself as he had been, trying to keep moving, shaking with the cold, high on acid, confused, and mostly wondering if anyone would come out for him. Then he saw himself again, kicking, propelling himself away, in any which direction. And then he saw himself again, pushed by the current in another direction, such that the versions of himself were multiplying. His descendants grew in number each time he blinked, and the effect was that he, the sight of his other selves, became an immense, congealed kind of smear. He would look around and see that, yes, he had been there, at the same time that he had been over there. And then he understood that he was here, too, in the stern of his fibreglass canoe, cutting through the waters in another direction altogether. He realized, too, that before these versions of himself, he had been upon the boat with Gerry. And then before that, on the road in the dark. It was as if his whole existence had been committed to a reel of magnetic tape, and this reel had fallen out of its container and the tape was spinning outward as much as it was spinning inward. There was no anxiety or fight or struggle. The falling of the tape hadn't been an accident. It was just a thing that was happening. He, his existence, was a kind of streak that, from a distance, seemed like pure and utter chaos. However, up close, examined and considered, it had a flow to it that was reassuring, even kind of majestic. Through all of this unspooling, this forwarding and rewinding, the beat of his heart, the pump and flex of its muscle. Sometimes his hands were in his pockets. Sometimes he was surrounded by old friends. Sometimes he was smiling, and sometimes he was crying. He felt himself at once, over and through time and over and through all of the distances of his small, stupid, beautiful life. He knew that he felt love, that he had love in his heart.

He looked away and continued paddling.

He realized that it didn't hurt as much as before. Today, for the next little bit, Boatswain Point was A and Herring Island was B, and to get there first meant to get halfway there, and within this half was another half, and so on, and yes, there was a destination, whatever that was, but it didn't seem likely, given this train of thinking, that he, and they, would ever truly get there, seeing as they were only halving halves, when you really got down to it. He and the girls and Gerry were the brushstrokes of colour upon a kind of infinite canvas, and these strokes of colour that they were, were also canvasses that would uphold more colours, because, in fact, they had already done this very thing.

Eventually they got to Herring Island, with Gerry hopping out into the pleasant warmth of the shoals and pulling the canoe to the beach. They lay on the sands for a little while and got sweaty in the sun, and then they went swimming. He told the girls to watch out for razor clams. About five hundred yards down the beach lay the carcass of a rotting seal. The boys out herring fishing had likely taken it onboard and shot it in the head. He scanned the Island, its rough trees and its smooth sand. His people had first come here from England during the reign of William IV, the sailor king. They had cleared the land and raised cattle and sheep and fished and built boats, and the Mi'kmaq would paddle out in the summers to visit, and they learned, over time and with a great deal of patience, to speak to one another with meaning.

He dug a shelf into the beach as long as his arm and about as deep as his hand fully extended, and then he set a row of rocks behind this. Gerry brought some grass and wood down from the bush, his legs slit and leaking with blood from the wild roses. Herring went to the canoe and got a junk of rope and put his lighter to it and the grass and bark. The tide continued to fall and Gerry waded out and started pulling up a heap of oysters. Gerry said, "Girls, don't tell yer mother 'cos this is totally illegal what we're doing." He found a shard of beer bottle and put this in his pocket. He set the oysters on the stones, the four of them huddled around this little, quiet fire, whispering to the world its tale of combustion, of release, and they waited for the heat to pop the shells open. Once in a while, an oyster would fall into the sticks of the fire, and Herring or Gerry would grab two longer sticks and use them as tongs to try and get the oyster out before it burst open and sprayed hot juice and shell onto their shins, and the odd time that this happened, everyone screamed and then giggled like mad things. They set the blackened shells in the sand to cool, their growth lines like miniature Zen gardens, and then Herring picked up each oyster that the fire hadn't opened and worked his shucking knife into the hinge, turning it as if it were a key in a lock, to reveal the flesh of the mollusk, all the parts of this remarkable little being. It was a neat little trick when he did it well. They squirted some lemons over the oysters and applied the few hot sauces they had brought. Gerry said, "There's just about nothing better than an oyster. My word, what a pleasure." He must have eaten about thirty of them, like an overheated dog at a bowl of cold water. He laid back into the warm sands, his belly a hill, his scribbled tattoos, and he napped, all brown and glistening, like a bead of syrup on the Queen's china. Herring leaned over to the girls and said, "See Gerry, there? He's solar powered."

The girls drank more pink lemonade from the Thermos and asked him about fishing. Marceline said, "What's a good tip for a beginner?"

"Remember," said Herring. "Where you get yer fish is where you'll get yer bait. And where you get yer fish is where the birds are."

Marcelina looked a tad puzzled. "But how do you get your bait?"

"You catch it," he said.

"But don't you need a bait for your bait?"

"Well, that's kind of true. Bait, by and large, is usually kind of skittish. A nervous fish that swims in shallow waters."

"So, he's afraid of the ocean?" said Marceline.

"If you want herring," he said, "you can rig up a line with a bunch of hooks on it to catch 'em. Or you can trap 'em in a little water bottle with holes at both ends. Or you can use nets."

Marcelina said, "But if you're fishing, you still need a smaller fish to catch a bigger fish, right?"

He could see that she was getting caught up on this point. He said, "Yeah, there's a pecking order to most things."

"Like lobsters will eat herring 'cos they taste good to them," said Marceline.

"And 'cos they're smaller, they can eat them," said Marcelina.

"Yeah," said Herring.

"And 'cos they're put in traps and dropped to the bottom."

"What eats lobsters, though?" said Marceline.

Herring said, "Well, humans do. Sometimes seals will get 'em. Flounder, white blacks and black backs, and cod will eat them, too, I spose. Monkfish. Monkfish are terrifying. Don't ever look at a monkfish. And, for that matter, spider crabs are bloody demons. Once you seen 'em, you can't unsee 'em. In all my years out at sea I've only ever seen three wolffish, too. They're pretty awful. Lobster are easier to get when they're young. They're born in shallow waters."

"So, they need protection?" said Marceline.

Herring nodded his head.

Marcelina said, "What do lobsters do all day?"

"Well, they mostly hide in cracks and stuff."

"'Cos they're scared of being eaten?"

"Yeah, something like that."

"Do lobsters fight each other?"

"If need be, sometimes, yeah," he said. "Sometimes they'll even eat one another."

The girls scrunched their faces. He rubbed more sunscreen on their arms and legs and faces. He scanned the horizon for Fisheries.

"What do you call a lobster with only one claw?" said Marceline.

"A cull."

"What do you call a lobster with no claws?" said Marcelina.

"He's a dummy."

The girls snickered. They picked up a few oyster shells and turned them over in their hands.

"Then you catch lobster 'cos you're a Herring?" said Marceline. She was teasing, and she smiled, quite pleased with herself.

"Something like that," he said. Her smile made him smile. "If you look down the throat of a herring, you can see a little mark that looks like a candle, which is how fishermen used to bring 'em to the surface. And sometimes if you look in their gills, you can see the shapes of oars."

The girls were shocked by this information.

"Everything that lives is marked by what hunts it," he said. He smoothed the bandages on his legs.

"Dad, are you a good fisherman?" said Marceline. Both girls stopped their investigation of the shells and gazed at him, the mackerel breeze lifting their red hair, exalted, as if they were the finest and most precious flowers in a garden.

"I'm none too bad," he said. "But mostly I'm a dummy, too." And then he leaped up. They screamed and threw the oysters at him, and he chased them away, his arms behind his back.

—

On their way into Boatswain's Point, Herring spotted from some distance what appeared to be a dog running down the middle of the road with a kind of slant to its gait, as if it were the blade of a plow. He assumed that it had been struck by a car at some point in its life. Probably when it was younger and had recuperated as best it could with unset bones to just get on with its business. As the truck got nearer, his foot off the gas and feathered upon the brake, and their paths seemed about to converge, the dog quickly swerved into the bleached and dead stalks of grass at the side of the road. The girls jumped to the window to get a good look at him. They realized that they were staring at a black fox. Herring stopped the rig. The fox stared at them, dark and thin, its coat in surprisingly decent shape, clean and glistening in the waning sun, its ears registering faraway sounds by flicking subtle adjustments this way and that, like the hands of some disoriented clock.

Marceline said, "Hey there, little fella."

The fox looked at them with thoughts of its own swirling behind its eyes.

"That's what used to be called a king hair," said Herring.

"He looks as if he's never been wet his whole life," said Marcelina.

"I'd say that's about right on the money," said Herring.

The fox waited for the truck to roll on before it resumed its path down the centre of the road, heading westward for a date with the setting sun.

—

The Acorns lived in a little farmhouse that had been built between the wars, on a swell of land from which you could see the lighthouse and much of the eastern sweep of the cape, the comings and goings of the lobster boats out of My Bonnie Harbour and My Bonnie River. There was a line of about fifty parked cars and trucks up the lane. In the grasses about their home were a number of blossoming cherry trees. Herring parked and the girls took off before him. He went around the back of the truck and fetched his toadstools. He was happy with how they'd turned out. They looked pretty good.

Glendon Acorn was a younger guy, in his mid-thirties, with a shock of red hair and a pair of thick, outmoded glasses that made him look like a Maritime version of Buddy Holly. He taught history at the university. His clothes were expensive and never far from an ironing board. He took himself seriously, and it seemed that the world had obliged him. Herring found him altogether foreign, and because of this, rather intimidating. Glendon's wife, Darling, was an artist. She made movies and had a casual blitheness to her, which she utilized to keep the force of the world at bay. Her hair was frizzled and unkempt, and she wore sneakers for every occasion.

Around the side of the house a big fire was roaring, and a glass machine was glowing and rolling hot dogs, keeping buns warm up top. There were people everywhere and coolers of beer set out and jazz music playing from a ghetto blaster. On the few wooden tables, lobster and potato salads and cheeses and sliced tomatoes and sauerkraut and pies. Fletcher Jordan's mother came up to Herring immediately and made a great fuss over his toadstools, and then a group of children enveloped her and pulled her away. Glendon and Darling came over and introduced him to Amos, bundled up and sleeping. He touched the boy's hand with the tip of his index finger.

He said, "Nice to meet ya, little man." They told him what was up, and he showed them his toadstools. He was terribly nervous regarding their opinion of him and his modest artistry, but they seemed to be rather surprised, even amused in the best sense, by what they saw. He had wanted them to be glad that they had invited an ignoramus like him, and so, he was pleased that this rite had gone the way it had.

"Help yerself to anything you like," said Darling. Glendon, who was the tallest man in Kings County by a good few inches, looked down at him and smiled nervously. Herring felt intimidated and wondered if all of this was a bit out of league.

Willy Lyon and Louis MacKenzie were stood by the fire, drinking shine, and Herring joined them. They nodded at him and smiled, passed him some shine, and he took a smell of it, cringed, and handed it back. He said, "That'd gag a maggot." The sky was getting dark fast. Jack MacLeod came up the hill and stood next to Herring. He was drinking a drink called the Chewbacca, which was a mixture of spiced rum and root beer. Billy Clow emerged from the dark trees about the property with an armful of logs for the fire. Leverett MacNeil came over. The children were playing hide-and-seek, and someone had handed out glow sticks and sparklers. Howard MacNeil and Eben Daley and Jimmy Beck shuffled up, and Rankin Jackson and Atwood LeLacheur came to the fire, as well. And for a time, it felt like they were all there, a closed and huddled ring of men before the light, and the darkness to their backs. No lips sought to occasion any talk. All was silent, aside from the sputter and surge of the flames. Bottles of rum and shine and lemon liqueur circulated. The will between them was good. Jack MacLeod said, "Well, that was about as much fun as the Last Supper." The men laughed, dispersed. Herring could see Deborah MacLeod and Selina Glover giving him the eyes from across the lawn.

Hot chocolate was served in little Styrofoam cups, and Herring made sure that the girls tucked into some hot dogs. They sat on a log, a tree that had come down in a storm a few years ago, while Glendon and his friends readied the fireworks. Out in the channel, a few lobster boats putted out from the Harbour to watch. They honked and everyone cheered, gave them a wave. The girls were hot and sweaty and were coming down from too much sugar. He could feel them on either side of him, their heat. The mosquitoes were out but not too bad. Pretty soon they'd be shivering.

Everyone cheered and clapped after the fireworks display, and then most of the older folks began to filter away. Chessel Glover came over and said hello. He had a pint of Russian Prince Vodka and was splashing it down his throat with relative abandon. Herring asked him how he was getting on with Stanislaus. Chessel said, "Oh, he's a fine horse. I don't have the bond that he and Dunbar shared, but I think Stan understands that I'm doing my best." And then Chessel said, "It all kinda worked out for the best, didn't it?" Herring said, "Well, not too well for old Dunbar." Chessel mumbled something. Herring asked him what he'd said. Chessel said, "Don't be forgetting about Dick Hume. Dick's body was still warm when ol' Dunbar was back at home tucking into his supper."

The girls were still fussing about with Treasure, running this way and that over the well-manicured grasses. Chessel said, "How are the girls getting along?"

Herring said, "No complaints. God, they're hungry little things. They left two cartons of milk out this morning. Wasn't I sour."

"Just like the milk," said Chessel.

"Huh?" said Herring. And then he said, "Oh, gotcha." They chuckled.

Chessel had a bowl of salt-and-vinegar chips. He offered Herring some. Herring said, "No thanks, there, Chessel. I'm sweating just looking at 'em."

A bunch of girls ran by, and Marcy Glover knocked into the back of Herring's legs, buckling him a little. He made sure she was okay, brushed her off, and sent her on her way.

Herring said, "Jesus, you Glovers are like stink on a monkey."

Chessel said, "Do you remember when you and Gerry were younger, you'd go to the hangar there in the River and load up yer sleds with airplane fuel? Well, you'd run out of fuel in about five minutes. That or the engine would blow and someone would have to come in another sled and tow ya idiots home. People didn't like it. Scared the horses."

Chessel finished his pint of vodka. Herring said, "Are ya walking home?"

Chessel said, "No, I like drinking and driving."

Glendon and his buddies were laying some thick into the beer and liquor. They had all gone to universities and played in bands. They had good skin and soft hands and unmarked postures. Herring listened to them talk for a while, then realized he had no idea what they were on about. One of them talked a great deal about mushrooms, and when he came to load the fire, Herring noticed that his fingernails had perfect little strokes of dirt beneath them, as if they were underlining something of importance. Some of them looked over at him, and then they would whisper amongst themselves. Herring didn't know what to do and was certain that he looked hurt and scared and even a little vulnerable. He went inside to use the washroom. When he finished, he wandered in the house a little, walked into the den and saw a room lined with books, strange and beautiful things that seemed to him to hold entirely new and individual worlds within them. He inspected the spines and was quite overwhelmed by the names and titles he found. It seemed to him that the whole of the world existed on their shelves, and here he was, just this regular PEI hillbilly trying to put his life back together, trying not to shit his pants at the realization that he didn't know anything about anything. Glendon came into the room to fetch a bottle of expensive tequila. Herring surprised him, and he froze a bit, like a statue.

"Yer a smart cookie. Do you mind if I ask you a question?" Herring said.

Glendon said, "I'm all ears."

Herring said, "This one time, when I wasn't too, too young, I had spread all these nickels and dimes upon my bed, 'cos I'd been saving them to buy something. Probably something stupid. A slingshot or an air rifle. I can't remember. Anyway, I was sorting them into five- and ten-dollar wrappers. There was just something about them being all laid out together that made me stop and think. The dimes, in comparison to the nickels, were so damn tiny, and yet they were worth more, twice as much, as ya know. And then, the nickels got to seem like they were too big to be even related to the dimes, except for they were all the same colour and even mostly made of the same copper. And the mattress was sagging with the weight of all these coins and there was just something odd, something deeply odd to me about all of this."

Glendon wiped his forehead with the back of his hand and said, "I'm a bit confused. What's yer question, exactly?"

Herring said, "Well, shit, I don't truly know."

He went outside and snatched himself the last dog from the machine. He loaded it up with the works, and as he bit into it, the condiments that refused to be contained burst free. He jabbed a hand out and caught a streak of plummeting relish.

They had tacked a white bedsheet to the side of the barn, and there was a projector going, showing one of Darling's movies. Herring stood behind the crowd of young folk and watched for a few minutes. From the bedsheet this blurred mass kept striking a line of glass windows in a sluggish and slowed fashion. The light was cool, but you couldn't tell where it was coming from exactly, such that one struggled to establish if they were on the inside or the outside of some building. He thought that the blurry thing might have been a bowling ball suspended by some rope, but you couldn't make out the rope. He didn't know how they'd done it. After the first strike cracked the glass, fine lines branching out from the point of impact, the blurred ball left the frame, only to reappear and charge the helpless panes again, each time increasing the scope and chaos of the cracks. This continued until the frames held nothing but eerie shards of glass that the bowling ball could not seem to extinguish. The ball was a brutal wrecking device, but after a certain point, it lacked any chance of precision. And eventually, the ball ceased, halted its torment.

Standing next to Herring, Darling still held Amos in her arms. "Oh, shit, silly me. Happy anniversary," he said. She smiled. The sky was now utterly black. She looked from the sheet to Herring and said, "It's about epigenetics."

He saw the girls by themselves at the fire, roasting marshmallows. Marceline pulled hers back from the flames and let her sister pull it off her stick. He walked over to them and felt the night refresh him, comb and blanket him as if he was soil being tilled. "C'mon, ladies, let's get you home," he said, and he scooped them up. The both of them fell right asleep on the drive home. He carried each one upstairs and got them to change into their pyjamas. Then he took Marceline into the bathroom and put her hand under the running tap. She groaned with protest. He said, "C'mon, ya gotta pee before ya go to bed." He carried Marcelina into the bathroom and got the water running. "I can't do it if it's cold," she said, her eyes closed and her frame limp. He got the hot going. She peed and then he carried her to bed. The two of them snoring as if locked into some strange endurance competition.

# TEN

Archie Beck stood, in his black braces, dander about his collar and shoulders like fallen leaves, as if he were a great elm in autumn, and he said, "Tonight's topic is forgiveness." Each person at this meeting, he said, knew that man was essentially good, that the spirit was willing but the flesh was weak. He talked about original sin and he talked about the apple, the fruit from the Tree of Knowledge. He said this apple wasn't the only problem. "Turns out, a lot of people were going to have problems with the apples rotting around the base of the tree," he said. This received a few polite laughs and snickers. He used this bit at every meeting. "You see, people know what is right and wrong. Ethics is a thing that's just kind of hard-wired into us. And when we choose to do wrong, to knowingly forsake our communion with the Divine, we experience guilt. And many of us here this very night know what it is to be fallen, to do wrong, and to resort to the bottle to drown our guilt."

Herring and Gerry had picked up Big Arbot Herring, and now the three of them were sitting side by side. Gerry didn't have much time for Arbot, didn't like being set next to the fellow, chewing on his donuts and slurping at his coffee like a cow at a trough, but he resolved to hold his tongue and not let the man annoy him too much.

Archie said, "Many of you know me. I had talent and ought to have used it. But I didn't do this. I was weak. I lied and I whored around and I drank to abate my guilt. I was scared of trying to work hard, scared and lazy of trying to be bigger than myself. After all, I'm just a simple farmer from the middle of nowheres. Who did I think I was? I turned away from that spark, the spark that I believe each of us has in our hearts, this electrical kind of glow that connects us to the whole universe. Looking back, it seems as if I swam for years, endlessly, and pointlessly, trying to find the bottom of any bottle that would tell me it was all okay, that I could be forgiven and start anew. That I could live a full life and serve my sentence at the very same time. I missed out on so much. And each time I missed something, a birthday, a funeral, a communion, a graduation, I became lowlier and meaner. Dark and deformed and subterranean." Archie wiped his mouth. "Now, I've thought a great deal about the matter of forgiveness. Many of us here tonight will not be forgiven our trespasses. But if you're able to retain yer sobriety this day, and then the next, and then the next, you will see improvements in yer life, in the way you interact with the world outside of yer head. And, perhaps this is the most important item of all. You will come to a place, like a kind of clearing in the forest of the mind and the jungle of the heart, of waters where the current subsides, where you will see that it is possible to forgive yourself, and to forgive yerself truly. From all of this wandering, and from all of this suffering, peace will take a form and reach out to you from the fabric of the universe, from the imagination of God."

Big Arbot just about had tears coming down his red cheeks. He was moved beyond expectation. Gerry's legs were bobbing. He leaned over and said, "Arbot, would ya mind taking off yer high-vis there? We're not exactly on a job site here." Arbot refused, said that at this point it was a matter of principle. Gerry said, "What's the goddamn principle here, Arbot? To look like yer directing planes?" Herring leaned over and said, "That's enough of that, girls."

Afterward, Isaac Cahoon came over to them in the parking lot. There were about a dozen people trudging about, hauling on their cigarettes, their cheeks just caved in. The atmosphere was about as lively as a funeral. Isaac began speaking to Herring about a former girlfriend who had taken cancer. She was dying. He said, "I'm a firm believer that the minute ya cut someone open and cancer sees air, sees the light of day, it starts to spread." Herring stood before the man, towered, in fact, such that Isaac was entirely within the shadow Herring cast, from the lights above the side door to the church. Isaac was agitated, smoking a mile a minute, pacing in his hobbled way, forward and backward, like a stunned fish in a bloody bucket. "I didn't think very highly of her," said Isaac. "She was lazy. A real mooch. We just argued forever about money. What was the point of it all? We could've just gotten along." Herring wanted to say something, like, boy, I know too well what you're on about, but he held his tongue and let the boy patrol. Isaac wasn't so much apologizing to him as trying to recognize that he had made some terrible errors. Herring wanted to believe there was goodwill and faith, there, in the person of Isaac, but he just didn't know, truth be told. He understood that this business of getting on with things, of repairing each path of destruction, was going to be supremely difficult. Hell, he didn't even have it in him to forgive a young fool like the one in front of him right now, and he liked to believe that he himself wasn't that much worse than Isaac. After all, he had been the one to maim him. He tried to understand that the bit of him he recognized in Isaac was also the bit of Isaac he recognized in himself. This thought, the way it sounded in his head, the symmetry and easy balance of it, made him suspicious of its authenticity. At least I'm trying to figure this stuff out, he thought.

Isaac said that the last time he'd been in Sleepy Hollow, he got around to reading two books a day. "Just real thin little things. There was nothing else to do. Lockdown was from eleven to seven and I was having trouble sleeping, so there was lots of time to kill, huh. There were plenty of Zane Grey books. Some Louis L'Amour, of course, but you could tell they weren't as thought out as the Zane Grey ones. Grey knew how to do plot, ya see," he said. "There were a lot of AA books, too. About men beating addiction by finding God. There was a book called *Burnt* that I liked a great deal."

Gerry was talking to Big Arbot. Gerry said, "I'm sick of being lost. I don't want this feeling anymore." There was real pain and sorrow in his voice. You could just about hear his heart crumple in on itself, pop and leak like a waterbed in a fight with a samurai sword, as he said what he needed to say, and even though they were out in the fresh air, the three of them felt that they were suffocating, that the air was somehow deficient, weak and scant, next to such an unattractive church, in this trifling place of holiness. Big Arbot was overwhelmed. His body was tight with it, his conversation all body, no speech. He looked terrified, too, because he'd never really thought about not drinking. He was like a thing trying to bust out of its shell, a turtle that embarks on some quest only to be run over by a truck a few yards from its objective. Sheila arrived and fetched Gerry. She waved at Herring. Herring could tell what the score was. And so, after this, he wasn't surprised not to see Gerry again for a while.

—

It was just after eleven in the morning, and Herring was at the Legion bar with Georgie Graham. Georgie was already sauced. He was speaking real slow, the breaks between his ideas so long, Herring thought he might grab some shut-eye. Soup and that Acadian fellow were over at the tables, setting up a game. Soup was talking about Haywire, and the other man was doing his best not to listen. Aside from the jukebox, it was quiet and cool. Edith was puttering, sorting out the till and getting the bar ready. She was drinking coffee. Georgie said, "I used to pal around with this military guy who was batshit crazy. When he was at the bar, he'd stir his drink with his dick, just so nobody would touch it when he went to the bathroom. And I mean, he made sure everyone seen what he was up to." Georgie slugged some Schooner into his belly. "I used to work with this one fella. We called him Tommy Two-Hammers 'cos he always carried two hammers around with him. Never used either of 'em. And as useless as a screen door on a goddamn submarine." Georgie slid off his stool. "You know, sometimes twice as much is really twice as slow, huh." He pushed a bit of hair behind his ears and went out for a smoke.

Edith was cutting something. Herring couldn't tell what. She seemed annoyed.

"Listen, Edith," said Herring. "I'd like to apologize for being a bit of a pain in the arse. Anyway, I've been thinking about things, you know, and my rudeness toward you has been bothering me for quite some time."

Edith halted what she was doing and braced herself against the edge of the counter. She looked at him. God, she's just a tub of a woman, he thought. Just a bag of milk. Herring could feel the nerves in him come right alive. He was beginning to understand that asking for forgiveness, if it was always to be this direct, meant that you really had to surrender yourself to the mercy of another. In truth, did he really want this woman's forgiveness? She trailed behind her a vast shambles of men who were idles and drunks, as far as he understood. Her brothers were thieves and degenerates. And anyway, when it came right down to it, he had more of a fight in him than her entire bloodline put together. Edith filled his glass with water.

"I spose it's all good and well," she said. "We've all done stupid shit when we're fucked up, myself included." His disquiet gave way to a tinge of anger. Edith put her head down, as if nothing had happened, which was mostly true. Herring figured that he'd just avoid this place like the plague. People didn't like the past being stirred up again.

"Well there, Edith," he said. "Thanks for hearing me out. I know it's mostly a drop in the bucket." Even though he'd only had water from the tap, he threw some coins into the tip jar.

She said, "Yer change is like yer charity, Herring. Just a drop in the bucket." Her sigh was audible, like the length of the gasp a trap can make as it breaches the waters. Well there, Edith, he thought, that was a tad melodramatic.

Herring walked up the stairs and opened the door, squinting in the sun. Georgie was there, watching a pair of Amish women steering their horse and buggy out of town.

"I guess they figured out a way to stop time," he said. And then he looked at his watch. "I had an Amish kid on the boat for about a week a couple of years back, helping with the banding, that I had to let go. He was one hell of a worker, but he had these warts on his hands that gave us all the heebie-jeebies. We worried that he'd give 'em to both us and the lobster. I heard that when they buy a new house they immediately rip out the plumbing and electricity. Now, you explain to me how that makes a whit of sense." Herring ushered Georgie over to his rig. He had an old diaper box with six boiled lobsters in it, all wrapped in a white plastic bag. "You mind giving these to Edith for me?" Georgie said it was no problem. Good, he thought. That'll show her.

—

A Sunday night in June, about fourteen years earlier, Nettie Gray was taking summer courses at the university, and she'd been out to a pub with some friends, to watch game 7, the Rangers beating the Canucks, 4-3 in overtime, to win the Stanley Cup. Nettie had had a few drinks and was driving home. It was dark and there were clouds in the sky. Coming through Kinross, she neared a rig whose brake lights flickered on and off in an increasingly erratic fashion. This made her nervous, so she kept her distance. The rig would brake and then accelerate as if it were trying to dodge squirrels and chipmunks, or as if high winds were bringing branches down on the road into Grandview.

As they entered the hills and began to ascend, the truck lolled to the right and sank into the dirt of the shoulder. The driver must have yanked on the wheel to try and correct, and then the truck was upside down and facing her, the brightness of its lights forcing her to raise an arm before her eyes. The rig seemed to rest for a moment, then began to succumb to the pull of gravity. Nettie drove past and parked at the side of the road, yanked on her emergency. There was a great holler of metal, like a deranged kind of cruise ship running into another, and she watched the truck slide upon its roof into the ditch.

She smelled the booze first. Then she heard the person in the cab struggling to get free. The air was as cool as a pint of stout. The front of the rig, to her eyes, was pretty caved in. She called out and the banging ceased. A voice called out, asking her to break the window so that he could get out. She knelt and saw that the fellow was pushed up right against the window. She said she was worried she might hurt him. "It's pretty late for that," said the man. "You got a tire iron handy?" Nettie was hesitant to strike the window of the rig. "Give 'er a smack," said the man. She swung it at the window and it cracked a little. "Hit it like it owes ya money," said the man. She took the iron and bashed it as hard as she could. She began cleaning the glass out of its frame. There was a knife on his belt. He asked her to get it and cut his seat belt. She did this as best she could, the two of them silent, their hearts pounding, wound by adrenaline, the night as surprisingly snug around them and their little scene as a pair of old denims. He pulled himself out of the window and lit a smoke. Once lit, he handed it to her.

They sat together for a while listening to toads croak down by the pond. In the woods an old clawfoot tub was just sitting there. Nettie said, "I know you. Yer seeing Bernadette Pollard." The guy blinked, rubbed his jaw. "Yeah, that's me," he said. They introduced themselves and he looked right at her as if she had been a fool to have helped him. After a while, Herring stopped shaking. He looked like he was about to fall asleep. Nettie gave him a little shake. His skin somehow both cold and hot at the same time, like a toe needing a second to figure out what's what with the water out of the faucet. She offered to drive him to the nearest farm, but he said that he wasn't too keen on getting into another vehicle just yet, so they walked to Mrs. Mars's farm and asked to use the phone. Nettie called Harland Miller, who had a tow truck. "Give me forty minutes there, Nettie," he said. Mrs. Mars made them tea and offered them some cookies. She asked that he sit out on the porch, didn't want the mess. But Nettie could tell the old woman was a teetotaller and, as such, just didn't have any time for drunkards. There were Catholics just down the road, and even though Mrs. Mars had never seen them with drink in hand, it did seem to her that they were drunk all the time. After a bit of strained quiet among them, the old woman told them that she was going back to bed. She said, "You're welcome to stay on the porch as long as you need." Nettie and Herring thanked her and there they sat, beneath the dark glow of the night, among the creaking pines. A skunk moseyed out of the woods and dug at the grass around the house, and then it shuffled down the lane, its white blazes and wiggling hips somehow imperious. They began to shiver in their chairs. "Well, I spose that's about forty minutes," said Herring. "We best be going."

They walked back to the road and waited in her car for Harland to show up. Herring was glad that no cops had arrived. His father was going to be some pissed, he said. Sometime after this, Herring got out of her car and started retching, thick fibres of spit issuing out of his mouth, and his guts making a sound like they were getting stepped on.

Harland showed up and said, "Jesus fuck, Herring. I'm just about done with ya." He hooked up his cables and flipped the rig, dragged it onto the deck of his rollback truck. All of this was a kind of strange dance, one that hadn't required a great deal of time to enact. Come sunrise, it would be as if the whole thing hadn't happened.

Herring said he couldn't find his wallet. With this, Harland refused outright to drive him anywhere. So, Nettie offered to cover the cost, which was not cheap at all. She said to him that she knew he was good for it, but secretly she worried that the very opposite was true. She tended to give her trust to people who had not earned it.

"How's the fishing going?" said Nettie. He said it had been good, but things were starting to dry up a bit, everything and everyone was starting to scramble. There was dried vomit in his red beard and it looked like he'd chipped a tooth. "Oh, no," he said, seeing her eye up his mouth. "That's just from this one time I was eating perogies. They were really tasty and I got a little excited." She noted that his ears needed a cleaning. And then he started telling her a story about driving home from a place in New Brunswick. Alma. They have the best Chelsea buns in the world there. Anyway, he had a strange, almost ominous feeling take him over that felt like he'd eaten something bad, something that was off. He slowed his rig down, and after about ten or fifteen kilometres, right when he was thinking that whatever he was feeling was ultimately stupid, a proper waste of time, a deer came out of the forest and stopped in front of him. "Deer are dumber than hell," he said. It was later in the year and his heater wasn't working, but he decided to roll down his window. He called to the deer, whistled a little. The deer just looked at him, seemed totally content to block his way. "I guess I was trying to have a moment," he said. He turned the rig off and the deer kind of snapped out of it and wandered away in the direction it had been heading. And just as he was firing up the engine, another deer ran full speed right into his door. "This thing was just on me, thrashing around. Broke my arm just below the elbow," he said. "There was blood everywheres. Thankfully, for the both of us, the window had been down. The damn thing just destroyed my door. It was injured pretty bad. I couldn't really do anything for it. So, I just watched it stumble off, hoping that a hunter would finish it off. I drove all the way to the ferry with a door that was just barely attached to the frame. My arm was barely attached, too. Some embarrassed, I was," said Herring. "When I got to the hospital, the nurses said I had deer hair literally knotted into my own. They tried brushing it out, but they couldn't get it, it was that bad. So, they asked me if I wanted it shaved off. I said sure. And then I guess the shock wore off and I just passed right out. And, what's more, for as long as I had that crappy rig, there were still deer hairs embedded in the upholstery. Almost stitched. It just never really went away."

He showed her how to get to his father's place out in the cove, and when he got out of the car, he stared at her hands upon the wheel, her engagement ring. His eyes alight and his breath slow and rumbling, almost sultry. He thanked her for what she had done. "I'm not certain, but I have a sneaking suspicion that life is like those damn deer." And in the morning, she found an envelope tucked under her wiper with cash in it.

—

The fisherman walked into the public library in grubby sweatpants, stained with fish and rust and dirt, and a pair of rubber boots. He looked like he'd been buried alive that very morning, truth be told. Some older ladies hummed and hawed over the romance section, and a younger woman and her two children sorted through the children's books and movies. Nettie could tell the man was nervous. His neck flushed red, and he looked as if he might begin to weep. He wandered around, went to the magazines, and after a painful amount of time, when the place had cleared, the man came up to her and fumbled with a question about the books there. The skin around his eyes had aged from years upon the water, squinting at the sun, and he was hunched a bit, in the way that draft horses were when they finally had to be retired. And he was kind of bald, but in a truly curious way that suggested the cool and sterile airs of the operating room. Aside from these things, he was still very much the same fisherman she had helped all those years ago. He said, "I'd like to learn how to think." Nettie thought he might collapse. She had a sense that if she could keep the conversation going, he would be okay.

She said, "Well, first things first. We're going to have to get you a library card." As they were doing this, she said, "Do you remember me?"

He said, "Yes."

"Now, I imagine it's philosophy yer after," said Nettie. "Unfortunately, we don't have any philosophy."

He said, "I'm at yer mercy." She found him a book and said there were worse places to begin from if he wanted to learn to think, said it might be a bit of a slog for him, but it was important that he punch above his weight, so to speak. These were good tales about men and women trying to navigate the world, and while she was signing out the book, he was barely able to contain himself. The air positively rippled with his energy. And without glancing at the book, he ran out to his truck.

He finally looked down at the thing in his hands, delicate but of great import. You could just tell. It was called *The Moons of Jupiter*, and it was by a person named Alice Munro. He was shaking with excitement. He flipped it open to a random page and read a sentence, without knowing anything about what was going on or who was who. He read, "She made efforts one after the other. She set little blocks on top of one another and she had a day. Sometimes she almost could not do this. At other times the very deliberateness, the seeming arbitrariness, of what she was doing, the way she was living, exhilarated her." He looked up, through the windshield. His heart trembled as if he'd been given access to some essential secret, as if he were a kind of Adam. That he should be reading a book struck him as miraculous.

A rapping against the window made him jump, and he dropped the book to the red dirt about the pedals. He rolled down the window. Nettie passed him his card. "Don't worry. I'm not a deer," she said.

—

Herring was out at the wharf. It was a Saturday, and even though he'd just woken up, he was still tired. He had a Thermos beside him, and his mind was off somewhere, thinking about what, he knew not.

Frankie Millar, who was Preston's cousin, and his daughter, Celia, were smoking pot in Frankie's red rig. Frankie was hard on everything, wives and boats and wallets, especially rigs, and its front bumper looked like a bunch of black jeans tangled up in the wash. Celia had been dropped off a few minutes earlier by her mother, Frankie's ex-wife. Her mother had no time for Frankie. She thought he was a plague. Celia's mother was spending the day with her granddaughter, who waved from the back seat as they drove off.

Frankie wanted Herring to go into scallops with him. He said there was good money in it, fifteen bucks a pound, up from ten the year before. Herring said he'd think about it, but he already knew there was no way he was going scalloping with Frankie this year. It was cold and the shucking just destroyed your wrists. You were always playing hide-and-seek with the ferries. One season he and Frankie had been scalloping, and a storm moved in fast, and all of a sudden this giant wave, as black as coal, came over the bow and crashed through the windows, just filled the cabin right up with water, and for an endless moment everything had been dark and silent, no sensations at all. You couldn't even tell if you were wet or dry, floating in space or on the earth, alive or dead, and then everything snapped back into place, like a broken bone set right. The electrical was all gone. They'd had to flag down the *Holiday Island* and get towed back to Wood Islands, which was especially embarrassing because Frankie's wife, Celia's mother, had been on that same ferry, and she'd stood at the stern of it, despite the snow and the cold, and had just stared daggers into him and Herring the whole ride back to port. At the end of a day of scalloping, no matter the temperament of the water or the skies, you just couldn't wait to step off the boat onto the wharf.

Leigh drove up in Dunbar's rig and joined Herring at the picnic table. Herring was watching a fly dart around in the hair of his arm. Leigh looked at him, the bags under his eyes. "Jeez Louise, ya look like me," he said. Leigh was still trying to figure out what to do with the *Pair-a-Dice*. He'd put an ad in the *Graphic* and at the grocery store and the post office, but no one had answered them. "Man, all of his traps are still out there. You think they're chock full of lobster?" he said.

Herring said, "Well, it's less than two weeks to Canada Day." He didn't know how scared of the water he still was. Canoeing was one thing, but being back in a boat was another kind of beast altogether.

"You figure it's pretty slim pickings?" said Leigh.

Herring said, "Yeah, I imagine she's pretty skinny all right."

Leigh said, "You ever think that life is like one of those video games where yer character doesn't really move, just kinda hangs out at the bottom there, and that it's everything else that moves around ya?"

"My word, Leigh, where did you come up with that? I've been thinking the same damn thing," said Herring.

Leigh was pretty chuffed with himself. He said, "I guess mediocre minds think alike."

He lit a joint. Herring declined.

Leigh said, "When I worked at the grocery store there was this old fellow. He did the turnips and complained all day about his shingles. I worry that I'm turning into that guy. It can happen so quickly. Yer whole life just kinda disappears away from ya. You lose yer energy and drive and everything becomes pain and misery. You gotta end things with a bang, right? Anyway." Leigh leaned his head, cracked his neck.

A white van, so immaculate it looked as if it had just been stolen from the dealership, pulled into the parking lot and rolled slow and aimless for a while, its rubber crunching the gravel with a deliberateness that pained the ear. You could tell the driver was trying to figure out the best place to park. Some of the factory workers, in their white smocks and hair nets, having a smoke break, pointed at it with gloved hands, disbelieving of its spotlessness. Venerable Mike, Zhaxi, Pema, and one other fellow that Herring didn't know got out and approached Herring. Venerable Mike and Herring were excited to see one another.

Venerable Mike said, "Well, your hair is coming in nicely."

Herring said, "Yeah, it's like a bunch of tide pools, I spose." The monks were also pleased to see Leigh, and they greeted him with what seemed to Herring to be reverence and warmth. The monks sat at the table with their shaved heads and their copper robes, their cheap plastic-and-foam sandals and their skinny arms, and the group of them made quite a scene, indeed. The fish warden, standing near the crane, just watched and scratched her head. They looked like the punchline to a joke she couldn't remember. They had a box of donuts in the van and one of them brought these over to Herring's berth.

Leigh asked them if they wanted a drag of his joint. They politely dismissed his offer.

Venerable Mike had a proposition. "We'd like to go out with you today, provided that you are free, and return the lobsters back to the sea as a showing of compassion." Leigh was quick to nod and pucker his lips, as if he fully understood both the principles and consequences bound up in this notion. He said, "Man, are we going to get roasted or what." Herring was more than a little baffled. The idea struck him as both profound and ridiculous. Venerable Mike saw that Herring was struggling and leaned in closer to clarify their intent. He said, "Obviously, we'll pay you for your time and your lobster."

Herring said, "Give me a sec here." He thought of Alice Munro and the passage he'd been memorizing since the other day, except that the *she* in the story, an editor and poet by the name of Lydia, who was on an island off the coast of New Brunswick, had now become him, Herring. He didn't let the idea of pretending to become a woman in a short story trouble him all that much. Somehow it seemed more reasonable than not. He said the words, as best he could remember them, in his head like a kind of sacred mantra. He could do this thing as if it were a block on top of one another. As if his experiences were courses of brick or cinder block that extended from the earth up into some sky. As if he was a pillar or column, some stalwart thing, that bore without complaint the substance and authority of some greater beam. He would have a day. And though it seemed arbitrary, what they were doing, the way he was living, exhilarated him. He wondered if Venerable Mike had an idea of what had happened to him. If he did, as surely he must, was this a kind of test? Was this an instance of the universe reaching out for his cooperation? Was this a kind of strange threat, a real violence, dark and once suppressed, reaching out, aiming for him, and now disguised as kindness? What was this, exactly? He tried to envision himself after having done this thing, and then he tried to envision himself, what he would do and feel, having turned down the whole idea. Herring said, "I'll take no payment and I hope you fellas have yer sea legs."

The six of them headed out into a light rain and a bit of a northerly. Herring figured the traps Joe hadn't been able to find were split between Crow Bank and the Giant's Thumb. The monk Herring didn't know was wearing a toque. He started throwing up pretty bad. Herring told Leigh where the buckets were. Leigh said, "I can't look at him, 'cos I'll start throwing up." Venerable Mike wanted to know if there was any way to ease his sickness. Herring said, "I don't think this works, but try looking out at the horizon." The monk tried this but his nausea didn't quit. He sat near the wheelhouse and just heaved and heaved, sounded like meat getting pulled apart by dogs.

Herring gaffed the first blue-and-white buoy and showed Leigh and the monks how to operate the hauler. Jack and Deborah MacLeod sailed by as they headed for another dump. You could see them just staring, mouths open, the wheels just spinning and spinning.

The rain stopped and the clouds thinned out. The sun got through and lay out upon the water, charged and artificial as tinsel, and everybody was able to stop shivering a little with the boat just bobbing as it was and no breeze. Herring forgot how comfortable he felt in his bibs. He didn't feel too nervous, but he kept an eye on things. Sometimes his bowels could go on him when he was overwhelmed.

So, they got the dumps in, and the trays were holding some lobster. He had twenty-five traps stacked at the back of the boat. Five had been too damaged to salvage, so he cut the heads out of them, and then Leigh sent them over the side. There goes at least a grand, thought Leigh. Herring said they had, give or take, about seventy-five pounds of lobster. To the northeast, just near where the Magdalen Islands would be, rain clouds were hovering, the line between them and the horizon thick and dense, rippling like a surgical scar.

There had been some jellies in a few of the traps and each time they picked one, Herring would rush this creature, as soft and as delicate as a newborn, to the stern, like some crazed midwife, and gently place it back into the waters, anointing the lobster.

The monks wanted to know about molting. Herring told them how they pull themselves in and then flex until they break out of their shell. How sometimes they will eat their old shell for calcium and to speed up the growing of the new shell.

Pema said, "Does this happen just once?"

Herring said, "No, I think it can happen up to thirty times." The Buddhists liked this idea quite a bit, crowded around one another, passing the molting lobster like it was something worth understanding, some symbol of impermanence or rebirth. "All right, all right, that's enough of that. Put him back," said Herring. The monks returned this lobster to the waters.

Herring and Leigh stood in the wheelhouse and drank some coffee.

Leigh said, "You know this is like cuttin' a strip off the top of yer bedsheets, stitchin' it to the bottom, and expectin' it to be longer than when ya started, right?" Herring just nodded, his untidy eyebrows crawling for his scalp. They watched as Venerable Mike sprinkled the lobsters, a few big markets and just a gutload of canners, with purified water from a large container. A tiny bell was rung and then they began a prayer to the Buddha. They followed this with a chant that was, in Herring's estimation, rather simple and quite powerful, calm and assured, as true as a well-worn path, though he didn't understand what they were saying. A song like this had likely never been performed out here. The one fellow had stopped puking. He was white as a ghost and a little shaky on his feet, but he was making the most of things. Herring ushered him over, made sure he was drinking lots of water.

A few other boats, the *St. Elmo's Fire IV*, the *Pleasure Seeker*, the *Strait 'n Narrow*, and the *Jenny Lynn*, all sailed over, crowded around as if there were an injured beast before them to be put out of its misery, and watched as the monks lowered each lobster over the rail and dropped them but a hand or two from the water, just pebbles into an aquarium. A number of these watchers were downright angry, just plumb disgusted at the spectacle before their eyes.

Eben Daley hollered across the water, "Ya know they're just going to get caught again."

Billy Clow said, "Just like yer Spargo, eh? Still tryin'a build that communist Utopia, eh, Herring?"

The men all laughed a great uproar.

Billy Clow said, "Yer dumber than a pocket full of bumblebees."

Herring didn't say anything, but he could feel the old edge coming up in him. He wanted to tell all of them to fuck right off. What was needed was restraint. Block by block, brick by brick. Just build something and hold it as it is. Rankin Jackson threw his boat into full speed and took a run at the *M&M*, swerving around the prow by a matter of mere inches. He swung hard and, like some crazed sculptor, into the face of the waters he cut a series of sharpened ringlets, then headed for home. Another boat left, and then the rest began to follow suit, a fleet of squat boats, accelerating, pushing themselves down into the waters. A line of reckless monks who belonged to another order, insisted upon another interpretation. They had about them a smugness that was easily offended. A delicacy that was guarded by posturing and bombast, by the best way it knew. Anyway, it was starting to get real hot and their catch would spoil.

As they came in from the run, through the greens and reds, Herring could see that there was a great commotion at the wharf, cars and trucks and the odd media van parked on the concrete, and a line of people just staring out at his boat. What they had done caused quite an uproar. Herring hadn't really anticipated this. He was anxious about being embroiled in something again. Amongst the reporters waiting for them were Minnie Carver and Grant Gallant. When he saw them he got real angry and slammed his fists down on the dash by the throttle. Somebody had wanted this business to be one hell of a story.

There must have been about thirty people waiting at Herring's berth. Evelyn and Kemp were in the background. Rotten Rick and his man were there, hands on hips. Joe was absent.

The last time there'd been this much excitement at the wharf not related to Herring had been when a beluga whale got stuck in the bullpen. It had been quite the commotion, children running this way and that like it was the midway at the fair.

Having to perform routine actions under so much scrutiny was both bizarre and brutal. Herring felt that only now was he being made to run the gauntlet, to face his jury as a condemned man. He felt caged in and the anger and terror in him was seething. He and Leigh managed to get the boat all situated and tied up without bumping the timbers too fiercely. The monks climbed up onto the washboard and then up the ladder. Some people in the crowd laughed at the sight of these foreigners, with their robes and inadequate footwear, struggling to hoist themselves up to dry land, slipping on the wet rungs. It did make for a rather singular spectacle.

The reporters moved in, as if a great weather system. The clicks of cameras and jostling of shoulders dissonant and intense. He and Leigh took their oils off and hung them up in the cabin. Herring tended to his knobs and dials, his mind racing for a course of proper action.

Venerable Mike and his brothers explained with polish and elo-
quence what their intentions had been. There was a general sentiment
of mystified indignation, and it put Herring in mind of the hallways
in high school. Herring and Leigh finally came up onto the wharf. He
looked at Minnie and she looked back at him. The crowd let Leigh
through to his rig. He was too connected to Dunbar Gillis to torment
any further. Leigh drove off, his tires squealing and coughing up gravel. Herring started hauling the traps up onto the wharf. Minnie and
Grant approached him as he threw a trap into the back of his rig.
"In the name of time, away with ya." He cocked a fist and lunged at
them, and they backed away, the pair of them with these horrified and
pale looks on their faces. And, almost immediately, he felt the anger
and frustration recede, then disappear, and he was left within himself, trapped just like before. He felt the shame and embarrassment
smack him and he felt hollow and puerile. Eben Daley came right up
to Herring and said, "Ya know yer just putting more money into my
pocket, eh?" Herring said, "What is this, the fuckin' Via Dolorosa?"
Billy Clow marched over to them and said, "Always making a scene."
And then he clobbered Herring, who went down like a bag of bricks.
Fishermen moved to break the affair up, but as they did, confusion
grew as to who was doing what, who was on which side. Someone in
the crowd said, "Oh, shit, here it goes again." The monks ran for the
van. There was some shoving and pushing, the tearing of fabric and a
great litany of curses. Herring received a couple of kicks to the stomach and these hurt him, took the wind right out of him like a bank
account being emptied with all the ease of a button being pressed,
and his body went on him. The forklift operators stopped, pulled open
their windows, and watched the heave of it all while a school of pinfish
in the bullpen, this kind of swirling concatenation that was very much
like the exploratory fingers of lovers, completed the outlines of something that was instantly lost.

# ELEVEN

Around the middle of July, Herring took compost from the side of the house and added it to the vegetable patch. The work was slow and hard, and he didn't really know what he was doing, just kind of running on the fumes of his intuition, but he figured that he was having some fun. He also figured that to mess up gardening was going to be pretty damn hard to do. He'd go out in the late mornings and turn some soil and watch the cat frolicking in the field. Then he'd sit and read for a while. Herring got his cucumber seeds into the ground before it got unbearably hot, spacing them as Fletcher Jordan's mother had instructed, and when he was done, leaning on the handle of his shovel, his arms just dripping sweat, he felt a contentedness that was remarkably pure. He didn't rightly know how gardening gave him sensations of such cleanness and clarity. He just felt it to be the case. Perhaps it was akin to witnessing a teacher explain some algebraic solution. Even if your mind couldn't absolutely comprehend what on earth was happening, your soul, the very flesh of you, knew it was true. Love was like this, too. Sure, he could have asked Emerson White over to do the work in about twenty minutes with his tractor and his harrows, but he had wanted to do something honest and hard, and even a little bit crazy. And so, when he'd placed his cucumbers, and took a moment to reflect on the sheer amount of work he'd completed, he felt something very near to a first love.

He cleaned up the basement and avoided the wharf. He lounged and got a decent sunburn. He swept the deck so much it was as if he'd sandblasted the darn thing. It took work not to do anything. He still needed to heal up. He was taking the time. He was nervous, too, about going out. Sometimes he'd look at the black mess on the side of the house and an explosion would go off in his mind. Once in a while, Jack MacLeod would drive by and wave. Herring would just look at the man.

Things were about as tight as he could handle. He took a box of paperwork into the Hagman Earlys office in Montague. They went through it and told him that he was delinquent. Next, he called the Fishermen's Association to inquire about some help with a workers' compensation claim. They said they could help him out, but it would take time. "As I'm sure you know," the woman had said to him. Joe and Euna came around and dropped off some macaroni and cheese and some beans and molasses for him. Leigh came out, too, with lobster and potato salad. Leigh hadn't found anybody to help him finish the season. So he'd asked his mother, Sally, for a hand. They'd been estranged for a while, but she was a tough cookie, didn't take any crap, and they finished the season on something of a high note, too, though nobody was really talking to him. Things weren't great down at the bullpen. They surely weren't terrible, but, no, they weren't too fun, is the truth of the matter. Leigh said, "You wouldn't believe the paperwork I had to do just to eke out the season. I practically had to write essays to the government. God, it was some awful, let me tell ya. Felt like high school all over again."

Herring kept the house clean and made some calls about repairing the sliding doors. A guy came out and took some measurements, gave him a quote, said the number was a real good deal. Herring went upstairs and pulled his wool sock out from under the bed and counted the bills. He and the window guy haggled for a bit, but Herring got real bored with this and offered to pay him the amount of his initial quote. The guy said they'd send round their installer, a younger fella, in the next few days.

Herring made an appointment to see Newton MacDonald. He showed up to his appointment a few minutes late and resolutely refused any kind of physical. Newton insisted, at the very least, on checking his blood pressure. Herring said, "Have at 'er, hoss, but I can tell you it'll be off." He shifted his weight on the examination table, crinkling the paper sheet. Newton slid his cuff over the man's arm and pumped it up. He checked the man's ears and asked him about his diet. He asked him about drink, and Herring just grumbled. Newton paused his fussing and stared directly at the man. He asked him, given what had happened out there, how on earth he was doing, because he could tell, he had a sense, that Herring wanted to cut right to it. The fisher said that he believed he was suffering from some kind of depression, and then, as if he'd received a blow to the genitals, he leaned into his arms, stiffly braced upon his knees, and sighed. Newton wanted to know more about what Herring was thinking, but he could tell the man was trained to be impenetrable, and therefore more than a little reticent to share even minor, harmless particulars. Even this simple utterance sounded like the greatest of vulnerabilities, like the fellow was some military general overwhelmed by howitzers and long without reinforcement. Herring wanted to know about medicines. He was open to the idea of taking something to see if it might alter the activity in his brain. He knew about serotonin reuptake, because a friend of his, Gerry, had taken them for a time. Though they just seemed to make him groggy, dopey. Newton had a rough idea of Herring's struggles with addiction, but he was nevertheless willing to oblige him, given what the man had just lived through. Newton asked him if he had any desire to see a psychiatrist, and without hesitation Herring said no. He'd had to talk to one of them in the hospital. It was all a bunch of mumbo-jumbo. And, quite frankly, it was more than a tad insulting. Herring had gotten pretty worked up relaying all of this information. Newton asked him to lower his voice. Herring mentioned that his father had been mortally terrified of doctors. One time, later in his life, he took a double hernia. Herring had come over to see what he could do for the man, laid out upon the floor, as helpless as a calf, and the best he could think to do was to make a kind of support out of the inner tube from a tractor wheel. His father had worn this thing till the day he died.

Herring had been trying to think about things, you know, to really think about things. About science versus survival, or some such duality. There was quite a bit going on in the man, thought Newton. Herring said, "Years ago, when I was trying AA for the first time, there was a woman there, just pullin' on a bottle of beer. Nobody said a word about it. But my goodness, the nerve. I've never forgotten it." Newton gave him a script for an antidepressant. Herring said, "It's all over but the cryin'." Herring asked him if he knew anything about philosophy. Newton said he'd read a bit of Nietzsche at university. "That's good," said Herring. "How do ya spell that?" And when he spelled it for him, though he couldn't recall if it was right, the man wrote it down on his script. "Hell of a name, but that's good, doc." He slapped him on the back, and Newton felt, very briefly, that the only thing holding him upright was the strength of his toes pressing down into his orthopedics.

—

When the window installer showed up, Herring was cutting the lawn. A faint bit of rain was coming down, and his boots were caked with grass. He was riddled with mosquito bites and looked like he had a pox. A gull had crapped on the tractor as he was doing his passes. The window fellow was tiny and drunk. A boy, really.

"Who's yer father?" Herring asked.

"Charlie O'Connor," said the boy. "From Five Houses."

"The same Charlie O'Connor who pitched a bottle of Gibson's Finest through the back window of my rig?"

"Yup, that sounds like my father," said the boy. "He's some terrible for sacrificing his bottles."

Herring was nervous about him operating tools and whatnot. He hovered about the kid for a few minutes, enough to annoy him. So, Herring had to just let him do his thing. He didn't want to piss the boy off and have him do poor work. But he also figured the kid didn't know how to do quality work. As far as he could remember, his signature wasn't on anything. If need be, he was prepared to make a stink. He figured that today this wave was going to break one of two ways.

Herring sat in the kitchen, drinking water, the cat nearby, waiting for a sunbeam to bask in. The fellow, who was probably in his early twenties, would work for about a quarter of an hour, swearing at the screws that wouldn't take or the drill that didn't have enough battery, then shuffle off to his rig. When he came back, the smell of him was ripe. Herring had to get up and leave. He went downstairs and read from the Munro. He looked at where the hole had been. It looked like an eye patch. There was a bit of quiet and it put him on edge. Herring walked upstairs. The sun was brilliant and you could hear the wetness evaporating, blistering. The glass fellow was up in the bedroom, rooting around for money, presumably. Herring scared the boy, and he tried at making a poor excuse, but Herring wasn't having it. He grabbed him by the collar and hauled him down the stairs. Luckily, the fellow was pretty cut, so he was mostly just dead weight. He dragged him into the kitchen and checked his pockets. The boy was red and breathing heavily, like a finger struck by the face of a hammer, but mostly he hadn't uttered a word. He was resigned. There was a light ding near the man's left hip and there it was, Euna's engagement ring upon the floor.

The boy said, "What can I say? I like shiny things. Must be the Indian in me."

"What do you know about being an Indian, you cocksucker," said Herring, and he walloped him right in the breadbasket. The lad let out a splendid rattle, as if he were a pair of bellows, and clutched his guts while he sank.

He drove the fellow down to the beach at the cove. The water was as still as a countertop. Drinking and smoking over by the sandstone promontory, a couple of Mexicans watched Herring drag the boy through the sand. Herring said, "Oh-la," and waved halfheartedly. He pulled the kid into the waters, scurrying crabs this way and that. The window fellow let out a holler, started slapping the water. He must have sucked up a great bit of water, because he took to coughing and spitting, screaming that he couldn't swim. When the water had passed his waist, and he was decently soaked from the struggle, Herring gave the boy a great push, this chaos of thrashing and kicking, and the fellow was pulled away from shore, his boots unable to find the bottom, his throat and jaw at the surface like a bow on a fiddle string, all vibration and passage.

Herring watched him, struggling as he was. There was no joy in this for him. In fact, he was nervous. It seemed the more he wanted tranquility, the more life was coming at him. About fifteen fathom out from shore a number of sea lions floated, watching. Herring cupped two hands around his mouth and said, "Careful there, O'Connor, they'll bite yer face off." The Mexicans remained seated, cigarettes burning from between pinched fingers. When the screaming began, Herring cursed his stupidity and ran back into the waters. He latched himself on the boy's legs and hollered that if he kicked him he really would leave him be. Herring pulled the fellow in until the seat of his denims were on dry sand.

He was coughing water and shaking and crying a wee bit. Herring allowed him a few moments to gather what composure he could, and then he dragged the boy over the sands and up the narrow path worn so by the spring runoff, and threw him in the back of his rig. He drove home. He gave the boy some clothes while his own were drying and helped him finish the installation. Herring told the boy that he would do the caulking himself. They finished and looked at the job. The boy slid the doors back and forth like he was showing them how to line dance, and then he put his right hand on the glass and said, "This is glass, but it's also sand. Most people don't understand that a thing could be two things at once, eh."

Herring saw him to his truck. "What about the money?" said the boy. Herring said, "I'll drop it off with yer employer." The kid didn't want to budge. An outboard was roaring up the river. An eighteen-wheeler thundered by, engaging the Jake Brake. The boy hopped into the driver's seat, wrote something on a pad of paper, and left.

——

For a while the only calls Herring got were about overdue bills.

—

In the first days of September, the remnants of a hurricane made landfall. Down at the harbour, the boys started shuffling their boats. Herring went down and watched the *M&M* batter and pummel the fenders on the wharf. The winds were remarkably intense, and Herring spent two sleepless nights pacing the house with a flashlight, waiting for something to give, for the roof to be pulled right off and a mighty torrent of water to be released inward. The cat got spooked and disappeared on him. He had two pounds of blueberries in his freezer. He ate these until he swore he'd never touch another blueberry again. This seemed like a great shame to him. The redfish and gaspereau in his freezer went bad. He loaded his rig and drove down to the cove and threw it all into the water, so that it looked like a school of fish trying to run up a shallow creek. Gulls swooped down and began thrashing at the surface of the water.

A great many power lines were down, and trees lay shattered across boats and sheds and some of the roads. He felled a Norway pine on the property and loaded up the basement with wood. He went to visit Sellar Hume out at the shore. Sellar was splitting a pile of his wood in the rain.

He said, "Hey, I know ya."

Herring said, "Sellar, you work too hard." His collie was sitting in the barn. Herring said, "You can tell he's smart as a whip."

Sellar said, "Yeah, I get him to do my taxes."

The old man showed him a giant American elm by his barn. He said, "The wind blew it right over on the first day. And then when the winds changed direction on the second day, they picked it up again and set it right back." Sellar put a four-foot level on its trunk. He said, "It's just about plumb, for Christ's sake."

—

He walked down to the beach early one morning and watched Agnes swimming for shore, her front strokes dark and angled scythes mowing through the waters. In the shallows, she stood up and walked in, her knees supplely rising and falling through the rising tide, as if she were a blend of rider and horse performing an elegant passage, her skin glistening and her hair disappeared beneath a swim cap. She was surprised to see him. They walked for a while, up the dirt lane to the shore road. The pavement was getting hot. He could smell the salt drying on her skin, the veins in her legs as bright as the tentacles of jellyfish.

She found his energy to be poignant, and it made her a little uneasy. Her heart was thumping in her chest. Agnes waited for him to say what he wanted to say. She wondered, very briefly, why she hadn't gone to see him since the incident. She had no need to explain herself to a man such as he. Agnes asked him if he wanted to come in for a spot of coffee. Herring said, "No, thanks." Agnes wished him a good day and retreated from his awkwardness. When she got inside she watched him out at the road, bent over, looking at something near his feet.

—

Herring season had begun. The few boats that were still interested in throwing money at the harvest were out, dropping their nets into the waters. One day, a coast guard helicopter flew over the wharf, and about twenty minutes later a herring boat that was set up to the gunwales in the water was towed into the harbour by Leverett and Lowell MacNeil. Lowell cut the rope as they neared the slip, and the boat crunched into the concrete of the Berlin Wall just next to the wharf. Somebody said, "Oh, that's not good." The volunteer fire department was already there, with generators and pumps, and somebody ran a line of rope from the boat to an awaiting tractor helmed by Sheldon Brehaut. The boat, which was from out of North Lake and captained by a Mi'kmaq fellow, was pretty well on its side. They had to get the water out of her before they could try to pull her over to the slip. It was chaos for a while. All of the women in the fish plant came out and watched, as the volunteer firefighters, in shorts and flip flops, began removing the decking so that they could get at the fish trays.

Herring said, "I'd say there's about sixteen thousand pounds of herring on there."

Leverett looked at all of the women and said, "Next time, I'm just going to sail out and set my boat on fire and wait for all the women to gather 'round. A drowning man isn't a single man for very long, I reckon."

There was water in the wheelhouse, and all of this hectic activity, bodies brushing the wooden rails, the light breezes of chaos, sent a covey of herring scales up into the sky, as if something that could not be saved was on fire.

It turned out that the trouble began because an engine casing had gone, and no one on board had noticed until it was too late. To make matters worse, the fish trays weren't properly braced, which led to them sliding all around the hull. The captain was standing in the background with one of the MacKays, just hauling on a joint to get some peace into him. Someone said, "Greedy fucker. Ya didn't even unload her." They snapped a few lengths of rope getting the boat up the slip so that they could get the crane onto the trays. Each time a rope went, Sheldon would holler out, "See, just like a bra on prom night." The boat was called the *Morning Dawn*, and Herring said, "Should start calling her the *Going Down*." He watched spiders rappel down the rails of the boat. Clarence Clements wandered by not long after. The captain had lost his credit card and Clarence found it on the asphalt. Clarence appraised the scene before him and showed Herring and Leverett the card again so as to reinforce the true cost of reckless-ness and inexperience. The fellow said, "And this, my friends, is why ya don't let Natives fish."

—

In October, the fellows went out in their punts, just north of the bullpen, and set their mud anchors and nets and their keg buoys for silversides. These were sold as lobster bait, as well as to zoos to feed their polar bears and otters and penguins. Gulls and terns would come and land on the compartment floats for an easy meal when the fishermen weren't out. When they were out, they stood up in their boats, hands on the tillers, their heads mostly down, solemn and bored, looking at the nets, heaving and flowing in the dark waters like bouffant dresses.

The potato harvest fired up, and the trucks began churning up the roads pretty good. On some of the more severe corners, especially out near the shore where the roads had a tendency to wind, potatoes would roll off the trucks and begin to accumulate, so that they looked like trail markers for some sacred route, some pilgrimage.

Herring met Kemp Reilly one day, and Kemp told him about coming back from North Lake about a week prior. It was early afternoon on a properly sunny Friday, and he passed Edith going the other way, swerving all over the road with a hole in her windshield about the size of a human. "Her eyes were just these plump things, as white as doves." Kemp's spidey sense got cooking real good, and about a kilometre down the road he found a young guy crumpled in the ditch. "Must've been out for a run," said Kemp. "I didn't even have to check his pulse." The RCMP found Edith about an hour later, still in her rig, just passed right out, the e-brake on and the transmission still in drive. Vodka bottles every which way. Kemp said, "Who am I to judge the woman. I've certainly driven drunk before."

Herring went down to the wharf and watched a boat bring in a two-hundred-and-fifty-pound halibut. The boys were pretty amped up about their haul, walking around the deck in disbelief. The fishing warden looked at her clipboard and said, "Well, that's the last tag." A jug of rum was passed around and everybody had a pull. The halibut hung there from the crane, one side dark and one side white, like a talisman of good and evil.

—

When Gerry showed up in his father's van, Herring was harvesting his cucumbers. Birds had picked at a great many of them, hollowing them out with their beaks so that they looked like auricles. Herring washed the cucumbers and gave one to Gerry. Gerry held it in his hands, this yellowed thing. He said, "The big crunch, eh?"

Gerry looked good. Some measure of age had come off him. He was lean and muscular in all the right places. His eyes were clean and clear, and his clothes fit him. His bridge was in and he smiled a lot because he liked showing it off. He'd been to anger management. There was a teenager there who used to beat up his own parents every night. "I didn't belong there." The nails on his fingers had shrunk and migrated from being wet so much, but they had also continued to grow, still required cutting, and the effect it had was truly odd to him. He'd look at them, this contrivance of a pair of hands, and each time he was more amazed than the last. He cut himself a length of cucumber and tried a bite. "God, these taste ignorant," he said, spitting out the flesh. "I'd say you've left 'em too long."

Herring said, "Aw, shit. Yer kiddin' me." He took a bite out of one and scrunched his face. "That is rank." Gerry said, "So much for that, green thumb."

Gerry said, "I seen a shark come up the Seal River a ways." He had also tried salmon fishing up in the Morell River for a while. He said, "It's only fly fishing from June first onward. I'm no angler, so I'd wait for the fishermen to go home, and then I'd sneak out. I could've done Leards Pond, but ya need a boat for that. I don't got no boat." Herring made him a bite to eat, some scrambled eggs and toast. "You gotta fish with the tide so that ya don't destroy the bottom. I prefer fishing for salmon earlier in the season, 'cos they're fresher in from the salt. Later in the season you just don't know how long they've been dawdling in the river." Gerry had a slug of some iced tea. He licked his lips. "Anyway," he said. "It's pretty good. All you really need is a good pair of sneakers and some dedication."

—

Herring was filling up the rig at Miller's when he noticed a large white trailer being dropped off at the wharf. There were a couple of rigs idling in the parking lot, water dropping from their tailpipes, a few old fellows walking around, looking at a big set of drawings. They'd stop every once in a while and point at something and then disappear into the drawings. Eventually they'd nod and continue walking until another notion took hold and they pointed at something else. A young woman in a white hard hat, with a little dog at her side, was smoking at a rapid patter, her knees just bouncing and her nails fluorescent pink, as she watched the trailer reverse beside the line of pine trees.

The next day he went over and knocked on the door of the trailer. As he stood and waited, he could feel the unevenness of the aluminum stairs.

Her name was Christine. She sat him down in the office part of the trailer and shut the door behind them. The beagle came up to him and sat between his legs. He asked her what the project was, and whether they were looking for workers, said that he didn't have a ton of experience in construction. He said, "I've got to let you know, if yer hiring me, yer also hiring my buddy Gerry. We're a twofer kind of deal, huh. I show up, he shows up." She said, "Oh, okay." She looked past him, at the light out the window, and then she rolled the pieces of paper before her up into a tight little cylinder. "Well, would he mind coming in?" Herring said probably not. "But if I get the job, he's gettin' a job, too." Christine scratched her forehead. There was a calendar behind her on the wall and each day of the month that had come to pass had a thick, black X through it.

Herring would have to go home and update his resumé, which meant he'd have to go home and write the thing out by hand. Then he'd get the girls to type it up for him. Wasn't going to be much on it other than self-employed and fishing, anyway.

When he exited the makeshift office, two young fellows and an old guy were setting up sections of a boom, unspooling the cables for this real ancient Dominion crane. A truck showed up with a clam bucket in the back. Herring stayed to watch them hook up the clam bucket to the crane, the cables twisting in the wind, singing with the strain of it all.

—

He drove to Belfast and worked with the girls to fancy up his resumé. Euna was sitting on the couch, drinking a bottle of non-alcoholic beer, wool socks in a pair of leather sandals. There was a jug of lilacs on the coffee table. He sat with her while the girls watched their television program. They were into British murder mysteries.

Euna just came right out with it. "How'd you do it? How did you live?"

He was surprised and impressed, because until now, no one he knew well had directly asked him about it. He fumbled around for a bit with his words. "Forgive me," he said. He realized he didn't actually know what he wanted to say. It was there, though. He just needed to crack away at it, take a few practice swings. He said, "Well, the truth of it is that, years ago, my father told me that yer only really wet when you get out of the water. I never really understood this, but it seemed to me there was something to it. So, anyway, I just stayed under the water as much as I could when I was out there. I imagined that I was a fish caught by the gills in a sheet of net. That the things that were horizontal were really vertical, you see? That I wasn't wet at all, but that, if I wanted to be, I was actually dry as a bone. The more I tried to push forward, the wetter I would become, and that if I became wet, if I tried to leave where I was, that this would be the thing to kill me."

"Like mind over matter?" Euna said.

"Yeah, something like that." He had his piece of paper in his hand. His name in the top left, and below, his entire life in a couple of paltry lines. "Now what do I do? I'm just kinda leftovers." He said, "You know, if I can be honest, I've felt dead inside for a long time. I guess I want to figure out how to live. It'll be tricky with the girls. I know I owe you quite a bit of money, but if you'd not mind helping me out, I'd be grateful. I spose what I'm asking for is a bit of patience, huh." With her free hand, Euna wiped the condensation off of her bottle, her fingers wet with it. "There was always this kind of power thing with us that I never liked," he said. "Like, I could feel it there, but I just couldn't find a way to talk about it. Do you know what I'm talking about?"

"Yeah," she said. "I know what you mean."

"It was like we were always fighting each other rather than working together," he said.

"I noticed it, too," she said. "A few months after we got married. It just kinda arrived. I guess I ought to have done more. Worked a little harder. I guess I was just lazy."

They were quiet for a moment, staring right before them. He could hear her blinking. Euna said, "I'm worried that I'm a piece of shit."

And something cracked between them, gently, like an egg meeting the lip of a bowl.

He said, "I worry about that, too. Sometimes I just feel totally rotten inside."

"I know that you'd do anything you could for me and the girls," she said.

"When I think about it, it drives me just about crazy." He looked at her. "You and the girls are the centre of the world to me."

"You're a warrior," she said. "I've always loved this about you."

"I'm sad. I'm lost. I'm miserable. I've burned every bridge I ever travelled across. And what's worse, it seemed like I knew what I was doing, the whole time. Like I had to make things as hard as possible, for some idea that I don't really understand. And yet, I still have this life in me." He truly missed her, missed her presence, her warmth, missed how her hairs would gather in their bed when they had made love. "What's wrong with me?" he said.

These ideas were deep in him, precisely because they had never been uttered. He'd pushed them down to keep them safe, to keep them secret. This was his way. Euna felt the magnitude of this little moment. She felt his body heave as he talked. He'd been broken again and again and again. Dashed against the rocks, so to speak. Euna took a few breaths and looked at him, so strange and yet so familiar.

"I don't know," Euna said.

"Well, at the end of it all," he said, "I guess you could say that I was willing to die so that people could eat. No matter all the stupid shit I've done, I'll always have this. Be able to say this about myself. And that's not nothing, huh."

Euna stood and walked over to him. She motioned and he took his shirt off and leaned forward. She inspected the back of his neck and the broad of his shoulders for blackheads.

"Pretty greasy back here," she said, her fingers pinching, then brushing the plugs away.

He said, "I wanted to tell you that I'm grateful for you. That I know you loved me as well as you could." He chose not to speak about her bar of soap, of how he had it with him when he went over, of how he'd cradled it in his hands, how he watched it go, of how the sea took it from him, slowly and in the smallest of increments, this solid thing that became a kind of cloud, as if it were burning sage, until his hands were empty.

Euna said, "Well, I'm grateful that at least you're flossing yer teeth these days."

—

It took them a few weeks to dredge the wharf. Gerry and Herring would stand out on a little raft with a sounding stick, while the crane dropped the bucket down. They hauled up everything. Old bicycles. A bunch of drive shafts. Timbers soaked in oil. Liquor bottles packed tight with mud. The crane would swing its load and release its burden into the backs of trucks, and the ground would be sprinkled with silversides, like a mountain range of jewels. They'd come back to work on a Monday and the minnows would still flop a bit if you poked them with your finger.

The work was hard on both him and Gerry, but it was a regular paycheque, every Thursday. Some of the guys wouldn't show up on Fridays, so the boss, this old guy from Ontario, said that he'd have to start paying them on Friday nights, just so he could get a full week of work out of everybody. There was always something different to be doing. Gerry would say, "I'm like a pecker. I just go where I'm shoved."

The boss walked around a lot, smoking and cursing and complaining about the government. The things in the world that escaped his sense were always reduced to conspiracies. He'd say that every day was just a newer set of problems. He'd been a diver with the navy, and all he had to show for it was a pair of bad hips and a heart attack. He got bored one week and bought an old submersible from some fellow in Florida. One day it showed up on site, this great white-and-yellow iron orb without propellers. The boss couldn't fit through the damn hatch, though, so the thing languished where it had been left. He praised fellows who picked up nails. For him, this meant an attention to detail and a dislike of waste. He'd say, "Those things are tire killers." Herring told him about all the times he had driven over his oyster tongs, the five nice little holes in his tires. The boss didn't like nervousness in a man. Consequently, he didn't think much of Gerry.

The project manager was an even older fellow, named Lloyd, who really ought to have been in retirement, because he'd had a string of minor heart attacks as well. He'd walk around with a little red book and a tape measure and hum and haw. Herring and Gerry liked him. Once in a while he'd buy them lobster chowder from Keeping's, and they'd talk about all the stupid stuff that had happened to them, except that Herring never talked to anybody about when he was lost at sea. He and Gerry didn't need to bring it up. Though it was always there, the whole thing had a peace to it, which both men seemed to understand and appreciate. Sometimes it's nice to have a secret. Lloyd was a Christian in the truest sense of the word. Some days he liked to talk about the soul and Gerry would say, "The only sole a man's got is on his feet." Herring didn't quite agree with this statement, but he kept his mouth shut. He had some secrets, too.

They drove piles with the crane. At lunch, the truckers would tell stories in the trailer about the prostitutes who frequented the stops. "We call 'em lot lizards," said one fellow named Walter. He was from Launching and was into motorcycles and golfing, didn't seem interested in ever really moving too fast. After a while, Walter got sick of hauling. The boss sent him home, and Walter lazed about, crushing tallboys and collecting pogey. Mostly everybody liked being there at the wharf. Having the work was just a real nice thing. There were some fights, of course, but again, there was a real sense of fellowship. Sometimes the boss would be yelling at a fellow, just right up in his face, and the fellow would say, "Ontario, if ya ever, I mean ever, growl at me again I'm going to knock yer goddamn block off." When they got onto the topic, the crane operator would say, "Just can't figure it out. There should've been a line of guys outside that trailer lookin' for work."

Sometimes the local dogs would trot about the site and the guys would hand them scraps of sandwiches. One fellow had thick fingers and long nails and would smoke pot in the bait sheds when the boss wasn't looking. He called his hammer the swing-bang. He ate pomelos at least once a week. Most of the guys had never seen something like this before. The fellow said they were like Asian grapefruits. He'd cut them right on the lunch table, squirting juice every which way. He'd been all the way up to Greenland for herring. He said the crew would hang two dead sheep off the bow rigging, and when the meat started to fall off the bone, that's when it was good to eat. Gerry asked him what it tasted like and he said, "You ever dip a rag in 5W-40 and try to swallow that?"

One of the guys, when he sneezed, which was often, always released five rapid-fire sneezes, like he was firing off a machine gun or something. One day he only sneezed four times, and that night he suffered a heart attack. He never showed up again. Another of the drivers liked to pass around photos of women's crotches, which he'd removed from old porno magazines. He'd present one to Herring, arch his eyebrows real high, and then say, huh, as if he was selling you something that you didn't really need or want. Like a time-share somewhere in Florida.

There was also this Acadian fellow who had the stomach of a dog. Sometimes at lunch the boys would gather around and watch him eat twelve raw quahogs for lunch. Just sit there, a kind of freak show, and pry them open with his knife. "I'd say, come tonight, his arse is going to be on the ceiling." That he couldn't read or write came to be common knowledge after a few weeks. Mostly everyone was surprised he was able to keep this hidden for as long as he did. He got everywhere by landmarks. If you needed him to go fetch something, a hydraulic coupling or a box of nails, you had to tell him to look for the gas station, hang a left by the old red house on the hill, and just keep driving straight till you hit the end. He got his wife to fill out his timesheets. She signed his cheques, too. Herring got to thinking about this arrangement and he said, "What a saint she must be." He meant it, because his body knew it to be true. He would picture her seated at the kitchen table, late at night, while her husband nursed a beer in front of the game in the room next door, ordering his life, the life of another, and he knew that these acts were holy intercessions. One time the Acadian fellow told him about fishing for smelts in his shack, and how a seal came right up through the hole in the ice with a kitten in its mouth that was still alive. He took the kitten and tucked it into his jacket and walked him home. The cat had been with him and his wife ever since. He'd refused to name the thing and cited some precedent that Herring didn't understand.

Herring lost a great deal of weight and got muscular again. He liked this, the joy of feeling the body grow strong all over. He'd find himself swinging a sledgehammer, pounding a two-foot bolt through walers and fenders, and he could just feel everything flex. He was bigger and smaller at the same time. He tore the skin on his shoulders off, from carrying lumber and steel, and as the skin tried to heal, the dead flaked skin looked to him like epaulettes. Some mornings he'd ride his bike into work from the cove, and his head would be dizzy and light, just swimming until that first cup of coffee. The other fellows made fun of him, but he didn't care all that much. After too many years of being alone, mostly he was grateful for the company. It was nice to be around people, to hear them whinge and complain. He'd get home so exhausted that he only had enough time to press some microwaved food into his mouth before he fell asleep, a filthy man on a grimy chesterfield or in a grimy bed, but he was getting a glow back, some of the jam of youth. His sheets on the line, stained with red clay, bore the evidence of this. One day he was welding a length of angle to the old Berlin Wall, and an ember landed on the cotton of his gloves and burned right through his flesh. There was this liquid that immediately started coming out that put him in mind of seawater through scuppers, and the wound looked like a woman's crotch. At night, he'd stare at it and feel the pain surge up the whole of his arm and make contact with his brain. He'd say, "I'm alive." Because, you see, he was alive. When Gerry saw the wound, he said, "It's a long way from yer heart."

Some of the guys, when their tape measures were out and they were putting something together, as if to excuse a fundamental lack of skill, would say, "We're not building pianos here." And others, as if to defend a lack of ethic, would say, "We're not building the Taj Mahal here." One fellow, who would count out eighths on his left hand while his other held his tape, the yellow blade of it drawn out upon a piece of lumber, would declare, "You only gotta be close with horseshoes and hand grenades, eh." He did this at least once a week, and Gerry would dutifully wait a few beats after the delivery of this line, then say, "I'm awful certain you're using that the wrong way." And the fellow would say, "No flies on you, eh McClellan?"

He thought about selling the boat and the licence. His father had bought the original licence from the Fisheries Office in Montague, in 1964, for twenty-five cents. Now, it and all the gear could go for well past a quarter of a million. He felt a nostalgia for his old life grow in him. A painful hunger in the belly. It scratched at him, like a deer through the ice. But he knew that if you didn't have a trade or work on the ferry, there wasn't much going on. He understood that he really didn't have much to bring to the table.

Meaney came out on a Saturday and hauled the *M&M* out, free of charge. They got the boat up, cradled on stands and the creosote sleepers, with a little tilt to her. Herring took the plug out the keel.

"You can have it if you want, Johnnie," said Herring.

Meaney laughed and said, "Nope, I don't want the headache."

Herring asked how Faustina was doing. Johnnie said, "She's prayin' a lot these days. You know, the world could end on a weekend and no one would be the wiser for it." Herring shook his hand and said, "Right, wrong, whatever. It is what it is." And Meaney said, "Well, it's not what it isn't, eh."

Herring and Gerry spent the better part of a day taking the mussels and barnacles off the hull and the prop with a pair of angle grinders.

Word was that Billy Clow and Jack MacLeod had hauled in a tuna, about half a ton. A shark had followed them all the way into the bullpen. Miles Mackenzie was out on the floating docks with a mackerel in his hand, going, "Here, kitty kitty."

Herring said, "Jesus, he's one special kind of fucking stupid."

Howard MacNeil and Clarence Clements were at the wharf, too, watching the show.

Howard said, "I had the record for the biggest tuna outta Rustico, for about thirty seconds. Mine was nine hundred and eighty pounds, and I fought 'er for fifty-nine minutes. Fella sailin' behind me caught one just over a thousand."

"'Member that foreign fella who'd come up every year, with a little donut-shaped raft thingy, there, and would go tuna fishin', insistin' that if he caught one, to just cut him loose from the towline. He wanted to feel the fight, and I spose to see how far a tuna could take him," said Clarence.

Howard couldn't place the name of the man, but, yes, he did remember him.

Billy said, "Back in the day you could put a herring on the gaff, and ya'd get a tuna jump right outta the water and take it off yer hook."

Gerry said he always enjoyed when you were jigging for mackerel and they'd do that. "Just a beautiful creature." Gerry recalled fishing with some cousins. How they had fought for their tuna all the way up to Chéticamp. Butchered it for $1.85 a pound. His cousin, Lyman, had looked up at the crew with this utterly disgusted look on his face, the shame of Judas Iscariot, his scrag marked with blood, and declared, "Never again will I kill such a fine thing for money. Never again." His gloved hands pinching one another, uncertain as to whether or not they might be trusted.

Years ago, Herring had gone to Keeping's and bought a shoulder of beef, and then he and Joe had sailed out for a shark. It was just catch-and-release, and a whole whack of paperwork, and nothing came of it, for they hadn't got anything. The deficit had been crushing at the time, but they got over it.

Billy said, "You know when you got a tuna defeated because they start doing their death circle under the boat to tangle yer line in the prop. That's when you know."

The fish warden said that there were only three tags left.

Jack said, "Fishing for tuna is better than sex. And, what's best, there's no complaining."

Billy started cutting the gut, running his hand through the crescent of its belly, while Jack put on shoulder-length gloves and began cutting the head off. The body was put into a tray of ice. Blood was everywhere, and for a while the head of the tuna sat on the wharf, shaded by a thick cloud of gulls billowing overhead.

—

Some nights Gerry and Herring would park in the lot at St. Mary's and watch the Catholics cross themselves as they passed the church. They drank water and crunched their way through bags of ketchup chips. They talked as openly as they could about Euna and the girls, Sheila and Susan and the boys. Regarding Sheila, Gerry would simply say, "God bless her hairy hole." They shared their shortcomings and failures. They spoke until they stumbled upon what it was that was truly bothering them, and then they would become quiet and wait for these thoughts to pass.

Gerry said, "A fella I know just told me, like, if the anxiety gets to be too much, you just put yer head between yer legs and wait for everything to pass." Gerry talked about his boys, Robbie and Mickey. "Boy, they're hungry fellas. The both of them go through four litres of milk a day," he said. "The thing about having kids is you spend nine months tryin' to get outta it and the rest of yer life tryin' to get back in." Gerry adjusted his collar and blinked his lids real heavily. He said, "The whole world is just hurry up and wait. Hurry up and wait."

A rig would approach from up the hill, and they'd call it as either a Believer or a Heathen. They made a game of this. Turns out they weren't particularly good at predicting what kind of vehicles Catholics drove. But usually, if it was a pretty beat-up rig, filled with fishing trays and ropes, the drivers would make the sign. Of this Trinitarian formula, Gerry said, "Boy oh boy, when I was just a runt, I thought for sure I'd wear my forehead out making the sign."

Herring said, "This fella was walking by the church, and he seen these two altar boys sitting in the snow. What are you doing, he says, and they say, Oh, the priest likes a couple of cold ones after mass."

Gerry opened a chocolate bar and bit into it.

"Teeth are holding up, I see."

"I'm just like a golden retriever pup," said Gerry.

Herring said, "I've lived my whole life like a bumped elbow."

Gerry said, "My life has been nothing but a serious case of the fuck-its." There was shame in his voice, timid and unsure, as if his body had grown another, younger tongue, which was now jockeying for position with the erstwhile one.

"You know, it's funny," said Herring, "when I was young I thought I'd be kinda extraordinary, that people would be in awe of me, for some reason I never quite figured out. As I've gotten older, it's turned out that I'm just no better'n mediocre." He laughed sharply. "Who did I think I was. How queer I am, eh. Some strange joke, I guess."

And then a memory rose and unfurled itself, like a boot tread in a cow patty, about how years ago there had been this real hole-in-the-wall bar in the harbour called The Cotton Club. Why it was called this, no one rightly knew, though it sounded vaguely like what a proper and self-respecting bar ought to be called. Anyway, Herring had shown up with his girlfriend, and Gerry was there, as drunk and as useless as ever, but somehow still kind of charming, like wet sandpaper. Herring went home early and left his girlfriend there. A few days later, he found out that Gerry had gone home with her. He'd never confronted him about it. Perhaps he ought to have. Perhaps this was the moment when the people he knew and valued, no matter the degree, lost respect for him. He wondered if Gerry recalled this betrayal, or if he even recalled this woman. He was awful messed up at that time in his life.

And then Gerry, as if he knew what Herring was thinking, said, "When I was just a squirt I had this real strong image of a house that was a circle. There's one of 'em out in Pownal. You know the one, right?" Herring nodded. "Somehow or another I musta got the idea into my head after seeing that place on the water there in Pownal, just by the Sugar Shack. I wanted to get a piece of land for myself and build one of these circular houses. It didn't matter where. I didn't really know why. It was just one of these things that gets stuck in ya. Like a vision of how the world ought to be. But I also kinda knew that if I did this thing, built this strange house, after it was all done, nothing would have changed. Like, I'd do this thing, and then, poof, so what? Anyway, years later, I was talking to some fella about this or that, and he told me that a round house means that the Devil has no corners to hide behind." Gerry looked over at him. "I wondered if I kinda knew that all along, ya know."

—

The sun had been down for a few hours. They walked out to Jack MacLeod's place with a bread bag full of dead mackerel. They gave one to the bulky dog chained to the stump, to keep him quiet, and then they pulled the hubcaps off of the rigs in the drive, put the dead mackerel in them, and pushed the caps back on. "There, that'll teach him," said Herring. Next year, if need be, he'd happily cut some of the man's buoys.

—

In the middle of the night he came out to see the boat, the ballast of its form illuminated by the moon, the sky dark and the tops of the trees jagged, tempered fangs. He put the wooden ladder against the hull and climbed up onto the deck. The wetness on all surfaces slight but somehow a safeguard. He stared at the boat and it felt like a stranger to him. He didn't know if it was a friend or a foe, and his instincts seemed unsure, or reticent, to help him sort this complication out. He pictured Gerry in high school, on the cross-country team, for he'd been a championship runner. As shirtless and shoeless as some messiah, just to rub it in to all the white boys with lawyers for parents and all the latest, most expensive gear, dashing all over the Maritimes, just cleaning up all the medals with these tremendous strides. A truly free and unbroken human being. Herring went to the stern and stood himself where he had fallen, where he had disappeared, the darkened ground below.

—

About November, Herring finally got the washing machine fixed and put four cords of wood into the basement, and then he moved into his father's old property out at the cove. The sky pitch black by suppertime. Snow was on the way. Euna and the girls moved back into the house.

The boys from the area took their dogs and their shotguns and bushwhacked to the rickety blind where the river crooks in Abney, and they dropped geese from the sky in such a gleeful running of booms that often these guns sounded as if they were tippers on some mammoth bodhrán.

At his father's old situation, mice had gotten into everything, and from the roof of the farmhouse, the trenches that the mice had worn, running to and from the house, made it all look like a great tangle of spaghetti. There was a family of skunks milling around who generally seemed to be lost. They were rooting for grubs and whatnot. He'd stumble upon them once in a while and receive the brunt and spray of their glands. Luckily, he had all of that tomato paste. After the first few got him, he took to keeping buckets of tomato paste outside and covered these buckets with the pieces of plywood that his setting routes were inscribed on. There was mint out in the garden, with big square stalks and whorled leaves that the frost hadn't killed, and he'd pick at this and eat it as he worked, cleaning up the place.

There were two pigeons in the barn that had spent years shitting on everything. Herring opened the doors for a few days, hoping they'd just pick up their things and leave, but they didn't. He fetched his father's old rifle and fired a few rounds off near them. They flapped their wings a bit and took to the air in the rafters, but then just returned to their roost up by the vent. When he had been a boy, he'd used that very same rifle to fold shags out at the cape. Their rifles would be just red with them. He'd never thought that he was taking lives. No, they were just killing shags as their fathers had shown them. Herring climbed up into the rafters and took his time getting a bead on them. He didn't like that he had to shoot them. There wasn't much left of them after the bullet had gone through. He shot one and when it had fallen, the other stood there, blinking, daring him. The pair of them laid out on the concrete like forgotten mittens.

It started to snow and the fellows were still out there, soaked and shivering on the waters, doing mussels, muttering about the ignorance of it all while they cleaned the socks.

He was up in the loft of the barn, and he found an old, deep wooden chest with his grandfather's military stuff in it. Some pictures and letters stained by water. At the bottom was a grenade. He was pretty sure it was live. Herring phoned Lillian, and she said he should call CFB Gagetown. He said, "Snow's coming," and then hung up. He called Gagetown and spoke with an explosive ordnance officer, who said they'd send a guy out to see what the situation was.

Murray Schellen arrived a few days later in a beat-up rig. He had an incredible moustache that looked like a kind of boomerang attached to his face. They drank some coffee in the kitchen and shot the breeze. He had a burgundy beret on his head and seemed allergic to sitting on chairs. His face was tired looking, as if he'd been doing trucker speed for a week straight, in anticipation of the apocalypse. Murray told him about this one house he had lived in. He said, "When we moved into the house on the base, the dog we had at the time would just stare and stare at the ceiling fan, transfixed. If we turned it on, the dog would just spook, and run away. We'd find her shivering on the bed. Couldn't get any air to flow through the place 'cos we didn't want to trouble the dog. In the summer, the heat was unbearable. I'd spritz the sheets with cold water just so we could sleep. Somehow or another, years later, I heard that the ceiling fan finally came down, made this real huge mess.

When I told my wife, well, she's my ex-wife now, she said, see, I told you the dog knew." Murray clamped two fingers into his moustache and pulled them downward, pinching the coffee out. He rubbed his stomach, content, warm. Murray told him about his last serious bout of diarrhea. He said, "Let me tell you, it was like hitting a turd with a tennis racket." Herring took him to the grenade. Murray held it in his hands, long and thin like the wings of a cherub, and confirmed that it was from the First World War, and that, yes, it was still very much live. "This is called a Mills bomb and this green band here means that there's amatol in it." Murray traced the green band with his forefinger and the paint smeared. He turned his hand around and looked at the mess of juniper on his finger. He said, "Huh, that's weird." Herring said, "My grandfather was the first fellow down at the wharf with an engine in his boat. He'd take the engine out of his rig and put it in the boat. When the season was done, he'd put it back in his rig." Murray surveyed the field out back. "You up for a bit of fun?" he said.

They dug a little hole about a foot or so into the ground. Murray patched a safety fuse into the grenade. They buried the dark egg with some measure of ceremony, their movements slow and gentle. Murray said, "To what base uses we may return. Why may not imagination trace the noble dust of Alexander till he find it stopping a bunghole?" Herring didn't say anything. Murray had enough character to scandalize every church hall in the Maritimes. The military tended to attract people who were of a certain species, as offbeat and bloodthirsty as vikings. Murray said, "You think I'm crazy, don't ya?" Herring said, "It doesn't matter to me where you get yer motor running, so long as you know where to park it." They filled the hole up and then Murray ran his spool back about fifty yards from the grenade to where a little hill of soil stood. This was to be a kind of shield. Herring watched as Murray went through a mental checklist. He extended his index finger first, and then another, and another, his hands freckled with green. He was counting. Murray looked at him. He said, "I'll let you do the honours." Herring put flame to the fuse and they watched it burn through the grass and dirt of the field, like an arrow that crawled, had legs. Murray was buzzing. Herring was nervous. And then there was a detonation and a giant plume of dirt and pressure spread upward and outward. A speckled cone that separated and aligned and then unified, shadowing all things beneath. The two of them stood upright, watching the debris float through the sky. A lowly and ignoble wave seemed to flood everything, like a great arm sweeping away a mishandled game of poker. Herring braced himself. He felt it right in his chest.

# Acknowledgements

to my father, Michael;
to my grandmother, Danny, and my grandfather, Ralph;
to my brothers, Adam (aka Spud) and Garth;
to my nephews: Sean, Liam, Alex, and Max;
to my mother-in-law, Lorraine Ada MacLean;
to Carla Rowan;

to Richard & Lindsey (and the boys); to Adam & Laura (and the girls) —
thanks for being my friends;

to the guys down at the wharf: Troy Jackson, Norman Ellis, Jerry
MacConnell, Doug Gallant, Jared Richards;
to Eugene Arsenault (for the confabs and weather predictions);

to the teachers (who changed everything): Sue Merritt, Kim Jernigan,
and Jacqui Smyth;
to Roberto and Cormac, Flannery and Clarice; Jorge and Gabriel;

to this town is small and the Banff Centre for Arts and Creativity;
to Julie Pellissier-Lush (for reading an early version and providing feed-
back);

to Séamus & Ciara;

to Talk Talk & The Weather Station (for the dreams);
to Loreena McKennitt (for her version of "Bonny Portmore");
to Simply Red (for "Holding Back the Years" on my wedding);
to Colm and Marilynne (for helping me with grief);

—334—

to Norma Lorraine MacIsaac & Elwood Bayfield MacIsaac;
to Edgar W. Parker & Lillian Gertrude Parker;

to Martin James Ainsley (for the edits);
to Julie Scriver (for the beautiful cover);

to Bethany Gibson (for the chance and for the trust);

to Norma Jean MacLean (for the future, among many other things).

Thank you all ever so much.


(Thèid an sgadan marbh leis an t-sruth.)